Darwin's Paradox:

A science mystery of international disease, diversity, and amateur scientists.
Pandemic Mysteries #1

J. Oestreicher
&
D.R. Oestreicher

Omega Cat Press — California

Omega Cat Press, independent publishing since 1990

ISBN: 0-9631755-5-6
ISBN-13: 978-0-9631755-5-7

1 2 3 4 5 6 7 8 9

"It is not the strongest of the species that survives,
not the most intelligent that survives.
It is the one that is the most adaptable to change."
— Charles Darwin

Dedicated to diversity:
cultural diversity and genetic diversity.

Also by J. Oestreicher and D.R. Oestreicher
Plague of Equals: A science thriller of international disease, politics, and drug discovery (Pandemic Mysteries #2)
Available in all Amazon stores
ISBN: 978-0-9631755-4-0
http://amzn.to/2jEwdyp

A book in the tradition of … Leon Uris, or James Michener: a big, sprawling adventure tale centered on a specific theme, with an almost Chaucerian cast of characters — Goodreads 5-star review

In this story, the scientists do what scientists always do … they find the truth. The truth is surprising to both scientific and non-scientific readers. Enjoy. — review by a research biologist

Amazon reviews

"…it takes you away and brings you back home, a little richer."

"The accuracy and humor of the conversation between scientists were amazing"

"…the tension between scientific discovery and social justice."

"…the science was on point."

"multiple story lines … everything ties in right at the end."

Table of Contents

PART I — RESEARCH

PROLOGUE

CAMROSE, ALBERTA CANADA

On the first day of kindergarten, Natalie Jenkins packed Ian and his three-year-old sister Lindsey into her pickup and headed to the elementary school. Shortly after her daughter was born, she received a small inheritance which enabled her to get a divorce and move 100 kilometers south of Edmonton just outside the small city of Camrose amidst a vast agricultural parkland.

Best decision ever. Clean air. Locally grown organic food. No crime. Friendly neighbors.

When Ian returned home from his first day of school, he complained of a sore arm. Natalie assumed something happened at school. She didn't believe in overprotecting her children. Ian had had his share of bumps and bruises, but after dinner he held his arm and rocked back and forth. He also had a slight fever, so she gave him some ibuprofen.

That remedied his condition until the next morning when he woke up crying. The pain now extended from his hand to his neck. He was trembling as she drove past the elementary school to the hospital in downtown Camrose. As she negotiated the short drive through city streets, she was grateful she hadn't chosen a more remote place when she was escaping her ex and urban living.

The doctors immediately checked Ian into a room in the intensive care unit. This prompt care did not soothe her. Instead she was frightened. Triage demanded they see the most serious cases first. Not a good sign. She loved Ian as much as she hated her ex whom he unfortunately resembled.

As they rolled him away, she followed and made the magical wish that Ian could exchange whatever he had with one of his parents, preferably her ex. She observed the lengthy exam until she remembered Lindsey was alone in the waiting room.

Exercising her personal mommy triage, she rushed back wondering what people were thinking of the mother who had abandoned her three-year-old.

She was hyperventilating, but relaxed when she saw the outgoing Lindsey regaling a gray-haired couple with stories about her bear and her moose, Fatty and Patty. The three of them, Lindsey, Fatty and Patty, had been fast friends and had had so many wonderful imaginary adventures that Natalie could ignore that the adorable stuffed animals were Christmas gifts from Lindsey's father. Ian's father. She no longer acknowledged any personal relation with him.

Fortunately, the vagaries of the oil field industries had sent him miles away, so such gifts arrived via Canada Post, and visiting was out of the question.

She was glad she decided to retrieve Lindsey when she did. The doctor returned shortly after. Again, this prompt action made her nervous. Even more concerning, the doctor didn't talk right away. First, she asked the nurses to watch Lindsey, and then led Natalie into a consultation room. After closing the door and offering a glass of water, the doctor sat behind her big desk. She spoke in a quiet voice, almost sounding like a funeral director, "My first thought was allergies, but Ian didn't respond to diphenhydramine, an antihistamine."

Natalie's frightened mind darted about while she tried to prepare herself for the bad news. She noticed that the doctor wore no makeup except for pale pink nail polish and possibly some clear lip gloss. Wondering whether this indicated a serious demeanor or a lack of care, she missed some of the explanation and what else the doctor had considered. Eventually, the doctor dismissed her, but kept Ian for "further observation." The terrified mother picked up Lindsey and, following the doctor's advice, rented a motel room in town.

After another anxiety-ridden consultation, she decided to stay in the hospital. The motel was just not close enough. She sat in the waiting room with Lindsey sleeping on her lap. Poor Lindsey woke up every few hours when the nervous mother went to check on Ian.

During the night, Ian developed tremors and spasms. He had trouble speaking. The night shift didn't want to do anything until the admitting doctor arrived in the morning.

Natalie seemed to mirror his symptoms. She was so scared and angry that she could barely speak. She tried to control her shivering to not scare poor Lindsey.

For just a moment she wished Lindsey's father had been there to share the responsibilities, but then she recalled, he had never shared the responsibilities when he had been there. That was never going to change.

Nothing happened until morning.

When the doctor arrived, everything went quickly. Several other doctors examined Ian, and they made consultation calls to Alberta Health Services. First to Edmonton, then Calgary, and ultimately to Sick Kids in Toronto.

The doctors considered epilepsy. Natalie had to run to keep up with the gurney taking Ian for an electroencephalogram. Little Lindsey was exhausted, emotionally and physically. After spending the night, Natalie found it easier to leave Lindsey under the nurses' watchful care. By this time everyone knew Fatty and Patty, and some of the nurses even contributed new adventures to the continuing saga.

Fortunately, or unfortunately, she couldn't think straight anymore to differentiate good news from bad news: it was not epilepsy.

By afternoon, she took Lindsey out for a healthy meal. She brought back Ian's favorite, KD, but he would not eat anything or even drink water.

Worse, he now had a rash and was itchy. She heard rumors about parents who had not vaccinated their children. Ian had had all his shots, but she now worried about measles, mumps, and chicken pox.

The doctors reassured her, "Ian's safe from those childhood diseases."

At this she just blew up, "Safe? Safe you say? What the hell is happening to him? Do something!"

They did something. They gave her a tranquilizer and had an EMS ambulance take her and Lindsey to their motel for the night.

———

Ian's symptoms worsened for a week until the doctors told his nearly catatonic mom that Ian was brain dead and they were taking him off life support.

She, Lindsey, Fatty, and Patty cried all the way home, not the least encouraged that the doctors, who could not help Ian, examined them both and assured them that they both were well.

The doctors put together a complete chart to send off to the Health Surveillance and Epidemiology Division at the Public Health Agency regional office in Edmonton.

Unknown to those doctors, medical examiners around the world received similar death charts. In Atlanta Georgia, the Centers for Disease Control (CDC) and, in Stockholm Sweden, the European Centre for Disease Prevention and Control (ECDC) both numbered their cases in double digits.

1. LILY

KATHERINE, ARNHEMLAND, AUSTRALIA

Lily ducked her head and wiggled the screen of her computer, trying to angle it away from the glare. Then she tried laying an unpainted canvas across the corner of the screen to block the light. "Casuarina Café" glared backward in bright purple letters on her screen. She finally scooted her chair to the end of the table and turned the computer screen sideways to the sun and the neon sign in the window.

Obrey said his customers liked the light, and he wasn't going to put in shades just to make a bat-cave for her, but Lily was pretty sure he just didn't want to pay for shades. It's not like there was a huge clientele in the shop; Lily was often the only one there, like today. He probably didn't have the cash. He drifted out from behind the counter and looked over her shoulder.

She put the last photograph of her newest artwork up on the Cooperative's sale site and typed the painting's description, size, and title into the boxes on the Coop's form.

"More bats," Obrey said.

"Of course," Lily said. "They are selling much better than my yam paintings."

"Because you do not love yams, as you love bats?"

"Maybe."

"You are so good with the colors; I am always impressed."

"Thank you." She knew he was doing his daily compliment, but it was still nice to hear her work praised.

"How many did you sell last month?"

"Three."

"A good month, Lily."

"Mm."

She saved her work, glanced through her other offerings on the site, then went to her **Bat Chat** page. Obrey drifted away. She found her mind changing gears with an almost physical growl: art to healing. Obrey to Ariq. Bats were the constant.

With the eight-and-a-half-hour time difference, she never knew whether she'd find Ariq online, but there he was.

 Dreamtime: Just updated my Coop page with a new painting.

 Mongol Bataar: Nice!

 Dreamtime: Another bat dreaming. I went out with my healer friend; she talked a bit about some leaves I had not heard of. I want to do a painting, but I am afraid to ask her if I can.

 Mongol Bataar: ?

 Dreamtime: The last time I did that things did not turn out well.

Lily's heart ached when she thought about the old women in Ngukurr she had been studying with. She still did not understand what she had done or said that had been so wrong. There was so much about her people she did not know. And there were so few willing to teach her.

 Dreamtime: How are things in New Mexico?

 Mongol Bataar: Not good. We had a death among our rehab patients with absolutely clean toxicology reports. Several others are ill with what looks like the same thing.

 Dreamtime: You are sure it is not simply old age?

 Mongol Bataar: She wasn't old. In her sixties, but that's not old. She had orthopedic surgery, nothing life-threatening.

 Dreamtime: Is your surgery pure?

 Mongol Bataar: I've done more tests, but there's nothing. It almost looks like rabies, but none of my patients or staff have been outside. And, anyhow, how could they all have been bitten by the same rabid animal—and not know it?

 Dreamtime: The illness was the same as before?

Mongol Bataar: Almost identical.

 Dreamtime: Mm.

 Mongol Bataar: Any alternative treatment suggestions from the Outback?

 Dreamtime: Send the list of symptoms in as non-medical language as you can manage. I'll need to translate it for my mentor. Maybe she has some ideas.

 Mongol Bataar: Sure. Worth a shot.

 Dreamtime: ?

 Mongol Bataar: A try.

 Dreamtime: Mm.

 Mongol Bataar: I looked at your new painting. I like it a lot.

 Dreamtime: Thank you.

———

Lily paid Obrey for her coffee and her computer time and headed out, her portfolio in one hand, her paint box in the other. She walked to her aunt's house, studying the way the red dust puffed up around her bare feet. It was always fascinating, how light and fluffy it was. At her mother's apartment in Darwin, there was often dark mud instead of dusty dirt. Here in Katherine, it alternated between very wet and very dry.

One of the first things she had done when she had gotten computer access was looked at maps of the Northern Territory, and then Australia, and then the world. In New Mexico, where Ariq lived, it was very dry and sandy. But the bats lived everywhere. There were bats for every environment, just like people.

When she turned the corner to her aunt's street, she was abruptly faced with a wall of people and vehicles. An ambulance was parked in the driveway of June and Papa Araminty. People in uniform were talking to her aunt Olivia and some other people who lived on Honey Ant Street. Lily saw her cousin Pana and waved. They met a little away from the crowd, and Pana put her hand on Lily's shoulder.

"It's June Araminty, is sick," she said.

"She was fine yesterday when I saw her."

Pana shook her head. "Not now." Lily's heart seemed to squinch up tight, and it was hard to breathe. June had been the one to tell her about the art Coop, and how to show her paintings online, and what kinds of prices were reasonable. June also was an artist, but she did modern paintings, in bright acrylics with no dots or x-ray styles, not like the more traditional things Lily had been doing.

Pana cleared her throat. "She's such a nice lady."

"Yes, she is."

They watched as the paramedics rolled June out on a narrow bed and into the ambulance.

"She's going to hospital?"

"I think she doesn't want to. She keeps asking for your Auntie Pearl."

"Does Pearl know?"

"She was here. She argued with the medic. I think she went home."

"I'm going to find her."

"You want me to put those in the house?" Pana reached and Lily handed her the portfolio and paint box.

"Thank you, Pana. I will be home soon." Her cousin nodded and walked through the crowd toward her mother's home, using the paint box in front of her to open a space between people. Lily could see Pana's fuzzy dark blonde head like a beacon in the mostly dark-haired crowd.

Pearl. Lily retraced her steps to the corner, took two left turns and walked until the street turned into a lane, and the lane into a path through the paperbark trees. The path ended at Pearl's house.

She could hear Pearl muttering to herself as she walked into the lean-to where Pearl had bunches and trays of herbs drying.

"Auntie Pearl?"

"Hey, Lily. You see all that mess out there? "

"They're taking June Araminty to hospital?"

"She does not even want to go, but there is no telling those people. They know so much."

The old woman looked up as Lily approached. Lily held her arms open and she and Pearl gave each other a big hug. Lily patted Pearl's shoulder.

"Maybe we can go later, and see June," Lily said, watching Pearl's face.

An eyebrow went up in the round, plump face. She looked at Lily. "You think we can take her some bush tucker?"

"Of course. She will be much happier with that than whatever the hospital tries to feed her." Lily grinned, and Pearl grinned back, hiking up her skirt so she wouldn't trip on it. Lily had been meaning to sew some new elastic into the waistband. The skirt was still good; it just didn't stay up around Pearl's waist anymore. As usual, the shirt the old woman was wearing didn't match the pattern in the skirt at all. Lily wondered if that was her artist's eye flinching or her mother's fashion influence. Pearl obviously didn't care.

"Let me see what I have here," Pearl said, and Lily stepped up closer to watch or hand her things. "She has bad fever, shakes, dry skin like a croc mummy." She pushed past Lily and started pulling things out of her drying racks. "You come help, now, see what I make."

"Yes," Lily said, and did so, taking careful mental notes on what Pearl was gathering and what she did with it. June Araminty was going to have a nice bush stew, that was what.

2. DR. BRIAN

R_X His daughter broke his heart for the second time. This time, because she wasn't dead. After years of searching, mourning, and therapy, he had had her declared legally dead and had moved on with his life. Now, there she was, alive, dancing in the South Pacific.

Doctor Brian, as he preferred to be addressed, had awakened when the sun rose over Fatu Hiva streaking through the volcanic peaks. Geologically young enough to trace jagged and sharp lines, but old enough to be covered in eroded lava as shown by the lush green vegetation, the mountains made a dramatic silhouette for sunrise.

His therapist, fearful of antidepressant dependency, had recommended the cruise. Now, after a week of serene oceans, tropical islands, and good food, he hadn't thought of his disappointing career and lost family for days.

After a room service breakfast of papaya, mango, banana, and pineapple accompanied by the blackest espresso flavored with Tahitian vanilla, he boarded the tender to visit Omo'a.

With no goal, he walked around the island and through the small town. He noted the obligatory post office with its ATM, a small food store that sold staples and a selection of candy for the children, and a clinic. A turtle—terrapin? —with a shell the size of a VW bug hood wallowed in damp sand, strands of seaweed draped over its neck. The palm trees, advertised on every website, swayed in the breeze. A few white clouds scudded across the very blue sky. Children were out in the schoolyard. There couldn't have been more than a couple of dozen of all ages.

Beyond the school yard, on the way back to the beach, was a small tourist market. He had no one to buy souvenirs for, but he still ambled in that direction, attracted by the sound of drums.

As he approached his seventieth birthday, he tired easily, so he gratefully took an empty spot on a shaded log, pleasantly surprised to find himself next to Jake, a friendly salesman he'd met on the ship. Jake's movie-star good looks weren't hurt by his scruffy unshaven jaw and bed-head hair—if that was what the young people called it? Every time Doctor Brian saw Jake, he felt compelled to smooth his own balding white hair and finger-comb his beard. He knew he was a long way from a "silver fox" the ladies might go for, but he wasn't ugly, either. At least not until he sat next to Jake. They waved to each other and returned their attention to the next group of dancers. Though the dancers dressed alike in palm skirts, colorful floral tops, and bare shoulders, they ranged in age from pre-teen to grandmothers.

A thirtyish woman with blonde hair and a deep tan attracted both Jake and Doctor Brian. Brian noticed her bright smile captured the attention of several other men in the audience. When she looked in their direction, Jake smiled back at her. As Brian stared at the long curly hair, the smiling face, he could feel his body tense. He was sweating and having trouble breathing.

This dancer reminded him of his ex-wife, the one who had turned his daughter against him. The two of them had disappeared twenty years ago, without even a "goodbye." In his mind, they had both earned the title of "bitches." They were impulsive and cruel—at least, they had been to him.

After years of therapy, he was beginning to let go; he was still not good at it. Since they had left long ago and were declared dead, one of his therapists had recommended a funeral. He purchased coffins and headstones. They were "buried" together, and he visited the graves annually on the anniversary of their disappearance. They couldn't be here, could they? They were dead.

His reverie ended with a loud drum roll. The dancers raised their hands and waited for the music signaling the dance to start. As with many of the dances he'd seen on the cruise, footwork was minimal. The hips kept pace with the increasing tempo of the drums, and the arms told the story. He stared at those arms, especially at the blonde woman's right arm. Against a dark tan were four distinctive v-shaped, white scars.

When he realized that he wasn't breathing, he gasped one long breath and leaned forward, shuddering. He recognized the scars as the unique signature of an external fixator. The exact pattern of scars left from repairing his daughter's arm after the accident. There was no doubt, now, the dancer was his daughter. Penelope was alive.

"Penelope!" he shouted.

She looked at him, their identical green eyes locked. She stopped dancing and blinked. He saw recognition in those eyes.

After the barest pause, she looked away and resumed dancing.

He jumped up and sprinted across the open sand between the tourists and the dancers. He reached his arms toward her. "Penny...*Penny*. It's your father!" He gulped back tears. "Time to come home."

This was a scene he'd dreamt of so many times. Sometimes during a hurricane, sometimes with explosions. Never with dancing. Always with Penny looking younger—as young as she'd been when he'd last seen her. And always with her arms out, rushing into her daddy's arms. He had never thought it would happen, but hope had lingered.

"Penny. Penny! Come home," he kept repeating.

As he approached her, she looked scared and backed away. "No. No!" she repeated louder and louder competing with the drums.

Brian felt a rush of movement behind him. Jake grabbed his arm, his shoulder. "What are you doing, Brian? Let's go sit down. You're upsetting her."

No, Brian thought. No one would interfere with his reunion, not after all these years. With strength that surprised himself and Jake, he swung his arms and knocked the younger man down.

He spun, picking up speed, and ran closer to the stage and Penny. Just as quickly, two large, bare-chested drummers stood between him and the frightened woman, big arms raised to block his charge. When he tried to push past them, one of the men hit him with a large drumstick. That was the last thing he remembered.

———

He awoke in what seemed to be the ship's infirmary. Jake was at his side, legs crossed in a stiff-looking straight-backed chair, a ratty paperback book in his hand.

"Ah! You're awake!"

Brian blinked, rubbing the lump on his head and wincing when he touched a tender spot.

Why was Jake here?

"Now, the reason they didn't treat you on the island is that woman you attacked is the town doctor. And that is just the beginning of your troubles. The cruise ship was ready to send you home. I promised to keep an eye on you; you can't walk around unaccompanied."

"Where's Penny?"

"The island woman? The doctor you attacked?" Jake shook his head. "She has no interest in seeing you."

"But—she's my daughter."

Jake's eyebrows rose at this, and he shook his head. "Maybe you should stay in the infirmary awhile, man."

But the nurse disagreed, needing to clear the bed to take in people who "are really sick." They kicked Brian out.

At dinner that night, Brian went on and on about his drunk wife, the accident, Penny's broken arm and long rehabilitation, the divorce, shouting, recriminations, lawyers, until one day, his wife and nineteen-year-old daughter were simply gone.

When dessert arrived, Tahitian vanilla creme brulee for Brian, and terrine of citrus fruit and Campari sorbet for Jake, it seemed like Jake had had enough.

"Listen, even *if* she is your daughter, she doesn't want to see you. Eat something to take your mind off her."

Brian was going to object, but instead he muted himself with a spoonful of heavenly custard.

Conspiratorially Jake whispered, "I recall you worked in drug research. Ever think of going back? I have a feeling there is going to be a sudden demand." He set down his spoon. "Let's go out on deck."

Research? This just depressed Brian more. From his worthless family, the conversation was shifting to his worthless career. Thoughts of his sore head and his resurrected and obviously hateful daughter both clamored for attention. He didn't want to listen to Jake's sales pitch. But he could use a friend. And what had Jake said about having to accompany him? They squeezed past other travelers out onto the deck. They leaned on the rail. Blue on blue, the sky, the sea.

Brian knew he could slip over the railing and not be missed until the ship was miles and miles away. It would be a fitting end to his lackluster life.

"Listen," Jake said. "I sell sequencers, expensive, high-speed sequencers. Do you know anything about DNA sequencers?"

Brian just sucked on his lip, feeling like a senile old man, and thinking of how the Pacific Ocean could swallow him.

"I am getting rich, very rich. These machines, hundreds of thousands of dollars each—people are buying them by the boatload. Labs that last year had no budgets are buying four or five at a time." Jake paused to glance at Brian. "Something big is going on, really big. I bet you have connections. Find out what."

Well, it wasn't exactly a sales pitch. Maybe Jake was right. Doctor Brian had done drug research for thirty years. If something big was happening, they'd be glad to see him. They'd need him.

3. NGA

LUAMBE, NIASSA, MOZAMBIQUE

The tablelands forest started to hum and chirp with life as soon as the tiniest edge of the sun lit the horizon. Nga Lind stretched and lay in the comfort of her bed for a few more moments, looking out the window. The forest had been cleared next to the mission buildings to reduce the fire hazard, but she could still see trees.

She was used to getting up early, but lately it seemed as though going to bed at the end of the day kept getting pushed later and later while rising time remained early. It was amazing, but she had no surgeries scheduled today.

Of course, the clinic's visitors would come along with sundry problems as the day went on, but at least she wasn't starting off already behind. And Halid was more and more helpful. She smiled thinking about the village headman's son. Halid seemed to be deciding he wanted to be a TC, too, and go to Maputo to get the training. Meanwhile, she was acting as his mentor because she wanted to help him and because he was helping her. A lot.

Two days ago had been a real horror, with two surgeries in the morning—setting and stitching a compound fracture that had come in during the night, and removing the wen from a villager's baby boy's ear. That had been interrupted by an emergency appendectomy.

She'd only had time to look at three people in the clinic after that. She'd set Halid to cleaning instruments while she wiped down the tiny clinic surgery. She'd sent him home, and then stole the time to eat a bit of leftover dinner before she fell into bed and sleep.

She stared at her mother's beloved flowered wallpaper that covered two walls of her room. Linnea had sold vegetables from her garden at the river trade camp for months to pay for the stuff, which had been ordered all the way from Johannesburg. Nga smiled, remembering the day the whole family had worked together to wallpaper this room and her parents' bedroom.

She could hear chickens clucking outside her window. She should get up—but the extra minutes abed felt luxurious.

Her rule was to stop at suppertime, or 6:00 P.M. She had to implement rules, or she'd have been in the clinic all day and all night, too. After 6:00 each evening, she was only available for life-threatening emergencies. The villagers could go to the traditional healer, Imrane. Who also happened to be her brother-in-law. Who also happened to dislike her intensely. He was fiercely traditional.

She needed help, but not Imrane's kind of help. She was the only technically trained healer within several hundred kilometers. People from five nearby villages came to her for help. God forbid if they ever had some kind of plague, like that rumored in northern Zambia. She wasn't even a doctor and she was swamped. What would a serious disease do to Mozambique's shaky medical system? She couldn't even imagine trying to deal with something like Ebola.

When she had gotten her Technical Surgeon's training in Maputo—after her little sister Mezi had almost died in childbirth— there had been promises of funding for more *técnico de cirurgia*—TC—like herself to be trained and sent north. But Niassa Province was a long way from Maputo. All the new TCs seemed to get lost well before they got up here. And she was willing to bet they'd never seen a real M.D. in the entire Niassa province.

"Nej, du överdriver—" no, you're exaggerating, she told herself in her native Swedish. "Surely there's one in Lichinga. She's just buried under her patients, so you would never see her." She laughed softly, tossed the covers back and went to brush her teeth.

At breakfast, Linnea asked little Muluzi to say grace. Imrane scowled at her, eyes bulging, a grimace twisting his lips. That was the image frozen in Nga's head when she closed her eyes and bowed her head. Mu, always willing to please his grandmama, complied in his piping five-year-old voice. "Most Holy High

Father, bless this food and our people, and lead us into the light of Christianity and protect us all," he said. "Amen."

After they had all murmured their Amens, Mu added, "Let's eat!"

His father scowled at him, then, but Mu just grinned and reached for the steaming bowl of corn porridge. Sometimes it seemed that Imrane was determined to show a severe face. The Yao villagers often laughed, and Muluzi and his big sister and his mother laughed with them, but their papa mostly scowled.

Nga kept glancing at him. Were his eyes bulging more than before? She wondered if he was in pain, but of course the man was never going to ask for her medical help. She had diagnosed Grave's disease and tried to get him to go to Lichinga for tests and medicine, but he was handling it himself, he told her. Whatever he was treating himself *with*, it had not seemed to make much improvement. The man was too thin and was sweating even as he sat here in the cool kitchen.

Mezi asked Teleza to pass the eggs. More solemn than her little brother, the little girl reached carefully for the plate of scrambled eggs and used both hands to pick it up and pass it to her mother.

"It's so nice to have you with us this morning, Nga," Linnea said.

"It's nice to have a hot breakfast," Nga said with a quick grin at her mother, serving herself a spoonful of the porridge. "Nothing scheduled this morning and no one in line at the clinic."

"Because I took care of them last night," Imrane growled.

"Who came in?" Nga wondered.

Imrane glared at her. "Kofi's arm itches. I told him to break the cast off, his arm is healed and the plaster is unnatural."

"Ah. And did he?" she tried to say it in a pleasant voice, curious what Kofi had decided.

"He did not. He says it has to stay until Monday." Imrane shrugged his slender shoulders. "What can a few more days do?"

"It's just to make sure his arm is completely healed," Nga said. So it doesn't go all crooked like Botte's did because you convinced *him* to take his cast off after only a week. But it wouldn't do to say that aloud and start a quarrel at the breakfast table. Nga caught her mother's glance, the pleading in her eyes. Linnea had had a hard time getting Mezi's family to join them for meals. Nga would not ruin that. She smiled at her mother then focused on her plate. Her father cleared his throat.

"We will need some help from the villagers to clean out the classrooms," Anson said. School would be starting up again in a couple weeks.

Linnea nodded. "Some of the children want to help with that," she said.

Their new teacher for the lower grades, Miss Anderson, had just arrived and was settling in. The older teacher, fifth to tenth year, had been here for several days, and was in her quarters behind the school building. The teachers did not have a real kitchen in their cottage, and Nga was surprised neither of them had joined them for breakfast. Linnea Lind traditionally fed the teachers and half the mission personnel at her big kitchen table. Perhaps they had eaten earlier.

Back in the clinic after a pleasant breakfast, Nga washed her hands and put on gloves and a gown. Using tongs, she removed her instruments from the glutaraldehyde bath one at a time, drying them and packing them into clean plastic pouches. Then she put them into their appropriate drawers and bins. Maybe someday they'd get an autoclave, but for now, the chemical bath was the best system they had for sterilization.

Giving thanks for the regular delivery of supplies—like the plastic bullets of hydrogen peroxide and boxes of gloves—she reached for a new pair of gloves, then emptied a bottle of hydrogen peroxide into a small tub of tea-kettle-boiled water. She used a new sponge, wiping down every working surface of her little clinic: exam table, countertop, cabinets, the plastic-covered chair. She emptied out the water, prepared a new batch with another bottle of peroxide, and repeated the procedure, finishing with the floor. She'd been rushed when she'd wiped things down last night, and hadn't had time to do a good job, lately. She was content as she sat outside on the stairs, enjoying the dry-season sun as the floor in her little clinic dried.

Halid showed up wearing only his hand-me-down jeans. His feet were dusty. She pointed at them, and he grinned, walking around to the outside washing station. He rinsed the dust off, and put on booties, careful to only step on the clean mats as he came back to her.

As she stood up, ready to go back inside to do her planned inventory, she saw a stranger approaching, one of the Luambe village boys leading the woman, who was limping along very slowly. She also saw Imrane looking at the woman, but he scowled and turned away. If she hadn't gone to her own village healer, she wasn't going to want a strange one to help. Clearly she had come for the medically trained clinician. Nga tried not to smile. She would have been happy to share treatment with Imrane, if the man wasn't so determinedly unpleasant. The combination of Western medicine with native treatment could be very powerful if they worked together. That did not seem likely to ever happen, though, not with him.

Halid called to the village boy and they chattered together as the old woman finally arrived, cradling her swollen wrist. Arthritis? Or broken? Nga went to work.

It was almost dusk when more strangers arrived in the village. Again, they passed the round village houses and approached the square mission buildings. It was a young couple, with a child. They might have been European tourists with their backpacks, sunglasses, and water carriers, but they shouted greetings in a Malawian dialect of Chiyao, the villagers' language. It was close enough to the Luambe dialect that Nga could understand them. Halid appeared at the edge of the village, looking at her.

The newcomers were saying something about plague. About leaving before it was too late. They seemed to be in good health.

Nga waved Halid off. She closed and locked the clinic door and walked out to speak with the strangers. Several of the Luambe villagers had surrounded the little family, and soon people from the mission joined Nga and the strangers, Halid among them.

"What plague, what sickness," Nga tried to ask in a space between rapid conversations between villagers and strangers. Everyone else stopped talking to listen to her.

The wife looked at Nga. "You are TC, yes?"

"I am," Nga said.

"Did you hear about Zambia, about the sickness there?"

Nga nodded. "I heard, but not very much."

"People are running from Zambia to Malawi now, sneaking past the borders."

"And then they take boats across the lake or walk through the trees to Tanzania, or to here," the man said. "Maybe they are sick, or maybe they are ahead of it."

The wife nodded. "Zambia has more than 700 dead already. My friend is a TC there. Or she was. She died last week."

Seven hundred dead? Nga knew they were isolated here, but she thought at least one of the mission workers would have heard about this on the news. Were these people confused? Or was the government suppressing information, trying to avoid panic or bad press? Zambia had its problems.

"What are the symptoms?" she asked, interrupting a villager who had begun to ask about a friend in Malawi.

"We hear it is a fever, dehydration, weakness. Nothing helps, none of the medicine Suzy tried seemed to help anything. Then she got it, and she died."

"Anyone recover?"

"Not that we heard. The only thing to do is get out of the way. We're going on to Pemba. None of the coastal towns are reporting any problems. You should go too," the young woman said. But Nga shook her head.

"My place is here, helping the villagers."

"If you wait too long, it'll be too late," the man said. "Think of the children," he hugged his son. "We thank you for the water. We'll be on our way."

Nga and Halid waved good-bye as the little family moved on. They planned to go south to the highway, then east to the coast.

She couldn't help but wonder if they weren't going to be at greater risk on the coast than Luambe village would be, isolated up here in the high tablelands.

4. ARIQ

ROSWELL, NEW MEXICO

Ariq Temuujin mentally reviewed the checklist for his presentation: architectural model of E-Ro city, laptop, projector, backup copy of his PowerPoint slides. He touched his waist to check he hadn't forgotten his belt and had zipped his fly. On a straight stretch of road, he looked down to check that his shoes matched. He leaned over to the rear-view mirror to confirm he hadn't nicked himself shaving. There wasn't a lot to shave, but on mornings like this, he couldn't be too careful.

His father had named him after his ancestor Ariq Böke, Genghis Khan's grandson, Kublai Khan's brother. Warrior blood flowed through his arteries, but today Ariq didn't feel it. For the hundredth time, he reminded himself that the Khans ruled the greatest Asian empire, feared by all, east and west, over 5,000 miles from Budapest to Shanghai. How could he allow a planning commission in the tiny town of Roswell, New Mexico, home of UFOs, aliens, and cheap souvenir shops, to rattle him?

Calmed down, he took a deep breath and turned onto Richardson Avenue. City Hall was just ahead. His hands had a death grip on the steering wheel. He hit the brakes to avoid hitting a crowd of protestors. "Earthlings Go Home," "Roswell for Robots," "Spaceports not Hospitals."

Avoiding the crowd, he drove right past the brick City Hall and around the block to enter in the back. Ariq Böke died a coward's death as present day Ariq snuck into the meeting room. To assure a stealth entrance, he left the magnificent model of the planned E-Ro city in his SUV.

Corporate expected Ariq to expand the ROC from twenty-eight beds to a health complex with hundreds of beds, plus luxury hotels, shopping, and recreation for their well-heeled clientele. PopulistHealth had been quietly buying up land east of Roswell, naming the project E-Ro, wanting it to remind their customers of SoHo in New York and SoMa in San Francisco. Eventually, they planned a thirty-six-hole golf course.

Ariq sat through the small-town planning commission deliberations to approve additional plastic aliens on Main Street, opening another theater to screen classic science fiction movies, and expanding a garage by adding another mechanic's bay.

He opened his laptop to review his presentation one more time when his chief financial officer Martina Hirsch arrived. She'd graduated at top of her MBA class from a third-rate college–but a 28-bed clinic in the desert wasn't exactly a resume builder. As usual, she dressed professionally, high collar, pale green suit, and impeccably-groomed short blond hair. She would assist with changing slides and answering detailed financial questions.

After a short break, the Mayor, Susanna Smyth, mispronounced his name. "Erik Tem-u-hin. I see you've brought your projector. That must mean another presentation. Our other business has run long, so I'd appreciate if you can make this brief."

Ariq walked to the lectern between the rows of chairs and the committee members seated at desks. He took a calming breath. "Thank you. I will do my best. As you know, PopulistHealth successfully completed the multi-million-dollar conversion of the abandoned East End Elementary School, and the twenty-eight bed Roswell Orthopedic Clinic is up and running."

One of the members, a dairy farmer named Jorge Casales, wearing a string tie with a turquoise slider and a straw cowboy hat, interjected, "Orthopedic Clinic! We already have a perfectly good hospital. I can't even recall why we approved a clinic for out-of-state rich people."

Ariq paused. "Your regional hospital is excellent. PopulistHealth considered that as a benefit of selecting Roswell, and now we can be an economic growth engine for Roswell and all of Chaves County. We've also helped local people. Remember that infant with pyloric stenosis? We– "

"Yes, yes, that was for one of your own nurses, wasn't it? You pick and choose and only take care of your own."

Ariq did a double take. That was Dee, short for Delores, Fuentes, who interrupted him. She wore her trademark embroidered shirt and braids, the image prominently displayed in front of her popular bakery and on all their pink boxes. The clinic was a good customer and generally she supported them.

At this point, Mayor Smyth hit her gavel. "Let's skip the presentation. You're here to ask approval for a six-story medical facility. We discussed this at lunch yesterday and decided that we're not approving anything taller than the dome on the courthouse."

Ariq frowned, imagining the planning commission eating tacos and burritos at the Star Track Taqueria while discussing the future of a multi-billion-dollar corporation's investment in their small town.

"But we've been talking with the planning staff for over six months and they never said anything. Besides you already have buildings taller than the courthouse."

The courthouse, over 100 years old, had a beautiful beaux arts dome covered in green tile, so he could understand wanting to keep it visible. But the commission's arbitrary decisions frustrated him. He looked to Martina for support, but she ignored him, concentrating on setting up the projector which clearly would not be necessary. He silently thanked the Buddha that he'd left the E-Ro model in the car. Today was not the day.

While he considered his next move, a small group of protesters ran into the hearing room dressed as aliens and shouting, "Shut it down. Shut it down!" The voices behind the plastic masks seemed to be high school students or younger.

The mayor's gavel came down again. Dee spoke up. "That's enough. We gave our word. We are not shutting anything down. But we are also not expanding until we understand the full story. We think you have more plans than you are saying."

Ariq looked toward Marti. She shrugged her shoulders. It seemed like the E-Ro plans had leaked.

"We do have bigger plans for the Roswell community. I came

to present those today."

Jorge didn't seem to be interested, "Roswell is a city of culture and traditions with a sound economic foundation based on agriculture and aerospace. We do not need rich people escaping from big cities." Many heads nodded their agreement.

Ariq had walked into a trap. They'd set this up over tacos and burritos. This was a disappointing day for Ariq Böke's many-times-great grandson.

Martina hung up her cell and wrote a hasty note to Ariq. He read the note and stopped. He stood limp in front of the committee, lost, wondering what his ancestor would do. In that lull, one of the aliens, a short one, maybe preteen, ran to the front of the room and grabbed the note, handed it to Mayor Smyth, and stood by hopping up and down.

The note said, "Another death last night. Two more sick. Must find a way to isolate guests."

When PopulistHealth planned the ROC, they chose Roswell as a place for families: low crime, good schools, museums, and clean air. All plusses when recruiting doctors. They also wanted isolation from sick people and strange diseases. They targeted people scared of MDRs and able to afford travel. Big city hospitals had a reputation as incubators of multi-drug resistant diseases. ROC wouldn't have any sick people at all.

Unfortunately, in the last few weeks, guests at ROC were getting sick…and even worse, dying. The clinic was not prepared to deal with this crisis. First, they needed more space.

Susanna passed the note to the other members.

Ariq spoke before they could. "An unknown disease has infected some of our guests. We have been in contact with the CDC in Atlanta. Diagnosis is difficult, as we have guests from all over the United States, and internationally. The sickness is a mystery. One person—no, two now–two people have died."

Their friend Dee seemed shocked, "When were you going to tell us? Is this like that movie? Outbreak? Are the feds going to bomb Roswell?"

Ariq shook his head, regretting that he'd accepted this job

when he could have had a nice position in Denver. Maybe he should have stayed in Med School as эмѳѳ wanted. He didn't use that mechanical, English word—grandmother. Only эмѳѳ expressed the warmth and tradition that she embodied.

He sighed. "No one is going to bomb Roswell! But we do need more room to quarantine potentially contagious guests."

Clearly, they weren't going to approve the new hospital; the E-Ro project was dead for the moment.

A good general knew when to call for a strategic retreat. There *was* something that would help, and getting an approval, any approval, would break their development moratorium. He'd use their concern based on Hollywood hype to his advantage.

"Next to the old elementary school, there is an abandoned motel. I think it was called The Area 51 Hideout."

He looked around. He had everyone's attention. Even the aliens were listening and nodding, antennas and springy eyes bobbing. "With your approval, we could convert the motel rooms to be private rooms to isolate our guests from each other and the people in town. We could institute BioSafety Level 1 protocols immediately and increase the level if recommended by the CDC."

The committee smiled at "isolate," and again for "BioSafety Level." Would the planning commission go for this, at least?

The mayor looked at her watch, turned left and right to her committee members, and used her gavel one last time, "Motion seconded, passed, meeting adjourned."

Ariq wondered what had just happened. Were they telepathic aliens? They hadn't even voted. But he wasn't going to argue points of order. Martina gave him a quick smile. Within a few minutes, they had gone from total prohibition to consent to acquire and renovate a second property. Martina knew as well as he did that corporate in Minneapolis had acquired the Area 51 Hideout long ago, and the refit was virtually complete. The approval was after the fact, but important.

He looked toward Marti and folded his hands together, like closing a book. She packed up the projector and stood to leave.

He looked at the committee. "Thank you. As you now know,

we have our work cut out for us."

He turned to go.

Jorge stopped them. "Just one minute. We hear that you have been housing bats in one of those old classrooms."

Ariq waited to see what the dairy farmer and amateur veterinarian would say next. The last thing he wanted was to discuss his small Chiropteran Research Center, really a grandiose name for a collection of a few hundred local Mexican Free-Tail bats and a handful of other species.

Jorge continued, "We have not approved anything like that."

Ariq gave a non-committal, "I understand," and continued to walk out with Martina at his side.

They would live to fight another day.

5. LILY

KATHERINE, ARNHEMLAND, AUSTRALIA

Auntie Pearl's face showed exactly what she thought of the hospital and what it was and wasn't doing for June Araminty. Lily didn't have much experience with *balanda* hospitals. She had seen five different native healers deal with various illnesses and injuries, and it seemed to her that the hospital was very clean, cold, and inefficient. She wondered if her **Bat Chat** friend Ariq would think the same thing, or if this was how they all were. No one was here with June, and that seemed very wrong. Everyone knew touch and human companionship helped to heal. She was glad she and Pearl had come.

June opened her eyes when Pearl's hand touched her forehead. June had tubes and bandages on her arm. Pearl was careful not to touch those. Pearl lifted June's eyelid and looked closely underneath. Then she felt June's neck and under the woman's arm. Lily watched, trying to hide her shock. How could someone so healthy look so suddenly like a stunned goanna? June's arms were limp, her skin a sickly shade of gray-brown. Her skin was dry and when Pearl pinched it the pinch mark took many seconds to flatten back out.

Pearl said something to June. It was a form of Gunwinyguan Lily did not speak. She and Pearl always spoke Alawa together. She tried to read their expressions and body language instead. Pearl was worried.

The old woman signaled to Lily. "She will try to eat," Pearl said.

Lily took the bowl of "bush tucker stew" out of the dilly sack and took the plastic cover off, musing about Pearl's willingness to use *balanda* gear to carry her treatment. The cover had fitted tightly and none of the medicine-rich stew had spilled, which was probably better than it would have done if they'd used a traditional gourd to hold it.

June's hand shook when she reached for the spoon, so Lily fed her, spoon by spoon, and June chewed and swallowed.

"Also, this," Pearl said when the stew was gone. She crushed a couple leathery leaves in her hand and put them in June's mouth. "Chew and spit," Pearl said, gesturing for Lily to hold the bowl in front of Pearl for the leaf scraps.

"Wild tomato?" Lily asked.

"Billy goat plum leaf," Pearl said.

June made a face.

When the leaves were chewed and spat out, Lily put everything away. She was pulling the string of the dilly sack tight as a hospital person came into the room.

"You should not be here," the woman said. Her nametag said she was a nurse. Lily knew the nurse did not have the same authority as a doctor, but did not know who had precedence, Pearl or nurse.

"We are leaving," Pearl said, her quiet dignity making the nurse smile.

"Thank you for visiting her. Tomorrow come a little earlier," the nurse said. "Visiting hours end at 7:30."

Lily nodded. "We understand." Though, of course, she didn't. How could there be hours for visiting? Why wouldn't people be able to visit the sick as the sick needed? Everyone knew touch and smiles of friends were important. How could the hospital want to limit such contact? She would have to ask Ariq why this was a rule in hospitals.

———

Pearl reached an arm back over the roof of the rattling pickup truck and pounded on the dusty metal.

Pearl's friend Gima stopped the truck and stuck his head out the window. "We are here?" he called.

"This is good," Pearl said, gathering herself up from the seats bolted to the truck bed. Using the side of the truck bed, she pulled herself to her feet, Lily's arm steadying her.

Meanwhile, Gima's son jumped out of the front and ran

around to the back of the truck. He opened the back gate and set down the short plastic stairs so Pearl could step down to the ground. Once the old woman was firmly on the road, Lily grabbed their water bottles, dilly bags, and her backpack and stepped down beside Pearl.

"Thank you, thank you," Lily said to Gima and his son, who nodded and got back into the cab.

Gima's dark brown arm waved out the window as the truck lurched back into motion and moved down the road. Lily held her hand over her face until the dust died down a little bit. When she uncovered her face, she saw that Pearl had headed off the road, toward a barely-seen path through the bush.

"Come, girl. If we are going to get fresh leaves and get back, we need to get started!"

As they walked along, Pearl occasionally pointed out something for Lily to pick and bring to her. Some were lessons Lily already knew from the Ngukurr herb-women. Some were new, or were of slightly different-looking varieties than the ones she had learned in lands to the east. A few items went into the dilly bags for June or for Pearl's supplies, the rest into Lily's bag, or discarded, their lesson complete.

"Did you find a place for drying your supplies?"

Lily sighed. "No, I'm still using the back porch of my aunt's house. I need to have my own place soon."

"Yes," Pearl said, nodding her head vigorously. "Or at least build a cover over your things; rain will ruin it all.

"I know. I plan to have a place by then."

"You go to the compound; you can build your own place."

Compounds of native people, like in Ngukurr. Lily sighed again. "Yes. But I am not sure that's what I want, Auntie." No electricity. No internet. She was not committed to the Aboriginal way of life. Yet. Maybe never. "It's difficult to explain, I just feel so lost."

Pearl snickered. "That is what the compound is for: to teach the ways of your country, so you are not lost."

"Ngukurr... "

"Those people are testing you Lily. You cannot just give up because they make an insult at you."

"Maybe."

Pearl laughed out loud. "Maybe I bring you to Warra for lessons. You will not say, 'maybe' if he is teaching you things, eh?"

Lily walked silently for a few moments.

"Who is Warra?"

Pearl laughed again. "Very smart man. He is sheepdog trainer for Karr Station. He can teach sheepdogs, he can teach Lily, eh?" She laughed and laughed, using the hem of her skirt to pat her eyes dry.

Lily wasn't sure if Pearl was insulting her or not. She made herself smile a small smile, and hoped the old woman meant it kindly.

"Oh! Supper!" Pearl pointed to a two-foot long goanna sunning itself on a fallen gum tree trunk.

Lily took her cue and picked up a good-sized rock in her fist. She crept silently up behind the fat lizard and whacked it over the head. It bounced off the log and thrashed a moment. Lily dropped the rock, picked up the goanna, and neatly snapped its neck.

"Good, good," Pearl chortled, then abruptly fell silent as Lily rejoined her on the path. Lily looked where Pearl was staring.

Ahead of them were soldiers, in desert camouflage clothes, rifles pointed at the two women.

Soldiers, in Jurassic Cycad Gardens?

Guns?

Lily glanced down guiltily at the goanna in her arms. Maybe they weren't supposed to be hunting inside the Park?

6. NGA

LUAMBE, NIASSA, MOZAMBIQUE

In the mid-day heat, Nga left Halid to finish changing the bandage on the baby's ear to take a telephone call. Her mother leaned out the back door of their house, holding the clunky old phone out. Nga nodded thanks and Linnea went back inside, pausing by the screen door to listen.

"Hello?"

"Nga? Hello, it's Ben Kalagho, do you remember me?"

"Yes, of course, hello Ben." He'd gone through training with her in Maputo, even though he was from Malawi. The telephone cord came up short as she tried to turn around, so she opened the screen and went into the kitchen. Her mother reached around her and closed the door. "What can I do for you?"

"Have you heard about this thing in Zambia?" Ben's accent was very strong. It took a moment for Nga to parse it. "Yes. We have heard."

"So we have no illness yet, but there are people crossing the border night and day, and I fear they bring the disease with them."

"Yes, I wondered about that. We had someone from Malawi up here yesterday, on their way to the coast. Said they were trying to stay ahead of it."

"Exactly," Ben said. "I am taking some friends and family to Maputo. I am in Lichinga right now, and I thought of you. You should go. You should take your family and your village and go to Maputo as quickly as you can."

"I'm not sure I can convince them… "

"But you must!" Ben's voice was frantic. "You are going to be overrun, Zambians here, Malawians there, and soon all are sick!"

"Ben, it's 2500 kilometers to Maputo from here. Even if I can convince them to go, we have no way to get there."

"I have seen this thing, Nga. It is very bad. It is very fast. It is very fatal. You do not want to wait for it to come to you. Go! Go now!"

"All right, Ben. I'll try."

"I want to see you in Maputo, very soon!"

"Okay. Thank you."

"Maputo!" he said, then hung up.

Nga looked at the phone, handed it to her mother to hang up. Linnea met her eyes. "Did you hear that?" Nga asked her.

"I heard him say Maputo," her mother said.

"Plague."

"In Malawi?"

"He said it is coming from Zambia, but he also said he had seen it, so I think it is in Malawi now, yes."

"What is it?" she grabbed Nga's hands.

"No one seems to know, but it's bad."

Linnea fell to her knees, dragging Nga with her. "Our Heavenly Father we pray to you for guidance and strength in this time of our need."

Mu and Teleza's heads poked around the corner, eyes wide. Nga shook her head at them, and they ducked back into the living room, where they were supposed to be finishing their Bible study, no doubt. Leza would be going to school in a few days, but Mu was still not ready. Learning to read from the Bible never hurt anyone.

School.

The village.

What should she do? Certainly she should tell them, tell everyone, what her friend had said. If this plague was bad enough to frighten a trained *técnico*, it was bad news. Some people might want to leave.

"Mother, I have to go." She pulled her right hand free and began prying her mother's fingers off her left hand. Her mother let go, but continued praying in a terror-stricken whisper.

Nga had spent years in prayer. She was no longer certain that it would do anything to help the people of Luambe.

She got to Salim to ask him to call a village meeting at the same time that a pair of strange men ran into the village from the west. They started shouting, at her, at Salim, at everyone. It sounded like Bemba, but Nga did not speak it well enough to be certain— she just recognized the accent and a few words. But it meant the young men were from Zambia, almost certainly.

They realized no one understood them and began waving. One reached out and touched the red cross on Nga's coat. She had forgotten she even had a lab coat that had the red cross on it— most of hers were from Maputo hospital, from the TC program. The young man grabbed her hands and tugged her downhill, away from the mission and the village and toward the creek. She met Imrane's eyes as the young men tugged her past him. He apparently was worried enough he forgot to scowl at her.

She tried to speak to the strangers in Chiyao, then Portuguese. Nothing got through. Finally she realized one of the boys was saying, "Sick, sick," in English. Dread washed over her, numbing her cheeks and throat. Plague? She stumbled and fell to one knee, but the young man pulled her up, practically yanking her arm from its socket. She jerked her hand from his and rubbed her shoulder, following them.

They arrived at the side of the creek. Under the shade of a small stand of scrubby pine trees, there were eight or nine people gathered around a heavy-set man who was lying on the ground. He was sweating profusely, panting for air, and moaning. Nga squatted beside him, put her hand on the man's forehead. He was very hot. She checked her pockets, but had none of her tools with her. She put two fingers to the man's neck along the jawline, finding a thready pulse. His throat convulsed, his eyes rolled up in his head and his eyelids closed, trembling.

"Sick how long days?" she asked in her very poor English, hoping they would figure out what she meant.

"Many days," one woman said. "Five." The woman's headwrap came loose as she shook her head. "Six, maybe. Him," she pointed to another man, who was kneeling beside the creek, scooping up handful after handful of water, "sick three day." She wrapped the bright cloth back around her head, looking determined.

Sick six days, the other only three. The other man, an old skinny fellow, seemed a little shaky, but otherwise not nearly as bad as the big guy beside her feet. She reached to his face again and lifted one eyelid; his eyes were not jaundiced, but they were threaded with hundreds of tiny red veins that were usually not visible. Irritated sclera. It could be from dust or dryness. Maybe it wasn't the plague. Maybe this man had just walked too far, too fast for his weight and general lack of muscle tone, and not enough hydration. It looked like maybe he had just fainted, though that didn't explain the apparent fever.

"When he drink water?" Either her vocabulary or her accent was wrong, because they did not understand this question. She pointed to the man still drinking from the creek, then pointed to the fallen man, miming drinking. "How long he have water?"

There was an incomprehensible discussion, and then someone produced a metal cup and held it up. Nga gave up on trying to talk; she nodded and pointed to the creek. The young woman went to the water and scooped some up. She handed Nga the cup and stepped back. Nga pointed to two of the huskier young men standing around and waved them toward her. They finally figured out she wanted the man to drink and he needed to be sitting up to do so. She got the water to his mouth, but he was unresponsive; it merely dribbled down his chin. She saw signs of him trying to swallow, his throat moved, but his mouth was clamped closed.

She needed to get him to the clinic, get an IV in him. She finally conveyed what she wanted, and three men and one woman picked up the sick man and had started up the hill when Salim's voice rang out.

"Not here!" he yelled in Chiyao. "Do not bring them here to my village," he said, facing Nga. Then he turned his gaze to the strangers and yelled at them. "Why do you come here, with your sickness? Why do you bring this to our land, to my people? Go away! Go away! You are not welcome here!"

Of course the strangers understood nothing of his words, but they were quite adept at reading gesture and body language.

It had taken Salim no time at all to forget about Christian charity. Meanwhile, Imrane their *mundunugu* stood and watched also, not helping these obviously sick people.

But it soon did not matter. Quite simply, while they stood there, the big man died. The woman who had been holding his left leg let out a wail, then all the women were ululating. Nga watched helplessly as the four people carried him back across the creek, and the rest of the people picked up their various burdens and the old man by the water, and returned the way they had come, the wailing gradually fading to just an odd sound on the breeze.

7. HALID

LUAMBE, NIASSA, MOZAMBIQUE

Halid put his hand on his father's shoulder, trying to offer his support. He did not want to anger Nga, his teacher, but his father was right. The sickness should not be welcomed into the village. If it could be cured, why hadn't their own *mundunugu* or TC helped them? Why bring it here?

"Salim, we need to have a village meeting," Nga said. She glanced from him to Halid and back. He could see how concerned she was from the tightness of her face. "We must consider moving the village closer to a hospital if this thing is coming."

Salim nodded. "I will call them," he said, then looked at Halid. "You can go up the hill and get Palana and Kofi and the others up there."

Halid nodded.

"I'll get the mission people together," he heard Nga say as he began jogging up the hill. He turned back, continuing to move uphill as he called, "Meet by the clinic?" Both Salim and Nga nodded. He waved to them, turned back around, and went on up the rocky path toward the small clump of roundhouses at the top of the hill. Kofi's family, including all five of his sons and their Luambe wives, had actually wanted the hot sunny site on the hilltop. The rest of the village was scattered on the long slope down to the creek, in the cool shade beneath the blackwood and cedar trees.

Halfway up the hill, he saw the unmarried village girls playing the circle game in the clearing in front of his sister Surane's house. He saw Gezy had pretended to wear a woman's headwrap today, weaving a bright scarf through her hair. Gezy did not look at him. Fazila did though, like she always did. He could see she was thinking of something to say to him, but he called out before she could say it.

"Village meeting, please tell the others!"

Surane stepped to the arched doorway of her roundhouse and waved. She was so much older than Halid, he felt he had never had much in common with her, besides their parents. "I'll find Yannic," she called. Her husband was probably off hunting; he might not even get to the meeting. Halid waved back and continued trotting up the hill.

He found Palana and her husband Kofi working in their vegetable garden. Kofi's broken arm was still encased in the cast Nga and Halid had made for him after they set the broken bone. The cast was soil-colored now. Palana's round face was dripping with sweat. Halid paused and looked at the small field, which seemed filled with beans, cassava, groundnuts and onions. Leaves he wasn't sure of could be sweet potatoes or herbs. Perhaps their choice of the sunny spot had been quite clever; Halid hadn't been up here for weeks—they had made a garden of the place.

He nodded at the couple, who had stopped their work and looked at him. "Village meeting," he said, and they nodded.

"Halid, would you mind going over the hill and finding Bemel and Sami? They are chopping up an old tree over there," Palana called.

Halid nodded.

She smiled at him. "Thank you! We will get the others."

Halid continued along the path past four other roundhouses and into the grass where the path faded out. He heard the sound of Bemel's good axe and Sami's bad one and headed that direction. He soon saw the two young men, bent over a fallen cedar tree.

"Hey!" he called. Bemel waved to him. "Village meeting!"

Bemel nodded, picked up his axe and headed toward Halid, Sami joining him as they moved past the pile of chopped wood. Halid turned and jogged back over the hill and down.

What did his village want to do? If they were going to leave for a hospital, probably in Maputo, they should go soon, if it wasn't already too late. Halid already knew he would go, but what about everyone else?

It took less than an hour for all the people to gather in the open

39

space around the clinic. More than 200 villagers, plus nine people from the mission.

Nga took the lead, telling them about the warning from the Malawi couple, Ben's telephone call, the man who had died.

"I do not know what this sickness is," she said. "I do not know if the man who died had this plague or something else." She paused, then finished, "It is killing many people in Zambia. The people with the man who died spoke Bemba like in Zambia. So…the sickness is moving. I thought it would not reach us here, so far away. But people are coming, and it looks like they're bringing it with them."

Halid could hear many murmurs as the villagers took in this news.

Nga finished, "I cannot decide for you what to do. But I will say this: if any want to try to get to Maputo and the big hospital there, I will go with you, show you the way."

Halid's father stepped forward then and spoke to his people.

He spoke a long time. As headman, he would stay here. He would protect the village as best as he could. Any who wanted to go were free to go. Any who wanted to stay would be protected.

Imrane interrupted whatever Salim had been taking a breath to say next, "I will stay, of course. You will have my care here." Halid was astonished to see the man's eyes shoot an ugly look at Nga. "The *téchnico* has no cure for this, but I do."

What? Halid leaned forward. Did Imrane know this sickness?

Salim frowned at the *mundunugu*. "Do you know what this is, then? Have you seen it before, where you come from?"

Imrane stared at Salim a moment, a sort of poison in his gaze. Then he turned and addressed the villagers as if Salim had never spoken. "My teacher gave me the ways of *my* people, your cousins the Makonde. I came here to help because you had no Yao healer. I learned many ways to stop fever, to heal using the gifts of the earth—plants and animals that offer medicines to help this—all the *mundunugu* ways."

"So you know what this is?" Halid interrupted him to ask again. The man had evaded his father's question. That wasn't right.

"I have not seen enough examples to know what this is exactly," Imrane said, obviously irritated by the interruption. "But I have learned to cure many, many fevers and chills. You know this," he looked around, meeting the eyes of several villagers he had helped. He did not look at the ones he had not helped, Halid noted—the ones who had come to the clinic, to Nga and Halid. "I gave up my life with my own people to come here to help you, and I say this is something I can cure. It is foolish for people to leave, and your headman should not allow you to!"

"Thank you, Imrane," Salim said loudly, and this time his voice rode over what Imrane had begun to say next. His father did not give the other man a chance to speak again. Imrane was not respectful. Halid turned to face his father, a few feet away, giving the headman his complete attention and prompting other villagers to do so as well.

"We do not know if this thing will come here to us," his father, the headman, said in his loudest voice. Every eye was upon him now, from village and mission alike. "If it does, it could be bad. If it doesn't—if we are safe here in our distant village, then surely there is no reason to go. But if it does come here, we are a long way from a hospital. Our clinic might be overrun, and Imrane might have too many patients to cure. The village healer for the Bembe speakers was not able to cure the man that died. So it could be better for you to leave, go where they can help many people at a time, go where the disease may not reach."

He opened his arms in a freeing gesture. "It is up to you, each family, each person, if you want to stay here, or if you want to do what several people have suggested: go far away, to maybe someplace safer, with many healer-doctors. It is your own choice."

"If any decide to leave, it should be soon," Nga added at the end.

Halid stood now between Nga and his father, torn about whom to follow. He had always wanted the medical training Nga had gotten in Maputo. But he also had wanted to learn his own people's healing methods. He'd asked Imrane if he could learn from him if Imrane would teach him. The man's flat refusal and his cold dismissal of Halid's interest still puzzled him. Now– his family was here, his father would stay. Salim and Anane stood next to each other, chatting softly with villagers who came up to them for advice, for reassurance.

Nga turned toward her parent's house. Mr. and Mrs. Lind stood with arms around each other. "We will stay," Halid heard Anson Lind say. "If plague comes all the way here, it is God's Will. But I will not ask anyone from the mission to stay if you wish to go with Nga."

Halid saw several of the more devoted villagers listening to the man who taught Christian ways. A few moved forward, toward Nga, a few toward Salim, where of course, Imrane stood also. Imrane stood still, looking like a scrawny stork, his head, his eyes darting back and forth between the groups.

Nga hugged her mother, then Linnea Lind's eyes closed as she clung to her husband, lips moving in prayer. Nga stepped away from her parents, toward her clinic, a small group of villagers moving with her.

Halid sighed, then walked over to stand with Nga. He'd been begging to go to Maputo for training. This seemed like an answer to *his* prayer. More villagers joined them, including Halid's mother Anane.

Anane's eyes were on her husband. Salim looked sad, but he nodded at his wife, glanced toward Halid then away again. Oh, that was it. Halid's brothers and sister were grown adults who could take care of themselves, but Anane would go with Halid. Because he was young, because he was unmarried, because they saw him as a child. He saw them smile gently at each other across the heads of other villagers. But a flash of anger washed through him.

He was sixteen years old! He was ashamed that they still thought of him as a child who needed his mother. Should he tell Anane he did not want her to go? He took a deep breath, readying his speech. And then he thought a moment more.

Was he a reader-of-minds, then? No, he could not say what

was in their heads. Maybe Anane simply wanted to go. Maybe she was setting an example for other village mothers. If he was old enough to be on his own, he should consider all possibilities. He needn't jump to the worst conclusion. His two sisters were married; their own families would decide what to do. His older brother had moved away to his own wife's village. So...why would Anane need to stay here? Salim would stay and she would go–the headman would stay with his village, while the headman's wife would go with the villagers who traveled.

Instead of speaking, he let the villagers distract him, let his anger dissipate. Who was going? It looked like a bigger group than he had first guessed.

Nga turned to her sister and Halid watched them closely. He had had many talks with the white woman who had married a native. Of course, she was born here, too, but she was not Yao. Imrane was not Yao either, so it was maybe a good match. Halid had asked Mezi about white and black, about pride and shame, about husbands and wives. He knew Imrane was not a good husband, he was not kind to his children, he did not honor his wife. Would Mezi dare leave without him?

Mezi stood between the two groups, holding Muzuzi's hand, her other hand atop Teleza's curly head. She and Imrane stared at one another. Teleza burst into tears, knowing something bad was happening. Halid held his breath.

Imrane's expression was appalled when Mezi turned and walked to Halid and Nga, leading her two children with her.

Anane's gentle voice lifted up out of the group around them. "We will go. But how shall we get there?" she asked.

8. DR. BRIAN

SOMEWHERE IN THE SOUTH PACIFIC

R_X Doctor Brian couldn't sleep. His reaction to discovering his daughter alive had uncovered so many feelings, feelings buried through years of therapy. He felt like he had PTSD. He relived the anger at his drunk wife for driving off the road and rolling into an arroyo fifty feet below. He still hated her for surviving.

Then there was the fear when he first saw Penny, bruised and bloody. He was so afraid she'd die. He could still see that ugly, mechanical structure with screws stuck through her arm. The cyborg erector set with the clumsy name: external fixator. For months, his daughter was a monster. When he saw the scars yesterday, it all came back to him.

He had wanted to hug his daughter, but the insult and indignity of her running away with her mother—the woman who had nearly killed her—overwhelmed him. She had deserted her father who had loved her and took care of her when her mother was drunk.

Now he regretted it all—trying to hug her, trying to reclaim her love. He was on a ship sailing south. He had lost his daughter again.

From a half-sleep of regret and fatigue, he heard a knock on his cabin door. He thought it might be room service bringing breakfast. He rolled out of bed and wrapped his lab coat that he used for a robe over the scrubs he wore for pajamas. He ran his fingers through the gray hair on the side of his head and looked in the mirror. He looked good for his age, some wrinkles, and a short gray beard. He touched the Doctor Brian patch on his coat and slid his feet into the ship's slippers. Alternately holding the furniture and rails he headed to the door.

"Coming."

When he opened the door, he saw Jake. What? He turned around to look out the window. It was too early for room service, and Fatu Hiva was outside again. They were still in Omo'a Bay.

"Jake? What's going on?"

Jake pushed in and closed the door. "We've got trouble. Three passengers and one crew are very sick. I spoke to the kitchen staff."

Brian had so many questions. He didn't know where to start. "How did you talk to them? None of them speak English."

Jake smiled, "I speak seven languages. Three from my childhood—I was born in Spain and went to school in Switzerland, so French and German. I even speak a little Basque, but I don't count that. For business, I've learned English, Mandarin, and Japanese. Finally, for occasions like this, I also know enough Tagalog. That's what a lot of the crew speaks."

Brian stopped listening part way through. Must be because Jake is in sales, he thought. He just can't give a short answer. Considering his next question with more care, "How are we in trouble? I feel fine."

"I've seen this before. They're going to quarantine the ship. We'll be stuck. I need to sell sequencers, and you need to save the world."

He understood immediately, and knew exactly what to do, "No problem. Just follow me."

Doctor Brian put on his shoes, grabbed his wallet, and headed toward the disembarkation level. As he expected, medical techs were preparing to remove the sick from the ship. He knew that before they quarantined the crew and passengers, they'd want to transport the sick people to a place where they could get better care and, more importantly, not die on the ship.

He followed the party to the infirmary. He introduced himself, "I'm Doctor Brian. My specialty is infectious diseases. If you'll give me and my associate…" He pointed to Jake, "some gloves and masks, we'll be glad to accompany these patients to the on-shore clinic where we will make a more detailed examination."

The ship's doctor, which Brian thought might be an honorary

title, seemed glad to hand off the sick people to someone else. His specialties were likely sea sickness and first aid.

Appropriately protected, they followed the four stretchers to the tender and headed ashore.

Jake looked at him with admiration and for once just kept quiet.

———

As the tender moved toward the dock, he counseled himself, "Do not get excited. The accident was long ago and had nothing to do with you. Penny is alive and happy. You are the father. Be happy for her. Live and learn. Let go and let god." He remembered his rage counselor saying, "All you need to know about God is that you're not." He nodded. That was correct, he believed that.

He practiced his breathing. He looked at Jake. Jake was bursting.

"Good job. You did it. We're off that floating death ship. Those people on the stretchers are really sick."

Jake couldn't sit still. He walked around the tender, stem to stern, from the bridge to the lower seating levels. Each time he passed Brian, he said something.

"Brilliant. Well done. It's great to travel with a doctor. Do you know what is wrong with these folks?" He changed the subject before Brian could formulate an answer. "Don't worry about being stuck on Fatu Hiva. I've already called for a small plane to take us to Papeete. From there, the world is ours. My next sales call is Sydney, then Delhi, and, can you believe it, Maputo, Mozambique. Even Africa has millions for sequencers. I told you I'm going to get rich."

Jake seemed to be a man of action, but Brian worried about details. "What about our luggage back on the ship?"

"This is not as rare an occurrence as you might expect. I'll contact them when we're safely in Papeete and our luggage will catch up to us in a week or two."

More details. Brian recalled Jake mentioning his wife. "What about your wife? You just going to leave her on the ship?"

Jake just laughed. "That's the funny part. Dee had always planned to spend a couple of weeks on Fatu Hiva. She'll join the next cruise."

When Jake headed for the airstrip, Brian went to the clinic and his daughter, shaking and sweating, but promising himself not to create another scene.

———

At the clinic, he was recognized from the previous dance incident; two large men blocked the door. He put his hands up, palms out, to signify coming in peace. He pointed to his name patch, "Doctor Brian."

Penelope looked up and stared at him. He stared back. She had her mother's prominent cheeks, small nose and mouth, but she had his eyes, bright green eyes. He just concentrated on those eyes. He smiled.

She walked up to him, "It is nice to see you. Please do not make another fuss." She glanced at his lab coat. "When did you become a physician?"

He didn't dare speak, but showed his palms again and blinked his green eyes.

She silently reached out and shook his hand. Tears ran down his face. "You haven't changed," she laughed. "You're still a pompous, arrogant old fool."

She pointed to the patch on his lab coat again. "Did I miss something? Are you really a doctor now?"

He smiled. Maybe his little girl was back? He shook his head. "No, not really. Sometimes I feel like a doctor."

"Okay doctor, can you help with these four?"

He shrugged his shoulders and tried to look contrite, "I doubt it."

"Here's the plan. We'll stabilize them as best as we can with IV fluids, antibiotics, and sedatives. Then they'll be flown to Papeete."

———

That night he had dinner with Penny and Jake. Brian started to doubt that Jake had a wife when he made apologies for her absence. He realized he'd never met her. Jake just went on to his story of international disease and how it was going to make him rich.

Having heard Jake's story before, Brian watched Penny. Dinner preparation and presentation seemed to be the responsibility of a native couple. They didn't seem to be servants, more like friends who dropped by to help.

He marveled at Penny's confidence as she managed the dishes coming and going, starting with an orange peanut soup, and then pork dumplings, various skewers, different noodles, stir-fried vegetables, many of which he could not identify. Dishes just came and went, with clean utensils and plates at various points.

He ignored Jake's tale and relaxed, playing the proud father home for dinner at his daughter's home.

One thing bothered him. Penny also seemed bored by Jake's story of selling medical equipment and getting rich. After some thought, he decided that she was just happy to see her father and found the salesman's story just interfering noise.

Penelope didn't say anything about her mother or how she ended up in French Polynesia. But beginning in Tahiti, she told her story. "I needed a job, so I told them I was a nurse. After learning to insert IV needles, I did well."

Being glad that Jake had finally stopped talking, he stared into her matching green eyes and thought, that's my daughter. Fearless. Intelligent. Up to conquer any challenge.

"I am very proud of you."

They were all drinking Hinano beer. After opening her second bottle, her fingers played with the label. She ended up peeling off the picture of the Tahitian girl. She continued her biography, "I took some premed courses at *Université de la Polynésie Française*. This led to a scholarship to complete my studies. I spent six years in France and came back here with a real M.D. and a government job which has taken me to various island clinics.

At this point Jake and Penny had a five-minute discussion in French. Brian just nursed his beer and watched his daughter's face.

Feeling encouraged by the happy reunion, he vowed, "I'm going to come out of retirement to help with this strange disease Jake has been telling us about."

Penny just stared at him. He couldn't read this reaction, so imagined that she was proud of her dad.

The next morning, she had another discussion in French with Jake, and they all exchanged contact information. Jake and Brian got on the small plane that would take them to Papeete.

Penny returned to her clinic.

Jake went off to sell sequencers.

Brian headed for New Jersey and Miller and Miller, one of the largest pharmaceutical companies in the world. They must be in a panic for trained personnel and would be glad to see him.

9. ARIQ

ROSWELL, NEW MEXICO

Before the sun could skim along the flat plain to the east, Ariq saddled up his pony and galloped west toward the ancient volcanos of the Sierra Blanca range. He leaned forward, pressing his ear against her neck. He could hear the steady heartbeat as blood pumped through her long carotid artery. The same artery a warrior targeted to silently kill—a person. Never a pony. White Ears kicked up a cloud of dust galloping across the gray desert before it colored red and orange with the sunrise.

Ariq held the mane with one hand and let his other arm dangle down, imagining he was carrying a bow like his Mongolian ancestors. This morning ride prepared him for the symbolic battle ahead.

While he visualized attacking the ancient cities of the Asian steppes, he fashioned a name for the mystery disease. Naming it after the clinic would be bad karma. It presented malaria symptoms—fever, chills, tremors—but it wasn't malaria. He also didn't want to advertise that they were clueless. In the end, he settled on IA, idiopathic ague, Latin for malaria symptoms of unknown cause.

Every morning, Ariq had a stand-up meeting with the staff. The no-sitting rule served two purposes. First, it kept things short and efficient. Second, mobility and openness, changing location each day spread his presence throughout the hospital. He modeled this on sunrise meetings Mongol generals held on horseback.

This morning he emphasized the approval of the Area 51 Annex to put a positive spin on the previous day's disastrous meeting with the city.

"Number one priority: idiopathic ague. What have you done? What's next?"

As usual, Nizhoni, chief nursing administrator, spoke up first.

Ariq felt a familial affinity for the Navajo nurse, her high cheekbones reminded him of эмээ back home. He'd read that the native Americans descended from Asian immigrants. Though separated by many millennia, he shared their journey.

"I have adjusted the nursing assignments to staff the new Annex. We'll begin moving guests tomorrow. Also, surgical face masks are now standard for all nursing staff when in guest areas."

Ariq gave a Nizhoni a small smile but inwardly cheered. He could count on her to set any discussion in the right direction.

She added, "I found masks that come in a variety of colors to help minimize the scary nature of this change."

"Good thinking," Ariq said.

Next, Lachlan chimed in. Lachy's blond hair, never in place, but also never sloppy, along with his blue eyes and square chin, gave him the look of a someone from a Foster's beer commercial rather than a young surgeon from Australia.

As a junior staff member, no one expected him to speak at staff meetings, but he seemed blind to such social cues. Everyone humored him, thanks to his youthful exuberance and excellent medical skills. "Now that we have the new annex, all new guests will start there. This will isolate them until they are evaluated."

Ariq had suggested something like this, but the doctors were slow to accept change. To be fair, being in a remodeled elementary school limited their options.

Since they had open-air hallways, standard for schools in the southwest, guests were transported in bubbles. The bubbles, called space suits in deference to Roswell sensibilities, provided sterile environments for the guests. Now with this mysterious disease, the space suits performed double duty as quarantine chambers.

"Will the doctors also wear face masks during their rounds like the nurses?"

The surgeons had resisted this, but with two deaths, Ariq felt he had to bring it up again.

Lachy frowned. "Yes, but we'll not be wearing the cute pastel ones selected by the nurses."

Marti laughed at this comment, before raising her issue. "We differentiate the ROC from other facilities with better service, fine cuisine, 24/7 visiting hours, and family-friendly accommodations. We treat our clients as guests, more like a hotel than a hospital.

"However, since the IA infections, we've had to restrict visitation, especially by children. Now with the Area 51 Hideout online, guests have private suites and we've restored family visits."

Ariq appreciated her concern for the guests. Finance was at the bottom of the hospital pecking order, an opinion reinforced by her responsibility for the physical plant, janitorial services, and waste disposal. She had suggested it was sexist to assign her these housekeeping jobs, but an informal survey by human resources, also under her purview, confirmed that this was a common practice, especially for small hospitals like the ROC. However, none of this made it easy for medical staff to take her seriously.

Ariq worried she was disappointed being stuck in the middle of the desert. She was single, probably past menopause, and generally very private. Marti rarely said anything—personal or otherwise. While the clinic was glad to have her, he doubted she had better opportunities.

Ariq had similar mixed feelings about his position. After graduating from one of the few schools that accepted foreign students from Mongolia, he stayed in Colorado and tried med school—for his family.

Эмээ, a small child when the communists took over, was a traditional healer. She encouraged his father into medicine, but with the influx of Russian doctors, the only opportunity was as a nurse. The family worked hard to send Ariq to the United States and were disappointed when he dropped out of medical school.

Ariq had a talent for administration but feared that his innate cold-hearted drive and ruthlessness made him unsuited to his job.

He justified his decision by his love of research, bat research. When PopulistHealth hired him, they agreed to a free day each week for him to pursue his investigations. The proximity to Carlsbad with hundreds of thousands of Mexican free-tail bats sealed the deal. However, he skipped his research days as many weeks as he took them.

He came back to the now. People were fidgeting, tired of standing still so long. "In the last month, two of our guests have died. And worse, they died of unknown causes. Like with the MDR outbreaks seen at general hospitals, people are starting to avoid us. Idiopathic ague must be stopped."

He wanted to close on an upbeat note. "With several new cases, we need to take special care using quarantine and isolation procedures. We can solve this problem. I want each group to go back and examine their house. Nursing, Surgery, Facilities. I expect daily reports from every department. No idea is too speculative. We're in Roswell. Check if we've been invaded by aliens."

Nervous laughter filled the room.

————

As everyone returned to work, he accompanied Joni to a nearby nursing station. Morning meetings were usually held near one, bringing the nursing staff briefly into the management circle. It helped everyone feel like part of the Clinic team.

IA cases were assigned to private rooms. Continuous electronic monitoring supplemented the regular rounds by nurses.

One IA case was nearby. Ariq, Joni and a small group of nurses put on gloves and masks and went to visit him. Ariq tried to see guests every day.

He looked at the chart with IA written in the corner in pink highlighter. Aside from that, the unremarkable chart included the guest's name, history, and vital signs. Ariq could see the guest was sweating and trembling.

The nurses waited a few feet back as he approached. "Mr. Elleich. How are you feeling?"

The gasping response was hard to understand. "My mouth is so dry…and I am cold all over." After what seemed like a supreme effort, he double-clicked his PCA and relaxed.

Joni tugged on Ariq's sleeve. He backed away, understanding

that Mr. Elleich had just used his Patient Controlled Analgesia to give himself two doses of morphine. No more talking for a while. They exited the room.

Just as well. Ariq felt drained and headed back to his office. He closed his door. Something told him that all the charisma, leadership, and management in the world wouldn't solve this. This would require science, research, insight, creativity, and, a thing he had no control over—luck.

Even though his family back in Mongolia wanted him to be a doctor, and his ancestors wanted a warrior, at this moment he felt drawn in a third unknown direction.

10. LILY

When the dust cloud settled a bit, they could see it was Gima and his truck again, coming back. Pearl was laughing as she waved him down. Gima pulled to the side of the road and slowed to a stop beside Lily and Pearl. This time the back of the truck was full of chattering people. Gima's son was riding in the back; Lily could see two old white heads inside, riding with Gima. The son jumped up to give Pearl one of the seats in the back. He and Lily sat on the floor with some other people Lily did not know.

Pearl waved toward Lily. "This is Lily," she said.

The very round woman sitting next to Pearl gave Lily a hard look. "Bat-dreaming Marra Girl," she said. Her voice was as hard as her look. Lily's insides shriveled to a small hard knot. Not again.

Pearl laughed. "There are no Marra girls," she said. "This is Lily. Lily, this is Kalinda Warramiri."

They nodded to each other, but the woman, Kalinda, did not smile. Kalinda turned and talked with Pearl. A wreath of wild brown curls framed the woman's plump face. She wore a shirt and skirt very much like Pearl's, though the solid red blouse looked good with the red and yellow flowers of the skirt. Realizing she was staring, Lily glanced around the group of people in the truck bed.

One of the boys next to Lily stared at the dead goanna in her lap.

"Dinner," Pearl said loudly. "From Lily."

Kalinda looked a little more kindly. "We have yams," she said.

The boy staring at the goanna said, "And we have billy goat plums."

"Good," Pearl said, laughing, "we have supper. We'll bake goanna in my stone oven, you come to my house."

55

Everyone nodded.

"Thought you said you'd be in the bush all day," Gima's son said. Lily still did not know his name. It was embarrassing.

Pearl scowled. "Soldiers in the Preserve."

At this everyone stopped talking and looked at Pearl.

"Say they have health problem there. Say we cannot go into the Gardens. Told us to leave."

"They were Americans," Lily said. Everyone looked at her. "They had American accents," she said.

"Whitefella soldiers at Mataranka, likewise," Gima's son said. "Maybe American, maybe not."

Mataranka. Where Lily's bats liked to nest. She scowled down at the goanna in her lap.

"They were catching bats, ones we saw," Kalinda said.

What were Americans doing with Lily's bats?

Lily raised her head to meet Kalinda's eyes. Whatever the woman saw in Lily's face made Kalinda soften. She nodded at Lily, a faint smile on her lips.

Lily nodded back. Maybe there was a little respect there for her. Maybe.

"I need to go back," Lily said.

"After supper, after we see June again," Pearl said. "Maybe your American friend can help."

Lily nodded. Then she thought for a moment. How did Pearl know about Ariq? For that matter, how did Kalinda know about Lily's bat dreaming, or Ngukurr?

The only link Lily could think of was…Obrey.

Of course. He was always reading over her shoulder when she was online at the Café. "Everyone's connected to everyone," she said softly. She heard Kalinda pause in her conversation with Pearl, then the chatter started up again.

———

Lily helped Pearl smooth out the hot coals in the pit behind Pearl's house. They lifted the goanna down onto the coals, then Lily used a couple branches as makeshift tongs to place a dozen yams around the lizard.

Pearl gave instructions to prepare a little stew of the plums, and they added the last of Pearl's small stash of sugar to the pot. The plums were very tart. Someone had promised to bring mangos to add to the fruit stew, but it was still nice to have a little sugar. Lily needed to remember to bring Pearl some sugar to replace the old woman's supply.

They left the supper to bake and took another bowl of bush stew to June Araminty at the Katherine Hospital.

June's skin still seemed very dry, and she was feverish, but she was happy to eat Pearl's medicine stew. Lily fed it to her again. While they were still there, they were joined by Kalinda and another woman.

"Good, you are still here, Pearl." Kalinda nodded at Lily. Then the three older women talked together in the language Lily did not know. Apparently it was all about June, because Kalinda, still talking, walked over and looked at June's eyes, and felt beneath the sick woman's arm.

Pearl's voice took on an angry tone, and Kalinda waved her hands about and yelled back. Lily finished giving June the stew, then glanced at Pearl to see if there were more leaves for June to chew. It took a few moments for Pearl to stop yelling and reach into her smaller medicine bag. She took out a different kind of leaf, which she handed to Lily whole.

"She should chew the whole thing and leave it in her mouth a little while time."

Kalinda shook her head. "Should not."

June opened her mouth, and Lily gave her the leaf on her tongue. June started chewing, then made a terrible face. "Gahh!" She spat the leaf out before Lily could catch it. It made a bright yellow stain on June's hospital dress. That maybe meant it was a black boab tree leaf, but Lily had never seen one before, so she wasn't sure.

Kalinda was still grumbling to Pearl, pointing to the stain and at Lily who was trying to clean it up.

"Enough," Pearl said. "Supper time."

They all walked outside to discover Gima's truck waiting to drive them to Pearl's. They left the truck at the turnaround spot where the road turned into a path, and all walked together laughing and talking to supper at Pearl's.

When they got to Pearl's fire pit, they discovered other people had already arrived. Someone was stirring chopped mangos into the plum stew pot. Someone else had turned the yams over and covered most of the goanna with a flat metal "lid" made from what looked to Lily like a car's hubcap.

More people arrived, dragging another log to sit on, and that Pearl could later use for firewood. Someone handed out bowls made of gourd and when those ran out, of palm leaves. People ate with their fingers, gesturing and talking with their mouths full.

Lily felt more at home than she ever had, talking to Pearl's friends, and laughing about the ashy goanna skin, and eating, eating and laughing as the sun went down, and the darkness fell.

———

Lily thanked Pearl for the day's lessons, then excused herself from the party. If she hurried, she could get to the Casuarina Café before Obrey closed up.

She bought a cup of espresso and fifteen minutes' computer time from Obrey, smiling at him as she took her cup over to the computer table. It was quite dark outside, so at least she didn't have to worry about glare from the windows tonight.

She was still a bit confused about the different time zones. Was Ariq still awake? Was he working? She logged into the **Bat Chat**, but he wasn't there. She noticed she had new e-mails, and went to her mail page. Ariq had sent a list of symptoms. As she read over it, Lily's skin prickled. It sounded so much like June Araminty's illness. Could they be the same? How could that be? They were halfway around the world from each other.

Lily sent Ariq a message saying she had received his list and would ask her herb woman about them tomorrow. Meanwhile, did Ariq know anything about Americans in Australia to capture bats?

Obrey drifted over as she finished her e-mail.

"So are you the big gossip, then?" she asked him.

He raised his hands, shaking his head. "People talk to each other, Lily. Always have, always will."

I don't, she thought. But maybe that was the basis for the problems she'd had—in school, and in Ngukurr—she didn't talk much. Not like her friends.

She checked the Coop page. Someone had bid on one of her older paintings. Only $A350, but it was one of her first ones, small and not very good. Maybe that was a fair price.

Obrey's voice was loud in her ear. She jumped. "Maybe I can show your paintings on my walls," he said. She turned to find he was so close, bent over her shoulder, that their noses practically bumped. She growled at him.

Awareness clearly came to his expression and he backed off and stood up. "Sorry, I was just looking. I like your artwork so much... "

"My artwork?" she said in a little, dangerous voice.

"Yes!" Obrey said, making an angry face. "I've been telling you this awhile now. And I want to put it on my walls so others can see it. You should be proud to show it off, and maybe it will even sell some more for you."

Lily shook her head. "Nobody in Katherine buys anything," she said.

"Maybe," Obrey said. "But they sure cannot buy it if they don't even know it exists!"

Lily found she had nothing to say to that. He was right. She logged off and picked up her cup and took it to the counter. "Do you need help closing up?"

"No. Just leave it there," he said, walking behind the counter. His body language said he was annoyed. Maybe angry.

"Obrey... "

"What?" his voice was flat.

"I will bring my unsold paintings here and help you hang them, if that is what you want."

He looked at her, chewing on his bottom lip. She liked the way his eyes looked. She discovered she was staring, blinked and looked down at her backpack.

"Can I ask a favor of you?" she said, peeking up at him.

He seemed surprised. "Of course."

"Do you think you could give me a ride to Mataranka? I know it is a long way, I would help with gas, or even if you can only take me partway, it would help."

His forehead crinkled. "Mataranka? Now? What for?"

"Americans. They're catching my bats, Obrey. I have to stop them."

He blinked a few times, then nodded abruptly. "Of course," he repeated.

He locked the Café then they got into his green BMW. He was so proud of his car. He'd bought it cheap from an English tourist who claimed it was hopelessly broken. Obrey took it to his friend Damon, and the two of them fixed it up. Lily smiled at him as he started it up and they drove out onto the highway.

"Please accept this," she said, trying to hand him two five dollar bills.

He waved her off. "Nope." He glanced at her, a crooked grin on his face. "I'd like you to 'owe' me," he said.

"Mm," Lily replied. What did that mean?

He stopped on the side of the highway at the Mataranka Park turnoff, as she'd asked.

"Be safe," he said. She thought it was a very non-Aboriginal farewell, but then, Obrey had been to whitefella schools, too. It was part of what they had in common.

She closed his car door firmly, but still as quietly as she could. If the Americans were camped nearby, she didn't want to alert them. "Thank you," she mouthed to him. He nodded.

She waved goodbye to Obrey and walked into the dark.

11. NGA

LUAMBE, NIASSA, MOZAMBIQUE

Nga spent the night preparing. She looked at the old national map her parents had, trying to figure a route. She called friends for suggestions. Then she helped Mezi pack for the children. They could not carry much; at least part of the journey would have to be on foot. So, a minimum of food, with the plan to gather somehow along the way. Gear and clothing for cold and heat. Hunting supplies. A few utensils. She thought of the Bemba speaker's metal cup. It was a good idea. Also some plastic gear, light, unbreakable. A cooking pot.

The entire time she packed, she knew they could not possibly be prepared for this journey, nor could the villagers that joined her. But they would do their best. Anane's question rattled around in her head during every step of her packing. They had no truck, no money. How could they get all the way to Maputo?

One piece of good news was a return call from her friend Shelly in Nacala. If they could somehow get their group to that town on the seacoast, her father's Fisheries boat there might take them as far as Beira. That would be a huge help. The boat was under repair, but they expected to set sail August 20th.

It was so frustrating. If they just had a bus big enough to hold everyone, they could drive there by tomorrow night. Instead, Nga wondered how on earth they could be in Nacala in five days.

Astonishing her, her mother came up with a solution.

"Look, Nga," Linnea said quietly, as was her usual way. The first mystery of their mother was her ability to gather the attention of the family, the mission, the village with her quiet way, while bluff Anson or loud, lordly Salim had to yell. Nga walked over and looked at the map where Linnea was pointing. "If you can get down to Unango, maybe by canoe, then you have a good road to go to Lichinga. In Lichinga is the train. It goes straight to Nacala."

"Yes, I planned the canoes. We cannot buy train tickets

though," Nga said.

"Once upon a time, a family came from Sweden this way," her mother said. "Poor missionaries, no money for train tickets." She smiled and met Nga's eyes. "We snuck on board. Those days, people rode on the top of trains, or inside empty cars, or on loads of shipments. I have heard it is still done this way. Nobody bothers about it. Only rich people pay to ride in the passenger cars."

Nga looked at her mother's face. It was hard to imagine Linnea Lind sneaking aboard a train. She met her mother's smile, then bent to look more closely at the map. She rubbed her eyes as the tiny print blurred. "Well, if that can be done, then the hardest part is getting from Unango to Lichinga."

"Maybe a truck or bus or some cars will pick you up. Or you must walk."

Nga thought of Muluzi's little short legs. "Forty to fifty kilometers. That is a very long way to walk."

"God will provide," Linnea said.

The second mystery of Linnea was how had Anson talked their delicate, aristocratic mother into leaving Sweden and coming here. Mezi believed God had something to do with it; Nga thought it was simply love. Perhaps they were the same thing.

Linnea smiled as her husband came into the kitchen. He walked over and put his hands on his wife's shoulders.

"I wish you would go with them," he said.

"My place is here," Nga's mother said, her quiet dignity lending such weight to the words that everyone knew Linnea Lind was staying at the mission.

———

Before the sun rose, Nga took her gear and walked out to stand next to the clinic. She had taken the least possible supplies from the clinic itself—a sort of minimal first-aid kit for minor problems. If anything major happened, she didn't know what she would do. Perhaps her mother was right, she should let go of worry and believe that there would be a solution, that God—or the universe—would provide.

She stepped out of the clinic, debating whether to lock it or not. She did not think anyone would bother it, but neither could they use what was in it. Villagers were beginning to gather in the open space around the clinic. She looked around at the serious dark faces, the few whites scattered among them like accent marks.

Mezi and the children were standing off to the side, making their farewells with Imrane. The *mundunugu* was talking to Mezi in a strong, loud voice. Nga could just imagine what he was saying. After a few minutes, she didn't need to imagine, as Imrane's voice got louder and louder. He was screaming when he said, "I am the husband, you must do as I do!"

Mezi made a face at him. Had Imrane forgotten the Yao ways so quickly? Women had many more rights than in other tribes, but Nga had thought that his Makonde people also were matrilineal, like the Yao. He did not seem to believe the traditions of either people—or at least he did not want to follow them. He picked up one of the bundles Mezi had packed and threw it uphill toward their roundhouse. "Go home!" Imrane yelled.

Mezi shook her head at him. She was holding her children's hands so tightly that Teleza squealed in pain. Mezi loosened her grip a bit, Nga could see the pressure from her fingers had left a red spot on Teleza's hand. Mezi raised her chin. "We are no longer husband and wife," she said clearly, loudly.

Around her, villagers moved away, and Salim stepped closer. The headman could not interfere in a divorce, but he clearly wanted to do something.

Mezi turned and stepped away from Imrane. For the barest moment, Nga felt sorry for him. The man had left his own people, had married a white missionary, had offered the villagers his knowledge and healing services, and now his wife had left him in the most public way possible.

But when he stomped forward and grabbed Mezi's arm, Nga no longer felt any sympathy for the man at all. "You cannot leave!" he screamed in Mezi's face. Mezi let go of Mu and Teleza's hands. The children ran to their grandparents, Leza clinging to

Linnea's skirt and Mu peering from behind his grandpa's legs while his parents yelled at each other.

Mezi used her left hand to peel Imrane's hand from her arm, and at this point Salim interfered, his daughters' two husbands and one of Palana and Kofi's boys helping him. They separated Mezi and Imrane, moving between them, creating a fence.

"This is done, Imrane," Salim said. "You no longer are married. And Mezi's decision to leave is her own choice, even if you were still her husband."

Choy said, "Think, man. This is not the way to convince her to stay, nor anyone else." Salim's middle son had always hung out with Imrane, was one of the closest things Imrane had to a friend. The two stared at one another a moment, then Imrane slumped. Choy slung his arm around Imrane's shoulders and pushed/led the man away. "Everyone is frightened," Choy said. "They'll come back home when this is over."

Salim and the other men moved away, leaving a hole where the people-fence had been. It was over, back to business, Nga thought.

She went to her sister, hugged her, and asked, "Are you okay? Do you still want to go to Maputo?"

"Oh, yes," Mezi said. "And my children with me." Nga could feel her sister trembling with reaction. Mu and Leza saw their father had left; they ran to their mother and aunt. Nga gathered Mezi's things from where Imrane had tossed them. She added them to her own small pile. Muluzu's dark eyes followed her every move.

Halid and Anane walked up, Anane balancing a bundle on her head, Halid with his modern backpack stuffed full. A few more villagers joined them, some different than those who had declared they were leaving the previous night. Still, the group was much smaller now than it had been then.

It became clear why, when a group of thirty or more came down the path from the more distant parts of the village. Spears showed above people's heads, bags and bright bundles contained everyone's best guess on what they would need or want. They were singing a hymn, one of the joyous ones that Nga also loved.

She sang with them as they joined her.

On the promontory behind and above the clinic, Salim walked out from among the straggly pine trees carrying his headman stick. He struck a pose, holding the stick firmly in one hand while he waved at his wife and son with the other. The singing quieted to a whisper, stopped.

"Is this everyone?" Nga called out to him. "Do you know?"

He shook his head. "More coming."

While they waited, a few people from the mission joined the group, among them the older teacher Mrs. Tately and Petyr Johansson, who at one time thought he would talk Nga into marrying him. He smiled at her, looking fit and ready to hike in his boots and safari hat. She couldn't decide if he would be a help or a hindrance if he imagined this was going to be fun, some kind of tourist outing.

The sun crested the eastern hills as a second group of villagers joined them. Nga's heart sank. They weren't going to have nearly enough canoes.

Her father apparently had thought about that. He disappeared and now walked out of their house with the key to the shed behind the school. He and Kofi and Cade opened the shed doors and dragged out the two rowboats the mission kept for emergencies. Compared to the native canoes, they were awkward tubs, but they floated and would hold maybe seven or eight people each. Some of the young men moved them down to the creek.

Despite Nga's determination to travel light, her father and Cade then returned to the group with a wheelbarrow full of canvas and burlap sacks full of rice, beans, corn, sweet potatoes, groundnuts, and dried fish. It looked like all the stored supplies the mission had on hand.

She was about to explain that they had to walk and carry everything for much of their trip when Salim came down from his hill and directed the villagers to put one sack in each canoe or boat. Salim was proud of the village surplus.

She was not going to argue with the headman, but it seemed

certain most of that food would go to waste. It would have to be left behind somewhere on their travels. But she said nothing. While they had the boats, they would eat well, at least.

Everyone walked down to the stream, some carrying or pushing canoes, some loading the rowboats. The water was low now in the dry season, but still deep enough that everything would float, even when overcrowded. It wasn't that far to Unango, they should be fine.

Nga grinned to see the rowboat bristling with spears as Bodie's group of young men got in. It looked like some kind of weird metal porcupine. Tub that it was, the porcupine moved rapidly out of sight once the young men put the oars to work.

She was counting how many people were still boatless when a final group came down from the village, eight people toting four more rough-finished canoes. The young men set the canoes in the water and helped people in. They apparently planned to stay in the village but had known there was a need and had made the canoes overnight.

Nga's eyes teared up, thinking of the work these young men had put in. She thanked Rana, who was the leader of this group. He would probably be the next headman since none of Salim's three boys showed the inclination. Everything else was passed down matrilineally except the headman position. That was patrilineal, or by contest. It seemed to Nga that Rana had already won. She smiled at him and the other boys.

She put her gear in the last canoe, where Halid was waiting along with his mother. Mezi's canoe was already gone, she and one of the older sons of Palana and Kofi taking up the paddles and pushing upstream. Sunlight filtered through the trees, making splashes of light and shade on Anane's face. The headman's wife looked as calm and good-natured as ever. Nga smiled at her, then turned back to the small group standing on the narrow muddy beach.

"Thank you again, Rana, Salim. Is that everyone?"

A cry through the trees answered her. "Wait! Wait!" A young woman ran down the hill to them, carrying her baby. It was Kimi with her little girl, Shaida. Nga's father had just baptized Shaida the week before. Kimi had been with the group last night, then changed her mind to stay, and now was here again. The young woman tossed a bundle into the canoe and got in next to Anane, still snuggling Shaida. Halid's mother put her arm around the young woman. Nga nodded to them, got in and took up a paddle. Halid grinned and dug his paddle into the water while Rana pushed them off from the bank.

It was hard to believe, but they were on their way.

12. ARIQ

ROSWELL, NEW MEXICO

Ariq couldn't sleep. He'd received an email from Minneapolis suggesting that his bats were the cause of the recent hospital deaths. They'd gotten an "anonymous tip." Now, in addition to the hospital's reputation, his job was on the line, and his research, and his bats. It was ridiculous. The bats were never anywhere near the patients. The people handling the bats, including himself, were not sick.

He contemplated the terrible infighting among Genghis Khan's grandchildren when the great Khan died. His namesake, Ariq Böke, was not the best politician; he lost out to his more famous brother Kublai Khan.

Ariq suspected the current crisis and his young age had emboldened someone on his staff. Perhaps this was the same person who had mentioned the Chiropteran Research Center to Jorge Casales on the planning commission. He needed to find the traitor soon, or he'd lose his chance. But much more importantly, he had to figure out the mysterious deaths before more people died. He knew his bats weren't the cause, but how could he prove it? On the other hand, if not his bats, what on the good earth was it?

He checked on his tablet: 5:00 AM, a good time to check in on **Bat Chat**. It was 9:30 PM in Australia, Northern Territory. Dinner would be over, so he had a good chance to find **Dreamtime** online.

He hadn't told anyone about his chats. His enemies had enough ammunition. He couldn't imagine what they might say if they knew he was asking medical advice from an Aboriginal girl with no formal medical training. Education, degrees, certificates, licenses were all important at PopulistHealth. As a medical school dropout and a descendant of an Asian healer, Ariq regularly reminded himself not to revert to his superstitious and unscientific roots.

However, as Hospital Director, he had to consider many points of view. After all, most of the people working for him had specialized education, especially the orthopedic surgeons who held much of the power. As a group, they tended to be arrogant and closed-minded. And they didn't know much about how to handle contagious diseases.

He was on **Bat Chat** for only a couple of minutes when he saw **Dreamtime** sign on.

 Mongol Bataar: G'day Dreamtime. Bad news here. Someone is trying to get me fired.

 Dreamtime: Can I help?

 Mongol Bataar: Can you send me what I need to use your healing methods? Nothing we have here is working.

 Dreamtime: I have to check with my mentor.

As he considered treating patients with folk medicine from Asia, he recalled the Mongolian legend of the bat. In the war between the birds and the land animals, the bat tried to be on both sides. In the end neither side accepted the bat and banished it to the dark corners. Would Ariq similarly be ostracized? He did not find the image of hanging upside down in a dark niche amusing.

———

Everyone stood in the open-air hall outside the ICU, formerly the school library. Ariq felt this was a good location to highlight the importance of the critically ill guests. The memory of Carl Elleich dosing himself with morphine still upset him. There had to be help. He would find it or die trying.

He was glad to see his medical director, Charles Thompson. Chucky avoided these meetings, sending a junior surgeon, often the ambitious Lachlan. His early morning surgery must have gone smoothly, as the doctor was back in a suit and his trademark bow tie. Ariq felt confident that Chucky was a supporter. The more meetings Lachlan missed and the less he knew, the better Ariq felt.

True to his modest style, Chucky deferred the medical update to Nizhoni. Joni reported on the guests. The strange infectious disease was sending doctors and nurses back to school.

"We've crossed out drug allergies, epilepsy, and some auto-immune reactions like acute inflammatory demyelinating polyneuropathy—AIDP, and Guillain-Barre. As you can see, we are well into zebra territory. We're hearing hoof beats, but none of the expected equines have arrived."

Joni's list of dead ends went on and on. Uncharacteristically, none of the men interrupted the middle-aged, native-American woman. Ariq took this to mean that idiopathic ague had baffled the medical experts.

"We collected the death charts and sent them to the CDC. I wouldn't be surprised if we made their Morbidity and Mortality Weekly Report. The MMWR is not the kind of attention we want, but it is the price of asking them for help."

Ariq agreed. No one celebrated a mention in the MMWR. Offering his best Mona Lisa smile, "I'm sure everyone is doing their best. Keep up the good work."

He knew it was a cliché response, but that was all he had this morning.

He noticed Martina taking in a breath as if she had something to add. He didn't trust the glorified accountant. She was certainly someone who might resent reporting to a younger person, especially one who didn't know much more about medicine than she did. This was the risk of being Hospital Director: both the administrative *and* medical staff imagined they could do the job better. He wondered, could she be the traitor?

He preempted her with, "The medical staff should continue their investigation. Spare no expense and bring in whatever specialists you feel you need. Thank you all. Let me know if you think a call to the CDC, administrator to administrator, might be helpful."

Some people started to leave. That was one of the risks of a stand-up meeting. Since everyone was already on their feet, it was easy to start leaving before any formal close.

He spoke up, "I know this meeting is going longer than usual. Yesterday I got a call from Minneapolis. They suggested that these deaths were caused by the bats in the CRC." The bats lived in one of the old kindergarten rooms, gloriously called the Chiropteran Research Center. He had personally purchased the sign on the internet. It was redwood and decorated with carved bats in flight.

"This was an unwelcome surprise, especially to think that someone on our staff had initiated an anonymous call all the way back to PopulistHealth corporate. If anyone has any scientific concerns, we'll research them ASAP. I'd like to know who was so disrespectful to the clinic. If you have any ideas, this is the forum."

No one responded, though no one seemed to be shying away either. The group continued to diffuse as people moved away.

"In the last twenty-four hours, we had another guest die, the Roswell planning commission has given us a vote of no confidence, and headquarters in Minneapolis has questioned our ability to deal with this crisis. Everyone is watching us. This is our time to shine."

Ariq remained until everyone departed. No one approached him.

These impromptu meetings reminded him of the importance of the non-medical parts of the business like the hospital kitchen and security guards. He'd added more professional security guards and the extended visiting hours. The initiatives increased guest satisfaction more than anything invested in the traditional areas of medicine or billing.

Roswell Orthopedic Clinic had round-the-clock visiting hours, and a world-wide reputation for a security detail that was efficient, courteous, and had extensive language skills. It was gratifying how many times the medical team benefitted from these in-house language experts.

Coming down the hall, he saw a gurney covered by a transparent plastic bubble. He recognized the two transportation specialists guiding the robotic vehicle. "Good morning, Maria and Harry. Where are you heading?"

"This is Mr. Yamaguchi. Dr. Thompson replaced his left hip this morning. We are taking him to a private room in the new annex."

Ariq proudly noted compliance with the new isolation procedures. He read every guest's admission documents. He bowed, "*Ohayō gozai masu* Yamaguchi-san."

The guest was awake, but still groggy from anesthesia. A subtle head nod was all Mr. Yamaguchi could accomplish. Ariq thought he detected a small smile.

Ariq checked the mobile monitor. Mr. Yamaguchi's temperature was elevated at ninety-nine, but his blood pressure and heart rate looked normal. The staff did not release patients from post-anesthesia care unit until their vital signs checked out, but he double checked to confirm no IA symptoms.

He followed them to the Area 51 Annex to survey the new rooms. They were very nice with accessible bathrooms, electronic monitoring, WiFi, cable, and four video monitors per room.

Once the transport specialists settled Mr. Yamaguchi, he walked to where the architects had installed a desert meditation garden in place of the kindergarten playground. Guests from around the country and the world were interested in the local flora but were rarely ambulatory enough get much beyond this wheelchair friendly exhibit.

While the garden reflected the desert, the clinic also boasted an artificial waterfall for guests during the day and visited by thirsty fauna during the night. The most famous visitor was a bobcat affectionately called Rosy by the night staff.

Beyond the garden was the small CRC which included cages for several hundred bats, a veterinary medical office, and his prize possession: an automatic DNA sequencer. The expensive machine was a surprise grant. He was using it to sequence the genome of the local bats.

Most of the CRC staff were high school students. With few

opportunities to do real science in Roswell, there was usually a waiting list. Each year, a few won science fair prizes in Albuquerque, and occasionally they even took national awards.

He interrupted a group of girls to ask, "Have you seen any of the regular hospital staff showing an increased interest in the bats?"

A high school student, Sofia, who'd been accepted to M.I.T. and CalTech with the help of her science fair awards, said, "That lady who always wears a suit has been asking questions."

Another student chimed in, "It's pretty funny. She doesn't know anything about science or bats. She asked about vampire bats, not realizing the closest one is over a thousand miles away."

Sofia added, "Don't worry. We were polite and didn't laugh…until she was out of sight."

Ariq wasn't worried about the students' behavior. It did make him sad that ROC staff could be so uninformed as to imagine bat bites might be the cause of IA. If the bats bit anyone, it would be himself or the CRC staff. Regardless, everyone who worked in the CRC, including all the high school student, received rabies prophylaxis shots.

That the bats had any opportunity to bite surgical guests was ridiculous. Besides, the Roswell medical examiner routinely checked for bat bites on all unexplained deaths. He shook his head. What was Martina thinking?

───────

Later in the day, Joni stopped by his office. In the southwest, it was often hard to distinguish Hispanic from Native American with the seemingly ubiquitous dark hair and dark eyes, but Joni always wore silver and turquoise jewelry to tip the scale to her native roots.

Today she was wearing a beautiful squash blossom necklace. Ariq recognized it. She didn't wear it every day. He closed the door before he started the discussion. "Do you have some ideas about the traitor?"

"I've noticed that Doctor Lachlan has been spending more time in the meditation garden than usual. It might not mean anything, but I thought I'd mention it."

"Thank you. How is your smart daughter doing?"

"I am so proud of her. I don't know the details, but she is working on a project for next year's science fair."

"Oh yes, I know it well. I have a feeling Jessenia's project will be very important. She wants to understand how bats can be carriers of so many diseases, but do not become ill themselves."

Joni had been head nurse long enough that she didn't let anyone talk down to her, "Yes, that has been the research direction since you arrived."

She also didn't mind reminding people that she'd been at the ROC since day one. Not many others could make that claim, certainly none of the current doctors or administrators.

"Of course, you're right. Jess is exposing bats to common human flu viruses to see if they develop immunities and pass the immunity to other bats. An excellent experimental design. I'm sure she'll be winning prizes next year."

Since Ariq did not have a graduate degree, he didn't have much opportunity to publish or get credit for his research. His satisfaction was the prizes won by the students in the high school science club, *los científicos*.

———

When he went to bed that night, he realized that his best hope for addressing the medical crisis was a girl in Australia. There might be a breakthrough from his staff, but he did not expect much from the ortho docs—not their interest or expertise. Another long shot was the CDC, hopefully something better than a mention in the MMWR—the booby prize for medical failure.

Musing on who was trying to get him fired and the CRC closed, he considered Doctor Lachlan, young and ambitious, and Martina, the past-her-prime accountant. He didn't know what to do next on that front. He reviewed the mystery books he'd read. All he could recall was that the first suspects were seldom the right ones. Did that reflect real life, or was it just something an author did?

13. LILY

MATARANKA & KATHERINE, AUSTRALIA

Lily stood near the road until Obrey's lights were gone. Once her eyes had adjusted, she headed into the park. She wasn't sure what the history was here—surely somewhere one of the Aboriginal peoples had stories about the creation of the pools at Mataranka. Surely someone had rights to the song and the paintings of the place. Such landmarks were considered sacred. But it had been made a National Park by the Australian Government for all to share. Mostly *balanda* tourists came here, to soak in the warm pools. Lily had begun coming once she learned about the bats, but she had never heard any of the people in Katherine or Ngukurr or Darwin say anything about Mataranka or bat dreaming like they did other places and animals.

She climbed between the bars of a wooden fence, holding her skirt away from the snaggly boards. There were tourist accommodations here, cabins and a big inn, but those were all dark. The soldiers had chased away the tourists, too. She moved cautiously toward the stand of palm trees where the bats liked to roost. Little Red Flying Foxes, scientists called them. Of course, they would be up and flying, getting their supper now. Except for the ones the Americans had caught.

There was a light on a stand in the middle of an open space. She crept around the edge of the circle of light. She glimpsed a couple military-looking vehicles, small and large. She made her way to the tarp-covered truck. She untied the tarp in the back.

She stood peering into the blackness inside the truck until her eyes could see cages, her ears could hear a slight rustling noise. Bats. Bats in cages. She tucked the bottom of her skirt up into her waistband to free her legs. Hands flat on the bumper of the truck, she swung her legs up, then climbed as quietly as she could up onto the truck bed.

It took several moments of fumbling in the dark before she

figured out how the cage closure worked. She glanced above her head at the tarp. They weren't going to just be able to fly up and away. She reached into the cage and caught up several soft warm bodies, leathery wings fluttering at her wrists. She turned and walked back to the opening she had made at the tarp "door." She reached out and tossed the bats into the air. They immediately caught air beneath their wings and flew jaggedly off into the night. She returned and emptied the cage, handfuls at a time, then got another one open. She had released a hundred or more bats when brilliant white lights suddenly blinded her. She froze, hands full of bats, blinking tears from her eyes.

"Oh, my God," a gravelly male voice said. "It's an Abo girl."

A nice voice responded, "Oz government said there were no native groups here."

"Nevertheless, here she is," said gravel voice. "How many fucking bats she let loose?"

"I speak English," Lily said, and there was immediate silence from the others. Perhaps she should have listened longer before she told them?

"Miss, those bats may be sick. They could be carrying a disease that is deadly to humans. We are taking a sample of them for testing."

"They are my country, my dreaming," she said. How much did Americans know about native Australians? Would they even try to understand? "You must not hurt them or take them away. They tell an important story."

"I'm sorry if they are your totem animal, but many lives are at risk. And we have permission from your government to collect and study them," nice voice said.

Totem animal?

"We cannot possibly sample them all, Miss. Some of your bats are still free here," gravel voice added.

She shook her head. No, they would not understand. But they did seem to be trying. "They are sacred to me. Each one you take is a bit of me, a bit of my country, the dreaming story gone."

She could see enough of them now to see several soldiers

holding huge torches— searchlights, maybe. Others held guns that were not exactly pointed at her, but not exactly pointed away either. One soldier had a fancy uniform. One man wore pajamas.

"I am very sorry it is a loss for you, but we must do this," pajama man said. His was the nice voice.

"Come down out of the truck, child," gravel voice said. He wore the fancy uniform.

The men holding guns did not say anything at all, but they moved back from the truck as she moved forward. They definitely were pointing the guns at her now.

Lily let the bats go she had been holding, making the soldiers jump. A couple tried to aim their guns at the bats. Then the bats were gone into the night.

Well, she had saved a few, anyway.

As she climbed down from the truck, sitting on the bed, then dropping to the ground feet first, she could hear gravel-voice and pajamas muttering to each other. She untucked her skirt and patted it down, while the two men argued.

"At least tell them to stow arms or whatever," pajamas said. "She is clearly no threat!"

"Civilians!" But uniform did shout an order at the men with guns, who moved back and put their guns away, rifles on shoulders, pistols in what Lily thought must be holsters of dark green webbing. Did they sleep with their guns, then, to be here dressed and armed so fast? Or were they up all night, guarding bats in cages?

Pajamas walked up to Lily and squatted down like he might talk to a child. Lily tried not to be insulted. She had had the same problem at school—she was short—people literally talked down to her. Sometimes it was meant as an insult, but often not.

"I'm sorry we are disturbing something important to you, Miss. But we must test them. They may be making some people very sick."

"I am not sick. I am with the bats very often."

Pajamas nodded his head, gray hair shining in the light. "It is true sometimes people do not get sick. But look," he reached and took Lily's hands in his own, turning them this way and that in the light from his torch. "There are scratches all over your hands."

"They did not mean to hurt me, they were frightened. They have never been in a cage," Lily said, pulling her hands back.

"I know, child, but the scratches can be the way you catch the disease. Or bites."

"They do not bite me. They never have."

He nodded. "But they bite some people, who get very sick."

He stood up and turned to the uniform man. "Can we just take her home? It's not like she broke any of her own laws."

Uniform's mouth tightened. "And if she's sick?"

"Your men will not be any more exposed than they already are. It will be just another local problem," pajamas said. "We need to finish these, our plane arrives tomorrow." He turned back to Lily. "Where is your home?"

She wanted to say, "Here," which was the spiritual truth, but she told the factual truth, the *balanda* truth, "Katherine."

They put her in a jeep with four soldiers and drove her back to Katherine.

Lily tried to ask the soldiers about the disease, what the symptoms were, what happened, but they pretended to not understand her. They rode in silence, then let her off at her aunt's house. She glanced back as she went through the front door. They drove off as soon as she was inside.

It was two in the morning, but her aunt Olivia was sitting bright-eyed on the sofa.

"I was worried about you," she said.

"I'm sorry, aunt. I was trying to help my bats, at Mataranka. There are Americans there, putting them in cages. I think they mean to kill them."

Olivia nodded, her face solemn. "I just worried, because Sophia saw you drive away with Obrey. And when you didn't come home, I worried more."

"I should have told you what I was planning to do. Obrey just gave me a ride down to Mataranka. The soldiers drove me back."

"I saw." Olivia was quiet a moment, then, "Lily, I must think about Pana, about her reputation. She is almost as old as you, and you set a...a wild example. Driving off with a boy, riding with men in a Jeep, talking to strange men on the internet."

It was like a slap in the face. "Do you think I would ever do anything to be ashamed of, Aunt? And that is the *balanda* way, to be ashamed to be seen with boys."

"It may be the *balanda* way, Lily, but it also your mother's way. What am I to think, what are others to think, when they see you do these things?"

"Pearl would never think anything of it. June would not jump to the conclusion I am free with boys!"

"They are not Pana's mother, Lily. I am. And you are a guest in my house. And do not tell me Aboriginal rules, Lily, when it was you who were asked to leave Ngukurr. They were not *balanda*."

Torn between trying to reassure her aunt and standing up and yelling because Olivia was implying things that just were not true, Lily clenched her fists and turned away.

"I know you are trying to protect Pana, and you have let me stay here out of kindness, Olivia. But I see that it is definitely time for me to leave." She stalked to her room.

Her mouth was dry, and tears threatened, but Lily succeeded in getting to her room without saying anything else.

Lily managed to catch Ariq for a Skype session, instead of just **Bat Chat**. She took advantage of their voice link to explain about the bats; her internet did not support video.

He had an odd accent, making her wonder what he looked like.

"Ariq, they were taking my bats from Mataranka! They had a whole truckload of cages. I freed some of the bats, but... "

"You're sure they were Americans?"

"Yes. The soldiers had American flags on their sleeves. They even said they had permission from the Australian government."

"Not your people's permission?"

"We don't have any authority, especially over that park. We have no government of our own, as you call it, that's not how things work."

"I'm sorry, Lily. I don't know much about Australian laws, but I'm pretty sure they had a right to collect the bats. You say they had guns?"

"Yes."

"That's odd."

"Is there anything you can do to stop them?"

"I'll look into it, I promise. I have a friend in the CDC, that's the only American group I can think of that might possibly have reason to go there and do that."

Lily's sadness deepened. It didn't sound like Ariq was going to be much help. She waited for the sound of his typing to stop.

"I spoke with Pearl today while we were visiting the hospital. June Araminty is feeling much better. Pearl doesn't think she had the same thing you were describing, though. Just the flu."

"Oh." He sounded sad now, too.

"I can still send you the herbs we used and how to prepare it if you like."

He sounded a tiny bit less sad. "That would be great, Lily. I know it's unlikely to help, but my staff has tried everything else, including some Native American healers' cures, and nothing is having any effect."

Lily bit her lip. "I have to tell you it is not just the medicine stew that is part of the healing. It is also…" something she couldn't even explain to herself. "How to say it? It's also about being there, touching, family and country and love."

Ariq was silent a moment. "All right," he said. "I will share that with my staff also. It cannot hurt, that's for sure." He sighed deeply. "We still aren't even positive where it's coming from. Some people want to blame my bats, but mostly because it isn't anything else." He made a funny noise, maybe like a squeak. "I wonder if that's why they were collecting your bats! But why would they go there– " he gave a small laugh.

"Do I need to fill out any forms for customs or anything?"

Ariq cleared his throat thoughtfully. "You know, I think we can get it here better and faster as biological specimens." He breathed softly for a moment. "Look, you have a hospital there, in Katherine?"

"Yes. It's very small, though. Katherine District Hospital."

"Airport?"

"Tiny. Very few commercial flights, mostly small plane charters."

"Okay. You are definitely on the backside of nowhere," he said, his voice raising in pitch. It changed his accent in a nice way.

"Oh, hey, this is very civilized. You should see Ngukurr. It's one-twentieth this size. When the right satellite's overhead, there's almost internet," she laughed.

"All right, let me look into some things. It would definitely help if you were still in Darwin.

"Help *what?*" she wondered aloud.

"I know, I know," he said. "You are definitely much happier now than when I first met you."

"Yes. And I know more, too. It might be easier to mail things, but I wouldn't even know about these herbs, this stew."

She waved goodbye even though there was no video, and they signed off.

———

Lily rinsed her skirt, noticing the hem had a couple rough tears and thin patches where she'd caught it on things getting herbs with Pearl. Maybe she should switch back to jeans, they were a lot more practical in the bush.

She remembered her first day in Ngukurr when her teachers Minnakenna and Jandry had looked at her in her jeans and tee-shirt and shaken their heads. And Pearl always wore skirts or dresses.

Mm. Maybe she'd just get a new skirt.

Aunt Olivia came into the laundry room holding the portable phone out to Lily. Her aunt was almost as beautiful as Lily's mother, but Olivia did not dress or do her hair and makeup like a fashion model, the way Adjana did. Lily secretly thought Olivia was prettier as a result. Olivia was stern-faced as Lily took the phone. She almost dropped it when she heard her mother's voice. Why should she be surprised? Who else would call? But it was like Adjana had been listening to what Lily thought.

"Hello, mama," she said, trying to put pleasant surprise into her voice.

Olivia stepped out of the room, giving Lily space to speak with her mother.

"I have a surprise for you, for your birthday!"

Birthday? Was it that time already? "Oh," Lily managed.

"I bought train tickets! You can come to Darwin, and we will have a party and presents, how does that sound?"

Uhm. Sounds like you think I am eight, not eighteen, mama. "That sounds like fun." It was weak, but maybe mama wouldn't notice.

"It *will* be fun!"

She needed to tell Pearl that she would be gone for a few days. But she kept not bringing it up, instead verifying once again, how to prepare the herbs she would need for the stew to send Ariq. She had gotten Pearl's permission to make and send it. The old woman had thought it was funny.

"Maybe probably not going to heal a *balanda*, you know."

"He just wants to try it. Who knows? It could work."

Pearl laughed and handed Lily a gourd to wrap with twine. They sat quietly together awhile, binding the gourds and knotting carry straps for them, then hanging them up to dry from Pearl's lean-to roof.

Lily took a deep breath. "Pearl, I must go away for a few days."

"To Darwin," Pearl said. Said. Didn't ask.

"To Darwin," Lily confirmed. "It is time to visit my mama."

"That is good. Family is good. Your Auntie Olivia is a kind lady, but your mama needs you."

"She bought train tickets. I'll need to stay at least a couple days to visit."

"That is right. Not to apologize for visiting family." Pearl laughed. "But also, you know, there is maybe something to do for

Auntie Pearl."

"Oh, of course."

"And Kalinda, if you don't mind."

"No...I don't mind. But I don't think she likes me very much. What could I do for her?"

"She likes you fine, Lily. It is your family she is thinking she doesn't like."

"Mm."

"Nothing you can do for that. But, she and I both need some things it is easy to get in Darwin, not so easy in Katherine, ever since the stupid *balanda* broke our trade chain."

"What do you need?"

Lily made a list, careful to write down exactly what Pearl said, and which shops to go to for each item. There was no mention of payment, and Lily understood that she was expected to contribute these things. She didn't mind paying for Pearl's, of course, because the woman was teaching her and helping her so much with finding her way. What she owed Kalinda was not obvious at all, and Lily was surprised to find herself a bit resentful. She sighed. The woman was Pearl's friend. She was one of the people. That would have to be enough.

Back at Olivia's house, Lily gathered her now-dry laundry from the line and folded it. She half-heartedly laid out her language tapes and notebooks ready to pack. She hadn't worked on Marra for two days now. Feeling guilty, she flipped the notebook open and memorized two new vocabulary words, then worked on her pronunciation with the tapes while she packed. She really needed to look at sentence structure again, but she would have time for that on the train.

She looked around the room. There wasn't much to it. A bed, a closet, a desk with a lamp, a desk chair. Maybe Pearl was right, she should try to build a place at the compound. It didn't need to be any fancier than this—a place to sleep, a place to paint, a dry spot for her herbs and canvases.

When she got back from Darwin she would look into what she

needed to do to get a spot.

Then suddenly she realized she would be in *Darwin*—just like Ariq had wished. She wanted to let him know right away, but she'd just have to make a quick trip to the Café in the morning.

Oh. But never mind a quick trip. She had promised Obrey she would bring her paintings tomorrow and help decide where they should hang in the Casuarina Café. She had totally forgotten about it, and after Obrey had driven her all the way to Mataranka, too. She started pulling paintings out of the closet.

Good thing the train didn't leave till 1:00.

BAT CHAT

PLUS FREQUENTLY ASKED QUESTIONS

? *Where are all the bats?*
  Many people report that they've never seen a bat. Unless they live in a polar region or an extreme desert, they share their environment with bats. Bats live on all continents except Antarctica and about 20% of mammal species are bats. This puts them in second place, as 40% of mammals are rodents. Primates are about 4%, dogs and cats together are under 1%.

  Most bats like the Mexican Free-tail and Brown Bat in North America, and the Pipistrelle in Europe, north Africa, and western Asia are small, weighing under ½ an ounce (14 grams). Fruit bats or flying foxes range from Africa across southern Asia and to Australia. These bats can be over 100 times larger with wingspans of almost 6 feet.

  With so many bats, why don't people reports seeing more of them? Simple, bats are nocturnal. In addition, many bats hibernate and migrate.
  http://www.defenders.org/bats/bats

 Batty: New to Bat Chat. I'm a docent at a zoo, but know nothing about bats What should I say when people say bats are sneaky and dangerous?

 Morcego: Tell then that bats pollinate mangos and bananas yummy

 Canuck: and that bats eat mozzies, lots of them.

 John Snow: Not dangerous. Only one or two deaths per year in the United States.

 Nina de la Ciencia: and bats are super cute

 Popo: Bats live everywhere people do. They are our friends.

 Batty: thanks, I'll use those

14. NGA

NIASSA PROVINCE, MOZAMBIQUE

Nga woke up chilled; she had lost her outdoorswoman's skills. She once had slept in the village every night. She'd grown up a tomboy, playing with the village boys while her mother had been busy with baby Mezi. She'd gone to school willingly enough, but loved the freedom of outdoors.

When she'd gone to Maputo for three years, it seemed that most of her toughness had abandoned her. Nowadays, she slept in her mother's house, and didn't much mind waking up to hot coffee, or what passed for coffee at the mission. It was more a thick herbal tea, but hot, and good.

After a night on the ground, she felt creaky and stiff. She got to her feet, rebuilt the fire inside the stone-lined pit the young men had built the night before. She filled a pot with water, then sat and rubbed her shoulders while she watched the water come to a boil. She made a pot of tea which she shared with anyone who wanted any. The families and singles woke up and got themselves around breakfast, then broke camp and picked up their gear together. Everyone was back on the water by 8:00 A.M.

They paddled smoothly through the morning, except for a ten-minute stop for latrines and stretching, that turned into a half-hour stop for the last four canoes, who had to wait for a small family of elephants to cross the river. Nga watched the matriarch of the little group stop mid-stream to smell the air, glancing at the nearby humans, then moving on into the forest. Her daughters, their children, and a young son followed.

When they pushed their canoe back into the water, Nga stepped into an elephant footprint in the mud. Her foot did not even go halfway across the massive pad strike. She climbed aboard their canoe and picked up her paddle, glad the old gray woman had chosen to ignore the *homo sapiens*.

They completely missed Unango.

Nga, running last in the queue of canoes and boats, leaned out to look past Halid. She could see Mezi's canoe, just a glimpse before it went out of sight around a bend.

They called it a creek, but Nga was certain this waterway was what her map called the Lucheringo River, which ran all the way up into Niassa Reserve and connected to the Rovuma River, on the border with Tanzania. If they had gone that direction, they wouldn't have had to paddle, but as far as she knew, no one had ever gone that way. There might be impassable waterfalls. There would have been hazards with wild dogs and lions and other beasts inside the Reserve. Plus, it would have brought them out at the coast on the Tanzanian border. Her map showed a very small town there called Lamiranga, about which she knew nothing.

Her decision to head south on the creek, even though it was a tough push upstream, was based on the idea that the good road, Highway 242, would lead somewhere useful. If they had to walk to Lichinga and the train, then they would at least be out of the bush while they did so.

Nga paused to rub her shoulders, and the canoe immediately slowed down. Kimi, facing her in the small canoe, held her baby out and pointed her chin at the paddle. Nga made the trade, holding Shaida, who cooed at her and smiled. Kimi turned around and began paddling. The canoe picked up speed again as the new mother's sturdy arms stroked deep into the water in time with Halid. Anane leaned over the side and scooped up some of the creek water in her cup. She took a few sips, then poured the rest over her head. The sun was hot in the places the sparse trees didn't offer them shadow.

"I think we are well beyond Unango," Nga said, to the others.

Halid's head nodded. "Plenty of water here, still going south," he said.

Might as well keep on paddling as long as they could. There had been a couple shallow spots, but nothing they'd had any trouble pushing past. Eventually that would change. At least if Nga's old map was correct—they were going to run out of creek before they got to the highway.

Sunset fell. Dusk came upon them, and Nga was relieved to see whoever had been running in front had decided to stop. A flotilla of canoes and rowboats were pulled up onto the western shore in a flat, treeless area. Halid guided them to the bank and jumped out, pulling the canoe a few centimeters onto the mud to get them out of the backward current. Anane climbed out, then the two of them pulled the small boat even farther up the bank.

By the time Kimi got out, some of the other villagers had joined them, helping beach the canoe, helping Nga and Kimi's baby out and up the bank. Ashore, Nga could see a bonfire had been started, pots of rice and fish were already cooking, and some of the boys were walking the bush, looking for what they could scavenge off the land.

Halid went back to the canoe after helping his mother up the low bank. He pulled a fishing spear out from along the outside wall of the canoe. He walked downstream a ways and stood in the cool water, searching for fish in the dimming light.

Nga turned back to the fire and took out her small bag of grain—field wheat, some wild oats. Then she remembered the sack of rice in her canoe. She went and got the sack, opened it, put a few cups into her pot, and retied the sack, double-knotting it. She scooped up water into her pot and went and looked closely at the fire. Someone had already placed wetted branches crisscross to hold pots. She added hers to the row.

Anane glanced at what Nga had brought and nodded. She took out her spice packet from her pocket and put some in Nga's pot. Salt, herbs, a little of what the Yao called pepperbark, and some chili seeds. She used a stick to stir it up.

Mezi's contribution was a bag of stringy carrots she'd pulled from her small garden back at the mission. Mu and Teleza each ate a raw carrot while Mezi cut up the rest and added them to a pot that already had other vegetables in it.

There was a small uproar out in the antelope grass covered field near a small stand of cassia trees. Awhile after the shouting died down, the group of boys who had paddled one of the rowboats walked into camp with bright eyes in the dark, and a jaunty step, and a reedbuck slung from a branch. They'd already skinned and gutted it, leaving the unusable scraps well away from the camp. They helped the older women butcher the beast into smaller pieces by the firelight and set them to roast over the fire. They gave the liver to Anane, as headman's wife, who thanked them and put the meat to roast over several green sticks.

"I'm surprised there was game so close by," Anane commented.

Bodie, the usual leader of this pack of boys, nodded. "We almost let it run away, we were so surprised! It was sleeping under the tree there, then jump! And we are all stabbing it." He acted it out for them as if they'd never seen a little antelope caught before, but everyone smiled.

The chatter of fifty people filled the air as they ate and drank their meals. Halid brought Nga one of his roasted fish, and she ate it, even though she was full of roast reedbuck, for who knew what tomorrow would bring?

"I don't think there is going to be anything left of this antelope, but I will pull and dry whatever's left," Anane said.

Mezi nodded. "It's pretty much gone already."

That was the general consensus. They could have some for breakfast, but the meat would spoil quickly. They might be out in the bush, but it was no different than what the villagers usually did. They did not have a refrigerator like Nga's mother, so they stuffed themselves when there was game, and maybe dried a little meat for later.

"I wonder how Ben is doing," Nga murmured. "How he is getting to Maputo?"

"He has a car to drive. He maybe is there already!" Halid said. He'd met the Malawian TC once when Ben and his wife had visited their village. Ben was probably more the reason Halid wanted to become a técnico than Nga was.

Nga nodded. "I wouldn't be surprised." She glanced over the villagers, who smiled and ate and talked. "But then, he missed this," she said.

Halid laughed. Beside him, Mrs. Tately grinned, but Petyr Johansson didn't seem to think it was very funny. He had been energetic when they'd left Luambe, but now he just seemed exhausted. He'd almost spilled his dinner onto the ground, trying to manage his plate and utensils with clumsy hands.

Abruptly Nga realized his palms and fingers were covered with blisters. He must have taken too long a turn at the paddles. She soaked a cloth in the dregs of her tea, tore it in half, and coaxed him into wrapping his hands with the pieces. The gentle herbs would help reduce the swelling and should soothe the pain a bit.

"No paddling tomorrow," she said, trying to sound stern. He just nodded, no argument at all.

———

Long before dawn lightened the sky, Nga was awakened by a disturbance in the camp. She saw a few other heads lifted up from blankets and sleeping bags, but only Bodie and Halid were actually up and dealing with the group of newcomers.

Nga blinked a few times, then crawled from her cozy blankets and built up the bonfire. She saw Palana and Palana's husband Kofi and their son Sami and Sami's wife talking to Bodie and Halid. Others who had originally stayed in the village had also now joined the travelers, mostly women.

"How did you get here?" she asked Kofi's wife, Palana.

"Kofi held his old canoe back, and Rana and his boys made another one."

Nga nodded. "Have you eaten?"

They had not. Nga found the remains of the roasted reedbuck and some leftover spicy rice. As they ate, Palana and Kofi told a very strange tale.

"Imrane and Salim had a big fight," Kofi said.

"It is like Imrane suddenly thinks he is headman," Palana said, indignance in her tone.

"But the worst thing is my brother Lendee shoved Salim," Kofi said. "And he would not apologize."

"Lendee did not even think he did anything wrong," Palana said.

"Because Imrane told him to," Kofi said, shaking his head.

Nga could almost feel Kofi's embarrassment. It was as if Lendee had gotten all the size that Kofi and Guta had not, but only half the brains. Usually their big brother was good-natured, but Nga had noticed lately that Lendee was cranky with both Kofi and Guta.

"Do you three have some kind of feud?" she asked.

Kofi shook his head. "No, just Guta has been friendlier and friendlier with Imrane. I think Lendee was confused that Guta and I did not agree. But it does not matter how confused he is, he should not be pushing the headman."

They all shook their heads in disapproval.

"They—Imrane and Guta—threatened that no one else would be allowed to leave the village, so of course, Salim yelled at them, and said anyone could leave who wanted to, and that's when Lendee pushed him, saying, 'No.'"

"I said I wanted to leave, now," Palana said, putting her arm around her husband. Kofi nodded. "And Sami and his wife, too, and some of the wives you see here now. So we left, in the dark," Palana said.

"I'm sorry this is causing so much trouble for Salim," Nga said. Halid watched her with worried eyes as she served the last of leftover dinner to Sami and his wife and three other villagers, women who had come without their husbands.

15. DR. BRIAN

LAWNTOWN, NEW JERSEY & WASHINGTON DC

R̶ Doctor Brian maintained a townhome in Lawntown, New Jersey: 2,500 square feet, three bedrooms, four baths, and room to entertain. He purchased it after he accepted that his wife and daughter weren't going to return. He kept it even after he retired. The location was in the same town as Miller and Miller corporate offices, and convenient to both Princeton University and Manhattan.

Like a chemist synthesizing a variant of an existing drug molecule, he replaced his wife's purchases with those of his own, atom by atom transforming the function, while maintaining the structure. For example, on his trip to India, he purchased a large silk carpet with a geometric design to replace a similar-sized one from China of a floral design. In the same way contemporary styles in leather and wood replaced French Rococo Louis XV pieces in the living room and dining room.

Before he left Papeete for Lawntown, he'd contacted his service to prepare for his arrival: check the car, stock the kitchen, and change the linens.

He arrived late and slept most of the following day. The next morning, he took his now classic 1999 BMW 323iC convertible and headed for M&M headquarters. The car still had parking stickers from before his retirement.

It was a short drive through winding back roads and past walled estates to the highway leading to the main campus.

Soon enough, the stone walls bracketing the Miller & Miller entrance replaced the chain link and razor wire that surrounded the rest of corporate park. The entrance had a portcullis and a half-timbered guard house in the Tudor style that was popular in the area. In this way, Miller & Miller advertised traditional Yankee colonial values, ironically drawing from a period that ended before the Mayflower arrived.

He barely glanced at the large sign harking back to the company's early 19th century German origin: "ATTENTION! No one admitted without proper identification and authorization."

He didn't slow down until he was beside the guard. The driver-side window was halfway down under automatic control. The sentry house and uniformed guard reminded him of old World War II movies. He expected clicking heels, and a salute with a crisp, "ACHTUNG!"

"Hey, Sam, nice to see you looking well. How are the grandkids."

"Wow, Doctor Brian. I haven't seen you in a while."

He inched the car forward. The guard clicked the remote to raise the barrier gate, also reminiscent of those WWII movies.

Sam turned back to Doctor Brian, "Your sticker is expired. You should do something about that."

"Sure thing Sam."

As soon as the gate cleared his car, he was through. Ignoring the speed limit signs and directions to visitor parking, he took a sharp turn away from the main entrance, kicking up gravel, and headed to the executive parking lot.

Once parked, he looked around. First he noticed how little the campus had changed since he retired. The same maple and oak trees placed among the broad expanses of turf, with mountain laurels and azaleas close to the buildings. He also recalled that this landscape was just a larger version of the house where he grew up in Purchase, New York. Both were close enough to Manhattan to visit the museums and theaters, but far enough to be exclusive and safe.

He felt that something was different. Not the dress code. The executives still wore suits and the scientists wore white lab coats. He thought there might be more women, but there weren't that many, and the company had been progressive in that way since the 1960s. After all, they had hired his wife as a detail man to hawk drugs to doctors around the country.

He could feel his muscles tense, remembering "Darling Darlene," making more money than he did while traveling around the country on expense account with her sample case full of drugs and, unfortunately, mini bottles of vodka.

Then it hit him: no briefcases.

He left his expensive ostrich-skin briefcase in the car and walked over to the Miller Mocha Café. After all these years, no one had thought to raise the prices—a large latte was still fifty cents. He took this as an indication that the drug business was still doing well, at least at headquarters.

Just as he was finishing his drink, he saw Doctor Leclerc, one of the research directors.

The research scientist was in his seventies, but with his short gray hair, it was difficult to see the true size of his bald spot. As he walked briskly through the café area, the overall impression was youthful vigor, maybe a cross between a marine and a professor.

"*Bon jour*, Doctor Leclerc."

Doctor Leclerc paused, "Why Doctor Brian, it's been quite a while. I thought you'd retired."

"I have retired. Been traveling around the world. Just came back from Tahiti."

"Nice." The director kept walking.

Brian pressed on, "I've heard rumors that there is a medical crisis." He paused, not knowing how much of Jake's rumors were common knowledge.

"A friend of mine sells sequencers, the high-speed ones, and he's noticed a spike in demand."

The director stopped.

"My friend thought—" Brian was uncertain, but he couldn't stop here. He spoke quickly, "Is there a pandemic, a suspected pandemic, or an urgent need for new drugs?"

The director pulled out his phone.

Brian smiled, "Who should I speak to? I'd be glad to come out of retirement if I'm needed."

"I was just checking my schedule. I should be running. I doubt we have a need of your individual skills on any of our teams. Since you've left, we've gone to a more collaborative research model. Probably not your forte."

Brian took a breath and tried to interject, but was unsuccessful.

"If you're willing to travel a little, I'd suggest checking in with our regulatory and compliance group in Washington. Ask for Julia Whitey."

"I've already traveled over 7,500 miles to—" He was going to question why a brilliant research chemist like himself should talk to the lobbyists and lawyers, but Doctor Leclerc was gone.

———

Doctor Brian walked down F Street to the Miller & Miller regulatory offices. He recalled that the company's lobbying operation spent five to ten million dollars annually depending on the legislative calendar.

He found the building, one of many three-story brick buildings designed with Federal architecture. The building might be new or two-hundred years old. Once inside, the interior was fully modern with bright colors, curved surfaces, and lots of surveillance electronics and cameras.

He walked past the unmanned front desk, ignoring the electronic sign-in kiosk, and took the elevator to the third floor. Finding Julia's office was easy in the small, but well-appointed, space.

Julia looked to be in her late thirties to early fifties. He found that as his years ticked by, it was harder and harder for him to guess ages. She might be of a similar age to his Penelope.

He thought of Penny. It would have been nice to have her with him on this trip. When she was younger, he would take her out of school for a week or two when he traveled on business. They'd had fun exploring together. She seemed to have a good time. This memory upset him. Her mother never took her on business travel, probably because she planned to drink, and who knows what else. Regardless, when the time came, Penelope ran away with her mother.

He happily recalled her small legs climbing the Great Wall of China. She'd brought home almost a dozen stuffed pandas from that trip, each one a little different. On another journey, they raced up the Tower of Pisa. Once there she had excitedly run around the top terrace, while he stayed on the high end, avoiding the area described in the guide books as, "cantilevers thrillingly over the grassy piazza." He fondly recalled that his travels were more interesting when she accompanied him, though a little scary.

Reaching his destination, he pulled his attention back to the present. Julia Whitey styled her red hair short and smooth. She wore a tailored fuchsia pants suit with medium height black pumps. As she walked down the hall, he noticed the bottoms of her shoes were bright red. He thought that that was something special, but couldn't recall what.

He waited in front of the office with her name on it, and when she arrived he put out his hand, "Hello Ms. Whitey. I'm Doctor Brian from Lawntown. Director Leclerc suggested I talk to you."

She shook his hand, maybe firmer than necessary at his age. "Yes, he warned me that you might visit."

He blinked, then continued, "I'm really a research scientist, but——"

He took a step back when she interrupted him, "Yes, I know. You're a smart guy, probably figured out that Washington's not the place for you. You scientists are all so straightforward. Here we need more tact or…"

When she paused, he completed her sentence, "Politics?"

"Of course, as you say, politics."

He frowned, mentally urging her to change direction, and she did.

"You have not wasted your travel south. I suspect that there might be an opportunity for you in Atlanta."

He knew she was referring to the CDC.

"Center for Disease Control? So there really is a major outbreak?"

She moved toward her office. "I don't know anything about that, but I've heard they're recruiting."

"CDC is a big operation. Over 10,000 people. Who do you think I should talk to?"

"Considerably more people than that, now. M&M cannot get

involved with CDC hiring, conflict of interest and all that. I'm sure with all your industry experience you have your own contacts."

With that she looked at her phone and slipped into her office. "Sorry I don't have more time. You were lucky to catch me. You should have called for an appointment. I'm expected at a congressional hearing shortly."

With that, she disappeared into her office, and he returned to his hotel in Dupont Circle to have the concierge arrange for travel to Atlanta.

16. ARIQ

ROSWELL, NEW MEXICO

Ariq received another call from Minneapolis. His frustration grew as he repeated the obvious answers to the obvious questions.

"As I've said already, the deaths are unexplained. We don't know what caused them."

"Yes, we sent everything to the CDC in Atlanta. The CDC doesn't know what is going on either. Feel free to contact them directly."

He resisted sarcastically adding, the CDC has nothing better to do than talking to hospital bureaucrats...

Moving from frustrating to insulting, the discussion morphed into an interrogation. Ariq became defensive. His inner Genghis Khan came out. He yearned for the ancient times of severed skulls stacked high at the city gates: a deadly warning most enemies heeded. "I'm sorry you're getting lawsuits. I'm doing my job. You have all the lawyers–do yours!"

The call ended badly, but he still had his job, so not that badly. He considered another staff meeting, however that would just disturb operations and accomplish little. He thought of prodding the CDC, but they were in the same position as he was and didn't need another interruption.

The phone rang again. He tried to ignore it.

Had everyone forgotten how to send email?

He didn't want to speak to another corporate hack or concerned parent or spouse. Somehow word had leaked out. He blamed the rumors on the Roswell planning commission, especially that dairy operator in the cowboy hat.

He didn't want to address the Outbreak movie or the government bombing Roswell again.

He didn't want to hear that the DNA sequencer guy Jake had found funding for another machine. He had more than he needed.

He didn't want to talk to any more reporters.

Another ring. Should have been in voicemail already. He answered, making a note to ask Martina about the voicemail settings. He pushed the speaker button. He knew he was going to regret this, but there was a saying: no cowards rode horses in the desert.

The caller began with just the words he didn't want to hear, "You don't know me."

Ariq waited and it turned dark just as he had feared.

"My father is a hip replacement patient at your facility."

And gloomy.

"I am concerned about the latest report in the MMWR."

Ariq didn't think the CDC had had time to publish the clinic's cases in the Morbidity and Mortality Weekly Report yet. How had she heard? "Who are you?"

"Sorry, I should have started with that. I'm Julia Whitey. I work in the regulatory and compliance group for Miller & Miller."

Confusion. Was this a concerned child or a sales call? The Clinic bought a lot of drugs, but he didn't usually get involved. In either case, how did this Julia get his direct number?

Ariq took a neutral approach. Listen. Listen, "What can I do for you Ms. Whitey?"

"Julia is fine."

"Okay, Julia."

"First, I must have confused you. You have not appeared in the MMWR. However, a few cases like yours will be published this week."

Ariq couldn't believe how much this Julia knew.

She continued, "More importantly, the number of cases nationally is growing, and they're not saying as much, but I believe many more cases have been reported globally."

He wondered if this explained those Americans that **Dreamtime** encountered in Australia. None of this was the ROC's—his—fault, and Minneapolis knew it. For the third time today he thought of stacks of decapitated skulls, in Minneapolis this time.

Careful not to admit anything, he asked again, "What can I do for you?"

"As soon as my father can move, I'd like him released."

Ariq needed time to think. "Okay, just give me his details. I'll take care of it personally."

The phone immediately rang again. **International**. Curious, he picked up.

"Сайн байна уу."

His father.

"Эмээ is sick. She is in the hospital. Can you come home?"

"She is strong. I have to be here."

His father sounded old. "I'm worried."

"Send me her hospital records. I'll do what I can."

———

Ariq listened to the gentle breathing of the sleeping bats in the Chiropteran Research Center. The CRC insulated Ariq from the frenetic activity of the hospital. He could think more clearly when he gave his brain something to focus on. Today he went online to review young Jessenia's research project.

As with much research, most of her results were not results at all. When she exposed the bats to human flu strains, nothing happened. The viruses had no interest in cross-order migrations. In truth, very few viruses were potent across a range of mammals. Most preferred a single order, or in many cases, notably *Homo sapiens sapiens*, a single species.

Ariq reflected that this experiment was designed to fail. The use of human viruses pretty much guaranteed it. However, high school students didn't have the skills or the time to develop genetic tools to isolate Chiropteran viruses. Human strains were readily available, therefore the easiest to test.

Real lab experience, even without real results, looked good on college applications.

Jessenia interrupted his reverie, "Are you looking at my lab notebook?"

"Yes. I hope you're not discouraged."

Jessenia laughed, "Oh no, Doctor Ariq."

He stopped her. Science was all about the details, and he took every opportunity to reinforce this, "I am not a doctor. Ariq is just fine. Someday you'll be a doctor."

Jessenia took the correction more seriously than he'd meant it. Her shoulders drooped and she stared into the bat cages. She continued softly, "I'll try to remember. Anyway, I don't need to win a Nobel prize or even the state science fair. I just want enough to make my college application stand out." She paused and her smile returned, "Like Sofia. She got into her first and second choices."

Ariq matched her stare at the bat cages, and his mind drifted back to the dead guests. He'd have to remember to check on Julia Whitey's father. Only half listening to the discussion he added, "It would be nice if we found something. These experiments could be important."

She seemed to have recovered from his rebuke and took out her tablet to check on her bats with the light of scientific inquiry in her eyes again.

Ariq wished that he could investigate the treatment Lily had discussed, but Australia was so far away and everything seemed to be so much harder and more primitive there. With his limited knowledge of Australian geography, he imagined her in a mud hut with a thatched roof and maybe a small creek. This picture made him laugh when he realized it was from some movie about the Kalahari Desert in Africa, not Australia at all.

Oh well, maybe he'd ask her about it next time they chatted.

His own research into bat immune systems and how they hosted so many diseases was temporarily on hold. He hoped it was only temporary.

———

Now that he knew that the deaths weren't specific to the ROC, rumors and people trying to sabotage him were less concerning. Still, their behavior had cost him that irritating phone call this morning. Also, he did not like his people going behind his back. It was best to address these transgressions as soon as possible.

He had lunch in the hospital cafeteria. The East End Elementary had been old enough to have a working kitchen. However, the Roswell Orthopedic Clinic required certain upgrades. Prospective guests received a tour of the stainless-steel counters, glass-front fridges, and huge black stoves and ovens. There was even a wine cellar for those patients not on opiates or other heavy-duty painkillers.

The lunch was a delicious Salade Nicoise, a healthy combination of local, organic veggies, free-range eggs, and sustainably harvested tuna. Since it was lunch, he drank herbal tea. In the evening, the cafeteria had a diverse offering of *cervezas* in recognition of their southwest heritage.

The same kitchen that served the guests fed the staff, often considered one of the staff perks. Next to visitor hours, food was the second most important factor influencing guest satisfaction. This was a strange business where non-medical things like visiting hours and food were often more important than the main attractions of surgeries and rehab, of doctors and nurses and medical expertise–which, after all, could be found elsewhere.

The first person he ran into was his head surgeon and medical director. Doctor Charles was in clean surgical scrubs, meaning he was on his way to an afternoon surgery.

"Operation soon?"

"Yes, a bilateral hip replacement."

This procedure was now routine, but Chucky had pioneered it, something the marketing folks never let fade into historic obscurity.

"I got a call from Minneapolis about our fatalities."

"I can't imagine why'd they call us. I've heard through the surgery rumor mill that we are far from unique. You might talk to young Lachy. Being recently out of training, he might have different connections."

"I'll look for him."

"He should be around. He doesn't have any surgeries scheduled this afternoon."

The conversation ended with some pleasantries and Ariq

moved on confident that the brilliant Chucky was not his problem.

The next person he ran into was Nizhoni doing her rounds, checking that all the operating theater nurses were in place.

"Everything ready for the afternoon schedule?"

She smiled. "*Si absolutamente.*"

"Do you recall a guest named Whitey?"

"Sure, Arthur Whitey. Just moved to the annex."

The closed door displayed a biohazard symbol. Joni put on gloves and a mask. Ariq did the same. He feared they'd find another corpse.

When she opened the door, he immediately focused on the vital signs monitor. Respiration, heart rate, blood pressure were all low, but not flat lined. Julia's father was sick, but still alive.

Joni went to the chart. Doctor's notes were electronic, but nursing notes were still on paper. "Definitely idiopathic ague. I see fever, tremors, and muscle aches. He can't tolerate anything orally. His nutrition is through an IV."

"He looks calm," Ariq added hopefully.

She looked back to the chart. "He's been sedated."

Clearly, Julia's father would not be released anytime soon.

"Is IA painful, then?" He remembered Carl Elleich clicking the button twice.

Nizhoni shook her head and shrugged, "*Si.*"

They silently left the room, discarded their gloves and masks in a ubiquitous biowaste containers. He couldn't think of anything to say until he remembered her daughter. "I saw Jessenia this morning and she's doing very well. No matter what happens, I am confident this experience will be good for her and her future."

Nizhoni gave a proud-parent smile. "Thank you. Did she tell you that she saw Doctor Lachlan and Martina walk through the meditation garden together?"

Ariq froze his face, not wanting to express the surprise he felt. He didn't think those two even spoke to each other. "No, she didn't mention it. We were talking about her research and colleges."

The nurse looked concerned.

"I'm sure it doesn't mean anything. Don't worry about it." He was going to add a hypothetical explanation, but he couldn't think of any business Lachlan and Martina had together. Just strange. He'd add it to his to-do list, along with Julia's father, Lily's treatment, Jessenia's research on Chiropteran immune systems, and…he suddenly realized he'd missed his horseback ride this morning.

The key to the Mongol victories was riding every day from the age of two. He'd try not to miss tomorrow.

17. LILY

KATHERINE & DARWIN, AUSTRALIA

Obrey had laughed and smiled more than Lily had ever seen him do while they were hanging her art. She was glad she had taken the time to do that with him. His subtle pressure for her to allow him to court her was always there, underlying every interaction with him. She was by no means ready to accept, but she wasn't ready to tell him no, either. He was a decent young man who respected her. Was that enough for marriage?

Lily stared out the train window, letting stands of gum and paperbark trees replace Obrey's earnest face in her mind's eye. She should put more trees into her bat art. Especially the palms where they liked to sleep, sometimes in bunches so large the tree branches broke, dumping startled bats into the daylight air.

She smiled remembering that, then noticed the woman in the side seat next to her, smiling at her smile.

"Boyfriend?" the woman asked. Her accent sounded like western desert.

"My bats, actually," she said, and the woman raised an eyebrow, then turned away. "But before that, it was a boy I was thinking about, you are right," Lily finished.

The woman looked back at her and nodded, a puzzled expression on her face.

They didn't look at each other for the rest of the trip, until the very end, when Lily was gathering up her things.

"Don't put him aside too long, or you may lose him, and your bats, too," she said.

All the hairs stood up on Lily's arms. By the time she thought to say anything, the woman was gone, and Lily saw her mother out on the platform waving and smiling. Mama was wearing a white dress with huge orange and purple flowers at the hem. And fancy high heels, of course.

Lily stepped off the train into a big perfume-scented hug.

"Hi, Mama."

"So good to see you!" Adjana reached for one of the bags Lily was carrying and Lily let her take it. "Do you have more luggage?"

"Nope." She raised the bag in her other hand. "This is it."

"That's a ripper, then." Adjana raised her arm with Lily's bag hanging on it and pointed to a handsome Asian-looking man. "Lily, this is Fei, Fei, Lily."

Lily smiled and nodded to the man, who smiled back and reached for her other bag. Lily handed him her backpack instead; the bag was full of the ingredients for the stew to send to Ariq and needed to be kept upright. The backpack just had her clothes and books.

"'Jana tells me you are quite the artist, Lily."

"Oh, thank you. Yes, some of my art is being sold at an artists' cooperative out of Cairns."

He nodded. "I saw that. Come, I'm parked over here." They followed him to a bright orange sports car. It was a convertible. It looked expensive. And very low to the ground, Lily discovered as she stepped down to get in. The back seat was tiny. They put her backpack and the bag Adjana carried into the boot. Lily was glad she'd kept the herb bag, as she tucked it safely down on the floor beside her feet.

By the time they arrived outside her mother's apartment, Lily's hair was blown straight up, or at least it felt that way. She noted her mother had prepared by putting a bright silk scarf over her head for the ride. She swept it off dramatically as she waited for Fei to walk around and open her car door and hand her out.

"So, a small surprise, Lily. I painted your room! No more baby animal wallpaper in the guest room!"

Lily had kind of liked the zoo paper, as she had called it years ago, but what could she say? It was her mothers' flat. "Oh? What color is it?"

It turned out to be yellow and orange. Lily had the feeling it was Fei's room, not hers. But she smiled and pretended to like it.

"Very fresh," she murmured.

"I thought you might like to wash up before dinner, Lily. We have reservations at a nice seafood place."

"All right, Mama. I'll get ready." By "wash up," of course, her mother meant, "Fix your hair and put on makeup and a nice dress." Which Lily duly did, wondering why she'd agreed to come to Darwin at all.

It was like her mother took only minutes to unravel six month's work of changes. Lily stared in the mirror, twisting a lock of hair around and around her finger. What would happen if she skipped the makeup?

At dinner, Adjana dominated the conversation, as usual. Lily caught herself glancing at Fei to see his reaction. He seemed to enjoy listening. Lily looked back down at her plate, remembering at the last moment to use her fork to spear a prawn, rather than pick it up in her fingers. She didn't talk much, but when she did, she made sure she swallowed her food first. Manners were important to Adjana. Whitefella manners.

"Lily, do you want to open your gifts here, or at home?"

Lily imagined all the people in the restaurant turning to watch her open her presents, and shuddered.

"At home, please."

Adjana laughed and finished her drink. "At home it will be, then, my heart."

Her heart? *As if*, Lily thought, one of Pana's favorite phrases popping into her head.

Her mother seated Lily on her sofa and got drinks for herself and Fei. Then she piled up some shiny-wrapped boxes next to Lily, smiling and excited.

The first gift Lily opened was a cell phone.

"I know you couldn't use it in Ngukurr, but now you are in Katherine," Adjana said, "and I thought it would be handy. Now I can call you, without—without having to bother Olivia!"

Lily gingerly lifted it out of the box. It could come in handy. It would have been nice to call Ariq a couple times when the Café was closed and internet not available. "It's fancy," she said looking at the instruction book. "Thank you, mama, it's very nice."

"Thank Fei, too," Adjana said brightly. "He picked it out and bought it."

"Thank you Fei," Lily said. He smiled gently and nodded. It really was nice of him. But she could not help imagining what Olivia would think about gifts from men.

The next gift was a day at the spa with her mother. Haircut, styling, dye work, extensions. Skin bleach and body massage. "Oh, you know, I've been thinking of doing something different with my hair."

"It's kind of straggly," Mama said. "You can dye it too if you want. Pana's is such a lovely color, maybe you could try that. I'm going to get rid of this black and go back to that kind of dark blonde, myself."

Lily nodded. "The blonde looked good on you. Thank you," she said. She was going to have to take a stand about the skin bleach, and they would argue, she was sure. Mama always had been a little ashamed that Lily's skin was so much darker than her own.

Really, what bothered Mama was anything that wasn't the whitefella way. Lily had no intention of lightening her skin. Maybe if she was pleasant about the other parts of the gift, she wouldn't hurt Mama's feelings so much.

The third and last gift was a flat box about the size of several sheets of paper—which is what it was. Lily tried to look excited as she glanced through the pages. Further down was a small booklet. "A passport?" she asked.

"You're going to need it, and I could get it for you as long as you were still seventeen."

Puzzled, Lily glanced at the rest of the papers. Why would she need a passport?

"I don't understand," she finally said.

Her mama laughed, leaning forward to point to a brochure.

"It's a scholarship! To this fancy art school in New York!"

Art school? Lily opened the brochure. Photos showed brick buildings in a cityscape, several art galleries or museums with walls of artworks, from very modern through musty-looking paintings of foxes and hounds—from England, she presumed.

"Fei and I sent them an application with links to your artwork at the Coop," Mama said excitedly, "and they wrote back all excited with an offer of a scholarship. They love your bats, Lily!"

"Oh!" Lily said, catching some of her mother's excitement. She tried to imagine herself in America, in New York.

It would definitely be a way to move out of Olivia's house.

"So when do you want to go to the spa?" Mama said. "Fei has to be at work tomorrow, so we could go then. And maybe the next day do some shopping."

"I have two errands to do while I am here. One needs to be soon, I have to mail something. But the other we could do on a shopping day," she said. She was with Mama; there would certainly be a shopping day.

"Let's do the spa tomorrow, then. We can shop and do your errand on Tuesday."

"That sounds like fun, Mama."

They spent the rest of the evening setting up her cell phone. Fei even showed her how to use the internet on it, "Even if there isn't WiFi, but watch your data usage," he said.

"Thank you so much," Lily said, thoroughly confused.

———

In the closet in her room were several blank canvasses. Lily pulled them out and laid them on the bed, considering. She wanted to find a form for the trees she had seen from the train. Most aboriginal artists did not code trees or bushes, but the ones that did signified them with an array of leaves, or a few branches, repeating the pattern in several places on each painting. She wanted her own style. She spread her old painting sheet out on the floor, careful to cover the nice orange and yellow graphic-design rug on the floor.

She pulled out traditional ochres, browns, black, yellow and tan. And some orange and red for Fei and Mama. She began painting.

As she suspected, it was very difficult to refuse the UV skin lightening. She ended up lying to avoid it. "It burned my skin so bad I turned all red last time," she said. "The healers say I'm sensitive to it."

Adjana's mouth compressed into a tight line.

"I'd rather be brown than red, Mama."

The cosmetologist agreed. "Some people aren't able to bleach," she said. "We'll use brightening makeup, find a foundation for her that will lighten, without burning."

Adjana's mouth quirked, but she nodded.

"It will go nicely with her hair, too," the makeup artist said.

Adjana gave up. "I do like the hair, but it seems too white, to me." She looked at the makeup lady's face, then back to Lily.

"It's fun," the lady said. "Marcy" her nametag read. "And the shorter length does a lot to make her face look more mature. We'll polish the look with some pale blush and highlighter."

Mama sniffed and nodded. "All right. I'll go get finished up."

Lily watched her mother walk away, her long hair now dark golden blonde, made longer and fuller and a bit wavy with the extensions Adjana loved. Lily's was now kind of the opposite. Short, white-blonde, straight. Lily had wanted to try kind of an Afro style; she'd had a dandelion-look in mind. But the haircutter had shaken his head. "It's not going to stand up like that, darling," he said, fluffing Lily's hair with his hands. "It's not stiff enough. We can gel it so it kind of stands up, but it won't bush out, not without constant care, and you wanted something that would look nice without a lot of work."

So they'd gelled it and lightened it. Lily thought it looked startling against the warm brown of her skin. She'd asked for something she could maintain in the bush, since she wasn't going to have product and straighteners at the compound, nor did she wish to maintain a closet full of beauty things, like her mother.

If she went to New York she might, though. New York would be all about the hair, the clothes, the whitefella world.

She sighed, and let Marcy the beautician finish her work.

———

Lily settled into her seat on the train, exhausted. She carefully put the two sacks of herbs under her seat and settled her backpack in her lap. She pulled her phone out of the backpack pocket made just for cell phones, which she finally had one of to put into it, and checked to see if the advertised WiFi worked.

It did. She found the **Bat Chat** site. Ariq wasn't on. She sent him an e-mail instead, with the shipping delivery information on the stew. She had called it "native art materials," as Fei had suggested. Anything marked "health product" would be stopped at customs and examined, may be confiscated, but art usually got a pass. She hoped the bundle would arrive in time to be useful.

Then she put the phone away and pulled her new passport from the special pocket the backpack had for that. She'd never expected to fill that pocket. She glanced through the pages. Her photo didn't really match now that she had her hair all white. That must happen all the time though. It shouldn't be a problem. If she even used it. She put it away and zipped its little pocket closed.

She laid her head back and closed her eyes. Her mind was all lizardy, darting in one direction and pausing, then darting another, tongue tasting the air.

Should she go to New York? Classes didn't start until October. She had time but needed to tell the school her decision. But, really, to go to an art school in America? What could they teach her about bat dreaming art?

No, she should she find a home at the native compound near Katherine, like she had planned. That would make Olivia happy. Her work with Pearl was very satisfying. And the old woman would be very disappointed if Lily dropped everything to go to New York. Of course, Mama would be very disappointed if she didn't.

Mama. Fei had offered her $A2000 for her new painting. It felt more like he was trying to please Adjana—Jana, as he called her—than that he liked the art. But did she care, if it gave her $A2000? And if she could get that much for a painting now, why would she need to go to art school?

More than anything, she needed to get back to Mataranka and do a bat count. She needed to write letters to the Park officials and maybe the Australian government, to tell them to leave the bats alone. She had seen the news headlines. Nobody even knew why people were sick, just that people were scared.

How could her bats be making people sick if people were sick all over the world?

Sunshine came through the window, making her drowsy. She let everything go and promptly fell asleep, her lizard brain basking in the sun.

18. NGA

NIASSA PROVINCE, MOZAMBIQUE

Nga tried to stay more up at the front of the group that day, hoping Highway 242 would be obvious when they arrived. They had clearly missed Unango, and as far as she knew, there was no other village or landmark along the creek until it crossed the road. If the canoeable water made it that far. They were going south, but it was upstream. It seemed backward to her, just wrong, even though she had lived by the stream all her life. Some atavistic part of her brain determined that south should be downhill, downstream. Why was that?

Things went well until a little before noon, when the two lead canoes, followed closely by one of the rowboats, went aground on a hidden sandbar. They tried back paddling, but even with the current's help, they stayed stuck.

When Padrit jumped out to push the boats off, he sank in loose mushy sand—he could not even get enough footing to push from, just sinking and swimming instead of pushing. There were no rocks or bushes or clay nearby to lay down to firm up his stand point. He scrambled back into the closest canoe and waved the other boat and canoes past.

"Maybe we can try pushing them off with the other canoes," Halid said. He steered their canoe to the opposite bank, climbed out, ran up the bank and grabbed a fairly large fallen branch from beneath a ragged old ebony tree. Back in the canoe, which Nga and Kimi held steady against the current, he managed to balance the log without capsizing the canoe. It hung off either side like a clumsy short outrigger.

"I think we should pass them and try to push from the other side," Nga said. "The boats will want to go downstream, of course." Kimi and Halid both nodded agreement.

They maneuvered past the three stuck boats, then Nga and Kimi paddled hard to stay in place while Halid angled the log and got the first canoe unstuck with one push and back paddling by the occupants.

The rowboat was very light, and the young men in it took up all the extra paddles and pushed backward. Halid hardly had to bump it with the branch and it was free.

The third boat, one of the rough-finished canoes, was heavy and floated a lot lower in the water than the others did. This meant it was stuck more thoroughly, and they fought to keep Nga's canoe in place at the same time Halid pushed harder and harder with the log. Nga couldn't imagine how the boat remained stuck if the sand was so slushy Padrit couldn't stand in it. Maybe there was a vein of clay holding the heavy vehicle. They tried again.

Halid lost his balance, lost the log, and both flipped into the water. It was a miracle the log hadn't smacked one of them before it tilted and dropped away. Then, of one single mind, Nga and Kimi chased after Halid. He scrambled back aboard with a big smile and a big bruise on his arm from the log, or maybe the side of the canoe when he went over.

Nga was tiring, and she knew Anane would not be able to help, her hands were too gnarled from arthritis. They once again paddled past the stranded canoe. She glanced upstream where a couple canoes rested against the eastern bank, watching and waiting for them. She waved to them for help.

"Maybe if we all three ram them from this side, the extra weight should push them back enough to come free," Anane said. She might not be able to paddle, but she was good at thinking.

The plan discussed with all the people involved, the three canoes pushed upstream, aligning themselves. Then they reversed direction, paddled downstream as close together as they could without tangling oars. They attempted to become a battering ram. At the last moment, they pulled paddles in and centered themselves, balancing their weight.

The three canoes did not strike exactly together, more like one, two, three—but it was enough. The canoe made a sucking sound as it broke free. All four canoes immediately began paddling, this time staying well to the east side of the narrowing stream, away from the sand bar.

Nga made a face when she realized her canoe was once again running last.

But less than a half-hour later they all had to bank their canoes and then portage around a rough little rocky waterfall. Above the falls, it was as if someone had turned off a faucet: the water was shallow and flat, all the canoes were scraping bottom on rock and gravel, and the heavier ones were barely making progress at all.

The rowboat of young men running in front finally pulled out of the water. They stood beside a huge old baobab and waited. All the rest of the canoes and the other rowboat pulled up beside them on the west bank.

"From here we walk, I think," another one of Palana's sons called. Nga thought it was Kez, but it was hard to tell, they looked so much alike.

She stood in the shade of the baobab and looked around. A stand of trees to one side, what looked like a once-plowed field to the other. She found a rock to stand upon for a better view.

"I think I see the highway," she called.

A couple people cheered.

———

They walked west on the highway for less than four kilometers. Where the highway crossed the rail line there were about forty or fifty people camping just off the road. Nga froze when it occurred to her that maybe they were ill, not camping. Was this an isolation field? She couldn't see any Red Cross personnel, but that didn't necessarily mean anything.

Their group of young men, Bodie in the lead, Halid beside him, approached the closest group of campers. Nga joined them, looking for sickness, listening to the talk. From here, she could see farther batches of people, from family-size to village-size. Things looked normal. Whatever that meant, Nga thought, envisioning big, dumb Lendee shoving Salim. That was not normal. It was like Luambe village had left normal far behind. She shook her head.

She was here, now. Enough problems were in front of her without going back to those in the village.

"Train comes tomorrow, we think." The man spoke Chiyao.

"Anyone sick?"

"Not in my group," the man said, indignant. "Others, I don't know," he waved an arm, "they are far away."

They weren't far enough to suit Nga, but maybe her group could set up here, since most of the others were spread out on the open fields nearer Lichinga town. From here, the town was a gray smudge on the horizon, a few huts and one brick building close enough to see details.

"Why catch the train here, and not in Lichinga?" Nga asked.

"They watching in Lichinga. Not here. Train slows down so slow here for the big turn south, and the highway crossing. And maybe to let people jump on, eh?"

"We have children and babies to carry," Nga said, and Halid nodded.

"How do *they* jump on?" Halid asked.

"You can do it," the man said. "One get on, hand over baby, other get on. You can do. Babies all the time on top of the train." He grinned, showing a lot of missing teeth, the remainder of which were yellow.

Nga was surprised. After years working with the Yao, she had come to expect good teeth. As a group, the Yao people had—usually had—straight, strong white teeth; they'd always been remarkable for their lack of dental problems. Well, maybe the man wasn't full Yao. Or there could be another explanation. Celiac disease, or sometimes diabetes, she remembered.

The young men set up the Luambe villagers' camp about twenty meters away from the next closest group. It seemed like a better position to Nga, since it was closer to the fresh water spring that apparently was the beginning of the "creek" they had followed in from Luambe.

More convinced than ever that they'd followed the Lucheringo River upstream to its source, or one of its sources, she looked closely at her map. There was another sizable waterway that ran to the north of them and joined the Lucheringo, close to the little waterfall they'd portaged around. They'd probably followed the smaller creek, because it went south. But that had been a good thing. If they'd successfully gone into Lichinga town from there along the bigger waterway, they'd just have had to walk back here for the train.

She left Anane, Halid, and Kimi to produce their boat's share of dinner and walked with her map back over to the other Chiyao-speaker's camp. The man seemed to know a lot about the railroad and how things worked. He might know what to expect once they managed to get on the train.

She glanced at her own villagers who worked efficiently to set up their camp. She felt an overwhelming surge of both affection and fear. She stopped walking, heart pounding. Why on earth had they followed her here? Was Maputo really going to be safer than Luambe? What if she was wrong? What if they were running from nothing?

What if what they were running to was worse? She took a deep breath and gathered her resolve, remembering the big Bemba man who had died.

Later, they gathered around the fire to eat. Mezi asked Teleza to say grace, and all the villagers paused while the girl finished. They were not all believers, but the Luambe Yao had always been polite. That was why it was so hard to believe the lack of respect Lendee had shown.

Nga ate, thoughtful. Lendee was a big man, but he had the mind of a child. His older brothers had always been his heroes. Had Guta goaded him into fighting with Salim? Had *Kofi*?

19. HALID

NIASSA PROVINCE, MOZAMBIQUE

Halid stared at all the people camped between them and Lichinga. How were all those people going to fit on the train? It was hard to imagine anything that big, that strong, that would pull everyone. He had seen pictures, of course, in his school books, and in old magazines Mrs. Lind put in the classrooms for everyone to look at. His people knew a lot about canoes, but not so much about trains.

His mother and others were busy gathering wood, building fires, laying out their blankets, watching children. He looked around the camp, watching his people settle into camp. He pretended to be the headman, keeping an eye on everything, so when some travelers from one of the other camps walked up and asked who the leader was, he said without thinking, "I am."

It was true enough, he supposed, though the man who'd spoken looked at him, a little dubious about the claim. But one of the women wasn't worried.

"Do you think we might borrow some rice or sweet potato?" she asked. "We came with food, but my bag was lost when the canoe overturned on the lake," she said.

"I think we have plenty," Halid said, proud of Luambe's surplus. "I will get some," he said and walked into camp until he found Bodie's blanket. Bodie had brought a sack of sweet potatoes from the rowboat. He filled his arms and returned to the others. "Is that enough?" he asked, looking at the woman who had asked him. She nodded, smiling. "Thank you, thank you." Her accent was odd, but she spoke Chiyao well enough. He nodded, and the trio walked back toward their own camp.

How had they managed to flip a canoe? Halid shook his head, then realized he had done it just like Salim would have. Embarrassed, he glanced at his own camp but could see no one watching him.

Bodie's group walked past him. "We are patrolling!" Jon called. Halid nodded. That would only last until supper, but there was really nothing to patrol from, was there?

A short time later his mother waved at him for dinner. He sat among his people, who were all a bit nervous about getting on the train in the morning.

————

Halid was not sure what awakened him. Perhaps a sound in the night, a break in the quiet insect hum. He sat up and looked about. The fire had died to coals, bright against the dark of camp. Only stars lit the sky. He listened to the deep silence. It had been a child sound that woke him up: he could remember it, a little squeak or whimper.

He got up and looked toward the spot Mezi had gone to sleep. His mother, Anane, was there. Mezi was. He saw who he thought was Nga. He saw Gezy and Fazila. But where were the two little ones? Where were Muluzi and Teleza?

Quietly, he walked around the camp, pausing to stare in the dark until he recognized faces. Half-moon light helped him pick out who was who. When he passed Kimi, she nodded. The young woman was sitting up, nursing Shaida.

Halid crouched down beside her. "Have you seen Mu or Teleza?"

Kimi's head tilted. "No." She glanced down at her baby, back up. "I think I heard someone walk through camp; I thought it was you or Bodie, keeping watch."

Halid nodded and stood up. Maybe they should have posted a guard, but they hadn't. He had seen Bodie sound asleep a moment ago, so it hadn't been him.

After a second search, it was clear that Muluzi and Teleza were missing. Halid shook Bodie awake and motioned for silence.

They walked away from the camp, out into the damp grass. "I think Imrane or someone came and took Mezi's two littles."

Bodie's eyes widened. "We should get to the river, quickly."

"Yes," Halid said. "I will go now; get a couple of the others, bring spears."

Bodie nodded.

Halid ran to the highway, sprinting down the road and then the short distance through the bush back toward the creek bank and the big baobab where they had left the canoes. Heart pounding more from fear that he would be too late than from the run, he heard Muluzi squeal, not too far ahead of him.

He rounded the copse of mulberry trees in time to see Lizzat holding Teleza by the hair. Little Teleza poked Lizzat with a stick. Lizzat let go and backed up, rubbing her hip. Teleza threw the stick at the woman, then ran to cling to Kadade's leg.

Kadade? Yes, standing in confrontation with Guta and Lizzat were Rana, Kadade, a stunned-looking Miss Anderson, and one of the other village women who had stayed behind in Luambe. Yet here they were. All holding spears, except Miss Anderson. The young woman holding Muluzi had a spear resting against her left shoulder, Mu held tight against her right. The little boy was weeping. He looked over the girl's shoulder at Halid, eyes dripping tears. Tema, Halid thought it was, holding the boy, but he could not see her face. Was she rescuing Mu or trying to take him?

"Go!" Rana yelled at Guta. He held his spear at an angle, not quite pointed at the older man.

"Not without Imrane's children!"

"I want Mama," Mu wailed. Teleza moved behind Kadade's leg and peered at Guta and his wife. Kadade's big hand dropped protectively atop the little girl's head. Tema, carrying Mu, moved beside Kadade.

"They will stay with their mother," Rana said. His spear point dropped until it was leveled at Guta's chest.

Halid stepped into view, followed now by Bodie and two younger boys with spears, lending their small weight to Rana and Kadade and Tema.

"You will not take them," Kadade said, his pose now identical to Rana's.

Kofi's brother, Guta. Halid thought it through. Had Kofi joined them earlier today just to help Guta get the children? Yet Kofi and Palana had both been asleep at the camp a few minutes ago. Or had they just been pretending to sleep? What about Guta's son, Sami, and wife? Halid turned and studied the bank of the creek. His eye caught movement from the canoe nearest the water. Yes, it was Sami. The man was crouched in the shadows by the boats. Halid nudged Bodie and the four younger men moved toward Sami.

Realizing he had been found, Sami stood up. He dropped his spear. Halid knew by himself he wasn't much of a threat, but even though Bodie and the other two were just boys, they knew how to use their spears. It was still at least two or maybe three against one. Sami held his hands out, showing empty palms.

Halid turned back to the confrontation between Rana's trio and Guta and his wife. The rising moon made a demon mask of Guta's face, shadows within shadow. Lizzat turned half away, her own face in shadow.

"You will pay for this," Guta snarled.

"No. But I think you will," Rana answered in calm tones.

Halid found himself doubting his own eyes and ears. It was as if a seed planted long ago had suddenly bloomed, turning Guta into another man. He was very glad for the presence of Rana and Kadade and the others. How could he have stopped Guta's family with just himself and Bodie's boys?

Well, it would be simpler for Kadade and Tema to fight, if they had to, if they weren't protecting the children. Halid removed Mu from Tema's shoulder, reached down for Teleza's little hand. He moved away from them all, starting to head back to the railroad camp.

He could feel Mu trembling, and Teleza's hand was sweaty. He picked her up in his other arm, cradling Teleza's head against his own. Mu reached out and grasped his sister's hand. Arms full of frightened children, he stepped out of the grass and onto the road. They were joined shortly by Bodie's two lieutenants, Jon and Gunnar, who looked over their shoulders often as they walked.

"Rana is running Guta off," Jon said.

Halid nodded. Before they made it all the way back to camp, Kadade and Bodie joined them.

"Rana and Tema will stay to make sure they are gone. They will find us later."

"You are coming to Maputo with us?"

"There is much news," Kadade said. His voice was sad. "But we will wait to tell everyone." He looked at Halid from the corners of his eyes, without turning his head, and Halid knew it was very bad.

20. ARIQ

ROSWELL, NEW MEXICO

Thousands of ponies stampeded across the plains. So many that individual hoof beats were indistinguishable within the dull roar. Enemies couldn't discern the direction of travel. The booming percussion surrounded them like thunder. Ariq knew the archers were adding their terrible shouts to the cacophony, but they also were indiscernible within the rumble. The ground trembled.

Then Ariq's sedated consciousness woke up. There were no ponies, no archers. Ariq had been listening to the rolling thunder of a summer storm. He looked at his clock. Three in the morning. The thunder continued, so he grabbed a pillow to bury his head and return to sleep. He needed his rest.

Before he could encapsulate himself, another round of thunder burst. His foggy brain complained, no lightning. No lightning? No lightning means no thunder, his science brain protested.

"Ariq! Ariq wake up!"

Someone was banging on the front door. The large wooden door echoed throughout his stucco and adobe house. Suddenly fully awake, he reflected that the thick adobe kept the noise, heat, and wind out, but when something got in, the massive walls trapped it in.

Ariq jumped out of bed and wrapped his *deel*, a going-to-college gift from эмээ, around the t-shirt and loose shorts he slept in.

"Ariq! Ariq wake up!"

Barefoot, he headed for the thundering door, trying to only step on his Navaho rugs for year-round the clay floor tiles were cold. He opened the door.

At first, he didn't recognize his caller. Nizhoni's hair formed a dark cloud around her head and shoulders. Clearly, she had not done anything with it. He had never seen her hair except in perfect braids or a tight bun or—Ariq didn't know much about women's hair, but he knew he'd never seen so much of it.

"Joni. What's wrong?"

The normally calm nurse, spoke fast in a high-pitch voice, "We called you. You didn't answer. We were worried."

"OK. But, what's wrong. You're not even on duty tonight."

"The one we visited this afternoon, Arthur, Arthur Whitey, is having seizures, violent seizures."

Ariq realized he wasn't going back to sleep very soon. He retreated to his room to dress but left the door open to continue talking.

"What have you done so far?"

She sat down, either exhausted or relieved. "Lachy was on duty. He called me! It took too long to find the EEG equipment and get it set up. Once we had it going, no one really knew what it meant. Nurses searched for the manual."

Ariq reflected that an orthopedic clinic rarely cared about brain waves. "Were you able to stabilize the guest? He's not dead, is he?"

She ignored him, "We didn't know what to do and we remembered that corporate was giving you trouble...but someone's life was in the balance. We called Minneapolis!"

Ariq didn't care about corporate paper pushers right now. "And...?"

They told us to get him to the regional hospital for an MRI scan and a consultation with a neurologist. "The ambulance left with full sirens."

By this time, he was dressed. "Good job. Your quick reaction might have saved his life. I'll head over to Chavez General immediately."

———

The emergency department had swallowed up Arthur Whitey. After Ariq completed a stack of forms, they sent him away. There was no neurologist on duty; they summoned the on-call doctor; please, come back later. He knew better than to hassle the ED staff.

Six o'clock was too late to go back to sleep and too late for his morning ride. He frowned. He would miss galloping in the sunrise two days in a row.

With their critical patient across town, the night staff settled down for the final hours of their shift. He doubted they wanted to be interrogated, nor that it would be productive.

Instead he called CDC in Atlanta, two hours ahead. "You must know something. I've heard an article is in the MMWR."

His CDC contact just dissembled with polite, bureaucratic denials. After almost a half hour and not one useful piece of information, he changed direction, "Well, I've been talking to an Aboriginal healer in Australia. It seems she has seen something like what I'm calling idiopathic ague, and has had some success with their traditional medicine."

Surprisingly, after so many denials, there were no denials that **Dreamtime**'s cases might be relevant. Sometimes silence communicated the most information.

Emboldened, he added, "She's sending me some herbs and instructions to try here. Are you interested?"

That brought some life on the other end. In such a soft monotone that Ariq could imagine her looking over her shoulder, the woman said, "Don't tell me how you are getting unregulated drugs into the country, and absolutely don't tell me about any unauthorized human trials, but if you get any positive results, I want to be the first to know. First. To. Know."

Wow, Ariq thought, Wow. This IA must be so much worse than I imagined.

He quickly agreed and after a few pleasantries and some more CDC denials and disclaimers, the call ended.

———

When he finally heard from Chavez General, Julia's father was in a coma and on a ventilator. His symptoms had rapidly progressed from seizures, ague, fever, and shivering, to severe tremors, rashes, itching, and mild hallucinations. For lack of an alternative, the medical staff had put him into a chemically-induced coma. Sheer desperation.

The ROC staff were doing their best to minimize mortalities, but Ariq would have preferred not needing to request outside assistance. Roswell Orthopedic Clinic plans did not include sick people.

Ariq felt guilty for not following up with Julia sooner. He hated to report inconclusive bad news. He now called without further delay. She answered on the first ring.

Once he heard her voice, he didn't know what to say. Holding back his anxiety, he found some words, which he delivered mechanically, seemingly channeled from some old black and white movie, "Julia, it is too late to release your father. He had seizures and hallucinations last night. He's been put in a protective coma at Chavez General."

He described the course of his condition and the current coma, leaving out the EEG difficulties, frantic calls to Minnesota, and the ambulance sirens.

"Have you considered rabies? You know my father's a veterinarian, so he's had rabies pre-exposure prophylaxis, but maybe this is something related. Vets are always concerned with rabies."

Ariq thought about rabies, again. Maybe the vet was exposed before he flew to New Mexico. Rabies had a notoriously unpredictable incubation period, from days to months. Certainly, rabies would be superior to a worldwide epidemic with a novel pathogen.

His brief respite lasted until his science brain asked, how would that explain the other cases?

Then Julia added another reason not to look for rabies, "He treated exotic species in the wild, so a cross-species pathogen is possible."

Ariq shivered. Zoonotic diseases can cause pandemics, bad pandemics. Lyme disease. Hantavirus. Ebola. Plague. Rabies.

Ignoring the evidence against rabies, she continued, "Since he's already in a coma, you might look into the Milwaukee Protocol for rabies. It's not perfect, but if it is rabies, you need to be ready to try anything."

Ariq thought of the earlier warning about unauthorized human trials. "I've been talking to someone in Australia." He was intentionally vague about his source, "They seem to have similar cases. They're sending me something that worked for them. Do you think I could try it on your father?"

She choked a reply, "Sure...if he lives long enough."

Ariq did not know what to say. She had just admitted her father might die. Ariq had some experience with bereaved relatives, but this was more like a hospice case, and he was lost.

Fortunately, she broke the silence. "You know he had me late in life and he's lived a full life. He spent years taking care of people's pets. When he retired, he worked with zoos to increase captive populations of endangered animals. His greatest joy was going on expeditions to release these animals back to their native habitats."

Her voice started cracking. With a few quick internet searches, Ariq found pictures of her father in Africa with some equines, in Mexico with condors, and on some coast with baby seals.

He knew he shouldn't raise false hopes, but he just felt so responsible. "We'll do everything we can. Maybe we'll get lucky. We'll find the answer."

Later he'd feel guilty for pushing this onto her, but he added, "You seem to have good connections. Let me know if you hear anything."

With that, they were both out of energy. The call was over.

He was in a daze until he noticed Lachy and Martina walking together. They seemed to be in a serious discussion just like nurse Joni had earlier reported. Ariq had had enough intrigue for the day, so he ignored them and headed to the CRC to spend some time lost in comparisons of human and chiropteran genomes.

———

He never made it to the research center.

He ran into his head surgeon in suit and bow tie, "I heard about the excitement last night. My protégé Lachlan did us proud."

The medical director's take on what Ariq considered a disastrous evening was surprising, even concerning. "Did I miss something? All I heard about was a lost EEG machine and a guest that nearly died until we were rescued by the hospital across town?"

"Follow me to the cafeteria. We'll have some of our excellent lattes and those flaky croissants, and I will correct your confusion."

They sat at a repurposed school-cafeteria table.

The chief surgeon sipped his coffee and leaned back. With his hands behind his head, he looked completely relaxed. "Remember that story about horses and zebras from med school?"

Ariq leaned forward, feeling like a first-year student, anxious and lost, and eager to prove himself. "Of course. When you hear hoof beats, expect horses, expect the common problems. Don't go looking for zebras, the rare diseases that take up pages in the textbooks, but are rarely seen in the wild."

Charles smiled. "Very good. Now the other side of that story is what you do when it *is* zebras."

Still smiling, he took a large bite of croissant. "It is the zebras that truly test us. Today we have a herd of zebras, and we are proving our mettle."

"Really?"

"No one expects much from us, a bunch of orthopedic surgeons who know little about sick people. But we showed them."

"Really? Two people have died."

"Zebras! Zebras! We're not talking about horses or your cute Mongolian ponies. These are zebras! The scorecard is different!"

Scorecard?

"The first challenge with zebras is recognition. Horse doctors kill zebras with their confidence and arrogance. Not us! We saw we were lost."

He finished his croissant, practically laughing. "Second, zebras require a team effort and an open mind. Did we try to solve this ourselves? No! We called Minneapolis. We shared reports to Atlanta. We sent our patient to the regional hospital. You even contacted a witch doctor in Australia."

Ariq wanted to defend **Dreamtime**, but he was thrown off balance by the surprise that someone else knew what happened on **Bat Chat**, *and* that the head surgeon thought it could be helpful.

He was further dumbfounded as Chucky exclaimed, "We might be the best zebra hunters yet." With a laugh, he added, "This is a big, bad zebra. I wouldn't be surprised if your bats and high school students were part of the solution, too."

21. HALID

LICHINGA, MOZAMBIQUE

 Halid got Miss Anderson to drink some water, but the woman would not let him or Nga touch her.

"Are you hurt?" Nga asked. But the woman did not answer, just hunched down lower on the ground and curled into fetal position. Worried about shock, Halid covered her with a blanket. Nga sat down beside her as Kadade roused the villagers. Then Rana re-joined them and helped wake people up.

The sun was not yet visible behind the distant hills, but the sky lightened as the Luambe villagers gathered together.

"I am sad and sorry to tell you this," Rana said, his voice firm and loud enough for all those gathered around him to hear.

Halid saw Nga's sister, arms around her children, face filled with dread. Anane moved next to Halid. He reached over and took her hand. Her usual peaceful joy at life had been replaced with worry and a deep frown. Halid knew his father had been left in a difficult situation. What news did Rana and Hadade have?

Hadade stood by the banked fire, lit faintly red by the coals. "I am sorry to say Imrane has gone insane. He is saying the missionaries, and Salim, and all the white people and the government have been telling us lies. That the old ways are best, with a strong ruler, strong traditions. He says all the women in the village are *his* wives now. All of them, are his. The foolish new rules, one man, one wife, are wrong and backward and have ruined our people."

"Ruined?" Halid heard Nga say.

Rana glanced at her and nodded. "It makes no sense, but he has convinced others. He– "

He broke off, staring beyond the villagers gathered before him. Off to the road, where five people were slowly making their way toward them.

"Dende!" Kofi called. Halid could see that indeed, Dende was one of those limping in their direction. Palana's youngest son. Halid started moving toward them. They looked like they needed help, but Halid was not sure he would trust any of Kofi's family again after what Sami and Guta had done. And he wasn't certain of Palana, either.

Kofi and Nga got to their feet and trotted toward the wounded group also. Dende was helping someone walk. Halid could see blood on their clothes.

Jojeza. Tonan and his wife, who was stunned-looking like Miss Anderson. Eslin, Bodie's older sister, who was limping badly, arm across Dende's shoulder on one side, Tonan's on the other. Her robe was bloody, her face bruised, her hand wrapped with a bloody rag.

Halid arrived, and Tonan nodded at him as he slid his shoulder under Eslin's arm in Tonan's place. Relieved of Eslin's weight, Tonan put his arm gently around his own wife's waist, guiding her toward the village group.

Kofi spoke softly to Dende. "Your wife?" Dende shook his head.

"She is gone. Imrane tried to take her and she fought. Lendee held me while Imrane ran a spear into her heart." He bowed his head, looked up. "There is worse news," he said.

Halid's heart went cold. What could be worse?

They limped into camp, and Halid helped Eslin sit down. He and Nga did what they could to help Eslin, while Rana and now Dende spoke to the group.

"They have burned the mission," Dende said. His eyes searched out Mezi, then Nga. He shook his head.

Nga looked up from Eslin and met his gaze. She seemed calm, as if she already knew what he would say.

"Mr. and Mrs. Lind are dead."

Mezi gasped, clutching Mu and Teleza even tighter against her, until Teleza squeaked. "Grandpapa?" she asked, her little girl voice carrying over the silent group.

"Grandpapa is gone to heaven," Mezi said, and visibly swallowed back tears. "Grandma, too."

"Why?" Mu asked.

The question the whole village wanted to ask. Why?

Mrs. Tately was openly weeping. She had known the Linds for years. Petyr Johansson awkwardly put his arm around the older woman, his own face a sad, shocked mask.

Halid was icy calm. If the missionaries were dead, what about the headman? What about his father? "Salim?" he asked, at the same time as his mother's soft voice said her husband's name.

"He was alive when we left, heading up to the old prayer cave. Surane and her husband were with him. His wounds are very bad," Dende said. "He told us to bring everyone that could move and catch up with you. Surane stayed to help Wayya, whose foot was almost cut off."

"They maybe can hold on there, until their wounds are better," Rana said.

"Or maybe we will see them come before the train does," Dende said. "There are still two canoes hidden if they can make it to them." He shook his head, looking at Halid. "He would not let us stay to help him."

Halid was ashamed that his father had only his two older sisters to help him. He should have stayed. But Dende was not ashamed; Salim had told Dende to leave, and he had done so, guarding these wounded remnants of their village.

"Salim," Anane said it like a prayer.

Salim had stayed, and Salim was wounded. That was right, that is what a headman should do. But it felt wrong, that they had abandoned him. Halid put his arm around his mother.

He could think of nothing more. His head was still. His heart felt like stone inside, a weight he was not sure he could carry.

He should have been there, not following Nga on some stupid adventure to become a medic. He should have stayed and helped his father.

Then he saw his mother's face. She was safe. Many others were safe because they *had* left. But...had that been the reason Imrane attacked now? Because half of Salim's supporters had fled the village?

If Halid had taken the traditional *mundunugu* training other Yao village healers had offered, there would have been no reason to accept Imrane into the village in the first place. But no, he had spurned the native ways, wanting to be modern, wanting to be a TC, like Nga, like Ben.

This was as much his fault as anyone's.

He turned to what he knew, what he could help Nga do. Eslin had been raped. She would not want him helping with that. So Halid tended to the powerful young woman's hand, washing away blood from the wound with hot clean water. The cut was deep. Halid could see the white of bone, inside the red of the wound, beneath the deep brown of her skin. He cleaned it, found his kit with sterile surgical thread, sterile needles.

Nga helped Eslin wash away the blood from her thighs. Mezi held a blanket over the proceedings, not to bring Eslin's agony before the eyes of all the young men. Anane brought her one of her own clean robes. Unlike Miss Anderson and Torane's wife, Eslin was angry.

"I will kill him myself," she said. "I will tear out his heart with my own hands."

Nga nodded, silent. She washed and touched gently. Halid tried to copy her, stitching the hand wound closed as gently as he could. It was difficult to believe any Yao man could do this.

But then, Imrane was not Yao.

"I wonder if it was the Grave's disease," Nga murmured. "A thyroid storm."

"Velvet beans," Mezi said. Nga looked at her, then back to Eslin, helping the young woman dress behind the privacy blanket.

"He was eating velvet beans?" Halid asked.

"To cure his unbalance, for energy," Mezi explained.

"He had pots of them, fermenting in his hut," Eslin said. "I saw them when he and Lendee dragged me there."

Nga scowled. Halid remembered that velvet beans were used for fevers and other ills in *mundunugu* work, but that they could sometimes produce hallucinations. It might explain some of the craziness.

After, he moved on to see what Dende needed.

What else could he do? It was too late to say, "Sorry, I should have stayed and helped protect you — "

He realized Nga was there but not there. Her body was there, but her mind was far away. She had just lost both her parents. Nga should have been given time to grieve.

Instead, the young woman continued to work among the wounded villagers, looking like a tiny white magic fairy, fluttering from group to group with gauze wings.

Halid finished bandaging the cut on Dende's arm. Nga came upon him in a cluster of people with Jojeza, Tema, Rana and Kadade. Dende had sat on the ground between them, scratching long bloody welts into his arms and legs, grieving for his wife.

Nga put out her hand to stop him, but the younger men shook their heads and stepped in her way. Halid gripped her shoulder, met her eyes. Dende needed to mourn.

She walked away. Hadid stayed, watching Dende's grief, sharing it.

Anane joined them. "Choy?" she asked.

There were expressions of consternation, then Jojeza said, "We think Choy has maybe pretended to join Imrane, to spy on him for Salim," she said.

"Or else maybe somehow he was convinced to join for real," Tema said.

Halid shook his head almost in time with his mother's head shake.

"Not Choy," Anane said. "As you say, he must be spying for his father."

"My brother pretended to like Imrane because my father saw he had no friends," Halid said. "He asked Choy to help make Imrane feel like he belonged, but Choy would come home every night and complain about things Imrane said. He does not like the man, and his wife likes Imrane even less."

"As to Guta, we passed him on the river," Dende said. "He lost his spear, throwing it at us. Sami just sat and watched. I hope wild dogs find them."

Jojeza nodded. "I think Guta was always part of this, telling Imrane his plan was good." Jojeza's eyes were fierce.

"Kofi?" Halid wondered. Heads shook. Everyone seemed to agree that Kofi was innocent of the conspiracy. "Good. He and Salim have always been close; it would have made my father's soul ache if Kofi turned on him too," Halid said.

"I think he loves Palana so much, he would never do anything to shame her like this," Jojeza added.

Halid watched Nga wander the camp, looking for people to help. The second time she stopped beside Miss Anderson, the young teacher accepted her help washing up, changing her clothes, drinking some water.

Mezi's eyes followed her sister. They were both mourning in the white people's way. Neither took the time to just grieve, to just honor the dead. It was one of the things Halid had never understood about Christianity or the missionaries. They seemed almost to rejoice in the death and the moving on to heaven of their people. Or at least they pretended to. He saw tears in Mezi's eyes, but the woman did not cry.

She had divorced Imrane, but still, the man who had fathered her children also had murdered her parents. That had to be tearing her soul into pieces, but he knew no way to offer her comfort.

The camp stayed quiet with shock, with mourning. Someone built up the fire. Someone cooked something. Some people ate. No one said grace.

After eating was pretty much done and cleaned up, Halid went to Nga and pulled her to her feet, led her to Mezi. "Please tell me the good things about Linnea and Anson Lind. The things you want us to remember."

Nga shook her head. "I cannot—not yet. I still hope they are alive. How could they be dead? It is not possible." Mezi nodded her head in agreement.

But Nga did sit down beside her sister. Muluzi crawled into

her lap, and she and Mezi each held a cocoa-colored child. That was one good thing Imrane had given them, his good looks: they were beautiful children. Mu's bright eyes looked over Nga's shoulder at Halid. He smiled gently at the little boy, then turned and walked away. There were others who needed help now, wanted it.

———

"Train coming," Bodie's voice carried over the group. "Everyone ready?"

Halid glanced around. Everyone was not ready. Mezi had taken her two children over to the small copse of coca trees the villagers had been using for a latrine, and not yet returned. Anane was still packing and re-packing her bedroll bundle. Others were slowly gathering up belongings. Nga took Kimi's gear along with her own, while Kimi anxiously rocked Shaida in her arms.

Most of the single young men carried a sack of the villagers' surplus grain that Mr. Lind had made sure they took. It was a good plan. Even if they couldn't cook on the train, they might be able to barter the raw rice or corn for some cooked food along the way. It was unlikely that any of the villagers had brought coin to buy anything with. They usually bartered.

Halid looked toward Lichinga. He thought maybe he could see movement, but not a defined train. They should have some time, yet. He jumped up and down, trying to see the train. Anane glanced up from her packing and gave the slightest frown. Halid walked over and picked up her bundle and tied it, adding it to his. Everyone began moving closer to the train tracks.

Halid kept looking back for Mezi. What would they do if someone was left behind? He should wait to board until he was sure all his people were on the train. He glanced around their camping area, checking again and again for stragglers, saw Rana and Hadade were doing the same.

The train whistled, and he could see it just coming into sight. He turned and saw Mezi and the children trotting back to camp. Mezi snatched up her bundle, handed it to Nga. They joined the others spreading out along the train track. The ground rumbled beneath their feet, and metal screeched against metal, clunks and bangs accentuating the train music.

Halid looked down the rails toward the big engine. He could see people already climbing aboard, shadowy figures next to the train, then gone. Many people already stood on the roofs of boxcars, waving and laughing. The engine went past, the engineer smiling at them; the ground shook, his bones shook, like the time an elephant herd had thundered past the village.

After all his worry, getting on the train was very simple. Halid tossed their bundles onto a half-empty timber car, then helped his mother and Eslin climb aboard, him trotting alongside. He watched as they worked their way to the ladder and got up on the boxcar roof with the other villagers.

Taking care of Miss Anderson as if she were one of their own sisters, Rana and Kadade and Bodie pulled the young woman aboard. Miss Anderson walked like a dead thing, but she would move where they gently pushed her. Soon she was climbing the ladder up to the empty boxcar roof next to Anane's, with Kadade in front of her and Rana behind. Bodie clung to the ladder beside the teacher, Halid could see his lips moving but not hear what he said.

He could not hear anything but the train.

Kimi didn't need to hand Shaida to anyone, she just stepped onto a short step at the front side of the car, grabbed the hand bar and pulled herself and her daughter on board one-handed.

Little Teleza got on without help followed closely by Mezi, who turned and looked at Nga, wide-eyed. Nga lifted Muluzi up, trotting beside the train. Mezi grabbed him. Halid closed in, in case they needed help.

Nga chased after that car, running a bit to stay even. She carried her and Mezi's things. Rana jumped off, grabbed the bundle and climbed back on the train. Mezi and the children had already climbed the ladder up to the roof where a knot of the Luambe villagers looked down. Rana tossed the bundle up, then backed down the ladder. Halid shouted encouragement.

Rana held out his hand, but Nga didn't need it, in the end. She caught the bar and jumped onto the bottom step. Rana moved out of the way and she climbed up, and Halid followed her, last to board as the train began to pick up speed.

He looked out over their campground. Salim had not come, Surane, her husband, and sister Wayya were still missing also. Nevertheless, Halid stood and looked as long as he could still see the campground, hoping they'd come at the last minute, hoping they had survived.

But no one was there—trampled grass trembled in the breeze, tree shadows stretched across bare patches of dirt.

The villagers were atop two boxcars, with just a few strangers mixed among them. They could not go home. This was Luambe village, now. Only their headman was missing.

22. NGA

LICHINGA & NACALA, MOZAMBIQUE

Nga lay on her back, knees bent, looking up at the clouds. Her mind felt empty, she could not seem to focus on anything, just…clouds.

One fat cloud looked kind of like her father, standing at the pulpit in the chapel.

She felt tears on her cheeks.

How could her father be dead?

How could anyone want to hurt Linnea, who was one of the kindest people in the world?

"There are twelve log cars," Teleza informed her. "I counted them!"

"Good for you." Nga stopped looking at clouds. She wiped her tears, sat up.

The train seemed to have energized her niece as much as it had diminished her nephew. Teleza's little brother was usually the exuberant one, but Mu had been pretty quiet ever since they got on board.

Nga thought about that a moment. Abruptly, she got up and looked around for Muluzi. He was sleeping with his head in Anane's lap. Nga lost her balance, sat back down and crawled over on her hands and knees. She felt his forehead. The boy was sound asleep. There was no fever.

Perhaps he understood what his father had done, that he would never see his grandma again, that was why he was quiet. Perhaps things were simply too strange.

Nga nodded at Anane then made her way back to her own spot.

They needed to remember to fill their water bottles at the stop at Cuamba station. Then they would ride all night. Depending on how long the stops were, they should arrive in Nacala around noon. She stared out at the trees that passed by, half hypnotized by the landscape.

Her heart beat in time to the train wheels clacking and the words her mind chanted: Mother is dead. Father is dead. Dead, dead, dead.

———

Nga woke from a disturbed sleep, the heat of the sun burning her pale skin. She put on her long-sleeved shirt, turned up the collar. Beside her, Mezi was talking to Jojeza. The sun was bright on Jojo's face, but Mezi sat slumped, face hidden in her own shadow.

"What if they need help?" Mezi said. "What if they are still alive?"

Jojeza's face was stony. Her slender dark arms were folded around herself as if she must hold herself together. She shook her head. "It is too late, Mezi, I am sorry," Jojeza said. "Too late for them. But there are many people here who need your help and Nga's help. Please do not abandon us now."

"Nga can stay. I could go."

"So Imrane can get his hands on you? You risk yourself and your children, for no reason."

"I could calm him down, maybe."

"Listen, Mezi. Imrane blocked the doors of the house. Then he put men on guard around the house. Then he set it on fire. He stood outside and laughed as it burned. We do not know what he did inside—if they were already dead—but there was blood on his robes." She bit her lip. "Anyone who tried to help was speared, or raped, or both. Afterward, after the house was ashes, Imrane sent Botte in to get their bones. He made his headman's staff– " she could not finish.

"Things have been bad with Imrane, but it is so hard to believe he would do this," Mezi said.

Jojeza shook her head. "He is crazy, like that elephant at Gurandi village, destroying everything."

"Maybe he would not have been so crazy if we had stayed," Nga said. "It is my fault, for saying everyone should go."

Mezi and Jojeza and Anane all shook their heads. "You did not

141

make him crazy," Anane said. "And you did not make the sickness come."

Maybe, but if she had not pulled away so many people who were friendly to Salim, Imrane would not have been able to do this. He might have gone crazy, but he would not have had enough power among the villagers.

How had the man convinced so many others that they should take over? That they should ignore tradition and all the years Salim had led them and led them well?

Mezi reached a hand out and gripped Nga's arm. "Nga, *Mother* said we must all leave. She looked upon this sickness as a sign that God had answered her prayers, given a way for us to escape. She *wanted* me to go, to take the children away to someplace safe. She wanted you safe."

Nga frowned. "Was he hurting Teleza?"

"Pinching," she said. "He would pinch her arm. He would mostly yell at Mu, sometimes hit."

"I saw bruises a couple times, but I thought you would say something if he was doing that. To my shame, I worried that it was you, trying to keep the children quiet maybe, trying to keep Imrane from yelling."

"I did try to keep everyone happy, but Mother figured it out. She made me promise I would leave as soon as there was a chance. Then she heard about Zambia. She heard it on her radio, on the news, so much sickness, so many people dying."

"She knew I would go?"

"She called Ben Kalagho, Nga. She begged him to convince you we must go. The news was so bad, we didn't think Ben would have trouble, because you already were thinking we should go. Then she helped me stand up to Imrane until we left."

No wonder Mother had been so helpful with travel plans, Nga realized. It had mostly been her idea. Linnea Lind was so quiet, so sweet, people never realized how strong she could be. Or maybe it had just been Nga who hadn't realized.

She thought about what Jojo had said. She carefully did not think about her parents' bones. It was too awful to imagine.

She sat in silence a few more moments, trying to get her grief under control. She got to her hands and knees again, moving to where Miss Anderson sat, looking at the scenery they passed with empty eyes. The young teacher should be in the hospital, with counseling and medical care. Nga felt so inadequate, so unable to help. Miss Anderson's first teaching job, and then this—

Eslin was angry and intent on revenge, but that was a better reaction than this cold, still, shock. Tonan's wife had begun to respond to her surroundings, her little family pulling her back from the edge of nowhere. But there was no one for Miss Anderson. Nga didn't even recall the woman's first name. Her mother would have chided her for that.

Linnea knew everyone's name and most of their birthdays. It was part of why people loved her.

Except for the one who didn't.

The train whistle pulled her out of reverie. They were coming into Cuamba. There would be at least a half-hour stop here, while the rail yard people attached the Lichinga train to the bigger one that came from Malawi. She patted her pocket, making sure the small bit of cash she had brought was there. It would be good if she could find some fresh food to share with the villagers.

They got off the train, used the toilets, washed up, filled their water bottles. Nga helped Kimi wash out the rags she tied on for Shaida's diapers. They would dry quickly in the sun on the rooftop of the train.

She found a baker selling loaves of brown bread that were still hot from round stone ovens. She bought everything he had. She found the Luambe villagers clustered together on the ground just past the eastern end of the station platform, enjoying the shade the building cast. She handed out loaves of bread, little warm bits of hope.

————

Her bed was hard, and it shook. Was there an earthquake? No, Halid was shaking her shoulder. She sat up. Train car.

"We are stopping, if anyone needs," Halid said.

She nodded. She saw no one else awake, even as the train slowed and squealed to a stop. She got off and refilled her water jug, amazed at the quiet. When she got back on top of the boxcar she checked again. Everyone was asleep.

The night, the train, it all felt disjointed, as if she was half in another dimension. The train started back up, shaking and rocking and rumbling. She did not fall back asleep.

The sun rose, and people began stirring.

They pulled into Nacala station at 11:00 a.m. The air smelled like ocean. Many of the villagers wrinkled their noses.

Nga was pleased to see the station was within walking distance of the docks. In fact, as she waited her turn to climb down the ladder, she could see a few ships docked, among them what looked like the fisheries boat in the picture her friend Shelly had once shown her. That would take them to Beira, where they hoped to board the Greenleaf boat, as her mother had suggested.

Mother.

She climbed down the ladder and walked to where the villagers had gathered.

"The boat does not go until tomorrow," Halid was saying. "We need to find a place to stay tonight."

Nga spoke up. "The refugee camp they set up last wet season is still here. They made it for the people who were flooded out. We should be able to go there."

"Where is it?"

"I'm afraid we're going to have to ask someone," she said. "And get a city map. I know Maputo, but not this place. But I also need to make sure our plans are still okay with the Fisheries boat."

"I'll find the camp," Halid said, "if you talk to the boat people?"

"Yes. That will work. I'll meet you there later. We need to collect food for the trip, everyone. Things that will last a few days. There should be a way to cook on the boat."

Anane nodded. "We will get food," she said. "I have some things we can trade—we have more than enough rice."

Nga nodded. She separated her bundle from Mezi's as Halid headed off to talk to people.

Mezi opened her bag. Inside the tiny pile of clothes for her and the children was a small brightly colored bag made from scraps of a cotton robe Nga remembered Mezi wearing until it fell apart. Her people had so little.

Mezi opened the bag, looked up at Nga. She dumped the contents out onto her hand. It was some jewelry she vaguely remembered her mother had. "She gave me a little money, but this should be worth more," Mezi said, handing Nga a bracelet and ring that sparkled, a gold pendant, another ring.

"Diamonds?"

"Papa gave them to her when they first met. Do you remember Grandpapa? He came to visit that one time?

Nga nodded.

"He had a nice house, some money. He was angry when Papa came to Africa, but he always loved Mother. He gave all this to Papa, to give to her. I think there was more, once. They used some of it on the mission buildings." Mezi handed her the empty bag.

Nga stared at the sparkling jewelry. "I wish she had come with us."

"Oh, Nga," Mezi said, putting her arm across her sister's shoulder and squeezing. "It will be all right."

Nga found she could not really look her sister in the face. No matter what Jojeza and Rana and Mezi said, it still felt like her fault. Her parents were gone. Her home was gone. And all the villagers were homeless now as well.

"I'll see you at the camp," she said, tucking the jewelry back into the bag. She put it deep into a pocket of her backpack and headed toward the docks and their ride for the next leg of their journey.

23. DR. BRIAN

WASHINGTON DC & CHARLOTTESVILLE, VA

℞ The concierge arranged for a driver to pick up Doctor Brian at 9:30 Friday morning. For short flights like this one to Atlanta, he had his suitcase expressed to the next destination. He found travel more relaxing without worrying about a big suitcase. His carry-on had his pills and a change of clothes. With four powered wheels, GPS, and WiFi, the clever little case could make its own way to the gate, like a modern-day butler. He just needed to follow.

In the open atrium of his hotel, he enjoyed a light breakfast of oatmeal, a half orange cut like a grapefruit, and finished off with a chocolate croissant and double espresso. He ordered this breakfast by rote, a compromise between coronary health and indulgence.

Doctor Brian recalled that he'd done his senior project on compounds that reduced cholesterol. He knew that several Nobel prizes had already been awarded for work with the strange compound that had been implicated in many diseases from gall stones to atherosclerosis and heart attacks. Once he graduated and was working at Miller & Miller, he had received some Japanese journal articles by Akira Endo of Sankyo from his father's investment analysts. This was to be his Nobel opportunity.

Though only a junior chemist at the time, he went right to the research director to pitch a cholesterol drug. He got a fifteen-minute time slot and raced through forty-seven hand-drawn slides. The director was polite to the bright young chemist but sent him on his way.

In a pattern that was to be repeated, the blockbuster development went to Merck instead. This was the bitter pill Doctor Brian swallowed with his faux grapefruit every morning.

The driver arrived early, while he was still enjoying his croissant and espresso. The driver suggested a take-away cup. Brian never drank from paper cups, so he ordered something for the driver instead. With a first-class ticket, no checked luggage, and his trusty electronic guide, he had plenty of time.

Every 10-15 minutes, the driver duly reminded him that Dulles Airport was over 25 miles and Friday traffic was unpredictable. With each reminder, Brian mentally reduced his tip and cursed the world's purveyors of superfluous warnings. Coffee is hot. Bacon causes cancer. Traffic is slow.

After feeding the remainder of his croissant to the pigeons, they went out to the car waiting in the circular driveway. Traffic to the airport was smooth. Doctor Brian congratulated himself for waiting long enough for the morning congestion to abate.

They arrived at Dulles an hour before his flight and he gave the driver a good tip anyway, just to say, "I told you so. We had plenty of time."

He ambled through the airport, taking the first-class line through security, and stopping for a Financial Journal at the newsstand, and a Massachusetts Journal of Medicine from the bookstore. His gate was in sight and he had fifteen minutes left.

Incompetently, they closed the gate fifteen minutes early and he missed his flight.

———

Annoyed but undaunted, he rented a car and headed for Charlottesville. It was Friday, and he wouldn't be able to see anyone at CDC until Monday anyway. The late summer weather was fine and he looked forward to a pleasant drive through the Shenandoah Valley and the Blue Ridge Mountains. He called back to the concierge in Dupont Circle to rearrange his hotels.

He took his time, admiring the wildflowers, yellow yarrow, classic oxeye daisies, and stunning purple-flower raspberries. At a couple of stops, there were even some early berries. Unfortunately, the small red berries were still sour—refreshing, but so sour his tongue seemed to curl.

His recent encounter with his no-longer-dead daughter stirred up old memories. In a peace offering or surrender, his parents had treated the newlyweds to a honeymoon through the beautiful

Appalachian Mountains. They had missed the wedding, a small event at the Purchase city hall with just a couple of friends for witnesses and, of course, baby Penny.

The honeymoon was a welcome vacation and the three of them enjoyed it. He remembered powdering Penny's baby cheeks with daisy pollen and her laughing. He had promised himself to make everyone proud with visions of Nobel prizes and articles in the New York Times.

The three of them often stopped to play in the flowers. Darlene laughed when Penny made a funny face after tasting a sour berry. Brian took another sour berry in memory of those happier times, unsuccessfully trying to forget his parents' subtle message that if he had married someone more appropriate and hadn't had a baby, the honeymoon would have been longer and in Europe.

By the time he checked into his antebellum B&B in Charlottesville, he was missing Darlene. Missing her for the first time in a long time. The flowered bedspread and chintz curtains reminded him of her.

It was five hours earlier in the Marquesas Islands. He called Penelope.

"*Fatu Hiva Clinique…*"

His heart rate jumped. He held his breath. He could feel tears coming. He almost hung up. "Can I speak to— This is Penny's— Penelope's— Doctor? Can I speak to the doctor?"

"*Le médecin est*— The doctor is with a patient."

He took a deep breath and collected his thoughts. "This is her father…*son père.*"

"*Une minute.*" The phone noise quieted as if it had been set down. He just waited, and waited. He wasn't used to waiting on the phone. He was looking at the red button when someone said, "It is not possible now. Call back in an hour. *Déjeuner* is in an hour." The phone went dead.

He wanted to go to dinner, but he had to wait.

He took out the Financial Journal. He wasn't interested in finances. He didn't even look at the quotes for his big holdings. He did notice a small article on health investments observing that medical equipment companies seemed to be experiencing an unexplained spurt in demand—especially DNA sequencer manufacturers. There was an anonymous quote from a salesman in India that sounded suspiciously like Jake.

That killed twenty minutes. He switched over to the MJM he'd also purchased at the airport. He noticed a survey of zoonotic diseases. There were several strange things about this paper. First, the time between submission and publishing was surprisingly short, as if the paper had not been refereed. Also, the paper was a joint effort of the CDC and WHO.

As he read the paper about various reservoirs of zoonotic diseases, he couldn't help thinking of Jake's rumors. Was CDC preparing medical researchers in advance of a large announcement? Was this like educating and funding scientists to study atomic energy in advance of the Manhattan Project?

Like his earlier experience with the cholesterol drug, Doctor Brian could feel the excitement that something big was going to happen. Maybe he wasn't too late for his Nobel prize. His meeting at CDC on Monday was going to be important.

In good spirits, he noticed that his hour in purgatory was up. He called Penelope again.

"*Fatu Hiva Clinique…*"

"This is Doctor Penelope's father. Can I speak to her?"

"*Une minute.*"

"Brian?"

"Yes, hello! I'm calling from the United States."

After a few minutes of pleasantries, he asked, "There is a zoonotic disease, something new, popping up around the globe. This sales guy I met on the cruise told me about it—and it could have been what happened aboard our ship."

"Yes, I've heard."

"Well, I'm going to leave my retirement. Did I tell you I retired about ten years ago?"

She didn't say anything and he was eager to continue.

"I'm going to help find a cure. Do you want to join me?"

"Brian, it's been twenty years. The other day you didn't seem even happy to see me."

Now it was his turn to be silent.

"I have to get back to work. Sick people. When you get settled somewhere let me know. We can talk some more."

He wanted to say, "I love you," but couldn't.

"Wait. Wait. Don't hang up."

There was no dial tone so he continued.

"Today I was in the Shenandoah Mountains." He told her about wildflowers and tart raspberries. "We had good times."

She said, "Of course I don't remember from when I was a baby."

"Well your mother will remember. Is your mother still alive?"

She laughed, "She was on the same cruise as you were. I guess you didn't recognize her."

He was speechless.

"She recognized you."

His brain went crazy. Thoughts of the honeymoon, his parents, Penny growing up, the drinking, the accident, Penny with metal rods in her arm, Nobel prizes— He couldn't keep track and he couldn't keep up.

He might have heard her say, "Are you still there?" and, "Well call when you get settled," or, "Goodbye."

When he realized the call timer had stopped, it was too late for dinner and he went to sleep in his clothes. He'd have to buy some pajamas tomorrow.

24. LILY

KATHERINE, AUSTRALIA

Lily went directly to her room without speaking to Pana or Olivia. She put her backpack on her bed, then took the two big shopping bags and separated out a small portion of each herb and bark and seed she had bought for Pearl and Kalinda, bagged and labeled them for herself, and put them in the closet on the shelf with her other herbs. It was getting pretty full.

It was hard to be in the house without speaking to her aunt and cousin, but she kept thinking about Olivia's face the night before she'd gone to Darwin. It was as if she had a disease Olivia feared Pana would catch.

Lily could not stay here any longer.

She changed her clothes, and with fresh resolve, picked up the two bags of herbs.

She'd go to the compound and deliver Kalinda's things, and see about getting herself a space there. The rules were she had a whole year to get something built, and by then she would know if that's where she wanted to stay or not. She could start with a simple tarp and lean-to.

She did not deliver Kalinda's herbs. When she got to the compound, Kalinda's hut was empty. Should she leave the bag inside the hut? Would the herbs stay dry and safe?

The old woman in the hut next to Kalinda's came out, pushing her blanket door aside. The woman spoke to Lily in a language she did not understand.

"Do you speak Alawa?"

The woman shook her head. She pointed at Kalinda's house.

"Is she gone?" Lily tried English. Most aboriginals understood it, even if they did not speak it well.

The woman nodded. "Hospital," she said, enunciating clearly.

"Oh, is June still there?" That was startling, she had looked much better the night before Darwin, and Lily assumed she had gone home days ago.

"No June. Kalinda!"

"Kalinda's sick?"

The old woman nodded.

"Okay, thank you."

The lady ducked back behind the blanket. Lantern light leaked out. It looked pretty cozy under the corrugated steel roof and curved walls, but the huts didn't have windows. They were basically just water tanks cut in half. The arc wasn't quite tall enough to stand up under, but you could sit or sleep out of the weather.

Lily wasn't sure that was what she wanted. She could paint outside when it wasn't too hot or raining or windy. But she might be asking too much of her own new little home to expect she could paint indoors. Maybe she'd go more traditional, build a roundhouse out of sticks and thatch. She stood a moment, considering.

Kalinda. Herbs. Well, she would just have to take them to Pearl's, and they'd probably go see Kalinda, and they'd figure out what to do. For now, she set the bag just inside Kalinda's hut.

She walked across the open space that had Kalinda's and the old woman's houses on it. Across from them was an ancient caravan without wheels. It had been there so long it had sunk into the dirt. Next to that was a lean-to with one rock and mud wall and a tarp spread down from it at an angle to the ground.

In between those two and Kalinda's, but set back from the open space, was a tiny *balanda*-style house. "Compound supervisor," a small sign said on the door.

She knocked on that door. Compound supervisor was a fancy name for the first family that had started living there. It was government land set aside for aboriginal peoples who had been displaced by construction, or disasters, or other problems. Problems like Lily's—people who had no tribal group because the government had stolen her grandparents' and great-grandparents' generations away to be taught *balanda* ways. Orphans. Stolen generations.

The door opened.

"You can come in, this is the office," a short round man said. He smiled at her, glanced at her bag and pointed to a chair. The office was a small room with lots of windows. It looked like Olivia's porch. It connected to the little house with the inside door he'd presumably come out of. He sat down behind an old gray metal desk.

"You want a space?" His eyes were bright, his smile almost bigger than his dark face. "Auntie Pearl said you might come."

"Yes," Lily said. "Do I understand right, that the toilet and showers come with my rent?"

He nodded and waved out one window. "Showers and toilets are over that way. You need to fill out these papers, with your explanation of why you need to be here. Most of the sites are $A30 a month. Some big ones in the back are 40. You must cook over a wood fire outside your hut, or you can use the *balanda* barbies out back there, there's charcoal," he pointed out another window to a picnic area with tables and steel barbecues. "Not allowed to cook inside your hut. There is one fire pit with a roof over there," he waved to a spot Lily couldn't see beyond a row of paperbark trees. "No cars or pets allowed. No motorcycles. No loud music from i-pod machines. Drums and rhythm sticks and singing okay."

"Good," Lily said, taking the application papers. "Can I use a tarp to make a lean-to until I can afford solid walls?"

"You can use the tarp. You can use thatch. You can use rocks or old bricks or rib steel. Nobody cares. Most just want a steel hut, like Kalinda or Rosie's."

Rosie must be the old lady next to Kalinda. Lily nodded. "How soon can I move in?"

"Fill out papers. Give 30 dollars. Then."

"Good. So I could move in tonight if I want?"

"Alla time sure," he said, nodding and smiling.

"Is there a place I can lock things up?"

He stopped smiling. "Not in native compound. Nobody take

anything."

Lily nodded. She'd have to rent a locker or something for her paintings. They couldn't sit out in the damp and dust. And despite what the man said, she knew what "nobody take anything" meant. There wasn't anything worth taking. She'd noticed that *his* doors locked. Anyhow, the various aboriginal peoples might be honest, but there were a lot of people in Katherine who weren't.

"So, how do I pay? Do they take Paypal?"

"They want you give me a check. Maybe later we can arrange something else."

"All I have is cash," she said. She was going to have to get a checking account. She'd been avoiding that, just using her savings account to deposit her art payments. It was interesting which pieces of *balanda* culture the "native" compounds chose to use. Checks? Maybe because it was a government holding—which meant, whitefella rules.

"Ya, cash is okay. I have receipts." He pulled open a drawer on his side of the desk and took out a pad of papers with carbon paper between. He started writing out the receipt, so Lily took her little tie-dye wallet out of her pocket and paid him.

"How many spaces are available?"

He smiled. "Many. Our space goes all the way back to Katherine Creek. Nobody even back there yet."

"Do I need to tell you which one I'm taking, or... "

His head was already shaking. He laughed. "Nope, nope. Just pick. If you don't like, pick one more, one more again. When you build, then that is your place."

She said, "Wonderful," in Alawa, and he laughed and nodded.

She filled out the papers. She passed them to him.

"Your name is?"

"Kutai. Kutai Djarrwark. Wife name Minka."

She stood and reached out to shake his hand in the *balanda* manner. He laughed and extended his index finger for her to shake. "Lily Waters," she said.

"I know," he said, laughing. "I know."

Lily set Pearl's herb bag down in the open central area near Kalinda's house and walked around. She realized the cleared area had a fire pit in the middle. A couple fallen logs served as benches around the fire. There were three other huts set among the trees or near the fire pit circle.

Most of the people had chosen to be close together, away from the trees. She thought about that and looked back and forth from the trees to the open area. It seemed like a couple trees between her and the afternoon sun might be helpful. And she wasn't quite ready to be on the town center, where people might be expected to gather as "family."

Stones outlined the "spaces" allotted to each person. She found a spot within sight of Kalinda's place, but not so close they'd be forced to speak every day. She still wasn't sure about Kalinda's friendliness level. The space was at the very outside edge of the center open area, with a big casuarina tree behind her. Casuarina, called SheOak by aboriginals, by her people. It seemed appropriate. There were lots of the long needles on the ground in her space. It smelled fresh.

She looked back toward Katherine Creek. There was a wood and thatch hut halfway between her and the water, all by itself. She saw through the trees toward the showers a bright blue tent. Maybe she could look at the tents at the big new Home Timber and Hardware DIY store in east Katherine.

She put the small silk scarf her mother had given her on the ground, sat on it, and looked around in all directions. She closed her eyes, breathed in the scent of gum trees, and paperbark and casuarinas.

Yes, this would do. She used some of the border rocks to hold down her scarf, marking her spot. She liked the way that sounded. Her spot. Her place. Her home. This might work better than she'd thought.

———

Pearl literally rolled on the floor laughing when she saw Lily's hair. "What happened? What is this?" She sat up again, and set down the dilly bag she had been knotting. She stared at Lily's hair as she got to her feet. She felt Lily's hair, running her fingers along the gel-stiff strands. "So strange," she said.

"Well. It was the best I could think of, given that my mother took me to the fancy hair place and insisted they do whatever I wanted as long as it was different from when I walked in. She wanted me to look—more stylish."

"Is that what that is? Stylish?"

"Kind of," Lily said. It had seemed fun in Darwin. In Pearl's little house, it just felt wrong.

Pearl pointed to the shopping bag. "Is that my Hoop Pine bark? And the liniment-tree leaves?"

"Yes. And Laurel nuts, redbush seeds, southern tea tree leaves, and… " Lily cocked her head, suddenly blank. What was that other thing? She started taking things out of the bags, sorting them into the ones she knew and the ones she didn't.

"Cooper's holly stems," Pearl finished.

"Yes."

"And Joe-Joe gave you the bark powders I asked for?"

"Yes, the thing you wrote down in Macassan. They're here," Lily patted the packed plastic bags.

"Good, good. Three kinds of trees bark powder, special from all the way in Malay."

"I left Kalinda's at her hut, but I hear she is now in the hospital, like June."

"She is in the hospital. Not like June. Much more sick." Pearl shook her head, looking sad. "They will not let me go in. The walls are all plastic inside, and the nurses wear… " she covered her mouth with her hand.

"Masks."

Pearl nodded.

"So we can't try to bring her healing."

"No. Not yet. Nice nurse says maybe tomorrow. Angry nurse says not ever."

"Well, that is too bad."

"Maybe Kalinda will die, with no help," Pearl said.

"I can't imagine what is wrong, that she became so sick, so fast."

"Mm," Pearl said. "Thinking it maybe was from the hospital, but they say they have nobody else so ill, so—." She shrugged.

Lily remembered Ariq's patients who died had become suddenly very sick. In his hospital. Maybe Pearl was right.

Pearl started re-packing some of the leafy herbs. "They can go moldy in the plastic," she said. "See if there are any more of the muslin bags in my cupboard, please."

Lily got the stepstool Pearl always needed to use, and put it down in front of the "linen" cupboard, Olivia would have called it. She looked on the bottom shelf, but there were no bags. Could Pearl have managed to get them onto the next shelf up? She was shorter than Lily, and Lily could not see over the edge. She reached up and felt around, found cloth, pulled it out.

"Ah, good," Pearl said. Lily helped her transfer the leaves from the plastic into the clean muslin bags. "So you going to build your own house your own self? Or you want help?"

"I just– " she met Pearl's eyes in disbelief. "I just *got* my place an hour ago, how did you… "

Pearl laughed. "I smell it on you," she said.

Smelled it? It was like the old woman had some kind of telepathy. Like all the aboriginal peoples had it.

But not Lily. It abruptly made her feel very lonely.

Pearl looked at her, smiling gently.

"Lily. Do you know what happened at Minyeri school? Do you know why the Ngukurr people ask you to leave?"

Shaking her head, Lily fought back tears. "Not really. Someone said something about my mother. Someone else complained about my bat dreaming. Then they said I was too *balanda*. Then they told me to take myself and my whitefella ways away."

"Come have some tea." Pearl turned on the ancient gas stove and lit a match. The flames made a *flupping* sound as they turned from yellow to blue. Pearl set her whistling teapot on the burner, after swishing it around and listening to be sure there was enough water.

As she put a big pinch of herbs into two battered Australian Navy mugs, she said, "There was a woman there who used to know your mother, to be friends with her. A friend also of Minnakenna Mambali's."

"In Ngukurr?"

"Not in the village, at the Minyeri school."

"Mm."

"So she had a little too much home brew one night, and told her friends that a man your mother knew said and did things to her that were not right. To her—not to your mother. And when she complained, the man said, 'Your friend said it would be fine with you.'"

"Mama would not say that," Lily said, then stopped. Why was she defending her? She knew what her mother did for a living. But, Adjana would not have set one of her friends up like that. "She is very careful to let her men friends know they are not to touch me. Only her. She has strong rules."

Pearl nodded. The teakettle whistled and she went to tend the tea. "That is what I would think from what I have seen of her and know of you. But Minnakenna said this woman would not lie about this, Lily. So maybe this man was a bad man, I don't know."

"The villagers did not even talk to me, or ask me anything. And Minnakenna was my teacher too, like Jandry was. I thought they knew me. They just… "

"Minnakenna told you to leave, like your aunt just did."

"Yes. Not even Kinney Renburr tried to help, and I had thought she was my friend. Now my aunt is upset, and for no thing I have done."

"So maybe soon time you need to decide which life you want."

After a long silence, "I am here," Lily said.

Pearl handed her a steaming mug of tea.

"Yes, you are," the old woman said, smiling.

"I may not have people's respect, but at least I will live and look like I want, not like– " some pleasure-lady, she had been going to say. Is that what she thought of mama? Tears sprang to her eyes, and she hung her head down so Pearl would not see.

The villagers had pushed on her in other ways, too. They did not like her using the internet. They did not like her painting her bat dreamings.

No one seemed to like Lily for just being Lily.

———

"You slept in the dirt!" Olivia said, hands spread in horror at Lily's appearance.

"It was my dirt," Lily said, looking away.

"You have a place here, you can stay until you have someplace."

"I do have some place. And I'm not going to stay where I am not welcome. "

Olivia looked really angry, now. She waved a hand, indicating Lily's dirty clothes, dirty hands and face. "You going to wear dirt all the time? That is somehow better?"

"I can wash the dirt. The dirt does not look at me with unfriendly eyes. I just came here to get my things," Lily said. "Oh, don't worry. There's a shower at the compound, I'll be clean and fresh, no one will complain to you about me." Why should you care anyway, Lily wanted to shout. You already think I am soiled, tainted, fallen.

Olivia's lips were tight. She put her hands on her hips, ready to speak again, but Lily walked away. She put a hand on Pana's shoulder as she passed, but dropped it quickly.

Pana just stood there the whole time, tears running down her cheeks.

Lily stuffed all her herbs into dilly bags. She had forgotten she'd hung most of her paintings in the Café. The only two that were left were ones she probably wasn't going to sell anyhow. Maybe she should just leave them here for Olivia to throw out? She stared at them, then finally shut the closet door. She already had plenty to carry, she'd come back for them, later.

Her backpack full of her clothes, her arms full of herbs, Lily made her way down the stairs. She listened and could hear Pana crying in the kitchen and Olivia talking to her. She went out the front door, closing it quietly behind her.

She was going to have to get a tarp, and some plastic tubs to keep the herbs in. Maybe it was time to ask Obrey for some help.

She paused, setting one of the sacks down on the dusty street. She reached around and pulled her new cell phone from its special pocket in her backpack. Thinking of Kalinda, she also wanted to ask Ariq about what his patients had experienced, whether being in hospital was part of the problem.

Glad she had taken some of the $A2000 and put it into prepaid international calling, she pressed the speed-dial button, and smiled as the phone rang on the other end. She picked up her backpack and walked toward the Casuarina Café.

"Ariq? It is Lily. This is my new phone. Did the package arrive?"

25. HALID

NACALA, MOZAMBIQUE

Halid saw a Mozambique Republic Police officer at the gate by the refugee compound. The MRP man did not seem to be doing anything, just standing there. He approached the man.

"Do you speak Yao?" he asked in that language.

The man shook his head, but held up his hand, palm out. "Wait," he said in Portuguese.

"Oh, I speak a little Portuguese," Halid said. He'd probably mangled the pronunciation, but the man seemed to understand.

"We have a Yao speaker at the other gate," he said, "If we need."

"My people need a place to camp tonight before we move on to Maputo," Halid told the man. "And maybe a few people who will need to stay here awhile because they...are hurt."

The MRP nodded and gestured inside the fence to a mostly empty area that held a few tattered cloth covered lean-tos and tin and cardboard shacks.

"Are there any rules? Anyone can go in or out?"

"This was set aside for refugees from the floods," the man said. "Now, anyone can use it."

"I don't understand why you are guarding an empty encampment," Halid said, stating his confusion aloud.

"Ah. Because the Nacala office of Mozambique Republic Police pays us to stand here," the guard said, a slight smile on his face. "People ride the train, sleep here, move on," he added. "We make sure it is safe."

"So we can just go in?"

"Yes, of course. Government asks no open liquor bottles in the compound. You can use the steel grills or the fire pits. Put your trash in the bins by the other entrance," he waved over his shoulder.

"Thank you," Halid said. The comment about no open liquor bottles did not sound very promising, but that needn't worry Luambe villagers, who did not drink. And, they would not need to stay here long. Most of them. Halid had already heard several people say they would not be going on to Maputo, despite having no place back in Luambe. Yet.

He walked back to the shady patch where most of the villagers sat and talked or slept.

"The camp is just ahead. We can go in, set up camp anywhere we like." He helped his mother to her feet and picked up their various bundles and bags. "There are guards keeping an eye on things."

Anane nodded. Halid realized his mother hadn't actually spoken since the night before. He shifted a bag to his other hand and put his free arm over her shoulder. "Surane will get them out," he said. It was not only his father stuck there, but two of his sisters and their husbands. "Surane has always been strong," he said.

She nodded again. "Her husband is good, too."

"If he hasn't joined Imrane."

This seemed to shock his mother. "Yannic would not do that!"

"I didn't think *anyone* would do that," Halid shrugged. "But it had to be more than just Imrane, Guta and Lendee. It's not anyone with us, except maybe Sami's wife–so who helped him?"

Anane's mouth opened, as if she would say something, but then her mouth closed. He could hear her teeth click together.

He cleared his throat. "Sami. Maybe Botte, but he's not much use." He nodded at the gate guard as he and the villagers walked into the refugee compound. "Maybe Wayya's husband can ask for shelter in his old village."

"Asraf does not have much courage," Anane said. Then, "I would like to stay in this spot," she said.

She sat down in the dirt beneath a dried up-looking blackwood tree–the only tree in the compound, though there was shade from a couple lean-to like shelters built of rough-cut boards along the fence. Posts, some fastened to the fence, a roof with no sides—

there was shade, which is where the rest of the villagers began unpacking, spreading out between the shade shelters and the tree.

"I wonder where we get firewood around here?" Mezi said, eyeing the blackwood tree.

"I will ask the guard," Halid offered, and both Mezi and his mother nodded.

Most of the villagers had not eaten since the bread they'd shared at Cuambe station early that morning. Halid wasted no time talking to the guard, who pointed him to sacks of what turned out to be charcoal along the fence. He picked up a sack in each arm and walked back to the Luambe village camp. So far, they seemed the only occupants of the refugee compound.

———

Halid was enjoying the strange smell of the ocean that floated into the camp along with the fog in the dusky light. Fog they were accustomed to, even fog with sunset light in it, but many of the villagers complained about the dead fish scents. Fresh-caught fish, cooked properly, had none of this odor about it.

Halid couldn't help but imagine old dead fish swimming through the fog. He thought he had actually seen one, then realized it was people, moving toward them through the thick ruddy light.

He got up from their fire, headed toward the people even as they moved closer to him.

"Salim!" he called. "Father!"

He heard villagers behind him, joining him, running toward their headman's group. Surane and Yannic, Wayya and Asraf, and a half-dozen or so young women. Salim was limping badly, but he had a weary smile on his face as his people clustered around him. Even grouchy Botte was there, though he walked separately from the rest of the group, only Sami beside him. Sami would not look up. His hands were empty. There were bruises and cuts on his face and arms. He would not meet any of the villagers' eyes. Was he here to kidnap little children again? Or had he gotten enough of Imrane?

Halid saw Kofi move toward his son, anger on his face. That was going to be *their* problem—though he saw Rana looking at them, too. If things got violent, Rana was going to have to break it up, since Salim was not doing well.

Halid offered his shoulder, which Salim took, resting his arm heavily across Halid's back. Anane put her hand on her husband's cheek, but did not actually kiss him in public, of course. But it was as if she had, since many of the villagers chuckled or jeered in their teasing way.

Halid glanced at Surane, who was helping Wayya hop along. Wayya's husband Asraf was on his wife's other side, also helping. A messy bandage covered Wayya's foot. Halid wondered where Nga was. They had work to do. His father groaned as they moved into the Luambe camp.

A lot of work.

He never did get Nga's help that night. She did not show up until morning. But she came with a lot of medical supplies she'd gotten from her TC friend here in Nacala. That was good, because Halid was out of sterile thread for stitching wounds, and he had no bandages at all.

She was surprised to see Salim and his group in the compound, but she did not apologize for being absent. "I spent the night at Shelly's," she said. "She has invited you to come see her clinic with me, today, Halid. And maybe we will bring some of these people for extra care."

She set to work alongside him, using boiled rags to clean various wounds, using fresh clean gauze to cover and protect. Salim's wounds were several days old now, it had seemed best to him to let them heal without stitches. Nga looked at the worst cut and frowned.

"This is so deep," she said, shaking her head. "Do you have any supplies to make Imra—uhm, a traditional poultice?"

Halid pulled the sack of herbs from his backpack and opened it. He pulled out Nimtree bark and dried leaves, and another leaf Imrane had told him was strong against infection. He stared at the leaves. Would Imrane have told him the truth? Halid glanced at Nga. She looked at him and what he held and nodded.

"He would not betray his medicine, I believe," she said.

Meanwhile she tore open an antibiotic packet and sprinkled some directly on the wound on Salim's upper thigh and buttock. She poured the rest into a cup of cooled boiled water and asked Salim to drink it all. He made a face like he'd swallowed sour root.

Halid used his fingers to break up the leaves, then added a few drops of olive oil. He mashed the poultice into a paste in his palm, then spread it on a piece of gauze. Nga helped him place the gauze over the wound. Together they wound gauze around Salim's body, holding the poultice to his hip.

Anane had moved closer with her blanket, screening the extent of her husband's wounds from the other villagers. Most of whom, Halid discovered when he glanced around, also gathered around injured people, cleaning wounds, offering food and peaceful conversation to those who had escaped Imrane's insanity.

There was a great deal of talk about going back, about retaking Luambe village. They needed to free the last few girls Imrane had captured as his "wives." They needed to take control of their home and make it theirs again. Rana was chief among those arguing for going back, of course. Not many were saying they should continue their flight from the plague, which at least at this moment was far less a threat to the village than Imrane was.

It turned out only fifteen of the villagers led by Rana were committed to going back to Luambe village soon. There were probably another dozen or so who wanted time in Nacala first, to recover and prepare before returning, which seemed to Halid a very good idea.

There were some undecided, as he expected, but still there were almost forty villagers who wanted to continue with the original plan: go to Maputo.

Still standing at the edge of the group, not part of it, Botte and Sami indicated they wanted to go to Maputo. Halid walked over to face Sami.

"Should we welcome hyenas into our camp?" he said.

Sami said nothing.

Botte spoke up in his rusty voice. "Imrane is insane. I am sorry for what harm I caused, but I will not stay with that man any longer."

"I think you are not too welcome to stay here," Halid said pointedly.

Sami nodded. Botte said, "That is why Maputo."

Halid grunted. "I will be watching you," he said.

Both men nodded, wordless.

Nga's voice rose, addressing the whole camp. "We have a space on the Mozambique Fisheries boat, though I have not spoken to the Captain yet, so I am not certain how many people we can fit," Nga said. "They can take us as far as Beira. We think in Beira we might get a ride from the Greenleaf people, since sometimes they move refugees of disaster to safe places, and my mother– " she gulped, then cleared her throat. "My mother spoke to them. Or I can try to find another train, if there is one from Beira to Maputo."

Salim nodded. "I am glad you will continue. This thing with Imrane should not make us forget why you were moving to Maputo in the first place."

Surane spoke for the first time. "The truck we rode on had other people running ahead of this thing," she said. "They said Malawi already has several dozens dead. It is still spreading. And they still do not know what it is."

Nga nodded.

Halid gingerly took a hot rag from the boiling water to clean his bloody hands.

"You might stay here, with him," he said softly to his mother.

"I am," she said. She met Halid's eyes. "I must."

He was on his own. He nodded. She'd just declared him a man. Finally. It was good to know his father would have her loving, strong support. He smiled at her.

He stood up and looked around the camp again. "The boat leaves tomorrow afternoon, with the tide," he called out, feeling proud he knew about tides and boats. "Let us all rest well tonight."

"Tomorrow I will speak with the Captain about supplies," Nga said, "and I would appreciate some of the younger men coming to help."

Of course, Rana and Hadade and Halid all nodded. Bodie sat quietly with his sister; he did not volunteer to join them, which surprised Halid.

"We will visit the Clinic again for more medical supplies and I will let Shelly know you have wounded here; she should be able to come by and change bandages, check on you."

"And," Nga added, "I need to sell some things, so we have some money."

Again, Rana and Hadade and Halid all nodded.

Despite all the loss and pain, Halid began to feel excited about their journey. He was already learning so much. Maputo was going to be great.

26. NGA

NACALA, MOZAMBIQUE

The Mozambique Fisheries boat looked bigger than Nga had realized, once she was walking up the ramp. "*Sun Fish—Nacala*" it said on the nose end of the boat. Boat or ship? Nga wondered as she climbed. Someone on the boat walked over to greet her as she stepped out onto the deck. "I am Nga Lind, with the Luambe villagers," she said in her best Portuguese, hoping they were expecting her. Shelly had been certain their ride was still going to happen, but she wasn't the captain—things might have changed.

"Captain Tola is in his cabin, if you would follow me, please."

Shelly Tola had been in Nga's TC class in Maputo. The last year, they had been roommates, since both of their prior roommates had dropped out of the program. Shelly had been very proud of what her father did on his boat. He was part of the very small group of people who worried about Mozambique's resources. The huge tourist industry—well, huge for Mozambique—ran sports fishing adventures all up and down the coast. Captain Tola kept track of licenses, monitored poaching, set license limits based on fish counts, and of course, counted fish.

The Captain's cabin was a small room with a built-in bed and desk. He sat on an old wooden chair, working on a computer, his back to the door.

"Captain, here is Miss Lind," her guide said.

"Ah!"

The captain turned out to be very tall when he stood up, towering over her. He had the look more of Zulu or Masai than he did anything else. Nga felt short. She could see where Shelly got her strong face bones and majestic height.

"Captain," she said, reaching out her hand.

They shook, his other hand covering their gripped ones.

"So you want to go all the way to Maputo?"

168

"Yes, we have about forty villagers—is that too many?" she bluntly asked as his eyebrows raised.

"Wow. I was expecting maybe twenty. Well. I think we can fit you aboard, if some do not mind sleeping in the hold and maybe on deck. But I will not be able to get you all the way to Maputo. I have limited fuel, so it will be to Beira only."

Nga nodded. "I cannot tell you how much I appreciate your help. Will there be anything we can do to help you in return?"

He laughed, his voice deep, his laugh hearty. "Count fish! And maybe some other things."

"I might be able to offer you a small amount of money, if that is also any help."

He waved his hands no. "My Shelly always spoke of how much help you were to her finishing the TC classes. If not for you, she might have failed, as so many did."

The *técnico* program had been so different from village learning, many of the students had had problems. "Shelly was so good at the hands-on portions of the training, I knew she would be a good TC."

Captain Tola laughed. "She is. They built her a whole little hospital here," he said.

"Oh, I visited there last night. It's wonderful."

His expression darkened somewhat. "They have much sickness there now, villagers and citizens from Nacaroa and Minguri, even Monapo have come here."

"We had them from Malawi and Zambia, at the village."

He shook his head once. "I hope we can weather this." He stepped outside his door and waved a hand up the narrow hallway. Nga went the way he'd indicated as he spoke. "So, we can cook meals all together, or I can give you a time for your people. My crew is only nine people," he said.

"I am sure we can include them when we cook," Nga said.

He nodded. "That would be helpful."

"And of course, we will clean the kitchen– " she looked at him. There was a special name for kitchens on boats, but she couldn't think of it.

"Galley."

"Yes, the galley, and anything else it would be helpful to have cleaned. Uh, also, does your computer get internet? I am going to need to find a way into Maputo from Beira."

"We have it here. Once we are under way, it is very unreliable, but we will put in at night in a couple spots where there is WiFi we can pick up."

Nga was vaguely familiar with what WiFi was from her time in Maputo. It sounded like she'd have a chance to do some research.

"I know I can go as far as Beira," Captain Tola said. "I am already asking around to see if there is another boat, or maybe a bus or truck from there. Um." He shook his head. "Wasn't thinking about so many people, though."

"I'll look also, if I can borrow your computer. I have some suggestions from friends, and my mother— " *Mother!* She took a deep breath, "—spoke to the Greenleaf people."

He nodded. "Good." After a few more details of space and jobs, she left the boat. She went to the refugee compound to pick up her escort of Halid, Rana and Hadade, but was first drawn into the villagers' conversations and plans.

———

It turned out there weren't going to be so many people going on to Maputo. Salim and others had been talking about what they might do to get their village back. They were planning a counterattack.

"I am less worried about this sickness than I am about what Imrane is doing to our people," Salim said, and Rana nodded his agreement.

"We think he only has about four or five men helping him now, and every night more women and girls are finding ways to escape the village. We must help, as soon as we can," Rana added.

Surane leaned forward, hands on her knees. "We were lucky, we caught a ride on the road outside Lichinga. There was not going to be another train for a week. But it will get here, and by then we will be ready to go fight."

Nga nodded.

"We rode a big truck full of vegetables." Surane's husband laughed. "They loved my 'primitive' spear, so I traded it to them. Not needing a spear here, but now I need to make another for home." He waved an arm. "No trees."

"We are finding out where trees are," Surane said. "And even if he waits until we are back at the canoes, he can make one then."

"So, I am staying here, with anyone who wishes to stay to go retake Luambe in a few days," Salim said.

"All right."

"Your boat leaves this afternoon?"

Nga checked the bandage on Salim's hip. "Yes."

"I think you maybe only will be bringing fifteen-twenty people," he said.

"Okay. I know Halid wants to go."

"Yes," Salim said, grunting as she swabbed antiseptic over his stitches. She did not like the looks of the long, deep cut on his hip and buttock. It was very red and swollen.

"Salim, you should go with us to the clinic here. They have proper gear to clean this."

"You are doing fine," he said.

Yes, but you aren't, she wanted to say. But one did not speak that way to the village leader. She would talk to Anane later, Salim would probably listen to her.

Nga put away her gear and collected the young men to accompany her into town.

———

"Our clinic was tiny, so you are going to see something much more like a small hospital than our little room," Nga said to Halid.

Halid nodded, eyes bright. Rana and Hadade hung back, making jokes about a man on the street who was wearing ragged jeans and a button-down shirt. Their own robes, so colorful in the bright sun, seemed much more natural, though Nga saw a number of people glance askance at their spears, which they carried proudly, but without any overt threat.

Shelly was standing over an instrument tray in an empty treatment room, a brightly-printed orange cotton robe peeking out from under her white lab coat. Her hair was pulled back in tiny braids, highlighting the strong bones of her face. She glanced up, saw Nga's group and was so excited she dropped an instrument back onto the tray and ran to enfold her friend in a huge hug.

"Hello, again!"

Nga introduced Halid, and the others. Shelly showed them around "her" clinic. Nga knew how she felt. Her own little clinic was left behind, probably gone now, and that was part of what had set her adrift. She didn't feel she belonged anywhere.

"You're definitely going all the way to Maputo?" Shelly asked.

Nga nodded. "I feel that it's the safest place. The number of people reportedly dying in Zambia and now Malawi is frightening. And Halid wants to take the TC program."

Shelly nodded.

"Some of the villagers are going back to Luambe, though, since we had that trouble I told you about."

Shelly nodded again. "Have you talked to anyone in his old Makonde village?"

Nga shook her head. "Well, maybe Salim did when Imrane first came."

"I see many Makonde here, and they have much respect for themselves and for the Yao people as well. It's a shame he used this sickness as a way to attack the village. I don't understand what could have provoked him. It is not typical."

"We are confused, as well. It may simply have been that Mezi divorced him—and he was getting revenge?"

Nga saw Rana nodding, beside her. "Just so," he said.

"But also, Shelly, he has what I believe is Grave's disease. And he has been eating velvet beans, to 'cure' it."

Shelly frowned. "Those are loaded with L-dopa. And, isn't that the bean that caused that problem in that Memba village a few years back?"

Nga sighed. "Well. We may just be making excuses for him being a crazy man."

"It certainly sounds like he went crazy. I'd bet on the velvet beans," Shelly said. "We know they can cause problems if not leached properly."

Nga met Halid and Rana's gazes. "*Tudo bem*, she said softly. "So, I was hoping you might get a chance to go by the refugee compound and have a look at some of the more serious wounds," she said, glancing at Rana again, then Hadade and Shelly. "They may be reluctant to try and come here." Did Rana understand how serious Salim's wounds were? Nga decided to say nothing further, yet.

"Of course," Shelly said. "And I'll check them for this flu thing or rabies, or whatever."

Nga grimaced. "I just cannot believe the World Health Organization—or someone, anyone—has not even figured out what it is," she said. "It's going to be bad, if they cannot find a cause and stop it. My God, the whole world could die."

Had she said that aloud? The young village men were still, eyes wide.

Shelly cleared her throat. "It has never gotten that bad, not even from the Black Plague. Most of Europe was hard hit, but many other places had no deaths at all."

Nga nodded, remembering their epidemiology and history lessons.

"I was thinking maybe you can join me here, once this is over," Shelly said.

By "this," she meant the sickness, Nga thought. Or was she talking about the village disaster?

"Has there been any announcement of symptoms, or treatment?" Halid asked.

Shelly shook her head. "No one tells Mozambique anything. But Daddy is listening on the internet, and I've been monitoring the TV, in the waiting room."

"You have a television? I didn't even notice it last night."

Shelly laughed, excited. "Yes! Come see!"

———

Halid chattered excitedly about the wonders of Shelly's clinic. "Of course, she is in a real city, not out in the bush," Halid granted. "Our clinic was just the right size for our village. Though it may be gone, now–"

Nga had to interrupt him. "There is a kind of shop where I can turn my mother's jewelry into cash, called a pawn shop."

Mother.

She bit her lip. "It's not in a very good neighborhood of town, and I may be carrying a lot of money back, so we will go there, make the trade, and then buy the supplies we need for both groups, those who go back to Luambe, those who go on to Maputo."

Rana nodded. Hadade grinned. "Maybe we can find a spear for Surane's husband." He and Rana both laughed.

They followed the directions Shelly had given her and found the shop. Nga realized she had seen similar places in Maputo, without realizing what they were.

She showed the man behind the counter what she had. She could see he thought the bracelet was very nice. He examined the row of diamonds, the clasp, the white gold mountings.

"MT50,000," he said.

"You mean MT100,000 new meticais," she countered, remembering what Shelly had said about bargaining.

He made a face. "Maybe in Maputo," he said. "Not in Nacala."

She thought about that for a few moments. Maybe she should save the bracelet for Maputo.

She showed him one of the rings, the pendant, and a gold bracelet, keeping back the ring that had a pink stone in it.

"What about these, instead?"

He looked at the pendant, pushed it aside with a grimace. The ring he spent more time on.

"New MT200 for both," he said.

"What about 200 for the ring."

"This is worthless," he said, not meeting her eyes, waving a dismissive hand at the pendant.

"No it's not, but if you don't want it, I'll take MT200 for the ring alone." Two hundred would buy a lot of food.

He chewed his lip. "What about the bracelet?"

"I'll save it for Maputo," she said.

He called to someone in the back in a language Nga did not know.

A very large, very fat man emerged from a back room. He turned sideways and ducked his head to fit through the door. He smiled at Nga, which gave his face a very merry expression. Like Sinter Klaus, she thought.

The man at the counter handed Sinter Klaus the gold jewelry. The big man then reached out a hand for the bracelet Nga was holding. She passed him the chain of diamonds. His eyes lit up.

"New MT100,000," Nga said in a firm voice.

Sinter's face told his thoughts. He did not reject that price out of hand.

"For all three," he said, and met Nga's gaze with a serious edge on top of the merry. "Bracelet, ring, locket."

That seemed good to her. "All right," she said. She really *could* give Captain Tola a useful amount of money for fuel.

The trade complete, she packed most of the cash inside a cloth bag and stuffed it in the bottom of her backpack. They stepped outside. She felt nervous with that much money. She had never seen so much in her entire life.

"Is there enough to buy Salim new robes?" Halid asked. All three young men looked at Nga's face for an answer.

"Oh yes," she said. "Whatever we need." Thank you Mother, she thought, and tried to blink away the sudden tears.

They moved down the street, looking at stalls and shops. It seemed they could have bought pretty much everything on the street, if they'd wanted it.

Still feeling nervous, she glanced behind her with blurred eyes, just making sure no one from the shop had followed them. It was a huge pile of meticais. She tightened both straps on the backpack and glanced at Halid. He nodded and dropped back a step to literally watch her back.

The found a couple robes for Salim and one more for Halid's

mother as well. Many of the villagers had left with practically nothing, after Imrane's coup. Nga bought several extra robes, Eslin and Mezi in mind. She herself had never taken to robe-wearing, preferring canvas pants or shorts and a knit shirt, but she knew Mezi would appreciate something new just for her. She found a wonderful little dress for Teleza.

She took a few of the bills and gave them to Kadade.

"Get what you want, and whatever you can think of we will need on the boat or at the refugee camp–food, drinks, supplies. Maybe you and Rana can take turns." He nodded and walked away, leaving Rana and Halid to guard her.

She noticed one of the outdoor vendors selling medical supplies. It was mostly bandages and aspirin and some outdated ampicillin. Probably stolen, from Shelly's clinic. It happened a lot in the bigger towns, they'd been told at TC training.

They made their way to the farmer's market that was set up near the train station. They bought some jerked meat, lots of fresh vegetables and some milk for the children. Halid got a small bag of sesame seeds and some spice bags for his mother.

"So, do you think most of the villagers are staying in Nacala, then?" she asked Rana as Kadade rejoined them, a big sack hanging off his arm.

"I am going on to Maputo," Halid said clearly. They all nodded.

"For now it looks like maybe twenty, twenty-five will go to Maputo, forty will stay here," Kadade said, and Halid nodded, wobbling his hand back and forth—more or less.

She nodded. "I want to leave some of this money with you for food and things," she said. "Should I give it to Salim? You?"

Kadade said, "Give it to Rana," he said gesturing toward his friend. "He is going to help Salim, until– "

"Until Salim turns over leadership to him?" Nga asked. That would happen eventually, especially if Salim's wounds didn't heal well. Rana was sensible and capable. He would make a good headman.

"Yes," Kadade said, and all three boys nodded, confirming that plan.

Kadade took one of the bags of food from Nga, carrying it easily against his chest.

"Our plan is to camp by the railroad track near Lichinga again, while Rana and Kofi go up and scout around and see what Imrane is doing," Kadade said. Except the word he used was not Imrane, but a twist on the man's name which in Chiyao meant something like "devil."

"I think the sickness may already be here, in Nacala," she said. "I feel I must tell the villagers this, that we are not fleeing only the 'devil,' but also the plague."

Kadade and Halid both nodded. "But we cannot just give up the village," Rana said.

"Yes, of course," Nga said. "I understand." They walked past the gate guard at the refugee camp. The man eyed the young men's spears as they entered the refugee encampment, but did not say anything. They were Nga's guards, and she had been happy to have them.

She found Rana and handed him a number of new meticais wrapped in a scrap of cloth. "The supplies money," she said, and he nodded, accepting the packet, and the responsibility as they had agreed. "You can ask Anane what you should bring to Luambe. Medical supplies for one thing, since Imrane probably destroyed the clinic. And food."

"No one will be there that knows how to use medical stuff," Rana said, a touch of anger in his tone.

Did he disapprove of Halid leaving? It was true that those who went back to the village would have no medical help at all. But Nga needed to be firm. That was their choice. She and Halid were going to Maputo.

"Bandages, iodine, you all know how to use those. I'll remove Kofi's cast before we leave today. Shelly from the clinic here will come by and check on Salim and anyone else who needs more help while you are still here."

Rana nodded, face grim.

She smiled at Mezi as they arrived, letting her know things had gone well. Little Muzuli ran up and tugged at the bag she was carrying, a big smile on his face.

"Did you get chocolate?" he asked, pronouncing it oddly.

Nga's eyes met Mezi's with a puzzled expression.

Mezi shrugged. "Someone gave him a little piece. Now all he can think of is chocolate."

Nga smiled. "I have some nice things," she said. "But I did not get chocolate."

"Aww."

Kadade laughed and swatted at Mu like a big brother. "But I did!"

Everyone laughed when Mu swarmed up Kadade's body like a monkey climbing a tree.

27. ARIQ

ROSWELL & SLAUGHTER CANYON, NEW MEXICO

At first light, he headed out along an arroyo that meandered behind his house. Like all desert life, his pony celebrated the dawn showers. She galloped a little faster and leaped a bit higher, splashing in the new puddles. With sunrise, the temperature would rise, the puddles would dry, and nothing would remain except some withering flowers.

Along the arroyo blue and scarlet morning glories burst into bloom. Farther out tiny flowers colored the damp desert floor a pale violet. Ocotillos, small clumps of six or eight incongruously tall, thin green sticks, waved bright orange-red flowers, competing with the splendor of the rising sun.

The desert loved the rain.

White Ears paused and tried to eat some tasty looking plants, succulent after the brief precipitation. Each time this happened, he pulled up on the reins and spurred her forward. There was little that was healthy to browse. Years ago, before over grazing and droughts, this area had produced black grama and other grasses, but now only sage and cacti remained. None of it was good for ponies, and the morning glory was downright poisonous.

Ariq looked up and saw a small group of bats heading south. Stragglers, he thought. He wished them a quick flight home before it got too hot.

Those Mexican Free-tails reminded him that he'd been ignoring his research. Today would be different. He turned around and headed into the sunrise and on to work.

Galloping along the sandy arroyo, he leaned forward and dropped his right arm. He was an archer prepared to conquer the Asian steppes. His inner-warrior recalled his discussion with Dr. Charles Thompson, senior surgeon and clinic wise man. That kind doctor's pep talk was encouraging at the time. Today, with warrior blood coursing through his veins, it all seemed like rationalizations and cowardice.

Today he wouldn't accept excuses from anyone, especially not himself. Today was a day for courage.

————

His phone beeped. A tracking app confirmed the package from **Dreamtime** had arrived in Albuquerque. If it was delivered today, he would go in, otherwise he was going to work from home.

Working from home meant no staff meeting, but he could still connect to the telemedicine robot to check up on patients, especially Julia's dad now that he'd been returned from Chavez General.

The robot was like that old Star Wars trash can on wheels, built on the same platform as those obnoxious carry-on suitcases that could be seen in funny videos on social media running through the airports chased by tourists with gray hair and the latest travel fashions.

The morbidity numbers were holding steady at two deaths, but seven were on the critical list, including three in comas. The comas included Julia's dad. Fortunately, he was still hanging on.

On the positive side, it was not hemorrhagic fever. There was none of that awful bleeding that attracted news crews. Though Ariq didn't talk about it, all that blood was one of the reasons he didn't make it through med school. He just didn't like blood, especially a lot of blood and raw red flesh.

His IA patients, the ones not in a peaceful coma, were in pain. Their faces were tense. Some were sobbing. Others had their eyes tightly shut and their teeth grinding with an eerie click-click-click. One patient had broken some teeth.

The doctors ordered pain medication, but even morphine PCAs were of limited success. Some patients didn't trust the patient-controlled-analgesia button. He made a note to see about putting more patients in palliative comas which seemed better for all concerned.

He was grateful for the robotic rounds. He could close his eyes and mute the robot without upsetting the patients and staff. In this respite of silence, he doubted that he was descended from Genghis Khan. He didn't feel the strength and resilience of a warrior, even on this day of courage.

Much of the clinic surgery was elective. Scheduled procedures were down and more were canceled every day. Even without any legitimate news, the internet spread rumors. Today, he wasn't concerned about the business. Full surgery schedules and occupancy didn't matter, only sick patients, their comfort and their cure.

With the Area 51 Annex, they had adequate space to quarantine and isolate the critical patients. Ariq made another note, to speak to Joni about teeth protectors and ear plugs for these patients if protective comas were not a viable option. The ROC was known for excellent care–in fact, the staff tended toward OCD, tending to these little things.

Ariq finished his telerounds in electronic silence.

He noticed that Joni had her nurses fully deployed among the critical patients, but the doctors seemed less engaged. No surprise. He had brilliant surgeons, but they were not the types that spent their vacations assisting Doctors with Helicopters bringing medical care to primitive villages or natural disasters. Like the clinic, they were not prepared for sick patients.

———

He regretted his decision to drop out of medical school. Two dead, three in comas, and a total of seven in critical condition. He abandoned his pride. People could think what they might, he couldn't just sit and worry.

First he called Minneapolis, "How many other locations are seeing idiopathic ague?"

"Idiopathic ague?"

He explained the symptoms observed at the clinic.

"Oh, we're calling that pseudo-epilepsy. Most hospitals thought they were seeing epilepsy until EEGs and MRIs convinced them otherwise."

Ariq didn't want to discuss naming. "Whatever. How many

hospitals?"

"I can't release that information. HIPAA confidentiality. Maybe half the hospitals. Can't say how many patients."

Ariq hung up after that evasive answer. Next he called the CDC.

The discussion followed the same pattern. They called the disease 3S for Sudden Seizure Syndrome. Beyond that they were vague, except for one instruction, "Rush us the death certificates, coded with the cause of death as COD-3S."

Ariq understood the message between the lines. Send us everything, but don't expect to hear back from us.

For all this aggravation, he was now positive idiopathic ague—he liked his name the best—was wide-spread and no one knew any more than he did.

Next on his call list was wise man Dr. Charles Thompson.

"Any ideas?" he asked, moving his cell phone to avoid some static kicked up, probably from his adobe walls.

Chucky had the best news. "I've taken the suggestion from Arthur's daughter and read about the Milwaukee Protocol. In brief, there is some evidence that a low-temperature coma can give rabies victims the chance to survive on their own."

"Really?"

"Well, we don't know if Arthur has rabies. We also don't know if rabies patients are helped by the protocol or from some innate immunity. However, the protocol of coma and antivirals such as ribavirin seems to be safe. Besides, he's already in an induced coma for other reasons."

"Does that mean you want to try it?"

"Already did it. Since the patient is non-communicative, and his daughter recommended it, I took that as informed consent and have already begun."

Ariq proudly said, "Thank you. Let me know what happens."

What if this works? His inner-scientist formed a hypothesis: maybe IA is a rabies variant.

He made one more call and received more good news. The nursing staff had determined that IA patients were becoming dehydrated and IV saline improved their comfort and vitals.

Ariq pantomimed firing an arrow. Roswell Orthopedic Clinic would save the world. Perhaps Chucky was correct, and they were great zebra hunters.

———

Then Ariq received two messages. One expected and one a surprise. Both cheered him after his morning telerounds.

First, a beep on his phone informed him the package from **Dreamtime** had arrived. He had been concerned that it would be stopped at the border, confiscated. After his discussion with the CDC, he even worried that the CDC might turn him in for smuggling drugs. Fortunately, the package arrived safely, contents apparently undetected.

A helpful person in the shipping department sent him a picture and a text, **Dangerous? Open for inspection?**

The package didn't look like the normal stuff that came through receiving. The normal stuff had corporate packaging, shrink wrapped or well-labeled cardboard boxes or those plastic shipping bags, with printed labels and an assortment of stickers: Fragile, Medical Supplies, Rush, Urgent, Danger, etcetera.

This package looked like a shoe box, worse for wear from its travels. The box was wrapped in brown paper, maybe a recycled grocery bag, sealed with tape and string.

He magnified the photo. The label was addressed to Doctor Ariq in black marker pen. He studied the return address: Liliadja Dhuwa Waters.

Dreamtime had a name…and an address.

He looked up Darwin, Australia. It was on the north coast, latitude twelve degrees south, practically on the equator. Even though it was winter down there, he expected it was hot, very hot.

He sent a text reply, **No. Don't worry. A gift from a friend. Tea and cookies or something.**

The other surprise was from Jessenia and Sofia, his two promising high school science students. Their text was simply, **urgent.**

It was not even noon and his work-at-home day was already

canceled.

———

The girls met him in the clinic parking lot. Jessenia was wearing thick gloves. Each student had their own gloves. It seemed like they carried them in their backpacks. She held out a tiny Mexican free-tailed bat. The little ball of fur seemed lost in the big glove. It was about three inches from its porcine nose to the tip of its tail. Ariq knew from experience that it weighed about a half ounce. Her thumb gently held down a spread wing.

These students had a lot of experience handling bats, both in the CRC lab and in the wild.

Sofia, the senior student, reached over and poked the little guy with a gloved finger to show that he was a male. He squeaked. In addition to his tiny male organ, he also had a tiny white plus where he had been freeze branded and the hair grew back white. The plus meant he was a Slaughter Canyon bat. "We found him while hiking the arroyo. Rain there last night. Flowers. Lots of wildflowers."

Ariq backed away. He didn't have his gloves. He was confident the two girls knew what they were doing and didn't need his assistance or advice.

Jessenia added, "He shouldn't be here in the middle of the day. He was flapping in a circle. Squeaking. He tried to drink from a puddle shaded by some scarlet morning glory."

Sofia jumped in, "Sick. He's sick. No sick bats allowed in the lab."

Jessenia, always the level-headed one, asked, "What should we do?"

Ariq thought for a while and then he laughed, a laugh of relief. This was good news. He'd need a bit of courage to take advantage of this lucky event, and today was a day for courage.

"Jessenia's been trying to infect bats for her experiment. Now we have an infected bat. Nature is running the experiment for us."

The girls looked puzzled.

"We've been trying to infect a bat to see how long it took to develop immunity and then how long it took for that immunity to spread throughout the colony. Here is an infected bat!"

They got it, "Now we hope he develops immunity."

"We'll go to Slaughter Canyon tonight, return him to his colony."

They looked at Ariq like he was a bit crazy.

Ariq was excited, "We'll call him patient zero. Put him in a carrier. In the meantime, he can stay in the CRC today, but separate from the others."

This would be a nice diversion. Sometimes science was just the best.

"Contact the others in the science club. *Los científicos* has a field trip tonight. No time to get Park Service approval and they might not approve anyway, so secrecy. We'll meet at the old drive-in theater at midnight. See if one of the moms can go with us."

Jessenia put the small bat back away with some water, covered the cage for darkness and walked toward the research center with its air conditioning. It was daytime, so he should be sleeping in a cool cave.

Before they went too far, he reminded them, "This is still an official outing. We need an adult chaperone, so ask around. No one goes without proper dress, water, personal first aid kit, and a signed permission slip. I know everyone's parents. No forged signatures."

The last comment was a club joke.

Ariq made a mental list of supplies. Check the fuel on his SUV. Mist nets. Biopsy punches. Forceps. Storage vials. Gloves. Sterilization supplies. He was glad that his students had been trained. They'd need to work quickly tonight.

———

After lunch, he concentrated on the package from Liliadja. In his head, he pronounced it lily-odd-JA or lily-odd-HA. Even before he opened it, he could smell the pungent herbs. He marveled again that it passed through customs unexamined. Liliadja certainly seemed to have a magical touch. He took this as a good omen.

It contained three numbered bags and detailed instructions.

The bag labeled 1 had chopped leaves of different colors. "Mash with a mortar and pestle, then drop into two cups of simmering (not boiling) water."

Ariq scratched his head. When had he last seen a mortar and pestle? Probably in a movie, maybe The Court Jester or The Princess Bride. He remembered the orthopedic mallets; they could substitute for pestles. He got a small one from the surgery prep area.

He went into the kitchen for a plastic bowl and the microwave. He microwaved the water in several steps to avoid boiling it. The herbs filled the room with a strong odor from the muddy, green mixture. Lots of oily resin scents, kind of like sage and maybe mesquite.

The bag labeled 2 had dust and yellowy chunks in it. "Stir this (bark powder & dried yam bits) into the stew after it has simmered for 10 minutes."

He had this. No problem here.

"Simmer another 10 minutes and let cool. Use before two hours are up."

The bag labeled 3 had several dried leaves. "After all the stew is consumed, have sick person chew a couple of these leaves two or three times, and spit out."

Oh, Ariq thought. The patient must eat this. So, none of his comatose patients were eligible. Julia's father had a feeding tube, but no way he was going to chew those leaves.

He tracked down Nizhoni and together they selected a patient awake and alert enough to go through what would be an ordeal— given how sick these patients were.

Hannah looked strong, being younger and in better shape than the typical geriatric, hip-replacement patient. She had been in a rock climbing accident on a 5.11 ascent in Last Chance Canyon, just a hundred miles south. The rescue helicopter had taken her to the regional hospital, but given the orthopedic nature of her injuries, she was transferred to the ROC.

She exhibited idiopathic ague symptoms shortly after her arrival delaying her knee surgery. She was an ideal patient for Lily's stew.

It seemed cruel to make a patient eat this mixture of bark and leaves, and then chew more leaves. Especially one that could barely sip water. It seemed so primitive.

The final instruction seemed a bit touchy-feely for Ariq's western training. "Someone must sit with the patient and talk to them, so patient knows caring people are there. Touch patient's shoulders, hands, side of face frequently before and after feeding stew. I hope it works! –Lily."

Ariq thought of эмээ back in Mongolia, and the failure of western medicine so far in this case; he decided to follow Liliadja's instructions to the letter.

Dreamtime called herself Lily. He liked the sound of Lily.

This Lily was an enigma. She was a healer with methods that might be thousands or tens of thousands of years old, but at the same time her writing was precise, her spelling and grammar exact.

While he made the stew, Joni woke the patient.

"Hannah? Can you hear me?" As strange as it felt, Ariq rubbed her neck under her beaded braids. He used a soft cloth to wipe the sweat off her brow and cheeks. She blinked, sighed, and maybe smiled.

He explained to her about the stew and asked her permission. She closed her eyes and grunted, then moaned. Considering her condition, tremors, and fever, he took that as consent.

He noted in her electronic chart, "Patient gives informed consent for the Australian Treatment." Joni glanced at the chart and gave him a questioning look. He winked, "This is a day for courage, not rules. This treatment has helped patients in Australia."

Ariq fed her the stew while Joni sat on the other side of the bed caressing her muscular shoulders and holding her hand. All the while they talked to Hannah and how they hoped she would get better.

The stew went well, but the leaves had a bad taste. She made an awful face. They counted aloud, "one, two, three," and she immediately spat them out on three. Ariq and the nurse talked with her for ten minutes before Joni administered something to put her to sleep and patted her hand until she drifted off.

When they got out of the room, the nurse turned and held him. At first he was stiff and uncomfortable, but then he was hit by the wonderful thing they had done together.

He held her and hiccupped with emotion. The two of them silently held each other for several minutes. Then they walked their separate ways.

———

Ariq napped in his clothes until the alarm went off at 11:30 PM. His SUV was packed, so he only needed to put on his hiking boots to be ready to drive to the abandoned drive-in south of town.

In addition to Jessenia and Sofia, there were three other science club members, two boys, brothers, and another girl. He collected their permission slips, nodded his thanks to the boys' mother, for driving and chaperoning.

"Here is the plan."

They all sat quietly.

"We want to see how a disease spreads among bats. How fast it spreads. Find out when an immunity appears. How fast the immunity spreads.

"Jessenia was going to do this in the lab, but we haven't been able to find something to make the bats sick. Now we have at least one sick bat!"

Everyone looked at Jessenia. She raised a small, blue cat carrier and smiled proudly.

"There are just a few of us, so we won't be able to sample many bats. Hopefully we'll see some more sick bats and have the enough data for Jessenia's experiment.

"We'll be taking punch biopsy samples. You all remember how to do that? I brought plenty of sample containers. Just remember to punch the wings away from any skeletal structures. We use the smallest punches and the bats should recover quickly."

Sofia asked if they were doing freeze branding tonight. He replied that that would have been a good idea, but they didn't have enough people or time.

There was a general murmur of consent, except one boy who seemed unsure.

"No problem, José. You'll be the lookout. We don't have park service clearance, so you find a high perch and call us on your cell if you see anyone approaching."

He turned to Mrs. Santana, "Can you stay with him?"

She nodded, "*No hay problema.*" This wasn't her first adventure with *los científicos.*

They got into two cars and drove south to Slaughter Canyon.

———

They dropped José and his mom about a mile before the canyon.

"Check your phone. Is your battery good? Does your carrier have coverage down here?"

The boy tapped his phone. "Three bars. Eighty-five percent. Good to go."

Once at the mouth of the canyon, Jessenia released patient zero and they organized into teams. The boy and the other girl held up the mist net and counted the little *fwops* as bats tangled themselves in the netting. After ten, they laid the net down for Jessenia and Sofia to get each bat loose, and take the punch biopsies. Ariq logged the samples on his tablet.

They used the finest mesh polyester nets so the bats wouldn't slip through or hurt themselves. They held them up on tent poles which were always in ample supply. Camping was the number one recreational choice among families in Roswell.

The operation was delicate because of the bats' small size. One hand the held the bat, and the other punched a tiny hole in the wing. Research had shown that bat wings regrew in a week with no long-term ill effects.

It went smoothly for the first three batches. In the middle of the fourth batch, Sofia squealed. Her bat escaped and after momentarily getting tangled in her hair, flew away.

Everyone in science club had had pre-exposure rabies prophylaxis shots and there was only a 0.5% chance of rabies anyway. However, with that scare, Ariq decided to call it a night.

Just as they were packing up, José texted, **ranger**.

They shook the net to free the last few bats. They turned off all their lights and hid amongst the desert chaparral. They just couldn't get caught.

Ariq ducked behind a small hill and imagined how fast he'd be fired. Trespassing in the National Park. Trapping bats in the National Park. Taking unauthorized biopsies. Maybe even endangering minors, but that would simply be punitive; he had permission slips.

The ranger parked at the entrance to the cave. A lizard crawled over Ariq, but he did not move. It seemed he was a warm and cozy place for the lizard. He made promises to whatever gods he could imagine and told himself that he'd be fine if it stayed out of his boxers.

The ranger flashed his light all around. It reflected off one of the car mirrors. Fortunately, they had had the foresight to park the cars separately.

Once he saw the car, he investigated more carefully. He found the boy. "Hey you. What are you doing out here?"

He shone the light in the boy's frightened face.

"I recognize you. You shouldn't be here in the middle of the night. There have been reports of bears, and I've seen a mother with cubs. You're local, so you know better than to fool with a mother bear."

The boy looked scared and didn't say a thing.

Ariq debated whether he should stand up and take responsibility for the students. It seemed cowardly to let this kid suffer on his own. Ariq started the day full of a warrior's courage, and now he was hiding behind a sage brush with a lizard camped in his pants.

Just then Jessenia jumped up. She put her arms around the boy and kissed him. "Please don't tell our parents. This seemed like a private place."

The ranger smiled. "I recognize you also. Get in your car and go home. This is not a good place right now."

The ranger followed them away, and no one moved until José called to say everyone was gone. Ariq stood up and shook the lizard out of his pants. Sofia couldn't help laughing. They collected the gear and piled into the remaining car. They caught up with Jessenia and her "boyfriend," waiting with José and his mom.

"That was a good night's work. See you tomorrow."

28. DR. BRIAN

BLUE RIDGE PARKWAY

R_X Driving along the Blue Ridge Parkway in the early morning, the eponymous haze imbued the ride with a dream-like quality. As much as he had hated Darlene in the aftermath of the accident, it was hard to hate her now that he knew she was alive, and even harder to suppress fond memories of Penny's childhood together.

When they married in the early 70s, Miller & Miller's business was booming. Both Darlene and Brian were making good money, and by the time Penny was ready to enter school, they were discussing private school or moving to a better district.

But on her fifth birthday, they still lived in that small two-bedroom house that had been a resentful gift from his parents. "We just can't have you raising our granddaughter in an apartment."

At her party that year, Penny was excited. In a blond Princess Leia hair style, she challenged everyone, girls, boys, parents alike, to a saber duel. "I have to win, I'm the birthday girl."

She spent the week up to her birthday obsessing about how she'd blow out so many candles. He had taunted her by threatening to get a big cake and separating the candles to the four distant corners and the center. She considered using a fan, a squirt gun, ice cubes, the candle snuffer that was only used for Christmas candles. In the end, she brought a cup of water, and to her parent's horror and secret amusement, she picked all the candles off the cake and dropped the flaming bundle into the cup.

Before she entered first grade, they had purchased a walled estate, three acres with a large 18th century colonial, but updated electricals and plumbing, and all the modern conveniences: dishwasher, automatic laundry, a built-in microwave oven. The property was on one of those secluded Lawntown back roads which combined exclusive privacy with convenience to Miller &

Miller headquarters.

He interrupted this pleasant daydream for lunch at a traditional roadhouse which still had a couple of rooms for rent on the second floor. He had the special: Appalachian fired chicken, with collards, grits, greens, and Appalachian slaw, which turned out to be more of a salad. He thought of renting one of those rooms afterward, but he wanted to be in Atlanta on Monday, so he grabbed a rocking chair on the front porch for a little shuteye, instead.

In the contentment that only comes from good southern comfort food, he took out his phone. He had nobody to call. The only one he could think of was Penelope, but it was too early. However, he did the next best thing. He entered her in his contacts as DAUGHTER. That felt really good.

After a short rest, he was on the road again and looking forward to his meetings at the Center for Disease Control and his triumphant return to chemistry—using his expertise and experience to save the world. He liked the sound of "save the world," almost as much as Nobel Prize. He recognized that retired for over a decade ago, and pushing into his 70s, he might need to settle for an advisory role.

While he considered his options, the road suddenly got steep and bumpy. He banged his head on the roof and he heard an explosion—air bag. That was the last thing he recalled.

He woke up in a sunny hospital room. He read the blood pressure and heart rate monitor. Pressure was 145/97. No real problem there, he'd probably missed a couple of days of his HCT pills. Heart rate was bouncing around in the 80s. He relaxed, he seemed to be okay and his vision was good enough to read the monitor, always a good sign after a head injury.

He took a breath through his nose. He could smell hints of hospital disinfectant and maybe orange juice. That was also a good sign. He also realized he was thirsty, another positive indicator. He listened to the beep of the heart rate monitor and then someone walking into the room.

The next step would be to check that he could move his fingers and toes, but he was interrupted by a nurse or a doctor.

"I'm glad to see you've woken up. You've been out for quite a while darling. We were worried."

He blinked at her. He was going to sit up, but he discovered he was strapped in. "What happened to me?"

"Well, honey, we all trying to figure that out."

He really wanted to sit up. "My vitals seem fine. Can you unstrap me? I'd like to sit up. And I'm thirsty…and hungry."

"Well, I'll be. Y'all lay like a dead man here for over a day. Y'all scare everyone to dickens. And now, with no thank you or by your leave, y'all think you're in some fancy eatery."

He wasn't in the mood for southern conversation or hospitality. "Can I please see my doctor?"

"Hold your horses. Is everyone in your family always in such a rush?"

He gazed at her with a puzzled look and shook his arms.

"OK, I'm gonna unbuckle you. Just wait until I get the rails up. When your wife, I mean ex-wife, was here, she warned us that y'all would be a problem."

Forgetting everything else, he tensed and said, "Wife?" That effort was exhausting and not as loud and forceful as he intended. He reevaluated. He might be in worse condition than he'd thought.

"Yeah. Wife. Darlene if I recall. Nice lady. Very nice lady."

The nurse raised the back of his bed and handed him the control. He found he could barely hold it, much less press the buttons. Resigned, he let himself sink into the bed. He noticed that his blood pressure and heart rate had spiked. He prescribed himself bed rest. He thought to laugh at his little joke, but a smile was all he could manage.

"You and that Darlene, two of a kind. Yankees I'm guessing. She was in a big rush. Flew in. Asked some questions. Signed some papers. And she's gone."

He didn't know if he was happy or sad. He whispered, "How

did you find my wife…ex-wife…Darlene?" It had been so long since he'd spoken to her, he was unsure what he called her.

The nurse laughed. "You funny. We looked at the contacts on your phone. Called your daughter. No great CSI genius needed."

The door opened. The nurse turned, "Here's that doctor you wanted."

He flipped his head toward the door. His vision blurred for a moment. Long curly blonde hair. "Penelope?" He fell asleep.

———

When he awoke, the room was full. The crash cart was next to his bed. Someone was rubbing the paddles. "Clear!"

Brian raised his arms, dropping the bed control with a clatter against the bed frame. "Wait, wait," he shouted in his weak voice.

The doctor with the curly blonde hair moved next to him. "Mr. Macalester. You need to calm down and stop scaring us."

He thought, scaring? I'm scared too. Someone held a straw to his lips. He drank some orange juice and thought that this must be a pretty good hospital, fresh orange juice.

"I'm sorry, doctor. What happened to me?"

He looked at her badge, "Neurosurgeon. Charlotte." None of that was encouraging. He could see his vitals on the monitor trending up again. Before the doctor could say anything, he whispered. "Charlotte. Shouldn't I be in Charlottesville?"

She put her gloved finger on his lips. "Your ex did warn us. Please just listen."

Just listening. OK. Easy. It took all his concentration to stay alert.

"Counting a few minutes ago, and the police report from where you ran your car into a ditch on the Blue Ridge Parkway, and your daughter's report from Tahiti, you've had three syncope episodes in the last week."

He had nothing to add, so he took her advice, or was it Darlene's advice, or Penny's? He just listened.

"Your history is problematic. Patients usually present with isolated syncope events. Your daughter tells us the first event occurred contemporaneously with a blow to the head. As the doctor who was there when it happened, she felt any diagnosis was conjecture at best, especially without modern diagnostic equipment…which was not available."

Penny *recognized* him immediately *and* observed his accident with care and concern. This caused a small upward blip in his vitals.

The doctor continued, "Here, the EMTs at your accident did not recognize the syncope incident, as their initial assumption was either drunk or falling asleep at the wheel. A quick test cleared you of drunk driving, so old-man-falls-asleep was their conclusion."

"Only after we spoke to your daughter was a neurologic etiology considered. Now given the event a few minutes ago," she pointed to the crash cart with the paddles still shiny with conductive jelly, "You will be here for a few days for observation and testing—at least.

Now that he understood better, Doctor Brian reconciled himself to being a week late to his rendezvous with CDC. Since the CDC and WHO were keeping quiet about the possible world-wide pandemic, he had time. The CDC would be happy to see him a week from now, wouldn't they?

Meanwhile this enforced vacation would give him time to think about his resurrected family. He wanted to call Penelope right away, but he didn't know where his phone was and he was exhausted by the recent talk. Darlene was a bigger problem; she had come to see him in the hospital. Why? How?

This time he closed his eyes and counted isomers of imaginary molecules until he fell asleep. He hoped peaceful thoughts of Lawntown and Matu Kiva would bring sleep and not summon the crash cart again.

29. LILY

Once again she asked Obrey for help. She showed him her phone and input his number. He smiled. "I like your hair," he said. "It's interesting."

"So far you are in the minority."

"Why? It makes you look like an elder, so wise."

Maybe that was why they didn't like it? On the other hand, Kutai Djarrwark didn't seem to think it was funny, like Pearl did. And Lily had decided she did not care what Olivia thought. Pana, of course, had thought it was wonderful, until Olivia started yelling at Lily. Poor Pana.

"You are quiet," Obrey said, turning the corner onto the Stuart Highway.

"Mm. My aunt and I had a big fight."

"I heard."

For the barest moment, she wondered if he meant he'd literally heard them yelling, somehow, then realized it was just, "people will talk."

"My cousin is kind of caught in the middle. She has no friends, so she's always looked up to me. Which is what Olivia is worried about. But this time my aunt made ugly accusations," she shook her head. "I'm not going to live there and fight against those kinds of lies."

"Well...because you left, people are saying what she said was true."

Lily looked at him, tears threatening to fill her eyes. "Why are people so willing to believe the very worst things? Do *you*? Do you think that is what I am like, sleeping around for money?"

"No. I do not. But what I think doesn't matter much. I'm just the guy sleeping in the back of my shop."

"Oh, no."

He shrugged. "I gave up my apartment. It's stupid to pay for

197

two places."

"I thought the owners don't allow you to use it for living space."

"They don't. But as long as I'm not obvious, they're willing to look the other way—I think because space is hard to rent. They'd rather keep me in there if they can."

"Maybe they charge too much rent," Lily said. She had no idea how much Obrey might be paying for the Café space, but it maybe was a lot. More than he earned, maybe. "You going to be able to keep the Casuarina Café open?"

"Not if my best customer starts using her phone instead of my computers," he said with a crooked grin.

Lily laughed. "No, I won't. I get reception only on Highway 1, and no WiFi." She thought a moment. "I did use it to call my friend in New Mexico yesterday, though. Sometimes he's not online—we've been exchanging emails, but I can see where the phone may be handy sometimes. Also, it makes a good light! I was using it last night to find my matches," she grinned, and Obrey laughed.

"Pretty fancy torch!"

They pulled into the parking lot of the big Home Timber and Hardware DIY store. The place had been built near the modern suburbs that had been slowly growing out of Katherine town. It looked a bit incongruous in the parking lot surrounded by bush and open forest.

"So—what do you need?"

"Definitely a tarp and some plastic bins. Maybe a great big bin to put my paint box and canvasses in. Some pots and dishes."

Obrey nodded. "I've only been there to the compound once, but it seemed rough."

Lily laughed. "Mm. Like we used to live. For 50,000 years."

"Oh, I thought it was only 40 thousand."

"*Balanda* lies!" Lily said and they both laughed. But Lily discovered she was wincing inside. Who was she to make fun of her people? If they *were* her people.

She thought about individuals. She would not ever laugh at

Pearl. The old woman really was wise. And kind, and funny. But she'd thought Minnakenna and Jandry were that way too, right up until they told her to leave.

Lily sighed and looked at the labels on the wall-ends. "Tarps, this way," she said.

Obrey grabbed a shopping cart, and it was full after the stop at the big plastic bin aisle. The store did not seem to have any boxes or bins big enough for her canvasses and finished work, though.

"Maybe I need to build a big box," she said.

Obrey stood still a moment. "I know what might work. Tintu and his family have a garden shed in the back of their yard. I bet we can get one here."

"Garden shed?"

"Big box, already built," Obrey said with a big smile. "Like a tiny house."

They eventually were told the sheds were outside with the plants and garden items, which made sense, Lily decided.

"Dirt?" they looked at the rows of stacked plastic bags. "Why would you need to buy dirt?"

"Maybe they are trying to make their lands bigger?" Obrey said, and even Lily laughed at that one, imagining some whitefella stacking up dirt in the yard to try and make more space around his house.

"Here's the sheds," Obrey said and waved "ta-da" at the row of tiny roofed houses.

"Oh, they're plastic," Lily said. "Mm, and metal," she added, feeling the side of one.

"Should be pretty water resistant unless you throw it in the river. They have a floor, so your painting gear is up off the ground."

Lily peered inside. There were a few shelves and some hooks to hang things. It was big enough to sleep in, if she needed to. She stepped back and looked at it. It was tall enough to serve as a wall for her lean-to. "Just attach the tarp at the top and pull it out," she said, demonstrating the roomy triangular space it would make. "This is just right." Ugh, but how much money?

They read the chart next to the sample sheds. The two big ones were ridiculously too big—and too expensive, of course. Lily was surprised to see that there were three she could definitely afford. "Thank you Fei," she murmured. "You bought me a house, even if you didn't know it."

Obrey lay down in front of the medium-priced shed. "You can definitely sleep in here, whenever you don't want to be outside," he said.

"I was hoping for a window, but I guess for $A400 it's really good." She examined the door handles. They had a small key lock. She could also put a padlock around the two handles and lock them together, if she wanted extra security. $A2000 for one painting was probably not going to happen again, but if someone stole her work she would have nothing at all to sell. And no income. It was worth buying a padlock. It was difficult to trust when she saw both sides of Katherine society.

She wiggled the tarp out from beneath the plastic bins. "Can you help me hold this?" They opened the tarp package and unfolded it. It could hook on the high side of the roof, cover the top of the shed and extend out beyond on one side.

"We can get poles, if you want it all open. Or you can stake it down if you like the angular look."

Lily nodded. "This will be exactly what I was thinking of."

"Maybe Damon can help build a window for you."

"Do you think so? That would be awesome!" she said, sounding like Pana. Awesome?

Obrey delivered her to the compound and helped carry her bins and pots and the bag of groceries they'd bought.

She stopped by the office, and knocked. Minka Djarrwark came to the door. "I am having a shed delivered here, is that okay?"

Minka nodded.

"They have to bring it on a big truck, and I know Kutai said no cars allowed."

"Okay for deliveries, just not alla time," Minka said.

"Good, because they'll be here in a half-hour. Sorry there was no warning, but it was now or not till next week," she explained.

Minka nodded again.

"Um, so, does a shed count as building my house? The spot I have now will be my permanent spot?"

Minka nodded, and waved her arm, bangle bracelets clinking, "Yes! You be sure it is where you like," she said.

Lily nodded. Obrey walked back to her space with her. "They seem agreeable enough," he said. "I honestly didn't think they'd let you live in a shed."

"Someone has a tent over there."

"Yah, I saw that. And the other, uh, huts."

"They try to welcome anyone that needs a place." Lily glanced at Obrey. "If they kick you out of the Café, you could come here to sleep."

"Is that an invitation?" he grinned sideways at her.

"Ah! Obrey, you could sleep in your *own* place. Thirty dollars a month."

His eyebrows raised up. "That's pretty cheap rent," he said.

"Mm. I should have come here sooner." She and Obrey walked all around the compound, down to the creek, back toward the dirt road, over to the path to the bridge.

"They keep the lights on in the bathroom all the time?"

"Yes. So I don't want to be close to that."

"Nor the smell," he added.

"That too. They keep it pretty clean, but still…." They walked back to where Lily's red silk scarf and pile of bins marked her space. "I think I like it here," she said. She sat down on the red scarf and leaned back on her elbows. Obrey squatted beside her. She put her head back and looked up into the casuarina tree behind—and over—her space. There was a dark crack where the biggest branch met the trunk. Lily got up and looked closer. "There are bats nesting in this tree! This is definitely my space."

"Nice," Obrey said, turning in a circle to look at it again. "Okay, well, I've got to go give Damon the key to my place. He's going to run the Café for me tonight while I drive you down to Mataranka."

"Thank you soooo, so much for your help," Lily said. "I could not have done this without you."

Obrey's smile was a little bit too smug to suit her, but he had been an immense help. He waved. "I'll be back in an hour or so."

"Okay. Thank you!"

Obrey's car pulled away from the compound office just in time to make room for the delivery truck.

Rosie came out of her hut and stood with Minka, watching the truck unload a little forklift. Lily showed the driver where the shed was going. The driver handed her a rake. "Get rid of all the rocks and branches, so we can set it down flat," the guy said.

"Thank you," Lily said, and went and began raking. She glanced over to see Minka and Rosie laughing as the little forklift lifted the shed off the truck and rumbled down the ramp to the ground with it.

Lily finished raking, and walked back to stand beside them after returning the driver's rake.

"Kutai will be sorry he does not see this," Minka said, grinning. "Big ol' hut, little bitty truck!"

"It's called a forklift, ma'am," the driver said.

"Forklift," Rosie said, pronouncing it carefully. Minka nodded.

Lily could not believe how good it felt to see her new home. The "river gum green" shed looked like it belonged there. She put her herbs inside the bins and covered them tightly, fitting the bins onto the shelves at one end of the shed. She left the pile of tarp, blanket, sleeping bag and liner, pots and pans and food on the floor. There was still plenty of empty space.

She'd take care of the rest of it when she got back from Mataranka. She put her lock on the shed door.

When Obrey returned, he had sad news.

"She's gone," he said, gesturing toward Rosie and Kalinda's huts. "Died in the hospital an hour ago."

"K—" Lily slapped her hand over her mouth before Kalinda's name could pop out. It was one of the people's biggest taboos. She knew elders at Ngukurr who would still not name the dead even after twenty years, though most would begin to say it again after four or five years. Except for the ones who had become whitefellas, and just said the name, and wrote the name, and tried to honor the name by speaking it aloud right away.

As though by telepathy, Minka and Rosie came out of their houses. "She died?" Minka asked.

Rosie just moaned when Obrey nodded.

"They would not let Pearl and me go to help her," Lily said. "We helped June. They should have welcomed us to help—! Why are they so stupid?"

———

On the road to Mataranka in Obrey's car, Lily tried to think of some way to thank him. He was adamant about not taking money from her.

"What about this," she suggested. "What if you take 10% of my sales if any paintings sell from your Café? The Coop takes 10%, so it's a fair amount."

"I thought you said they wouldn't sell in Katherine," he said, a crooked grin on his face.

"I think they probably will not, but if they do…."

"All right," he said. "That sounds good."

They rode in silence for a while, then both started to talk at once.

"I wish— "

"Does Pearl… "

They laughed. Lily waved him on.

"Does Pearl know that that woman at Ngukurr was sleeping with that other woman's husband?"

"Oh." Lily shook her head. "I have no idea."

"Because I think she would be a little more ready to fight for you if she knew the villagers were holding to a double standard."

"Mm. Maybe."

"I still don't understand why they think it is such a, uhm, taboo," he said. "Certainly Olivia slept with lots of young men before she chose Tonda as her husband."

"Oh." Lily could not believe Obrey would even have that information, much less share it. "How do you know?"

"My papa is the biggest gossip in Katherine, Lily, as I'm sure you've heard. He talks to everyone, *alla time*." He glanced at her, crooked-grinning again. "Your aunt was considered a very good catch, she's so pretty and clever. Everyone was surprised she chose Tonda."

"I was under the impression she had no idea who Pana's father was."

"Well, she's not proud of it, I think. Tonda turned out to be a petrol-sniffer. He died two years after Pana was born."

"Oh. I did not know that." She rubbed her face. "I did not know that at all."

"Well, my point is that young women are *supposed* to sleep around, young men are supposed to visit lots of young women. Now. Since we don't have so much kinship and arranged marriage rules, it's the only way to find a mate." He shrugged. "So why would Olivia be so angry if she thought that's what you were doing?"

"But, I'm not."

"I know, but could that be why? Because you *aren't* trying to find a husband?"

It was suddenly very awkward to be talking about this with her most likely candidate. "Mm."

"And I wonder if it wasn't that, plus guilt, that led to you being banished from Ngukurr."

"I don't know."

"Ask Pearl. I think if you just ask her straight out, she'll tell you. But I bet she doesn't know about the adultery."

———

Obrey dropped her off with a smile on his face, and an airy wave. She quietly walked toward the pools, the trees, the bats.

"You're still here?" she shouted, when she saw soldiers again.

The soldier with the fancy uniform waved a dismissing arm at his men. "Stand down," he said, then turned to Lily.

"They're still in cages!" she said, trying not to shout. "How long does it take to kill a couple hundred bats?"

"What? We're not killing them. We're just collecting samples for the CDC."

"And killing them."

"No, child," pajama-man's voice said from behind her. "We aren't killing them. Just taking samples. We let them go when we're done. The bats are fine."

Lily turned to look at him. He stood at the entrance to a white tent. He was wearing a thin white coat, like they wore in the hospital, and gloves on his hands like the hospital people, too. He had a white mask over his mouth and nose. He was wearing a white hat with a plastic shield over his face, like the dentist Lily's mother had dragged her to had worn. He was holding one of the Little Red Flying Foxes in his hand.

"Come, look. I'll show you exactly what we're doing."

Glancing at the soldiers, who were now ignoring her, Lily took a step toward the man, then stopped.

"I thought you were leaving, you said the plane was coming the next day."

The man blinked, thinking through what Lily said. "Ah," he nodded. "We needed to get some samples back to headquarters right away for testing. Now we are gathering additional samples from as many bats as we can."

It was Lily's turn to think it through. She stepped forward into the white tent. "I'm not a child," she thought to say. "I'm just short." They moved toward a table set up at the back of the tent.

"Ah," the man said again. He held up the bat, wings spread. Lily saw two tiny holes, one in about the center of each wing. "The holes will heal closed in a few days. Meanwhile, they can fly just fine." Then the man grasped the bat by its feet, slid a bag up over it, pulled a string to close the bag, and walked back to the tent opening, holding the bag by the string. Lily moved aside. He handed the bat to a soldier that now stood outside the tent. The soldier walked over to the trees, opened the bag, and shook the bat out. Wings opened wide, the bat caught itself on the air, and

205

fluttered up into the nearby tree, apparently unharmed. The soldier was wearing a white mask and gloves, too, but not the plastic face-guard thing.

"See?" pajama-man said. He looked at her, then removed the glove from his hand and reached his hand out to Lily. "I'm Dr. Darnell."

Lily shook his hand. "Lily," she said.

"Hello, Lily. I'm with the CDC, the Center for Disease Control in the United States. Do you know where that is?"

"Yes."

"Okay. Sorry, I don't mean to sound patronizing, but I have run into several aboriginal people out here who didn't."

"Mm," Lily said. "They were probably just pretending they didn't. We aren't as isolated as everyone seems to think." Or as stupid. But sometimes it was helpful to pretend stupid. You found out things from what the *balanda* said that they might not have spoken about otherwise.

"Okay," Dr. Darnell said. "Well, I'm just trying to keep things friendly and get my job done. I haven't been able to get an assistant here– " He stopped in the middle of taking another bat out of a cage and turned to look at her. "How old are you?"

"Eighteen."

"Oh, wow. Sorry, I was way off. But– " He must have pursed his lips, because the white mask pouched out. She could see his forehead crinkle while he was thinking. "Can *you* help me? You seem comfortable with the bats. It would go so much faster if you could take them out of their cages, and then send them on afterward." He bit his lip. "I'd be able to pay you a small wage for your help."

"Do I have to bag them to take them out? Could I just carry them over and let them go?"

"Oh. Oh, yes, you handled them before. That would be fine, if that's what you would prefer."

"How do you make the holes? Does it hurt?"

He showed her a thing that looked kind of like a fat pen. "It's a punch. I'm careful to put the hole in the wing surface where there are no blood vessels or nerves. So, no, it doesn't hurt them."

"If I help they will get out of the cages faster?"

"Oh, yes. Definitely."

Lily thought about it another moment. As far as she could see, it would not violate any dreamtime sensitivities. And it would mean the bats could fly free sooner. "Good then," she said. "Show me what to do."

30. NGA

NACALA, MOZAMBIQUE & INDIAN OCEAN

In the afternoon, their good mood extended past farewells, plans and boarding the *Sun Fish*. Nga introduced the twenty-four villagers plus six children to Captain Tola.

"Halid is our acting headman," she told the captain, and he nodded, shaking hands with the young man. Halid beamed to be called a "headman" even if it was only temporary.

"Welcome," the captain said. "This is First Mate Bill Gaio. You will mostly be talking to him about where to go and what to do. Also this is Tomas, who cooks for us, and will gladly turn cooking duties over to you once he shows you how the galley works."

Jojeza stepped forward. Nga said, "This is Jojeza. Jojo will be in charge of our meals." Tomas smiled at her, and she gave a little bow.

"We have these foods," Nga pointed at the crates and bags the villagers had loaded aboard. "Perhaps Jojo and Tomas can tell us where to take them."

"We have refrigerators and stowage in the hold," Bill said. Tomas will show you."

"Good," Captain Tola said. "We leave the dock in an hour, so if there's anything last minute, get it now. Otherwise I want everyone aboard and ready."

Feeling a little silly, Nga bowed to the Captain. "Thank you again."

"Shelly will be here to say goodbye in a few minutes," he said. "I think she planned to bring something to share with everyone."

Indeed, as he finished speaking, Shelly ran up the ramp, her arms full of baskets and bags. "Snack!" she called.

The baskets were full of breads and rolls that smelled delicious. Some had cheese, some a dusting of sugar. And some had chocolate.

Mu danced around Shelly making kissing noises. All the

villagers were grinning as they picked from the baked foods.

"Thank you so much," Nga said, hugging her friend.

———

Life aboard the *Sun Fish* was so different from Luambe village that Nga thought some of the villagers might die of homesickness. Mezi and the children and Halid were fine, exploring everywhere, talking to the crew and learning about parts of the boat. Others, like Miss Anderson and Petyr Johansson seemed to be in a fugue state, standing around staring a lot, not talking, not eating much either. Nga kept a close eye on them.

On the second day out of port, they began counting fish.

"We have an imaginary grid over the ocean here," Bill Gaio explained. "We take samples in certain squares of the grid, count and weigh the fish, release them and move on to the next assigned square. We will do seven separate sections on our way south to Beira. Seven more, further out to sea, on our return to Nacala. Each section measures four pulls of the trawling nets. Then the computer will help us estimate all the fish in this part of the Indian Ocean based on our samples."

"Okay," Halid said, bright-eyed. "Do we count every fish?"

"You will each have a specific kind of fish to look for. In the same way we grid off the ocean, we will have sections of our holding tank assigned to you. You will count only your kind of fish in your own section. This is why we must keep the glass walls of the "aquarium" clean and unscratched. We also weigh the fish, for a secondary, mixed count."

"There is a scale in the aquarium?" Nga asked.

"Yes, a giant scale. We adjust for the water weight to get a tonnage of fish."

"It doesn't seem very accurate," someone said in Chiyao. Many of the villagers nodded in agreement. Nga translated.

"Over time," the First Mate said, "we have a very good estimate of whether certain species are increasing or declining, and by how much. Captain Tola adjusts licensing accordingly."

Nga gazed at the somewhat murky waters of the aquarium

hold. The *Sun Fish* was a very specialized fishing boat. When the counting and weighing were done, the entire aquarium contents were released back into the Indian Ocean. Then pumps began filling the huge tank again. It was amazing to her that the machinery existed to do all this.

The crew hauled in the trawling net, and the villagers stood well out of the way as the cranes lifted the huge mass of captured, flopping fish over the aquarium. The crane lowered the net into the water, released it, and fish immediately swarmed every which way in the enormous tank.

The First Mate handed out big plastic-covered sheets of fish photos to the Luambe helpers. Nga's fish was dull yellow and gray speckled, with extravagant tail fins. She hoped she'd be able to pick it out of all the others. Bill and other members of the crew passed among the villagers, making sure they understood what section and fish they were counting.

One of her fish swam out of the mass and she marked her clipboard. It was kind of fun. Completely politics- and medicine-free work. Completely innocent fish.

Yellow tape marked the borders of Nga's section. She stared at the roiling fish, counting roman-numeral style on the card on her little clipboard. The crew gave them an extra ten minutes on the first "pull" of the trawling net. The rest of the six-hour day they only had fifteen minutes to count their fish in their section, then the aquarium was dumped, the boat moved to the next grid cell and the tank refilled. The trawling net was refilled, the boat stopped and sea-anchored, and they counted again.

Four pulls. Nga found 78 of her fish, about twenty per pull.

By the end of the day, she was more than ready for supper.

Jojeza and Miss Anderson had spent the afternoon in the galley, with a little volunteer help from the younger women. Somehow Jojeza talked to Miss Anderson, and was able to get her to follow simple directions. They added fresh herb-steamed sea bass to the villagers' more usual menu of baked cassava, calima beans and rice. The crew gave rich praise for the meal, and Nga was content that the remnants of Luambe village were doing their share.

———

She was not able to do anything about securing transport for the next leg of their journey until the fourth night aboard the *Sun Fish*. They anchored offshore of Quelimane town, and the captain was able to get good WiFi reception. Nga checked with Shelly and with Ben Kalagho to see if they had any news. In the end, it was Captain Tola who helped them again, seeming to follow hints from Nga's mother.

Dead mother. The pang was deep. She took a deep breath to counter it.

Captain Tola said, "The Greenleaf boat, *Arcturus,* have decided to take some refugees to Maputo from the Beira area. They would be willing to add your small group, especially if you can help them out with any kind of donation."

"Yes, I have some money."

"They also need food and clothing. My crew have been gathering canned goods and some clothes, so if you have anything you can add to that, it would probably be enough without the cash."

Nga nodded.

"We'll be in Beira in three days. They'll be expecting you."

"I cannot thank you enough."

"Your people have been quite helpful. We have been able to move along faster than usual this run, so do not think it has been all charity," he smiled. Nga noticed a tiny chip on his front tooth. It was almost exactly the same chip Shelly had. She found herself wondering what they'd eaten that caused such a thing. Fish bones were too flexible. Maybe bits of rock in their beans?

She and Mezi went through their little stash of clothes. Mezi gave up a couple of the children's things that were on the verge of being too small, along with one of her older robes. Nga had a couple of shirts and a pair of shoes. It wasn't much, but maybe the new refugees had even less than they did.

Halid contributed one of the robes they'd gotten for Salim that he had strongly disliked, as well as one of his own robes. He'd taken to wearing only jeans, tee-shirts and flip-flops, like the crew.

They also still had bags of the village surplus they could share—dried fruits, sweet potato and fish, beans, corn and rice. She could add some medical help, too. If that wasn't enough, there was still most of the cash left from her mother's jewelry. She actually was able to smile, thinking how happy Linnea Lind would be to know how much she had helped. They were going to Maputo.

31. LILY

They still had not emptied all the cages when darkness fell. Lily worked as quickly as she could, preparing the bats for Dr. Darnell, then releasing them afterward. They chatted together, Lily asking questions about the testing. It seemed so much like what Ariq was doing. Why did they need the bat samples? What could they learn from them? What good did it do?

"Bats are amazing," Dr. Darnell said, and Lily liked him better for that. "They carry the viruses that cause many diseases, but they don't get those diseases themselves."

"They don't get sick," Lily said.

"Very rarely. Like with the rabies virus, many bats, in fact most of them, all around the world, might carry the virus. But only a half of one percent of them get the disease." He looked at her. "You understand percent?"

Lily nodded. "I graduated from high school in Darwin," she said.

"Ever think about University?"

"My mother suggested it," Lily said. "I took a computer class at the University outpost in Katherine. But I don't want to be an imitation whitefella," she glanced at him. His attention was focused on the bat, but his expression was neutral. "I want to learn about aboriginal things, too."

Dr. Darnell nodded. "Some of your people are very wise."

"Yes," Lily said with a small smile, thinking of Auntie Pearl.

There was a scratching at the tent wall, and a voice near the doorway cleared his throat. "Doctor," the man said. It was the boss soldier. Sergeant, Dr. Darnell had called him.

Dr. Darnell finished the second punch, put his tools down so the tips were in the flame of the always-burning Bunsen burner and turned to the Sergeant. "Yes?"

"One of my men is sick. Do you think you could take a look at

213

him?"

"Well, I'm not a physician, Sergeant Palmer."

"I know, but you're as close as we've got, and Private Glenn is very feverish. Gave him ibuprofen, it didn't help."

Lily took the finished bat to the door and let it go.

"I can look at him," she said surprising herself. "He may have the same thing as June Araminty."

The Sergeant's eyes widened, and he sputtered.

"We'll both go," Dr. Darnell said. "Though I don't know how much help we'll be if the man is truly ill."

Sergeant Palmer looked back and forth between Lily and Dr. Darnell, the bright light from the pole in the yard casting his flickering shadow against the white tent. Then he shrugged. "Can't hurt, I guess. He's over here," he said. "We've isolated him in the supplies tent."

Lily waited while Dr. Darnell looked Private Glenn over. "Definitely fever," he said.

She glanced at the sergeant, then moved to the other side of the cot the soldier lay on. She reached forward, glancing at the man for permission. Private Glenn watched her hand approach his face, but he didn't say anything. Lily laid her fingers on his neck beside his jaw. The heartbeat there was light, erratic and fast, just as June's had been. From the touch, she could also feel and agree that the man had a definite fever. "May I look in your eye?"

"Uh, yah, okay."

Lily gently used her thumb to push the closest eyelid up to reveal more of the eye. There were a lot of tiny red veins, confirming he was dehydrated. His eye had been dry awhile.

"Fluids," Dr. Darnell said at the same time Lily said, "He needs water."

"IV?" the sergeant asked.

"He can drink," Lily said, "so he should drink."

She looked at the other two men. "There's a small clinic in Mataranka town," she said. "It's probably closed up for the day, but we can wake the nurse up."

"Is there a physician there?" the sergeant asked.

"No, just a nurse most times. They send people who need a doctor to hospital in Katherine."

"Do they have more people sick like this in Katherine? Like your friend?" Dr. Darnell asked.

Lily nodded.

"We'll keep him here," Sergeant Palmer said.

"I have had good luck with a native-plant stew," Lily offered. "It cured June. She is home, safe, now. But K— another lady they would not let us tend to, she died this afternoon. She did *not* have the stew. It may mean the stew helps."

"But did she have the same thing?" Dr. Darnell asked. "The same sickness?"

Lily nodded. "Looks the same, acts the same. Anyhow a few native herbs will not hurt him." She pinched the soldier's skin and showed the Sergeant and the Doctor how it stayed pinched awhile before returning to normal. "Much dehydrated. Stew would help." She shrugged. "But it's up to you; I know you like hospitals better than native healers."

The scientist and the Sergeant exchanged a look.

"I guess it won't hurt anything, if we try that," the Sergeant said.

"Easy for you to say," Private Glenn muttered.

Lily smiled at him. "It tastes like vegetable soup; I think you won't mind. Mostly." She looked at the sergeant. "I need a small pot and fire," she said. "I have herbs with me." Nice and fresh, too. Obrey had laughed, helping her collect them. Auntie Pearl was running out, since she'd used her supply on June and another woman who had gone to the hospital but had left already.

Nobody wanted to stay in hospital.

When the stew was ready, Sergeant Palmer helped the soldier sit up on the narrow cot. They stuffed a pillow and some kind of canvas cover behind his back, propped up against supply cases.

Lily squatted by the cot. "Do you want to eat it, or should I feed you?"

"Uh. I'll try," he said. His hand was shaking but he took the spoon the sergeant had given her and scooped up some of the green-brown stew.

He tasted, made a face. "Needs salt," he said.

Sergeant Palmer looked at Lily. "Salt okay?"

She nodded and the sergeant disappeared, returning a few minutes later with a blue cardboard salt shaker. He shook some into the stew and Private Glenn stirred it in.

"Better," he said.

"He can probably use the salt," Dr. Darnell said. "He's sweating so much."

"There's a lot in the bush plants," Lily said, "but it may not taste like it."

"I'm closing down the bat tent for the night, Lily," Dr. Darnell said. "We will have to finish in the morning."

Lily thought sadly about the hundred or so bats still in cages in the canvas-covered truck. She nodded. They'll be free tomorrow, she promised herself.

"Aren't we about done here, anyhow, Doc?" Sergeant Palmer asked. "We caught more bats that were already holed than we did fresh ones today."

Dr. Darnell nodded. "Probably can be on our way tomorrow or the next day."

"That's good," the sergeant said.

When Private Glenn finished the stew, Lily took the bowl from him. "Another thing," she said. She showed him the two Billy Goat Plum leaves. "It tastes terrible," she told him with a grin. "But you should chew them three or four times then spit them out into the bowl. You might want to have water ready to drink."

He nodded, reaching for the cup of water the sergeant had set nearby, and watched while she crumpled the leaves, releasing their pungent scent. She reached forward, and he obligingly opened his mouth. She put the leaves in his mouth. He chewed only twice and made a terrible face.

"Chew, chew!" she encouraged him.

He did so, while she leaned forward with the bowl. As soon as the bowl was in front of him, he spat the leaves out and grabbed the cup, swallowing down all the water and reaching for the pitcher to pour more.

"Okay," he said. "That is just nasty!"

"I know. Sorry. It really will help with the fever, and to…mmm…'set' the stew." She settled back into the folding chair. "It's okay if you sleep now. Later if you wake, or in the morning, I will make more."

"Really?" Private Glenn said. "Maybe I'll be better tomorrow."

Lily didn't say anything, noticing how his hand shook as he set down the water cup. "We believe that it helps if someone sits with the sick person, so I will sit here, if that is okay?"

"I don't care," the sick soldier said. "I'm going to sleep."

Dr. Darnell stuck his head inside the door opening. "Lily, I think your phone is ringing?"

Lily jumped up. That was the funny drumming sound she had just barely heard earlier. The ringtone she had set for her mother: rhythm sticks.

She went to the bat tent and grabbed her backpack. She took it back to sit beside Private Glenn while she got her phone out. "Hello, mama."

"Where are you? I've been trying to call."

"Sorry. I'm at Mataranka. Cell phones don't work very well here."

"Well, you need to get back to Katherine. Olivia is sick! Pana called me from June Araminty's house," her mother's voice sounded panicked. "Someone needs to take care of Pana. Someone needs to go see Olivia!"

Lily could feel her heartbeat speeding up. "What is wrong with Olivia?"

"Pana says it is the same as June's was. The ambulance came and took her away. Poor Pana is crying, because they would not let her come with her mother. She has no one, Lily, she needs you."

"I have no way to get back to Katherine from here, until tomorrow. I already told Obrey I was spending the night."

"Lily, Pana said Obrey is in the hospital also."

"What?" Lily jumped out of the chair.

The sergeant, who had apparently been standing outside, said softly, "I'll sit with my man."

Lily nodded and walked outside. "Obrey's sick, too? He was fine this afternoon."

"I guess he went to visit Olivia, because Pana called him at the Café. He passed out in the hall on his way in. The hospital wouldn't let him leave."

"Oh, no! I need to get there!"

Why did Lily have to be stuck down here when her family and friends were ill? She definitely needed to be in Katherine. But it was over 100 km. away; it would take her hours to walk. Days, maybe.

Dr. Darnell came out of one of the plain tents, his lab coat and gloves and mask gone. Beneath he just wore regular clothes, tan pants and a blue-striped shirt. He looked at Lily, and cocked his head.

"Do you need a ride?" he asked.

"Oh," she looked at him, "hold on, mama." She nodded at Dr. Darnell. "If you can, yes, please!" she said, her eyes thanking him. "Mama, I have to go," she said into the phone. "I'll call you when I get to the hospital." She hung up, meeting Dr. Darnell's eyes. "My friends and family are sick. I need to go to them."

"Okay. Well, we flew in here, so I don't know much about this area. How far is it to Katherine?"

"Just over 100 kilometers. Just over an hour," she said. "Good road."

"Okay." Dr. Darnell stuck his head into the supply tent. "All right if I check out a jeep?" he asked the sergeant.

Lily reached inside the tent to get her backpack as the sergeant said, "Sure, why not? This whole thing just keeps getting crazier and crazier." He caught Lily's arm as she turned to go. "Will you come back?" He pointed with his chin to Private Glenn. "For him?"

"Yes, if I can. The guy I usually ride down here with is one of the people who's sick."

"Maybe you want to spend the night in Katherine, Doc," the

sergeant said.

"I'll see. That could prove helpful," he said.

One of the first things he said once they pulled onto the main highway was to ask if she thought he could visit the Katherine Hospital with her.

"I have no idea," she said. "I guess we could pretend you are someone's friend. They haven't been very nice about letting friends in, though. Maybe you are Olivia's long-lost brother."

Dr. Darnell nodded. "Sure." He glanced at Lily, then back at the road. "And is there such a brother?"

"Not that I know about," Lily said, "but the nurses won't know that either, they're mostly *balanda*."

He waved a hand. "You all seem so…connected," he said.

"Mm. Well I am not. My mother and aunt are not. My grandmother was a stolen generation child, you know about this?"

He nodded.

"So there is a lot of…brokenness, rupturing, from this. All my grandmother's songlines were lost, except one. She taught me the yam dreaming, but I never had a ceremony or any of the other things that would have made me part of my tribe—well, there *is* no tribe, now. It was broken to shards. So my mama decided to stay in Darwin, and my aunt moved to Katherine, and I don't know where I am."

"I see," Dr. Darnell said. "Well, you've obviously learned some healing."

"From Auntie Pearl. But she is just a friend, not a real aunt, like you would say."

He nodded again. "Well, I hope the herbs work."

It was Lily's turn to nod. "Yes. They have so far."

32. DR. BRIAN

BLUE RIDGE PARKWAY

℞ Doctor Brian blinked his eyes. He'd fallen asleep again. He looked out the window to the distant trees. Afternoon, he guessed. He shook his right arm. The plastic bracelets were annoying. He had a white one with his name, a red one for his allergy to adhesive tape, and the yellow one for fall risk. He'd already spent more than a couple of days and was more than ready to leave, AMA if necessary.

The phone rang. "Hello, Doctor Brian here," he answered.

"Really? This is Doctor Penny, and I've told them that you are not a doctor, not an M.D., not a Ph.D., not any kind of doctor, so you can stop that foolish doctor stuff." Only his daughter talked to him like that. He pretended she hadn't said it.

"I'm ready to leave. They've taken so much blood and run so many tests, if they haven't found anything yet, they're not going to. I'm out of here. I have more important things to do."

He thought about the global pandemic Jake had told him about. They required experienced people, not patients filling beds for cover-your-ass diagnostic tests.

She spoke rapidly, "Look, my clinic is pretty busy today, so this is going to be a short call. First, you're not leaving. You're scheduled for another test."

Talking to Penny was exhausting. She never listened. He was too tired to fight, and after twenty years apart, he didn't want her to leave again. "OK, one more day, but no more CTs. I get claustrophobic when they strap me down like that. They already did it twice. That's enough."

She sighed. "They had to check for cerebral hemorrhages. You're supposed to be smart. You know that. You had two head injuries. Fortunately, your brain is fine." She added in a whisper, "Or as good as it has ever been."

That was good to hear. The nurses wouldn't tell him anything, and the doctors...well the doctors were rare and rushed. "What is planned for today?"

"Cardiac Angiogram. They suspect vasovagal syncope or ischemic heart disease from atherosclerosis."

That was terrible. "I don't want heart surgery, no pacemakers."

"Listen, Mr. Macalester, it's been twenty years, but you haven't changed. You're still the arrogant pain-in-the-ass that drove mom—first to drink, and then to leave."

He shouted, "I didn't make her drink! And after she almost killed you driving drunk, why didn't you stay with me? Why go with *her*?"

"I'm not having this discussion. Get your angiogram and I'll talk to you tomorrow. I told you. Patients waiting."

"Well, can you tell them to stop drugging me?"

She said, "*Au revoir.*" And his phone stopped counting the seconds. 05:47.

He collapsed into the bed, imagining about the welcome he'd receive from the CDC when he offered his services.

He just needed to get out and drive to Atlanta.

———

Soon enough two men with Transport Department badges were rolling Doctor Brian down the hall. They were nice enough to raise the rails and not strap him in, but he didn't think they knew anything important, so he just rehearsed his interview with CDC.

"Yes, over thirty years of experience."

"Of course, both for clinical trials and full-scale production."

The first thing he noticed was that the cath lab was cold. He was sure he'd turn blue and be shivering in minutes. It didn't help that he was tired and stressed and drugged. He repeated his commitment to check out in this morning.

The Transport Department transferred him to a high-tech lounge chair. They wheeled the gurney out.

A nurse came in to explain the procedure. He knew the general idea, so he didn't listen except when she promised him some warm blankets. The cardiologist would insert a catheter into his femoral artery and thread it through to his heart, and he would be on his way.

Once he knew the blankets were coming, he calmed down. They attached him to monitors, inserted an IV, and buckled some safety straps. Happily, his arms were free and the straps weren't too tight. It got real when she shaved a patch on his groin.

The machine looked a lot like one of those planetarium projectors that turned every which way. He was in the belly of something from a sci-fi film.

When she finished shaving, he got nervous. He thought about this thin tube entering his crotch and somehow traveling to his heart. Suddenly this seemed like a bad idea.

The doctor came in wearing a large lead apron. She looked so young. Brian blurted out, "Have you done this before? How old are you?"

The young lady, looking even younger than Penny, just laughed. "I've done this hundreds of times and have never lost a patient in the chair. Just chill. Chill…that's cath lab humor."

He looked at her more closely. She had his Macalester cheeks. There might be blonde hair under her cap. He just wished that Penny was here. Heck, anyone. He'd even be happy to see that chatty salesman from the boat, Jake. But Penny was on Matu Kiva, Jake was probably in Africa, and Darlene…Darlene had visited less than a week ago. Who knew where she was now. He didn't think he wanted to see her anyway. It would be such irony if he died before the crazy drunk did.

The doctor threaded the catheter.

"Stay still." There was silence for a few moments, then she grunted. "Hmm. When you were a tiny fetus, your femoral artery decided to go differently from most people. I'm going to pull back and try another path."

Now that it was happening and he couldn't feel anything, he relaxed. He even tried a joke, "So no GPS?"

She laughed. That lightened his mood. "We just wander around like a drunk in the night. We always find our way home."

He didn't like the drunk reference, but he smiled. The doctor was sweating. The nurse came over and wiped her brow. He thought how doctors were among the last manual laborers. Doctors and dentists.

Farming, manufacturing, construction, even most food preparation…all automated. Anyone who could sit in front of a computer console could do it. But here was this doctor, cardiac specialist, more than a dozen years of training, and she was sweating from physical effort. Doctors and athletes. Strange.

Once she reached his heart, the planetarium projector spun and spun, taking pictures from all angles. And then it was all over.

It seemed anti-climactic. The nurse unhooked him, and the Transport Department returned him to his room, where a welcome supper was waiting.

———

The next morning, bright sun and something smelling better than hospital food woke him. Barbeque, but not sweet, more like sour, tangy. He opened his eyes and there was Jake.

"I thought you were in Africa or India or someplace far away."

Jake laughed. I know it's early, but I couldn't let you escape North Carolina without sampling some Lexington barbeque—pulled pork at its best."

He placed a bun stacked high with savory meat and slaw in front of Brian along with a bottle of shocking red soda.

Brian took a big bite. After all the hospital food, the flavors exploded in his mouth.

"Good isn't it. None of that tomato-sweet Texas stuff. Vinegar and mustard, barbeque as God intended it."

Brian took another chomp. "But what's in the bottle?"

"Another local delicacy, Cheerwine. A bit sweet, but goes perfectly with the local barbeque."

Brian settled in to enjoy his early lunch, knowing Jake would have a lot to say, as usual.

"I was in the neighborhood. I told you that business was hot. My customers in Maputo wanted fast delivery, so they just ordered over the phone to save time. I came back to the U.S.

instead. Business is booming here too. Lots of orders in the big cities, and even orders from small places like Roswell, New Mexico. Roswell, aliens visited us, New Mexico. Even they are buying sequencers. I'm going to be so rich!"

Brian interrupted him, otherwise he'd just go on and on. "Why are you in Charlotte?"

"Just thought I'd visit you. Bring you some authentic southern cooking. Believe me, I know hospital food can kill you. True around the world you know."

This went on for another fifteen-twenty minutes. Brian couldn't get a word in, and besides Jake never answered questions any way. He told his stories. Brian ate his sharp, sour sandwich. Jake was right about the Cheerwine. It all tasted so good, and he felt so good, he doubled his resolve to leave.

He thought he'd ask Jake to drive him to the airport for the short hop to Atlanta, but Jake disappeared before he could get the conversation around to it.

It was 11:00. Penny had been calling every day. She wouldn't call for a couple of hours and he wanted to leave before the call. He buzzed for the nurse.

33. ARIQ

ROSWELL & SLAUGHTER CANYON, NEW MEXICO

It had been a couple of weeks since the planning commission fiasco, when Ariq stopped at the 3D to pick up a morning treat for the staff. Dee Fuentes, owner and planning commission member, greeted him in a pink apron emblazoned with the likeness of her face, braids, and embroidered blouse. "Morning doctor! Today's special is sage-scented shortbread."

"I guessed as much. The shop smells like the morning desert."

Dee laughed, "You get it! That's the grand marketing plan of Desert Dessert Delights. Each time you visit the desert, you think of us."

"Works for me. Four dozen please."

She passed his order to the young man behind the counter. As the pink boxes of cookies stacked up, he thought that four dozen seemed like a lot, but they smelled so good and it didn't hurt to maintain good relations with the town, and specially the planning commission. The model of E-Ro city sat on his kitchen table reminding him each day that PopulistHealth owned a lot of land east of town.

Everything at 3D tasted just fabulous. Dee specialized in recipes using local plants. He'd never seen any 3D sweets go stale. If the staff was full, they could always share the local treats with out-of-state patients.

Dee handed him his stack of pink boxes, "Have you gotten that outbreak thing under control?"

He remembered she was worried about the government bombing Roswell. "We're making progress. You can rest easy. The big cities have far more cases than we do. Roswell will stay under the radar."

She wiped her hands on her apron leaving flour tracks, then grabbed his shoulders. "*Gracias a díos.*"

Both Lachy and Chucky grabbed a couple of cookies each before the meeting started. He hoped that two surgeons in attendance was a good sign. Nizhoni was also smiling and in high spirits.

When she saw the pink boxes, she picked one up and played the good hostess, passing shortbread around the nearby nurses' station.

Martina didn't seem to have received the happy memo, looking as dour as ever. She stood near Lachlan. Minneapolis had called again about the bats, and he still suspected this odd couple of something.

As much as he hated it, the group had established a pattern to open with the mortality report. He didn't hate the report itself, he just hated that people were dying in his hospital and he couldn't do anything about it.

With each morning's mortality report, he again felt bad that his hemophobia had caused him drop out of med school. His fear of blood, people cut open, wounds and needles, were nothing compared to death.

Death. Death reminded him that modern medicine was just the current version of myth and superstition. A hundred years from now doctors would look back on today's medicine and laugh. Science helped in the long run. He mused that scientists didn't have to watch people die.

When he dropped out of med school, эмɘɘ chided him. "Every time someone dies you're going to regret this. Whenever death wins, it's on you."

In his mind, she went on and on, never stopping.

The mortality report started badly. One more patient had died. Dr. Charles handed him the paperwork. It was his penance to contact the family. He looked quickly to check if it was Julia's father. It was not. It also wasn't the young rock climber Hannah.

Carl Elleich…Carl Elleich had died. Ariq recalled him dosing himself with morphine. He tried to think that his pain had now ended. But to tell his family, "He was in pain, but now it's over," sounded just cold and heartless. His warrior ancestors might have been able to do this, but it aggrieved him deeply.

He quickly calculated, four dead, two in comas, and six more just ill. An even dozen was good news. The containment efforts—gloves, masks, isolation—must be working. No new cases in almost a week.

Now the two surgeons looked to Nizhoni. Lachy smiled, "To honor the work of our dedicated nursing staff, we've asked Joni to continue the report. Joni paused and took a bite of a cookie. Ariq thought this must be something good, for all the drama.

"Last night Arthur Whitey woke up. His fever broke. He is showing signs of recovery. A preliminary neurological examination indicated no residual deficits after over a week in a coma."

Everyone cheered. Not only those in the meeting, but also the people gathered around the nurses' station eating cookies.

Ariq hugged Joni, and Chucky, and Lachy, and even Martina, though the middle-aged accountant seemed uncomfortable. He made a mental note not to do that again. He hugged some others. There was lots of hugging and maybe a little unprofessional air kissing.

Ariq waited for everyone to calm down. "Do we think that the Milwaukee Protocol for rabies helped? This man was a veterinarian and had up-to-date pre-exposure prophylaxis. Do we think that saved him?"

Even though no one specialized in infectious diseases, everyone, even Martina, had been reading up. Even the nurses seemed to be considering his question.

He added, "We haven't heard from the CDC. Do we think this unknown disease is related to rabies?"

Dr. Charles, the senior person, spoke first. "We can think whatever we like. I'd recommend, recommend strongly, that we don't say anything to the CDC. We're required to inform them about deaths. But beyond that, getting them involved rarely helps."

Martina asked, "If the Milwaukee Protocol helped, does that implicate rabies? Couldn't that treatment, which has no known mechanism, work on something else?"

He thought for a moment and agreed, "Good point. The Milwaukee Protocol is closer to folk medicine than science. At this point we're happy for any recovery regardless of the source, but we can't draw any conclusions."

He thought, if Arthur recuperated from a folk treatment, what about Hannah? Had Lily's stew, another traditional therapy, helped? Was there hope?

With a general nodding of heads, that was the end of the discussion. Everyone returned to their regular activities. Ariq noticed the pink boxes were empty. He took those empty boxes as a challenge. He thought about getting six dozen cookies next time.

———

He wondered about Hannah. She wasn't on the mortality list, nor on what he now thought of as the miracle cure list. He walked to the Area 51 Annex.

Hannah had not deteriorated. He took that as a good sign. He regretted that Lily hadn't been able to send more supplies. Hannah's treatment had exhausted all the stew.

He entered Hannah's room. With the desert in bloom, someone had taken it upon themselves to provide fresh flowers. The blue and red morning glories spilled out of two vases, one on each side of her bed.

The two vases were something of a trademark at the clinic. If a patient had flowers, they shouldn't need to roll over to see them. The volunteer staff maintained a large collection of abandoned vases for this purpose.

Ariq visited her every day. At first, he'd felt awkward, but now it felt right to sit at her bedside and talk to her. While he spoke, he patted her muscular shoulders, rubbed her hands, and wiped the sweat from her cheeks and brows. It wasn't scientific, but he thought she was sweating less.

"We all wish you well and want you to recover."

"You are looking better."

"We are planning a party for when you feel well."

Thus, he talked to Hannah as Lily had instructed. He imagined

Hannah getting up and walking out of her room. He imagined Lily walking into the room, smiling.

Эмээ would have been proud of him, but his internal scientist just laughed. Each day he visited Hannah, эмээ's memory grew stronger. Unfortunately, her scorn for not completing med school also gained strength.

———

After the close call on that first night, the new plan was to get an ordinary backcountry permit for Rattlesnake Canyon and take advantage of the back-country camping rules.

Campsites must be located at least 100 feet off established trails, 300 feet from any water source or cave entrance and a half mile or 2,600 feet from any road or parking lot.

This suited them just fine. They established a campsite out of sight and beyond the reach of regular ranger patrols. After a fun cookout, they set out to hike the five miles to Slaughter Canyon. Having all grown up here, there was no chance of getting lost, even in the dark of night. Ariq made sure that the students wore snake gaiters or high boots.

On the fourth night, about half way to Slaughter Canyon, they heard a noise to the left, and a couple of noises to the right. They turned off their lights, so their eyes could adjust. Everyone was quiet.

Ariq pointed to the left. There was a black bear. Following their training, they all stood tall and bunched up in a group to appear as big as possible, and made a lot of noise to discourage approach. The bear kept coming toward them.

Everyone went franticly through their packs, but no one turned up any bear spray. Bear spray was 98% effective, but only if you had some. They expected the bear to avoid them. Something was wrong.

They loudly sang, *The other day, I met a bear, Out in the woods, away out there*, with as many verses as they could remember. Slowly they moved left and right, trying to move out of the bear's path. Nothing seemed to work. Sofia and Jessenia turned on their lights and scanned the woods for an escape path. Sofia yelped, and Jessenia pointed to the right.

Two bear cubs. Everyone realized their inadvertent mistake. They'd broken rule number one: never get between a mother and her cubs. The group moved perpendicular to the line between mother and cubs. The mother kept advancing toward her babies.

Once the group was out of danger, Ariq located a couple of bear spray canisters in a separate pocket of the emergency pack. Now they were out of danger and armed.

They posted a sentry with a cell phone and bear spray. Since their cars were far away, their presence was small. The one time a ranger patrolled the area, they were virtually invisible.

Scientifically, the data was exciting. The first night, the one the ranger interrupted them, they found three bats with traces of virus out of 34. By the second night, the total was eleven out of 44. On the third night, the data showed thirty-three out of 47. Clearly the virus was infectious and spreading, spreading fast.

The real excitement of that previous night, and the thing that had everyone in high spirits tonight, was that when they got back to the lab, their testing showed that two bats exhibited immunity. Sequencing found mere traces of viral DNA. The virus had infected these bats, but they were fighting off the infection. The bats' immune systems were working on the virus, but how fast? Tonight's data would give a hint. Would there be six or sixteen immune tonight?

They did one extra round of collection just to be sure. They trapped and biopsied 54 bats before they started the hike back to their campground.

34. HALID

BEIRA, MOZAMBIQUE

By the time they reached Beira, Halid never wanted to see another fish. Counting fish had been so boring, and his eyes felt permanently crossed from peering through the thick glass of the big tank. They'd had some kind of fresh sea fish every night with their dinner, different types that the crew discussed as if the fishes were gourmet selections fit to serve a king. To Halid, after the first couple days, they just all tasted like fish.

He recalled the little antelope Bodie and his crew had caught so many days ago with great fondness. One of the first things he planned to find in Beira was some fresh greens for steaming with a little dried meat. His mouth watered just thinking about it.

Others seemed to be feeling the same way, for as Beira town came into sight, a number of the Luambe villagers cheered. Halid lifted Muluzi up and sat him on his shoulders so the little boy could see, too. He'd been frustrated much of the trip by the railing of the boat being above his head. He'd found a peek hole or two where the anchor chain or other gear went through the railing, and there was a short mast pole Mu could climb to look out. He kept getting in the way, but the crew had been quite patient with him.

Halid had expected a town the size of Nacala, but Beira was huge. In the distance, he could see tall buildings, taller than trees. There were few green or open spaces amongst the concrete. The city seemed to hum, the sound reaching all the way to the docks like an undertone of drum and insect music. The villagers stared, just as they had stared at their first sunrise over the ocean.

The sunrise stunned all of the villagers. Most of them still stopped what they were doing to watch each day when the sun came up. The golden ball edged over the line of deep gray-blue water, at first the merest glimmer of light, then sunrays sprang into the sky and the globe became visible, gradually rounding as it seemed to float up to the sky. The water was endless, the blue consuming all the other light. Sometimes clouds puffed around or streaked the sky, but mostly it was the impossibly huge sun, sea, and sky, with nothing to block their view.

On the other hand, Halid, and others he talked to, missed the silhouettes of hills, rocks, trees. While the colors varied, and the weather, there was a sameness to the kilometers of water that made his soul ache for the sound of wind through the grass, the creak of a tree branch, and birds whirring and chirping.

Beira was not that, either.

———

Dende moved up beside Halid at the railing, his arms full of village supplies. The young man set the gear down and went below to the galley to help Jojeza with another load. Halid had been talking to him. He missed his wife, but felt no particular urge to return to Luambe village. He had chosen to go to Maputo mostly to help the others who wanted to go—and because Nga had helped heal his wounds and he felt he "owed" her.

"I am sure you have no obligation to Nga, or to me. It is our job."

Dende shrugged.

"So, you are thinking you will stay in Maputo?"

Dende met Halid's eyes. His mouth puckered and he shook his head. "Captain Tola has offered me a place here. When they return to Nacala, one of the crew will be leaving for college. They said I might take his place, if I like."

Halid shook his head. "You enjoy this boat, all these fish?"

Dende shrugged again. "The fish are okay. I like working with the crew. The *Sun Fish* is a tiny village; I would like it to be my village, since they seem to want me to stay."

"Well, good for you," Halid said. "What about Roberto?"

"He's going on to Maputo with you." Dende looked away. Had Dende and his friend had a fight? They hadn't been seen together much lately. At first their shared misery of lost wives had seemed to bond them, then later Halid thought perhaps it had gotten in the way of their old friendship. Now they barely spoke to one another.

"Good, then," Halid said. "Thank you for your help, and I'm glad you've found a place."

Dende nodded, turned, and walked away. That was all the good-bye that happened between them. Halid frowned as he turned back to look at the other villagers, many of whom were staring at the scrubby trees that grew in the swamp area bordering one side of the port. Then the *Sun Fish* bumped against the dock, the Beira tugboat moved away, and the dock workers raised a short ramp to the side of the *Sun Fish*. Halid picked up several bundles, glancing around for Bill, who was going to guide them to where the *Arcturus* had docked.

Hoping there would be time to get a little shopping done, Halid stepped onto the docks of Beira with his villagers. Mezi and her children, Kimi and her baby, Jojeza, Tonan and his wife, Miss Anderson, the others: all of them seemed delighted to step onto the relative stability of the dock. Nga looked up from talking to Teleza and smiled at him.

Bill showed up with a small hand truck. Halid helped him load the heavier sacks of supplies and people's gear onto it, then took turns pushing it up the slightly rocking dock toward solid ground.

"Do you think there is time for us to get a bit of shopping done? We could use some fresh vegetables and fruit, milk for the children."

"I'm pretty sure the Greenleaf people will have taken care of that, but you would have to ask them about shopping," Bill said. The first mate had been kind to the villagers throughout the trip, but now Halid imagined the man was freeing himself of a burden as he turned them over to Ms. Cora Davis, liaison for the *Arcturus*.

"Hello," she said, holding out a hand for Halid to shake. He did so, introducing himself and Nga. "How many people do you bring?" the woman asked. Halid thought her red and white head wrap clashed with the bright orange and turquoise of her robes, but her smile was nice.

"Twenty-three now, and six children."

Cora nodded. "Good, and do you have food or shelter or clothing for yourselves or to share?"

Halid nodded. "But I was hoping we could shop for some fresh fruit, greens, milk. Mostly we have dried foods."

Cora smiled. "That is excellent. We need all the food we can get. I believe Captain da Cunha plans to depart early in the morning. That will give some time to run to one of the markets today, but you will need a guide. Beira is very confusing."

"Good. That would be very good. We also have some extra clothing, but not much. And no shelters."

"All right, we will arrange some tarps for you, since you will need to camp out on the stern deck; there is temporary room in the passageways if it is very stormy, but good weather is predicted for the next week so we should not have that problem."

"We are used to sleeping outdoors," Halid said. Were some of the refugees so pampered they required indoor cabins? "Will we have access to the galley?"

"There is a schedule being prepared so each group has time to cook and eat. We ask you remain flexible about the hours, but it will be fair."

Halid blinked. Apparently, the other refugees complained about everything; Cora seemed to be pre-empting any issues the Luambe villagers might bring.

"Should you be called 'Halid's group'?"

"Luambe village," Halid said.

"Have you any sickness among you?"

"No, just some wounds from a fight."

Cora Davis scowled at this. "There is no fighting aboard this ship. Captain will put you off in a rowboat."

"We did not choose the fight, we simply defended," Halid answered. "We just want to keep to ourselves and have safe passage to Maputo."

She nodded, making notes on the form on her clipboard.

Halid was suddenly glad all the young men with spears had stayed in Nacala. They'd help take back Luambe village. They would not be welcome here.

Shopping in Beira turned out to be a big project. None of the farmers' markets were close to the docks. Cora assigned a young man named Allon to guide them through the maze of streets to the western edge of the city.

Botte, of all people, had volunteered to come with Halid. The three of them walked past a sort of village within the city, made up of huts built from stucco mud or stone or wood walls, all with corrugated tin roofs. People living there eyed them. Strangers, go away, they seemed to say.

Halid saw several instances of sickness, where people were lined up on cots or blankets on the ground. Workers wore face masks, moving among the unresponsive patients. A few seemed to have IVs with what looked like clear solution feeding through. Glucose, maybe? Halid did not dare move closer to find out.

Allon crossed the road whenever they came to one of these impromptu clinics. He turned down another street when they approached an especially big group with what Halid estimated to be several hundred sick people. He wished he had a face mask, and one for Allon and even for Botte.

They made their way to a market, finally. Hundreds of booths made of tarps and scarves, some few with corrugated tin roofs, others made of old boards, protected the farmers' offerings from the sun. Botte was more help than Halid had expected, choosing the best of the greens, some nice papaya, some gourds that could be split open and steamed, in case they didn't have an oven for baking.

Halid spent freely on the food, but was more cautious when it came to the blanket Botte wanted.

"It's not for me, Halid," Botte finally said, a grim expression on his face. "It's for Miss Anderson. She has been shivering every night. I am sure it will be no warmer on this boat than it was on the last one."

Halid looked carefully at Botte's face, searching for untruth, but the man seemed genuinely concerned about the teacher.

"Kimi and her baby could use one, too," Halid said. "I think the wool is heavy to carry, but it is the warmest and strongest."

Botte nodded, turned to the small stack of woven wool and picked out two. Halid paid for them. Half the money Nga had given him was now gone.

"Is there milk anywhere?" he asked Allon.

The man nodded. "Later," he said, in strongly accented Portuguese. "Later we get milk. On the way back."

They were puffing and tired by the time the *Arcturus* came into their sights again. Once aboard, Allon handed the several sacks he had carried to Halid, who took them to where Jojeza had erected a lean-to made of a tarp and a portion of the railing. She grinned at Halid.

"It's dry, at least."

He nodded. "Good. Is there a refrigerator for the milk?" It had been interesting learning what others did about fresh milk for the children. In the village little ones had nursed until they were two, then if milk was wanted, they simply milked one of the village goats. Here, that was not possible. Halid could see why the Linds had loved their refrigerator, even though their old generator was a constant problem. Had been.

Jojeza showed him the "cool room" where the vegetables and fruits went. Each group seemed to have its own area marked off. There was also an "all groups" section, where Halid deposited one sack of greens and some of the papaya. He recognized a village sack of rice and one other, that had come all the way from Luambe.

Then he went and found Nga and tried to give her back the rest of the money, but she would not take it. "You should keep it, who knows what will happen next?"

He thought about that only a moment before nodding and tying it into one of the little sacks Mezi had made from robe scraps. He stuffed the sack into his jeans pocket.

Nga sighed. "Now I need to find out what we are to do about laundry," she said. "We're out of clean diapers again."

"Who do we talk to? Ms. Cora?"

Nga nodded. "Yes. We're not to bother the crew. I tried speaking to some of the other villagers, but we didn't seem to have any language in common." She shrugged. "Just as well, they seemed unfriendly."

"Worried, most like."

"I suppose."

Strain etched her face. He gauged she had lost about five kilos since the start of the trip. Had she been eating, or only worrying?

"I just hope no one gets sick. It's almost another week to Maputo."

35. LILY

KATHERINE & MATARANKA, AUSTRALIA

As they drove, Lily could see the reception on her phone getting better. She checked the app that showed what time it was in Roswell, New Mexico. It was 1:30 in the morning for Ariq. With a sigh, she turned off the phone and put it away.

Dr. Darnell glanced at her with an eyebrow raised.

"I have a friend in the United States. A bat friend. But it's the middle of the night there."

"You could send an e-mail."

"I just got this phone, I don't know how to use it for e-mail. Anyhow, that's my excuse to go to the Casuarina Coffee House and Internet Café, to see my friend Obrey. Who's in the hospital, now." She bit her lip.

The scientist's lip curved in a half-smile as he asked, "Is Obrey a bat friend also?"

"No, just a friend." She blinked and realized he was more than "just" a friend. "Maybe almost a boyfriend."

"Ah," he said. "Where's this bat friend, in America?"

"Ariq is in New Mexico, near the Carlsbad Cavern bats."

"Really. Hm. That's where my crew and I are going to go next. CDC wants me to sample those bats. They've been done many times before, but not recently."

"I think Ariq has done it. He described taking samples for this project some of his students are working on."

"He's a professor?"

"No. He runs a hospital."

"Interesting."

———

They stopped at Lily's new house on the way into town, intending a brief pause in their journey to the hospital. But there was a big group of people talking and cooking around the fire pit, and K—'s

238

hut was open, with lights shining inside. Lily realized they were honoring she who had died.

"It's kind of like a wake," she murmured to Dr. Darnell. "The woman who died recently, whose name we do not say aloud, she lived here. So they honor and celebrate her here. She has gone back to the dreamtime, it is a good thing. But to say her name is to try and pull her back, to keep her here in this time. That is not a good thing." He nodded his understanding.

She introduced him to the group. "He is studying medicine and native contributions," which wasn't exactly what he was doing, but it was what they would understand and accept. They were silent, a few nods or other acknowledgments.

Incongruously, he bowed to the group. Pearl laughed and Minka took his hand and led him to one of the fallen tree benches, conversation rising up around him again, while Lily pulled Pearl aside.

"Olivia and Obrey are in hospital."

Pearl blinked. "I did not know that. I need to get herbs, to go to them."

"Yes, and I do, too. I have a few supplies here, but I was thinking, she would not want hers to go to waste…?" She nodded toward Kalinda's hut.

Pearl nodded. "No, she would not. I will get some things, we can make stew here, then eat whatever food's ready, then go to the hospital." She rubbed her belly. "Have not had anything since yesterday."

"Oh! I have some food I can share, and I'll get my new pot. Good time to start curing it," she said.

Pearl headed off to what had been Kalinda's hut, and Lily went to her own. She took all her spare clothes and crammed them into her backpack so she could wash them back in Mataranka later. Then she used an old dilly bag to carry all the herbs she had that would go into the stew. She needed to keep some aside for the sick soldier, Private Glenn. If she could get stew to Obrey tonight and tomorrow first thing, he would begin to heal, she was certain of it.

She didn't realize until she walked back to the fire pit that she had been fitting her healing plans around getting back to the bats and finishing the job with Dr. Darnell. Well. She "owed" him for the ride. If he'd been native, she wouldn't have worried about it; everything was shared, everything went around in a circle, through the dreamtime, and back. But the *balanda* did not think that way.

———

Lily looked up June's number and asked for Pana. "Oh, we were just leaving to go visit Olivia," June said.

"All right, we'll meet you at the hospital," Lily said. "We have lots of Pearl's stew to give out."

"Good," June said. "Pana is so worried."

"Tell her I'll see her soon." She pressed the "end" button.

Beside Lily, Pearl nodded her head, smiling. "Good. She needs to see her mama."

"Olivia and Obrey are sick, but I need to go back to Mataranka with Dr. Darnell tomorrow. Maybe Pana could stay with you?"

"Or June. We find out."

"Okay."

They had crammed their pots and containers of stew into a couple old plastic shopping bags. The herbal scent filled the cab of Dr. Darnell's jeep.

"Do you like the baked yams, Dr. Darnell?" Pearl asked.

"The yams were good. The grubs were a lot tastier than I imagined they'd be," he kind of shuddered when he mentioned the witchetty grubs.

"Rare delicacy," Pearl said, laughing. "Usually only found in very hot desert. Friend of friend bring them, along with funeral stick."

"The stick will be carved and placed to honor our friend," Lily explained.

Pearl laughed. "You teach him alla time things?"

Lily smiled and shook her head. "Just a little," she said.

Pearl laughed.

Then they turned into the driveway of Katherine District Hospital, and she stopped laughing. There were ambulances all over, and many cars blocking the driveways and parking lot.

"I did not know we even have so many ambulances in the whole district," Lily said. She glanced at Dr. Darnell. "Are you sure you want to come in with us?"

He nodded. "I brought a mask, just in case," he said.

They managed to park in the dirt outside the regular parking lot. Lily and Pearl gathered their containers of stew, spoons, and leaves, and headed inside.

Nurses and doctors rushed around, pushing rolling beds with patients in them, or helping others to sit down in the open waiting room.

Lily nodded to the friendly nurse and asked where Olivia and Obrey were.

"I really can't let you back there, today," she said.

"Are they under the tents already?"

The nurse looked at a list on a clipboard on the counter in front of her. "No, but they aren't doing well, and there are so very many– " then she was called to assist someone with a lady who had fallen down.

Lily cleared her throat and turned the clipboard to face them. Three pairs of eyes rapidly scanned the list. "Obrey's in 304," Lily said.

"Olivia Waters in 308," Dr. Darnell said.

They walked down the hall and turned left into the 300's corridor. Nobody paid any attention to them in the chaos.

Lily glanced in the door of room 304. Obrey was sitting up, drinking some water from a plastic straw in a plastic cup. He set it back down on the over-bed tray. She stepped into the room and he looked up, waved at her, put a finger over his lips. There was another bed in the room with him, with someone asleep on it. There was no space for a chair; even the bedside table had been pushed out into the hall. Lily set her things on the floor.

"So I go away for a day, and you fall down?" she said softly.

His smile was fragile, but it was a smile. "I had to have some way to get you back here," he whispered.

She took out a bowl and poured some of the still-warm stew into it, from one of Kalinda's large containers she and Pearl had used. She motioned feeding it to him, but he took the bowl and spoon from her hand.

"Go see to your aunt," he whispered. Lily nodded. She left her things; Pearl would already have stew for Olivia.

She made her way to room 308. There was only one bed in the room, surrounded by Pana, Pearl, and Dr. Darnell, who stepped aside when he saw her. He had his mask over his mouth and nose, but she could see his eyes were tight, his forehead frowned.

When he moved, she saw her aunt. She stopped and stared. Pana's little hand was grasping her mother's tightly, but there was no answering pressure from Olivia. Her aunt looked completely wasted away, the bones of her skull standing out as if she had already died.

"She's so hot," Pana said.

Pearl leaned forward with a spoonful of stew. "Open your mouth, Olivia," she said gently. Olivia's eyes popped open. She leaned her head forward, opened her mouth, and accepted the spoonful of stew. She chewed a little, swallowed with difficulty, but opened her mouth for another bite. Then she saw Lily.

Her eyes became very angry. "What are you doing here?" she yelled in a hoarse, shaky voice. "I told you to leave!"

It felt like a wave of hate from her aunt washed over Lily. "I am leaving, Aunt Olivia. I am gone."

Pearl would give her the stew. Lily would take care of Obrey.

She went back to 304. Obrey shook his head as she came in. "I could hear her all the way down here," he said. "I'm sorry."

"So am I," Lily said. "But Pearl will help her." She tried to find the good in it. "That means I get to help you," she said.

Obrey smiled his crooked smile. His smile turned to a scowl when she fed him the Billy Goat Plum leaves.

"Gah! I know what that is, that is so I want to get better and not have to taste those again!"

"That seems to be the general belief," Lily said, thinking of

Private Glenn's similar reaction. "June didn't make such an awful face."

He shook his head. "Maybe she's used to it."

Lily pinched his skin, felt beside his jaw. "You have fever, but not as bad as June's was."

"So maybe I'll get better?"

Lily nodded. She stroked his face, his neck, his shoulders with cool gentle fingers, as if pushing disease back, away from him.

"I'll try to come back tomorrow morning with more," she said.

"Don't bother. It's crazy here. I'm going to go to the Café and sleep in the back. Damon's still covering for me, but if he gets this too, I want to know right away."

"Okay," Lily said.

"In fact, if you can–" he broke off as someone came in the room.

Lily turned around. She introduced Dr. Darnell to Obrey.

"I'm not a physician doctor, I'm a science doctor," he clarified. "But I will say you look a lot better than Lily's Aunt Olivia."

Lily nodded her agreement. "He's thinking of leaving the hospital."

"Especially if Lily is going to come and give me stew," he said. "I don't know how this thing is infecting everyone, but I don't think being here is good. It's almost like being here is causing it."

"They still don't even know what it is," Lily said. "But June got it before anyone ever came to the hospital. She was one of the first."

"True."

"You can ride in the jeep with us, tonight," Lily said. "But tomorrow we have to go back to Mataranka. I will be gone all day, maybe more, so you are stuck at the Café."

Obrey nodded. He removed some pads and wires connected to his wrist and sat up. "Give me a minute to find my clothes and get dressed," he said. "But I think I can drive myself home."

"Is that a good idea?" Dr. Darnell wondered as he and Lily went out into the hall. Lily rubbed her cheeks. Her eyes were tired. In the few moments they stood there, a dozen people went past, sick and well, on their own two feet and not.

Obrey came out in his jeans and tee shirt, flip flops on his feet, his keys dangling from his finger. Pearl joined them with Pana.

"June and I will sit with her," Pearl said. The old woman looked Obrey up and down. "You going home already?"

"Might as well be ill where it's quiet," he said. "Lily plans to come back to treat me in the morning?"

Lily nodded. Pearl nodded.

The five of them pushed their way through the throng in the admitting area waiting room.

It was beginning to feel like the whole world was sick. The dry, relatively quiet air outside was a relief.

"Are you okay to drive, Obrey?"

"I have to. Don't want to leave my car here. You can't drive. It's just a few blocks, I'll be fine."

"I'll be by the Café to check on you in the morning. Call me if you need anything," Lily said.

The remaining four climbed into the jeep. "Where to?" Dr. Darnell asked.

———

The morning visit with Obrey was much easier than the visit to the hospital had been. Damon was wiping down the counter when Lily walked in, trailed by Dr. Darnell.

"Hey, Lily," Damon said.

"How is he?"

"Complaining that I'm doing everything wrong," Damon snickered. "So, I guess he's getting better."

Lily gave Obrey his morning dose of stew and sat next to him, watching him eat it.

Again, she touched his shoulder, his arm, his face, thinking healing thoughts, murmuring words of healing, of hope. He dutifully chewed the horrible two leaves and spat them out, then nodded at Dr. Darnell, and went back to his cot in the back.

"Better, but still tired," Lily judged.

"Yah. Heck of a thing," Damon said.

"Thank you for taking care of things for him," Lily said.

"He'd do for me," Damon said.

Lily gave him $A10 for a little computer time and bought herself and Dr. Darnell a couple of lattés. She wrote to Ariq what had been going on, then got off the computer.

"Back to Mataranka?"

Lily nodded. "Thank you so much, again, for driving."

"It was interesting," he said.

As the jeep headed back south, Lily thought through the last few days. Her life had suddenly become so eventful, she really missed the quiet meditation time she was used to on her own.

Pearl had planned to take Pana back to visit Olivia and deliver more stew that morning, but June called from the hospital to say they'd tented Olivia. No one could visit her now.

Lily had hugged Pana, unsure how much the younger girl's understandings were around dreamtime, and how much were around *balanda* ways. Her cousin seemed sad, but resigned.

"Auntie Pearl will take care of you," Pearl said. We will go and get your school clothes ready. School starts soon!"

Pana might have to start High School without her mother, but she would start it with Pearl's love and Lily's best wishes. And a little money from Lily's savings. Pearl would share everything she had, but it wasn't much. That was a way for Lily to help, too. She was fortunate she could sell her paintings.

Lily closed her eyes as the jeep went over a bump, then turned onto the highway back to Mataranka.

She hadn't realized she'd fallen asleep until her phone rang. She sat up and fumbled around for her phone.

"Hi, Ariq!"

"You have any more of that stew for me?"

"I can send more. But not for a few days," she said.

"I wish you could bring it to me."

"Mmm," Lily said. "Maybe I can work something out."

"Come to America. Help me with my bats. Give my patients stew!" There was laughter in his voice, but he also sounded serious.

"I'm thinking about it," she said. "I'm sure airfare costs more than all the money I have in the world."

"I'll buy your painting, the one with the pond thing in the middle and the red dots."

"I think that's not enough, though," she said.

"Six hundred fifty dollars U.S. goes a lot further than Australian dollars."

"Okay. I'll think about it. It's still a lot," and it would be 10% off the top for the Coop.

"Well, I'll think about offering more, then."

"I can find my way there, but I'm needed here, Ariq."

Ariq was silent for a moment, then he said, "How are your bats?"

"We'll probably finish with them today," she said. "Dr. Darnell said maybe they are leaving today or tomorrow. They are going to your place, the bats at Carlsbad. "

She glanced at the doctor. He gave her a quick smile and nod, then looked back at the road.

"You said your friend was better?"

"I plan to call and check on him later, but yes. He left the hospital. How are your patients?"

This time the silence on the other end lasted a lot longer. "Not so good," he said. "It's awfully hard to find a cure when you don't even have a diagnosis. The only thing that has remotely helped was the stew you sent, and maybe induced coma."

"I thought that was true here, too. I gave Obrey stew, and he is better. But Pearl gave my aunt the same thing, and she was worse today. They put her in the tent thing, no visitors. Last time they did that, the lady died."

"Well. Sorry to hear that. I hope your aunt gets better."

"Thank you, Ariq. I hope your patients improve." She tried to end on a happy note. "Have fun with the Carlsbad Caverns bats," she said.

"I will. And think about the painting and the airplane. I'm really desperate here."

"Yes. 'Bye."

She leaned her head back and thought about trying to sleep some more. She'd spent a big part of the night talking to Pana. If Olivia died, Lily and Pearl would be all she had. How could Lily go to the U.S.?

Was she always going to be torn between two places?

BAT CHAT

PLUS FREQUENTLY ASKED QUESTIONS

? *Are bats related to birds?*
Bats and birds are not related. Powered flight is an example of convergent evolution where unrelated life forms evolve similar adaptations to similar environments.

Flight evolved at least four times. Pterosaurs preceded bats and birds by 50 million years. The fossil record indicates the independence of the three large flyers. A single finger distinguishes pterosaur wings, while all bird fingers combined into the wing structure.

Bat have their fingers spread apart, the most detailed wing structure. Bat wings are so unique that their order name, Chiroptera, means hand wing.

The first evolution of flight? Insects, who preceded all the others by 150-200 million years.

https://justcallitresearch.wordpress.com/2015/10/01/evolution-of-flight-by-chiroptera-aka-bats/

https://justcallitresearch.wordpress.com/2015/10/05/bat-wings-chiroptera-o-science-biology-anatomy-evolution/

Kitty: Has anyone heard about a strange sickness, maybe rabies?

Syms Covington: Something is out there. Anyone think it has to do with bats?

Radar Rat: Here go again. Every time they can't explain something, they blame it on bats.

Nina de la Ciencia: Totally unfair

Morcego: Same here. People get sick. Bats Bats always bats

Canuck: Whatever it is, it killed my son. I don't think it's bats, they should look at everything

Batty: Something is happening We get more visitors to the bat exhibit every day Everyone is interested in bats

Radar Rat: We should all spread good stories about bats. Killing insects. Pollinating plants. Bats are at risk if the public panics. Post bat-positive stories.

36. ARIQ

ROSWELL ORTHOPEDIC CLINIC, NEW MEXICO

Ariq had put off calling Julia Whitey as long as he could. Her father had been regaining strength and clarity every day. Soon her father would be able to make the call himself. Ariq wondered why he'd been dreading the call. After all, her father was in recovery, so this should be a good news conversation. Should be easy.

On his morning gallop, he figured it out and committed to making the call before Arthur could do it himself. His trepidation went back to dropping out of med school. His pride wanted to believe that even without the certificate, he knew enough to understand the medicine.

He feared she was going to ask, "What was wrong with him? How did you save him?" Ariq didn't want to say, "I don't know." In all his years at ROC, he'd never had to do this. He'd always had answers.

When he arrived in the office, he summoned all his Mongol warrior courage and called. The phone rang. Someone answered, "M&M."

"Julia Whitey please."

"She's in a meeting. Can I take your name and have her call you back?"

He had been so prepared to talk to her, he didn't know what to say. "Oh...okay. I'll call back," and he hung up.

Feeling anxious about Julia, he suspiciously eyed Lachy and Martina walking by his office laughing. Lachlan's interest in accounting seemed odd. One of Martina's responsibilities was to counsel employees about retirement plans. Were they laughing about investment options? He doubted that.

They looked into his office. He met their stares. But then his phone rang. He looked down at the caller ID. It was a 612 number, Minneapolis. He assumed it was PopulistHealth, but it could be

249

anyone. When he looked back, Lachy and Martina had disappeared. Did they know he was going to receive this call? Were they waiting to see the phone ring?

He picked up and heard the annoying assistant. This was the third or fourth call. He looked for Martina again. Still gone. He should have spoken to her before this.

"Ariq? I trust it's okay to call you Ariq." He didn't feel very friendly, and this petty bureaucrat hadn't given his own name. Regardless, Ariq waited in silence.

The voice at the other end of the line continued, "We like to keep things informal here at PopulistHealth, keeping the lines of communication open." The voice paused for a breath, then rushed ahead as if he had memorized this for a high school speech class. "I took your suggestion. We like suggestions from the field. I called all the hospitals. Back to you now."

This did not sound good. Ariq waited for the bomb to drop.

"There are rumors of a big CDC announcement after the weekend. We want to be ready. What can you tell us, so we'll be prepared?"

Ariq's mind spun in circles. Had Martina called the CDC in addition to calling Minneapolis? Lachlan would never do something like that. Surgeons were too proud and independent to talk to the CDC. Somehow this seemed bigger. He hoped it was something bigger. Something that had nothing to do with his small hospital in Roswell, New Mexico.

He had told Dee from the planning commission that Roswell would be unnoticed. He hoped that his assurance was correct.

The caller droned on, "Skeletons in your closet? Something you've kept under your hat? Cats in your bag?"

Now Ariq was confused, but the hemorrhaging of clichés stopped, so he had to say something. "We're clean. You know everything."

That response, so patently false, felt safe. No one knew everything. If accepted, it was an implicit agreement to not have a substantive discussion—and it worked.

"Well, I'm glad we had this talk. I'll check you off on my

report."

What a relief. Maybe the calls had nothing to do with his management or Lachlan or Martina. Ariq was still suspicious of their whispering and laughing, but Minneapolis seemed concerned about a bigger picture.

No sooner had this call ended than the phone rang again. He almost didn't answer, but he recognized the caller ID.

"Hello Julia. I just tried to call you."

"I know. That's why I called back. Good news?"

He quickly reviewed how he was going to answer all her questions…brief answers…with confidence…and not opening the way to an in-depth discussion.

"Yes, your father is recovering and should be able to call you himself later today."

"That's great. I'll look forward to his call. Thanks for letting me know. Bye."

Ariq almost dropped the phone. With the anxiety of talking about her father out of the way, he recalled that Julia was a Washington lobbyist and plugged into the rumor mill. Before she had a chance to hang up, he quickly spoke, "Julia?"

"Yes?"

"Do you know anything about a big CDC announcement next week?"

In a condescending tone, she replied, "You know they're in Atlanta, right?"

Ariq hated when anyone talked down to him, so he pretended it was a joke. "Keeps them out of Beltway politics, doesn't it?"

"Yes, mostly yes." She paused. Her voice sounded almost cheery. Either she was still relieved that her father was recovering or she had some juicy piece of news to share.

"They're in Atlanta, but the World Health Organization is right here in Washington. There's going to be a joint announcement. Not only WHO and CDC, but also the ECDC - European Centre for Disease Prevention and Control."

"Do you think it has to do with the rumors about people dying of a rabies-like disease?"

"Where did you see that?"

Ariq regretted that he mentioned anything. Now he'd have to admit that the doctors didn't share much with him, that he got his news from social media. He felt like such an outsider. He couldn't think of a diversion, so he just said it: "**Bat Chat**."

She laughed. "**Bat Chat**? That's funny. Just between the two of us, and as thanks for saving my father, I think those bat nerds know something."

———

Ariq headed to the Chiropteran Research Center. On the way, he saw Martina.

"Martina, could you walk with me for a while?"

"Sure, Ariq. I heard about Hannah. I'm glad she's improving, but aren't you concerned that we're experimenting with superstition and magic?"

Her accusation hurt. He was too drained to be polite or politic. "If you have concerns about what I am doing here, you need to talk to me, not PopulistHealth in Minneapolis or the CDC. I'm still your boss. I will not put up with disloyalty or insubordination."

She walked next to him in silence. The silence of guilt?

He balled his fists. "There is a lot going on and I have no time for politics. If you intend to come to work next Monday, you must come clean. Now."

They were almost to the CRC, no one was around, the meditation garden was empty, so he continued. This was the moment to say it all, "I've seen you scheming with Lachlan."

There it was. He had put all his cards on the table.

She stopped and turned to face him. Her face softened like he'd never seen before. She took his hands. She looked years younger and she moved so close he was afraid she intended to kiss him. He leaned back.

"Ariq, you are a wonderful boss. For as much as you go on about Genghis Khan and warriors, I've never seen any ruthlessness in you. All of us love you very much."

Now it was his turn to be silent.

"I'm going back to the hospital and you should continue to the CRC. Have a good weekend. You'll understand soon."

With that she turned around and walked away. Ariq continued to the CRC, completely confused.

———

Sitting in the CRC, looking for a distraction from politics and medicine, he reviewed Jessenia's progress. After that fourth biopsy collection and the close call with the bears, he told them they had enough data for the science project. The seniors would be leaving for college in a few weeks, so packing and goodbyes put the science on hold.

Jessenia was only a junior, so she still spent a few hours a day preparing samples and running them through the sequencers. Thanks to Jake, they now had three sequencers, all dedicated to a high school science project. By brute force, they knew the sequences for their bat virus and the antibodies.

When the students weren't running sequences for Jessenia's project, sequencing runs for the Mexican Free-tail bats took up the slack. With these modern machines, the complete genome would be ready soon.

Ariq noticed Jessenia had been quiet and had run the same samples over and over.

"Jessenia? Stuck? Problem?"

She looked so small, a high school girl in torn jeans, an *Hecho en Mexico* t-shirt, her black hair in a ponytail, and sandals. Here was this girl who would have looked just right giving change for hamburgers or bagging groceries, standing among millions of dollars of high-tech equipment, examining screens, and adjusting parameters.

She checked that everything was running properly then turned to Ariq. "The first three days went so well. We saw the expected exponential increase in infections, and with the third samples a few bats developed immunity."

Ariq followed her experiment. Even with everything else happening, her work held his interest. "Yes, I recall. So now what?"

She looked like she might cry. "The last set of samples are all the same. *Every* bat is immune. Makes no sense. I've looked for contamination. I've reprocessed the samples. I've been very careful. Three times now, I get the same result. It seems like we sampled the same bat 54 times."

She tried to laugh. "Couldn't have done that. The bat's wing would be like Swiss cheese. The tiny thing would be dead."

That didn't sound right, but the beauty of high-school science, really any science, was that the expected results didn't matter. They only needed to collect good data, and not mess up. If they could find an explanation, a solid conclusion, that would be a plus, but it wasn't required.

"I agree," he said. "We expected a few more bats with immunity. The first few bats took days to develop immunity."

She finished his thought. "The immune system should work the same in the other bats. Immunity should continue to take a few days. The infection curve and the immunity curves should match, with immunity delayed by a few days."

"But that's not what you're seeing?"

"No."

"Don't worry. Let's call the science club together and I'm sure someone will have an idea."

She seemed to like that plan. Before he left, he could see her rapidly tapping on her phone to set up the meeting.

Happy she had calmed down, he still worried that their effort had been wasted. How could they have gotten such weird results?

37. DR. BRIAN

ATLANTA GA

R̲x̲ Brian's cardiologist came in before housekeeping cleared away the bootlegged Southern brunch. Brian rolled the bed table away as if to suggest the barbecue and Cheerwine belonged to someone else.

The doctor ignored the remains. Brian smiled at her. He suspected good news. She wasn't wearing scrubs. She wore white linen pants, and a short-sleeved silk blouse with a bright floral pattern that reminded him of Tahiti and Penny. He assumed this was a casual visit.

"Your angiogram yesterday was pretty good. Despite your obvious poor eating habits—" she waved her hand at the table.

"Not me. I don't eat like that. A friend of mine brought that. When in the south and all that."

The doctor responded with her mellow southern drawl, "I thought you were just passing through. Do you have friends in Charlotte?"

"Oh no. I think he lives in Geneva. He was just passing through also."

She furrowed her brow and gave a brief shake of her head, as if to show that she'd met crazy Yankees before. She let it pass. "Well. As I was saying. Your arteries are not perfect, but good enough for someone your age. Stents or an angioplasty are not indicated."

Brian sat up. "Great. I need to head to Atlanta today."

She held her hand in front of him in a not-so-fast gesture. He stopped as much because of the barrier her arm formed, as by the surprise to see such definition and development of her biceps. The show of strength reminded him of her previous effort with his misaligned arteries.

"I had heard that you were eager to leave. Today is my day off, but I came in personally to give you my recommendation."

She crossed her arms, flexing her biceps, "Three fainting episodes in a week. The most recent was caught on our monitor—ventricular tachycardia."

He knew where this was heading. In another of those close, but no Nobel prize drug investigations, he'd worked on a cardiac arrhythmia compound. Ultimately another company released Amiodarone for this indication.

Unfortunately, Amiodarone would not be a get-out-of-the-hospital pill. The first doses required close observation and hospitalization.

As if talking to herself, she continued, "You should really get some more tests: another EKG…an echo cardiogram…thallium study."

He sat up trying to look strong. "I really need to get to the CDC in Atlanta." He hoped mentioning the CDC might help his case.

She mused, "You probably have ventricular arrhythmias and need an Implantable Cardioverter Defibrillator."

He knew the implant operation would be even a bigger delay than the Amiodarone observation. Now he wondered if he should have suggested the drug.

Before he could say anything, she added, "With your clean arteries, you could delay if you promised to avoid high stress situations, and schedule an operation at a location closer to your home within 30 days."

Brian tried to disguise his happy surprise. He turned and let his legs dangle off the bed. "No problem. Thanks for your understanding and excellent care." He stood up grabbing the bed to hide his lightheadedness.

She didn't notice.

That night he was sleeping in a nice hotel in Atlanta and finally reunited with his suitcase.

———

The following morning, he took a cab to the Center for Disease Control. The campus looked like a large hospital, six and eight-story buildings, with lots of windows and parking spaces. The

Darwin's Paradox

architecture exhibited some curved facades, but mostly represented the governmental utilitarian school. The grounds looked well-tended, and there was no shortage of flag poles with American flags.

He had the driver tour the campus until he located the National Center for Emerging and Zoonotic Infectious Diseases. He paid the cab and walked into the reception area. He had checked LinkedIn, and had the name of an old friend who was now a deputy director. This was one of the benefits of age. His friends who had not retired had important positions.

He founds his friend's office on the directory and walked up to the reception desk. "I'm here to see Director Gereben." He gave Gereben a promotion, not that the guard noticed. The guard checked his identification, he signed in, and the guard issued a visitor's badge. He took the elevator to the sixth floor.

When he got off the elevator, he looked around trying to decipher the office-numbering pattern, but before he figured which way to turn, he spotted Dr. Gereben—evidently on the way to the restroom. He ran up to him, and reached out his hand, "Mark. Good to see you after so long."

The tall man adjusted his glasses and looked at the visitor badge. "Brian Macalester…. It's been a long time since Miller and Miller. How's your wife, and daughter, if I remember correctly?"

Not wanting to get into a lot of personal details, he said. "Daughter, that's right. She's a medical doctor now." He had to designate *medical* doctor, because at a research place like this most doctors were the Ph.D. variety.

"Nice. What brings you to CDC?"

Brian recalled Mark was always very businesslike. That's probably why he was a Deputy Director, and Brian was retired. "Actually, I was hoping to see you."

"Well, you're lucky to have found me. I'm leaving this evening for Geneva."

Brian guessed, "Big announcement at the World Health Organization?"

Mark continued walking, "Yes."

"Well that's why I'm here. I heard some rumors and thought you might need an experienced chemist."

They walked into the men's room. Mark looked around, and when he saw that they were alone, he stepped up to the center urinal and spoke quietly.

"I appreciate your offer, but you've been out of practice for a while. I remember the announcement of your retirement in M&M Medical Memos. It was a while ago."

Brian stepped up to a mini-stall two to the left. He lied, "I've kept up my reading. I still get the journals."

"Sorry to be short, but this is a very busy time and as I said, I have a plane to catch. Bottom line? From what I recall of your reputation at M&M, I don't think you'd be happy here."

The two men flushed in unison.

Mark seemed a bit embarrassed by his blunt pronouncement. Without looking at Brian, he added, "I suggest you go to Doctors with Helicopters. They have an office here in Atlanta and might have something…if you really want to get involved. I warn you this is a big shit-storm and you'd be advised to stay out of it."

There was nothing more to say. The men washed their hands. Brian stood in front of the dryer waving his hands, to give his friend time to exit the room and go wherever his important job would take him next.

———

The meeting at Doctors with Helicopters went better. People crowded the reception area. Most looked in their thirties and forties, young medical doctors. There was also a crowd in their twenties, athletic, smiling men and women. He listened to their chatter.

"I'm not a nurse, but I've been a Vet Tech for three years."

"I hear the big announcement will be early next week."

"I'm a certified EMT, but that's so boring. I'm not cut out to be an ambulance driver, I want to see some real action."

Adventure seekers. He did see a few who were his age. He filled out the forms on an old desktop computer and waited.

He noticed that the interviews were short. They seemed to last ten to fifteen minutes, but most everyone left with a smile and a big envelope.

When it was his turn, he entered a small office. Just a table and two chairs. Looked like an interrogation room from a low-budget cop show. She tapped her phone and looked up. "Mr. Macalester, welcome to Doctors with Helicopters. Please have a seat."

She swiped her screen for a couple of minutes. He assumed she was reading his information. "Chemist. Any experience with clinical trials?"

That was a surprise. Clinical trials? Did they already have approved investigational drugs? That's not what he expected. "Yes, as the chemist doing optimization, I interacted a lot with the people running the trials."

She smiled. "Nice to have someone with that experience. Most of the people we see are long on enthusiasm, but short on experience."

He sat a little taller. This was a much better interview than the bathroom at CDC.

"We have a perfect spot for you: Maputo. The only catch is we have really limited resources. You'd have to get there on your own. Our budget can't even afford coach tickets."

He didn't know where Maputo was, and he certainly didn't want to fly in coach. He'd be happy to buy his own ticket. "No problem."

He was going to ask where Maputo was when she stood up and handed him an envelope. "Get there as soon as you can. All the information you need is in here."

She reached out her hand to shake his and walked to the door. After the disappointing meetings at M&M and CDC, he was glad to be going, even if he didn't know where.

———

He went back to his hotel. It turned out that Maputo was in Mozambique, Africa. All he could recall was an old Bob Dylan song that he hadn't heard in forever, but now he couldn't get it out of his head. *"I like to spend some time in Mozambique."* He laughed to himself thinking, "Is that what wins a Nobel prize?

When he met with the hotel concierge to arrange flights, he began to wonder if this was such a good decision. He planned to spend a couple of days visiting Penny. It seemed like it was on the way. That was before he realized that nothing was on the way to Maputo.

The flight to Tahiti was fine. He could leave tomorrow afternoon and arrive in Tahiti at midnight local time. He'd fly first class and sleep. This was starting to look like fun.

He made a quick call to Penny and she even agreed to meet him in Papeete. But then he tried to book a flight to Mozambique…to spend some time in Maputo. That song came back again.

The concierge frowned. None of the web sites he used would book a flight to Maputo. It was a "You can't get there from here" sort of thing. After working at it for a couple of hours, he'd found he could leave Tahiti early in the morning and land in the morning in Japan. There was a dateline involved, so he wasn't sure of the day, but by that point he didn't care. There were still no direct flights to Maputo. His second ticket was to Johannesburg via Hong Kong. Once in Jo-burg a third ticket got him an hour flight to Maputo.

He purchased the tickets. He was committed.

The next morning before his fight he went shopping. Mosquito netting, bug spray, Cipro, SPF 50 clothing, water purification tablets, hiking shoes, another suitcase, extra underwear, extra phone charger, power convertors, electrical adaptors. He didn't know how long he'd be there, but felt he should be prepared.

He had a nice dinner on the plane and went to sleep in his comfortable bed in the sky thinking more about seeing Penny than what might happen when he finally arrived in Maputo. He hadn't even opened the Doctors with Helicopters envelope.

38. LILY

KATHERINE & MATARANKA, AUSTRALIA

Back at Mataranka, Lily found that the soldiers had gathered only a few more bats. Lily gave the sick soldier, Private Glenn, some stew and did the touching healing ritual. He looked much better today, almost as good as Obrey had. She had enough herbs left for one more helping of stew for him.

She helped Dr. Darnell most of the morning. When they took a break for lunch, she went down to the biggest pool and did her laundry. She enjoyed the quiet. Usually the pools at Mataranka were filled with tourists. In a way, the soldiers and Dr. Darnell had helped the bats, clearing all the *balanda* guests out of the area, at least for a while.

She bathed and put on one of the clean but still damp skirts and tops and washed her last set.

Obrey was healing; the soldier was healing.

Olivia was not. It was a puzzle. She could explain Obrey, because he was still enough of a traditional person he could touch the dreamtime, she was certain, and that might be what helped him. Olivia was so *balanda*, and so angry all the time, perhaps she could not. But if it was only the dreamtime that made the difference, why would the American soldier be getting better? Surely he didn't have a dreamtime connection? And K— had died, the most traditional of them all.

She sighed, listening to the breeze through the palm trees, the sound of the water falling into the pool.

She'd had a dream of teaching Pana about the bats, that they could create ritual, walk the songline and dance the bat dreaming together. But Olivia had brought that plan to a halt. Maybe the dream wouldn't die if Pana got to live with Auntie Pearl awhile.

If Lily went to America, she would not be able to share that time with Pana.

She thought about that awhile.

What if she brought Pana with her?

They wouldn't be here, in their country, but they would be near some bats. And away from Olivia.

But Pana was going to want to be with her mother, of course. That was a silly plan.

She sighed again.

———

Dr. Darnell and Lily finished taking the samples from the last batch of captured bats. Lily released the very last bat into the air with a sense of satisfaction. Her dreamtime connections were free again.

Later, they sat around the fire, eating the last of their meal, along with the cold baked yams Lily had brought.

"One last serving of stew to your soldier, then back to Katherine," Lily said.

"Lily, thank you for helping with the bats and with Private Glenn," Dr. Darnell said. "I wanted to talk to you about New Mexico," he went on.

Lily looked at him.

"I still have no assistant, and we will be moving straight from here to Carlsbad without going to the CDC offices, where I might have been able to commandeer someone."

The Sergeant cleared his throat and then nodded, without saying anything.

"I know your friend in New Mexico is in Roswell, which is very close to Carlsbad."

"Yes, I looked it up on Google Maps," she said. "It's where Ariq's team goes to get bat samples also, at Carlsbad. Mexican free-tailed bats."

"Well, would you be interested in coming with us? I know you need to get back to Katherine tonight, but our flight home arrives tomorrow, probably early afternoon. If you get back here, we would be happy—I would be happy to have you join us and work as my assistant for the Carlsbad sampling. Then you could meet up with your friend."

Lily sat and blinked, thinking about it.

"Of course, you would need to figure out how to get back home here on your own, since we will be moving on to Atlanta when we are done. I can offer you a small payment for your time helping us."

Ariq had offered to buy her painting. How much would a ticket back home cost?

But what about Pana?

"I would be glad to get to New Mexico, but I need to think about it. My family and friends here also need to be considered."

Dr. Darnell nodded. "Of course."

In the end, it was Obrey and Pearl who convinced her to go.

"You might be able to help them figure out this sickness," he said.

"You may never have another opportunity this good to go," he said.

"Pana," she said.

"Pana cannot go, with her mother so ill. And if Olivia dies, Pana will need to be here, will want to."

"I should be here, too."

"Not after Olivia threw you out."

Lily sighed and nodded, "That is true. She was so angry, in hospital."

"I know. Well, you 'hang out' with soldiers, and with bats, and with me. You're a little odd, Lily."

She made a face and saw he was laughing. Then he got serious again, glancing at her, then back at the road. She was so glad he felt better, was up and about again.

"This is about *you*, Lily. You and your bats and what you want to do."

She wanted to help Pana. Pana was with Pearl.

She wanted to help Ariq, and Ariq's bats, and Dr. Darnell. They did not have a Pearl. She wanted to go to New Mexico.

Pearl smiled when Lily told her the possible plans. "I feel guilty leaving now, but I would feel worse if I did not go," she said, and Pearl nodded.

They packed dilly bags of herbs for stew, hands working while they talked.

"Pana is much like you were, when you and I first came together. The dreamtime makes its own touchings—it is all together, all connected. There is a reason she is here, with me. She will be fine. These things you want to do with her will need to happen later if they happen at all. Pana needs her own country, Lily, not yours."

Lily's breath caught. Was she pushing on Pana, like her mother pushed on her?

She could not decide for her cousin. Pana needed to find her own way, just as Lily had—was still doing.

"You are trying to please your mother and Olivia and Ngukurr and Pearl," she smiled when she said her own name. "When are you trying to please Lily?"

"Mm."

———

The plane was not a passenger plane with lots of seats, like Lily had seen in photographs. It was a big empty space that they drove their jeeps up a ramp and inside of, and loaded Dr. Darnell's equipment and sample cases on pallets like a warehouse. It had a row of seats on either side of the open space. She had room to sleep or sit on her portion of the bench.

It was very noisy.

She tied her backpack and dilly bags to the "cargo stowage" nets, as the Sergeant showed her.

She tried to listen to language tapes, practicing Marra. At least no one could hear her if she made pronunciation mistakes. Then the tape machine ran out of batteries and she finally gave up on it and lay down to sleep.

Maybe she could get the tapes converted so they would work on her phone. She knew people read books and listened to music on their phones; why not language lessons? Maybe she could ask

Sissy if they had more modern recordings at Minyeri school. Maybe Ariq could show her how to make that work; he was good with computers and things.

Still thinking about what New Mexico was going to be like, she fell into a bat dream and slept until they landed.

39. DR. BRIAN

PAPEETE, TAHITI, FRENCH POLYNESIA

R̶x̶ He tried to roll over before he realized he was in the airplane…flying to Tahiti. A bright flash through the few open window shades, followed by a thunder clap, announced an electrical storm. Next came the turbulence and the captain's announcement to fasten seat belts.

In the best circumstances, he rarely slept through the night and he was now going to be awake for a while. He raised his window shade. Nothing. Nothing below. Nothing above. Just the eerie reflection of the plane's lights off the haze.

He felt a chill. He'd been sweating. But the chill was colder and deeper. He'd been dreaming. It all rushed back.

A car sped along the Hutchinson River Parkway. 4:00 AM, northbound, no traffic, eighty miles per hour. Penny at the wheel. Darlene passed out in the back seat.

The details were so specific and the image so sharp, but were they true?

"No, no, no," Brian screamed in his dream as the car turned onto the depression era off-ramp designed for half the speed of the rushing car.

This is what had woken him up. This old nightmare, one he hadn't had in so many years. It always confused him. Was the accident caused by Darlene or Penelope? Who should he blame? Who should he hate?

He rolled over twice before it registered that he was in a king-size bed in his hotel in Papeete. He vaguely recalled landing at Faa'a International Airport. A sleepy driver met him and shuttled him to his hotel. He checked-in and a polite hotel porter escorted him to his room. Now, after a much too short night, the Tahitian sun lit the room through a small opening in the closed curtains and he could hear younger tourists on the beach just beyond his lanai.

The phone rang, "Are you coming to breakfast, I've been

waiting for you."

"Sorry, sorry. Long trip. Short night. Be there in a jiffy."

Hearing Penny's voice brought it all back in a flash. The car spinning out of control, becoming airborne, crashing. The crisp, crunchy sound of breaking bones. Then the image of Penny's arm with wires and rods through and through, so she was part broken person and part bird cage.

"Good morning. Sorry I overslept. I've been so looking forward to spending today with you."

She wore a black skirt and a solid yellow blouse. She stood out from all the tourists in their big floral designs. Her mother had worn yellow, said it went with her blond hair and tanned complexion. Even with all her travel and living in New Jersey, Darlene was always tan. Penny looked so much like her mother.

Darlene and Penelope shared a room in the hospital. Penny with her bird cage, and her mother just bruised from bouncing around in the back seat without a seat belt. His eyes flashed back and forth between them. Horror. Anger. Pity. Blame. He had nothing to say. They had nothing to say.

"I'm so happy that you are doing well." He reached to touch one of her chevron scars, but stopped. It felt inappropriate and a little weird to touch her.

"Do they…the scars hurt?"

"That was so long ago. Everything's fine. You saw me dancing, didn't you?"

His mind was bouncing around. He kept reminding himself that he had all day, to take it slowly. "There's going to be a big announcement next week. World-wide pandemic. I don't know all the details, but I'm signed up to help."

She smiled at him. "I've heard the rumors."

Encouraged, he continued, "I going to help Doctors with Helicopters in Africa."

Now she frowned. "Aren't you supposed to get an operation for your heart?"

He'd forgotten that he'd spoken to her every day from the hospital. The voice on that phone was his daughter. This person across from him was someone else, a vision, a younger Darlene. He was having trouble connecting them.

"I think that can wait. I want to help, be useful. They need me."

She took an ice cube from her water glass and placed it in her coffee cup. After stirring it, she picked up the cup, ignoring the handle, holding it like a glass in both hands.

First, the mother-daughter crash. Second, the shared hospital room. Finally, that last breakfast concluded the troika of nightmares. Darlene sat across from him cupping her lukewarm coffee in both hands. She had smiled, "Have a good day at work."

As many times as he replayed this final deceit and betrayal, there was never a, "See you tonight," or an, "I'll miss you," and certainly no, "I love you." That was the last time he saw her.

But this wasn't Darlene. It was Penny. He wanted to invite her to come to Maputo with him. They'd certainly need as many doctors as they could get. But he didn't. Instead, he asked, "Where's Darlene? Do you think I can see…talk to her?"

He still didn't believe Darlene had visited him in the hospital. The nurses said she'd been there, but he'd been asleep. It could have been anybody…nobody.

She reached over and took his hand. It was warm from the coffee cup. Her green eyes connected directly to his. "Maybe another time."

That was how the day went, fragmented conversations, brief connections, and more flashbacks. He considered canceling his flights to Maputo, but he didn't.

Doctors with Helicopters needed him. His family didn't. He had important work to do. They had so many medical people to help the sick, but they'd need a chemist to find the cure.

40. ARIQ

CHIROPTERAN RESEARCH CENTER, NEW MEXICO

Monday morning. The previous night, **Bat Chat** had been all about the big joint WHO-CDC-ECDC announcement coming from World Health Organization headquarters in Geneva. Geneva was eight hours ahead of New Mexico, so Ariq didn't sleep and skipped his morning ride, to catch it live.

At 7:00 AM, still only 3:00 PM in Geneva, with plenty of time remaining for the announcement, he decided to go to the clinic. His phone sat in the passenger seat connected to **Bat Chat**.

He didn't want anyone to disturb him during the press conference, so he parked away from the main doors and snuck into his small adjunct office at the CRC.

Never being one to waste time, he walked over to check the bat genome sequencing. Before he reached the consoles, the silence struck him. That comforting sound, the growl and purr of science he called it, had stopped. The console proudly announced **Sequence Tadarida brasiliensis complete**.

Thanks to Jake's mystery grants, his three DNA sequencers had analyzed the first complete genome for any chiropteran species: Mexican free-tail bat, or *Tadarida brasiliensis*. He also had partial genomes for a flying fox from Australia, and a pipistrelle from England. Along with this, the Internet hosted several other partial sequences from other chiropteran research projects around the world.

He wanted to celebrate, but no one at the clinic cared. *Los cientificos*, like all high school students on school vacation, were certainly asleep. He thought of **Bat Chat**, but the posts already flew by at double speed spinning theories about the expected WHO press release. The big question and fear: Will they blame the bats?

His sequencing announcement could wait. He suspected his data would be more in demand after the WHO announcement. Nothing else would explain why all that money had suddenly come available. Idiopathic ague, money for sequencers, bats, the big announcement. They all connected. Jake wasn't surprised by the grants. Somehow Jake knew before anyone else.

With a complete bat genome, he was ready for the next phase of his research: a comparison of the bat immune system to other mammals, specifically *Homo sapiens*. Since chiropterans had branched off from other mammals 50-70 million years ago, he hypothesized that their immune system might be different, more primitive maybe.

On the other hand, the vertebrate adaptive immune system evolved in fish around 400 million years ago, so all mammals should be similar. Soon enough, he'd have the data. He'd know. Debates belonged to philosophy. Data made science.

With no announcement forthcoming by 9:00 AM, or 5:00 PM Geneva time, he figured there was a delay, or the announcement was just a rumor. Before he headed over to the main building, he set up some BLAST queries to search for chiropteran analogs to human immune genes.

Basic Local Alignment Search Tool or BLAST analyzed *configs* from the DNA sequencer. National Institutes of Health developed and maintained the program. It had all the knowledge about genes, proteins, and functions. He hoped BLAST would uncover something…important.

He took a roundabout path back to the administrative offices. The meditation garden exploded with color: fluorescent purples, bright oranges, fiery reds. The sweet air smelled of rain. Nothing compared to late summer mornings in Roswell with a light breeze off the Sierra Blanca range to the west.

As he approached the intensive care unit, he heard noise coming from the cafeteria and staff break room. As he approached closer, he could make out individual voices, happy voices. Curiosity led him to forgo a stop at the ICU. He went directly toward the cafeteria. The noise came from the adjacent staff room.

When he entered, he first noticed pink boxes. So many pink 3D boxes that he imagined someone had taken his unspoken challenge to order so many sweets there would be leftovers. There were also balloons and a foil banner.

The balloons proclaimed *Congratulations* and *Best Wishes*. The banner screamed *Engaged*. Engaged?

Then he saw the writing on the staff white board. *Lachlan and Martina!* Surrounded by hearts. The young orthopedic surgeon and the middle-aged accountant were just walking to the front of the room by the table of pink boxes, hand in hand, accompanied by children, lots of children.

He stood at the door.

Martina began. "Thank you all. We're so happy to share our engagement with you. We also want to introduce our family. On my right are my teenage twins, Alejandra and Roberto."

The two looked a little embarrassed and kept plenty of room between their mom and each other.

Martina pulled them close. "You don't need to be bashful. You've met all these people before."

They made you're-embarrassing-us faces and as soon as she let go, they retreated to the cookie table.

Lachlan continued, "My three are over by the cookies with their new big brother and sister."

He pointed to three children who appeared to be preschoolers, dressed in jeans and t-shirts. All wearing androgynous, medium length haircuts. Three redheads.

"They are Abigail, Bruce, and Caitlynn."

The crowd applauded and shouted for pictures.

Lachy called the children over and phones flashed at the new blended family.

Ariq blinked. Who knew?

He quickly grabbed a cup of coffee and made a toast. "Congratulations both Lachy and Marti. We all wish you the best." When he shook Martina's hand, she gave him a small apologetic smile. "We wanted to keep it quiet as long as we could.

Ariq drank his coffee, watching the staff's excitement with great amusement. Things were certainly looking up. This explained the staff intrigue. Martina and Lachlan had been exchanging lovers' secrets, not conspiring against hospital management.

His bat genome research was in the hands of BLAST.

The announcement loomed ahead, but whatever happened, Jake might find a grant for faster computers for the CRC's genome searches.

All of this didn't overshadow that Lily was on her way. He had much invested in this girl from the Australian outback and her stew.

In the excitement of the celebration and the embarrassment of jumping to the wrong conclusion about Lachy and Marti, unbiased science once again took control of his actions. For the moment, he felt no conflict between Lily's stew and his genomic research. Both 10,000-year-old treatments and the newest research technology coexisted.

———

The science group met that afternoon. Jessenia presented her findings. Ariq was proud. Were it not for the fact that they all looked so young, most of the boys barely shaving, and all of them having that insecure posture and affect of teenagers, this could have been a real scientific colloquium. This was not some superstitious gathering in the desert.

Much wisdom had evolved in the desert: ᴈмᴈᴈ in the Gobi, Lily in northern Australia, and now Jessenia in the Chihuahuan Desert. He felt something mystical about deserts.

The Gobi reminded him that he hadn't received ᴈмᴈᴈ's medical records. He took that as a sign of her recovery.

Everything was going so well, except for no Sofia. She was leaving for Pasadena, California in a few weeks, so Ariq expected her to be looking forward, and preparing for the next phase of her life. It seemed natural for her interest in *los cientificos* to be waning. Still, since she had been such good friends with Jessenia and interested in the other girl's project, he was surprised that she missed this meeting.

No one had expected the sudden propagation of immunity the

data showed. He had trained them well and they were first skeptical of their own results. There could be no science without good data.

Following Jessenia's lead, they considered contamination. They went over everything about the night they'd collected the samples. They confirmed that they did not duplicate samples; nobody took biopsies from bats with punched wings. They stored each sample in a new sterile vial. Each time, they broke the green seal, inserted the sample, and closed the vial with a red seal. They checked and double checked every step along the way. Each person had followed protocol.

They considered the bear encounter as a risk, but it had occurred before collection, so there was little chance that this was the problem. Regardless, someone retrieved the collection box and double checked each bottle for cracks or chips.

Then they reviewed Jessenia's sample prep and sequencing protocols. They didn't have the expertise to create DNA probes, so they had brute-force sequenced the samples. It was not efficient, but avoided the complexity and possible errors of dealing with probes. Thanks to Jake and whatever WHO would announce later, they had more DNA sequencers dedicated to a high school science project than ever before, so brute force had been possible.

After a couple of hours, Ariq ordered pizza, and made a pronouncement. "It's time to change directions. You haven't been able to show that the data is wrong. Now assume the data is correct and formulate a hypothesis to explain the data."

The room was silent.

In the back of the room, a couple new ninth graders whispered back and forth. They shouldn't have been at the meeting until school started and they were in high school, but here they were.

"You say it."

"No, you."

Everyone stared at them until Jessenia spoke to the girl, "Betty, what do you think?"

Betty looked at the boy. He stepped back a half step and shoved her toward the group. She pushed him back and hissed sotto voce, "I'm telling your mom." Then she turned to the group. "Um. Looks like the immunity is contagious. Really contagious."

There were a few laughs and a couple of kids commented, "Is that even possible?"

Since no one else had any ideas, and the pizza had arrived, they adjourned the meeting and ate their pizza.

Ariq thought the idea might not be that crazy and decided to post something on **Bat Chat** to see what the bat geeks thought. The idea made him nervous, sounding a bit magical to him. It reminded him of sweat lodges and healing dances.

As the teens filtered out, he stopped Jessenia and spoke to her in a quiet corner, "Do you know where Sofia is?"

"Haven't you heard? Just before the meeting she brought her mother to the emergency department."

———

Ariq spent the rest of the evening with Sofia and her mother Louisa Cortez, ensconced in the final individual suite in the Area 51 Annex. Louisa had the familiar symptoms, fever, tremors, and muscle aches. The staff administered a cocktail of antihistamines, analgesics, and anti-inflammatory drugs. Ariq reviewed the chart after each nurse visit, hoping that someone smarter than him had a solution.

Once again, the thought of Lily flying across the Pacific with her herbs brought solace. Hopefully she had enough for both Hannah and Louisa.

He did his best to comfort Sofia while she held her mother's shaking hands. He kept busy fetching ice chips for Louisa and a variety of dinner options from the hospital cafeteria for Sofia. In the end, Sofia didn't eat anything.

Close to midnight, the doctors decided to sedate Louisa. Sofia fell asleep in a chair, and Ariq walked across the parking lot to his small black SUV–which looked more like a hearse tonight. Each light pole attracted a swarm of desert insects, and the insects in turn attracted bats.

He drove slowly and carefully, looking forward to some sleep.

Just as he pulled up to his house, his phone beeped with an official announcement for a press conference for 9:00 AM Tuesday in Geneva. Ariq's sleepy brain did the calculation: 1:00 AM tomorrow. He glanced at the time and corrected himself: 1:00 AM today.

He just had enough time to make some strong coffee before the event.

PART II — DISCOVERY

WHO PRESS CONFERENCE

WHO HEADQUARTERS, GENEVA, CH

Dr. Kipchirchir stood in front of the circular table surrounded by a sea of United-Nations-blue chairs. It was an un-American 9:00 AM Geneva time, long before most Americans were up, assuring no live coverage by any major networks or cable channels. When the steering committee had seen the panicked anticipation on social media, they delayed twelve hours to deliver their report during the late night, early morning news lull in North America.

Dr. Kipchirchir started with some background, sounding like a BBC newsreader, with his deep calm voice and British public school accent.

"Two years ago, through twin programs of treating dogs and humans, we dared to hope that one day we'd add rabies to the list of conquered diseases. Inspired by the eradication of smallpox, the international public health accomplishment of the 20th century, governments and non-governmental efforts were bearing fruit. Human deaths from rabies decreased 50% during 2010-2013."

Dr. Kipchirchir summarized the different efforts mounted to remove dogs as a vector for rabies, and have post-exposure prophylaxis vaccines universally available. Much of this was verbatim from the WHO Rabies Fact Sheet available in six languages. The press listened politely.

"Two years ago," he echoed his opening, "we observed a rise in rabies-like symptoms not associated with traditional animal exposures."

He reviewed the difficulty of diagnosing rabies due to the highly variable incubation period and initial symptoms shared with so many other diseases.

Finally, he made the proclamation everyone was waiting for, "We are calling this new disease Aerosol Infectious Rabies or AIR in English. Here is what we know."

All the reporters stopped talking.

"Several Chiropteran species, indeed most, are capable of contracting this disease, passing it among themselves, and acting as an asymptomatic reservoir. A small number of humans contract AIR from bats. Most people contract the disease from friends and family. The disease has the typical variable incubation period and during that time the patients are mildly contagious. As the name suggests, AIR propagates through airborne infection such as coughing, sneezing, kissing or even close conversation."

The room erupted. This was the worst-case scenario.

The rest of Dr. Kipchirchir's talk was about face masks and respirators, hand washing, and other public health recommendations.

Somewhere in the middle of that, he delivered discouraging news to the privileged, "The expensive pre-exposure rabies vaccinations used by veterinarians and people in contact with wild animals are not effective against this new strain."

He also slipped in between some routine pronouncements, "The hot spots for AIR are sub-Saharan Africa, southeast Asia and northern Australia, the eastern Mediterranean from Lebanon to Crete, and the southwestern United States." For unknown reasons, AIR infections had not made it to South America in appreciable numbers.

Dr. Kipchirchir finished with, "There is no reason to panic. AIR spreads slowly, requiring multiple exposures over time. You cannot catch it walking though crowds, sitting in a theater, or riding on an airplane."

1. NGA

MAPUTO, MOZAMBIQUE

As they entered the port, Maputo looked very different to Nga's eyes. She had lived here for three years, almost ten years ago. She ought to have recognized something. Then she realized they were viewing the city from the opposite side she had seen on her original arrival as the TC bus drove into Maputo from the north. She remembered all the TC candidates cheering as the city came into view, kilometers of houses, sheds, huts, and multi-story buildings seen from the bus windows, all so different from their own little villages and small towns.

That bus had done wonders to ensure that native peoples from all over Mozambique could get to the school at the *Hospital Central de Maputo*, but when it had crashed and sunk in the big storms two years ago, the government had not replaced it. She wondered how many students were here in the *Técnico de Cirurgia* program now.

The Greenleaf ship passed floating platforms with dredging machinery. Miss Davis explained the Maputo Port Development Company was deepening the harbor, so bigger ships could bring trade to Mozambique's shores

The *Arcturus* neared the wharf, then tugboats tediously docked the ship in its assigned spot. Halid joined her at the rail to watch the end of the docking process.

"Our people are ready. They have spent the last hour helping the other refugees pack up." Halid shook his head. "Why do we seem so much better organized than other villagers?"

Nga smiled at him. She wanted to say, "Because of you," but she also didn't want to give Halid a fat head. He was already pretty full of himself after being "temporary headman" for two weeks.

"Perhaps it is the Yao way," she said instead.

Halid smiled.

Their trip from Beira to Maputo had been calm—almost boring—but she had welcomed the chance to rest and help Wayya and the other Luambe wounded who had come with them.

One of the sailors had offered stargazing sessions each night, and she and Halid and several others from Luambe had taken advantage of that to learn about constellations and navigation. Only one young woman from the other refugee group had joined in these sessions—the rest had stared with big eyes, or had turned their backs.

When the other villagers began to show signs of the illness, plague or flu, whatever it was, they had clustered even closer together, keeping separate from the Yao group. Nga was relieved. None of her people had become ill and she wanted it to stay that way. Greenleaf crew had worn face masks around both groups of refugees, but no one said anything about quarantine.

Nga made sure to thank the Greenleaf captain and the Liaison Cora Davis again and again when they left. The Luambe villagers had ended up sharing a lot of their food with both the crew, who appreciated "family style" cooking, and the other villagers, who had brought so little with them. Ms. Cora had been grateful the two groups had gotten along without squabbles, and she relayed to Nga Captain da Cunha's thanks in return.

The ship was docked, the gangway run out, and people began getting off. Nga saw some gurneys on the wharf, ready to take sick patients to the hospital. She looked further and grabbed a wheelchair with the words *Hospital Central de Maputo* stenciled on the back. Wayya would be able to ride and that would help get them across the many blocks they needed to walk to the hospital. She was puzzled by the availability of gurneys and wheelchairs, but no accompanying hospital personnel.

She asked Halid to gather the Luambe villagers together at the east end of the dock while she made sure the other refugees had someone to guide them. None of them spoke any of the languages she did, so they did not communicate with her, but she seemed to be the only one present who spoke enough Portuguese to ask the dockworkers for a guide for them. If such a person could not be found, she worried that she was going to have to lead them.

Did they even want to go to *Hospital Central de Maputo*? She did not know. Finally a young man dressed in hospital whites ran up and began speaking with the headman of that group. He got them organized and moving together, pushing the gurneys with their sick people, carrying children and small sacks of gear, so Nga left him to it, trotting down the dock back to her own group with a sense of at least partial relief.

As with every other day, her primary concern was the health of her own villagers. They needed to find to find a safe place in the city quickly. None of them was prepared for Maputo.

On the positive side, Halid seemed to have matured by years over the weeks of travel. He was a big help, fat head or not.

She approached a dock worker and asked, in Portuguese, the shortest way to exit the dock areas. He frowned at her a moment, then waved another man over. Nga repeated her question.

"Where are you going?"

"*Hospital Central de Maputo*." She pointed in the direction of the hospital, in downtown Maputo.

He explained they should follow the road along the docks until they could cut over to *Avenida 24 de Julho*, before they got to the botanical gardens. Otherwise—

"There's a cliff, yes, I remember."

"*Avenida Guerra Popular* should get you over."

"This road goes through to there?"

"Yes. It curves into the Guerra just as it ends. If you are in a parking lot, or see the ferry docks, you went too far."

Nga nodded. "Thank you so much." She took a deep breath and tried to remember to relax her shoulders. She'd been holding them so tight up against her neck, they were starting to cramp. She could do this. They'd get safely to the hospital before dark. But it was kilometers to walk. She smiled at Halid, trying to reassure them all. She took over the job of pushing Wayya's wheelchair, to slow herself down so the children did not have to run to keep up.

They moved as a group through the mostly deserted streets away from the big ship wharf, past warehouses and parking lots packed with new imported cars, toward the distant clump of trees that was the *Jardim Botânico Tunduru*.

She sighed in relief when they found *Avenida Guerra Popular* and turned away from the water. The slight uphill made pushing the wheelchair more difficult. She worried that her exhaustion might mean that she was becoming ill with AIR.

———

When they finally arrived at the Hospital, it was not a relief. The entire area around the building was a chaos of refugees in parking lots—buses and ambulances trying to get through, and cars stuck amidst clumps of pedestrians trying to go one way or the other. She finally saw someone in hospital whites and wearing a face mask who seemed to be directing people. She moved through the crowd, making space in front of her with mildly aggressive pushes of the wheelchair. Wayya's hands on the arms of the chair were clenched tight, her face half a wince of pain, half appalled at the seeming wall of people in front of them. Nga patted her shoulder and nudged their way through.

The young man in whites turned out to be a TC, not a doctor or nurse, but that made sense. Why waste those medical skills out here directing traffic? Wondering how much authority the TC had, Nga got his attention, explained they had wounded, but no one sick, and wondered if there was an empty ward or refugee space for those not ill.

"A separate place, where there is no sickness?" The TC shook his head, his eyes tight above the mask.

"I am a *técnico de cirurgia*," she said.

That seemed to make an impression. The TC stepped up onto a box she hadn't noticed and looked around the area. He pointed toward the left side of the Hospital entrance.

"Take your people there. Maybe they can help you." He stepped down off his box and turned to speak with the next person who pushed in front of him.

Nga turned and made sure Halid was looking her way. She pointed to where they were moving next. She started off in that direction, slowly pushing through the crowds, around gurneys, past clumps of people sitting on the ground, nursing babies, eating snacks from baskets, combing their hair. Nga could feel her legs shaking as she moved step by halting step.

Beside the stairs into the main hospital entrance, there was a group of TCs and people not wearing uniforms or lab coats, but with name tags or business suits. All wore face masks.

"It's called AIR, Airborne Infectious Rabies," said a muscular man in a tight-fitting suit. Sweat droplets stood out on his forehead, ran down his neck, wetting his collar, his face mask. "They announced no treatment plan or cure, though some people have reported that the Milwaukee Protocol seems to help. It is a virus. It is airborne, hence the name. We should use CDC-certified N95 respirators to be safe, but there are virtually none available. These," he pointed to his own mask, "do not seal around your nose or mouth, and can only filter large molecules. They can only prevent contact with patient fluids from coughs and sneezes. Nevertheless, we are asking everyone who works around AIR patients to wear one, unless you have already been heavily exposed."

The TCs and other uniformed or badged people around him nodded their understanding. Mr. Suit pointed to the far edge of the parking lot to the north. "That area is to be set up as a camp for those groups definitely showing signs of AIR." He pointed the opposite direction, where refugees filled a small park-like open space. "Somehow we need to clear that space and make it available for those groups who do not have sickness."

Nga looked that way. That was where the Luambe villagers should go, but there was a flood of people passing over it. How would they be able to make a space in that mob?

"Nga?" a voice said in her ear. A big deep voice.

She turned and practically fell into the embrace of Ben Kalagho. "Oh, Ben, it is so good to see you!"

His mask crinkled as he smiled and hugged her. Beside him his wife Catia waited, then also hugged Nga, then exclaimed over Wayya in the wheelchair.

"You made it!" Ben said.

"Just now," Nga said. "We are looking for a space to settle."

"Are any of your people ill?"

She shook her head. "Though I am shaky and exhausted, perhaps the first signs?"

Ben's big hand felt her forehead, her neck. "No fever," he said.

Well, that was good. Nga took heart, and promised her body a good rest, now that they were in Maputo. Just a few hours more, until Luambe had a safe place to sleep, and she could let go.

"We do have some wounded, like Wayya, here," she said.

Catia was examining the bandaged stump of Wayya's left leg.

"I am hoping amidst all the chaos, we still might be able to find a prosthetic for her, and rest and help for our other trauma victims."

"Were you attacked on the way?" Ben seemed shocked.

"No. It's a long story. First I must get them settled somewhere safe."

"How many people?"

"Twenty-three, and children."

Ben frowned, then nodded. "I think we might have something. Please follow us." He and Catia turned and made their way around the group of people around Mr. Suit. They walked behind the short garden planter to a ramp. Nga was so grateful not to have to wrestle the wheelchair up the stairs that she burst into tears.

Without a word, Ben took the handles of the wheelchair and pushed it up the ramp. Halid came up beside Nga and looked at her. She saw Mezi and others also looking at her with concern.

"It's okay," she said, hiccupping. "I'm just glad to be here at last."

2. ARIQ

ROSWELL, NEW MEXICO

Ariq watched the press announcement live in the isolation and comfort of his living room. He nursed his coffee sitting in a backless wooden chair like the ones he grew up with. Both combined to keep him alert. After all the rumors and deaths, nothing surprised him, not even that he lived in a disease hot spot.

He feared for his sick patients. Once the CDC declared the ROC to be an outbreak center, evacuating them to somewhere else or bringing in additional help would be impossible. Southern New Mexico, never in the mainstream to begin with, now stood alone and isolated.

Sadly, the health of his patients hinged on a medical director from Mongolia and a traditional healer from Australia. He felt so lost.

Still dressed, he went off to bed, but couldn't sleep, thinking about tomorrow. After what seemed like hours of restlessness, his phone buzzed.

Arrived at Carlsbad. See you in a couple of days.

This was the best news. Lily had made it across the Pacific. He rolled over and went to sleep.

"The press conference said that rabies vaccines are not effective against Airborne Infectious Rabies, but I've asked Martina to check our inventory anyway."

Martina smiled, either pleased to be central to the morning discussion, or still in the glow of her engagement. Ever efficient, she already had the numbers. "We have our normal inventory levels, ten series of each."

Nizhoni said, "Despite what they said on the news, remember that Arthur Whitney recovered. Hadn't he had rabies shots? Wasn't he a veterinarian?"

Chucky added, "I've been doing some reading. Rabies vaccines have few side effects. It seems to me that they advised against them because of the cost."

Ariq agreed. "Regardless of the announcement, our experience with Arthur Whitey indicates they could help. I trust our actual experience more than some proclamation intended to prevent world-wide panic and a rush on anti-rabies supplies." Staff nodded.

Encouraged, he took the leadership reins, "Forget the cost. If there is a chance to save lives, use everything in the inventory and order more…though I doubt we'll get any."

Moving to the next step he asked, "Who will benefit? We have ten vaccine series for pre-exposure, like Arthur had. We also have another ten for immediately after someone received a bite from a rabid animal."

Nizhoni, always thinking of her patients, pursed her lips in an angry face. "But we can't identify patients until it is too late for either of these. With AIR there are no bites."

Ariq thought about her daughter Jessenia, but remembered that all the students working in the CRC had been given the shots.

Lachlan joined the free-for-all. "That's a good point. We should give the rabies shots to spouses, offspring, or intimate partners of the AIR patients. Since the disease is airborne, once we observe symptoms, the cases will have exposed their partners. It might not be too late for them."

"OK, we can do that until we exhaust our supply. For the pre-exposure treatment, we'll treat the nursing department. Martina will organize a lottery."

Martina wasn't smiling any more, but she didn't object.

"Any other pressing topics?"

Lachlan jumped. It looked like he'd received an elbow in the ribs from his somber fiancée. Everyone got very quiet. "We've been discussing a destination wedding. Someplace not too far or expensive, like maybe Las Vegas… "

He took a deep breath, "…but now with this crisis, we're staying here. If anyone has any suggestions, please let us know."

The wedding planning offered a welcome diversion. Murmured suggestions ranged from national parks to the deserted drive-in.

Ariq and Joni put on gloves and masks. Before the wedding venue discussion ended, they began their morning rounds.

At the first room, they observed Louisa Cortez's condition, starting at the oxygen at her nose, moving down to her feeding tube, electrodes across her chest, IV in her right arm, and heart rate, oxygen, and blood pressure clip on her ring finger. Each morning he regretted anew abandoning medical school, but he'd picked up enough to read Louisa's chart. Severe tremors. Heavy sedation. Prayers.

It didn't really say prayers, but that's what he thought. Since she wasn't in a coma, he hoped that Lily's stew would make a difference. He shuddered and wondered if he had finished his education, would he have had a more scientific idea than this girl from Australia with her weeds and touches.

On the sofa sat Louisa's frightened daughter. He could see tears stains on her mask. He walked over and sat down beside her. "Sofia, how are you doing? Did you sleep last night?"

She wrapped her arms around herself like a protective cocoon. "I'm so scared. She's all I have. She has to get better."

Joni turned to Sofia, "We're doing everything we can to keep her comfortable and help her get better."

"Do you want to go home for a while, maybe take a nap?"

Sofia didn't budge. Seeing no reaction, Joni tried, "Jessenia can go with you. Later, you can have dinner with your mom and spend the night here, or you can sleep over with Jessenia at our house."

Sofia squeezed her eyes shut to hold back her tears. She said, "Yes, I can do that," but it was unclear as to what she'd agreed to.

He gave her a smile and patted her shoulder. "That's a brave girl. Do you want me to have the EMTs drive you home?"

"No thanks. I'll walk. It's only a few blocks."

While Nizhoni checked all the tubes and changed the IV saline solution, Ariq went ahead to check on Hannah.

Walking to Hannah's room, he pondered the irony that after dropping out of med school he was caring for a patient, but not with what he would have learned in medical school. He was administering traditional techniques he learned from an Aboriginal girl in Australia. The internet compounded the paradox. The latest technology distributed healing knowledge that might be more than 10,000 years old. The crowning incongruity was that each day his patient seemed to be improving.

Hannah looked peaceful, like the pain and tension had left her. He sat down next to her and started talking to her, telling her how wonderful she was and how much he cared for her. He wiped her brow. She was still warm, but her fever had broken.

He held her hand.

Then he understood, and his face covered with tears. It started slowly, but soon he was sobbing. He bent over, resting his head on her bed, his tears spotting the cotton blankets.

His brain realized what his body already knew: The spirit had left her body. Lily's stew hadn't worked. His patient was dead.

Nizhoni found him there. With the gentleness and compassion of an experienced nurse and mother, she separated the living from the dead.

———

As an escape, Ariq went to his CRC retreat and reviewed the BLAST analyses of the Chiropteran genome. Happily, no one's life was in the balance when he examined DNA sequences. Even better, he didn't have to understand the patterns, BLAST did that for him.

He had a couple of PCs expropriated from accounting and admissions; they didn't have the specs for data analysis. To limit the computational load, he'd modified the standard NIH scripts to compare his bats against just two mammals: a 'generic' *Homo sapiens* and the ever-popular lab mouse.

He marveled at the comprehensive NIH list and was just a little jealous of their obvious access to extensive computer power. To manage with his resources, he had to comment out other primates, mammals like rat and pig, and non-mammals like fruit fly, zebrafish, yeast, and rice. The menu of available genomes seemed to be an almost endless assortment of genera, species, and sub-species. He didn't understand the details, but he had a layman's understanding and a creative imagination.

BLAST lived up to its reputation and suggested several interesting results. At least he thought they were interesting.

———

Since Ariq didn't have any research credentials, he had to find a way to get some credentialed scientists to look at his results. At first, he thought of his warrior ancestors and imagined kidnapping some scientists or taking over a CDC lab and holding people hostage. He recalled pyramid mounds of skulls erected to convince cities to surrender.

Rejecting thirteenth century violence, he setup an online news conference for that evening, really a glorified chat room, a social media event, streaming video.

Before the meeting started, he saw a half-dozen graduate student types, a couple of bloggers, and maybe one legitimate reporter online. The students could have been proxies for some real scientists, but that was the most optimistic interpretation of the general disinterest in his event. More lead time and promotion might have drawn a larger audience, but he hadn't had time.

"I have been researching bats—Chiroptera—for several years. Last year, when they were first implicated in a suspected pandemic, I was granted several of the latest DNA sequencers. I now have data for the complete genome sequence for the Mexican Free-tail Bat or *Tadarida brasiliensis*."

Evidently some of the participants were live tweeting his conference. After he implied his research addressed Aerosol Infectious Rabies, the number of participants doubled.

"Without getting too technical, I ran BLAST using the Chiropteran sequences. I wanted to know how bats managed to harbor so many viruses without getting sick. The literature suggests that bats are reservoirs for over 200 different diseases, many of them dangerous to humans. Now AIR is suspected to be one of those."

He now had over 100 followers. He started to worry, because he didn't really know what he was talking about. However, if his theory was correct, it could be important, but only if the right people looked at it and figured out the details.

His great, great grandfather, Genghis Khan, would have been proud of him as he bravely went forward, fearless and against all odds. He took a deep breath and relaxed. This was one of those rare times when he felt his warrior ancestry was working to help the people he was responsible for.

"Over fifty million years ago bats split off from other mammals. I looked at their immune system genes and the MHC— that is, the major histocompatibility complex. I found that while some sequences were analogous to other mammals, others were different, while BLAST still identified them as immune functions."

He started to see questions coming in over Twitter.

"What are the genes in common with murine or primates?"
"What MHC differences do you see?"
"Is your DNA data available?"

He didn't know how to answer for the first two, the questioners obviously knew more than he did. However, he made a note to announce the public availability of his data.

Taking another deep breath, he charged ahead with the statement he'd been reviewing in his head, "Bats have survived relatively unchanged for fifty million years. They have an immune system that protects them from viral diseases. When they split off from the other mammals, they took the better immune system."

Twitter exploded.

"Nonsense. You can't tell that from DNA data."
"OMG How did anyone trust him with a sequencer?"
"This is all conjecture."
"ROFL—All fantasy."

He rushed to his conclusions fearing he was going to lose his audience. "Bats can repel virus attacks because they have more immune genes and more B-cells and T-cells. By hosting all these viral strains, bats benefit from horizontal gene transfer like bacteria."

With that Twitter really blew up. The questions and comments scrolled by so quickly that he couldn't read them. He got the sense that many people thought he was a fool. It was too late to worry about that, he had people dying in his hospital. Nonetheless, Ariq feared that if they all laughed at him, he'd never get help. It was time to stop before he got himself in deeper.

"Thank you all for attending. Globally we are at a tipping point and something must happen. I am making all the Chiropteran sequence data publicly available."

He gave out file names and access to his cloud storage.

Overcome with anxiety of inadequacy, he apologized. "I am aware of the deficiencies in my education and background. I welcome review by those with more expertise."

To the shame of his warrior self, he went on, practically whining, "On a personal note, I have already seen too many people taken by AIR, and would be happy to accept abuse from a hundred of you, if only one can find an answer in the data."

"Thank you."

———

Ariq couldn't sleep. He tried a midnight burrito scavenged from leftover rice and beans, and for a touch of glory, locally-grown jalapeños. With a full stomach, but still wide awake, he gave up trying to sleep. He took a quick shower and drove to work.

The clear night stars faded as he approached the well-lit clinic. He ignored the staff parking area and entrance, coasting into the empty visitor's lot, and walking to the main entrance. Once through the gate, he followed the stone wall to the meditation garden, and the white sand path around to the back of the reception building.

The quiet felt lonely and isolated. Nothing happening in Roswell. Elsewhere so much was going on. Lily would soon arrive with more stew. But Hannah was dead, and all he could do was wait helplessly praying for Louisa to survive. The sun had risen high in Europe and real scientists were working in their labs. Dawn had reached the east coast. The NIH and CDC surely hummed with research.

In Roswell, he sat at the top of the stairs leading to the fountains. There sat Rosy, the clinic's semi-adopted bobcat. She crouched below the largest waterfall batting the frothy water with her large paws. She licked the water off her fur and washed her face. After an undulating stretch ending with her stubby tail, she stared toward him. He gazed back into her golden eyes, sparkling in the dim moonlight.

"Rosy, what do you think?"

She made a small noise and leaped to the top of the waterfall. She lapped the water, once again looked at him, and settled down to clean her hind legs.

"Do you ever feel like you're in the wrong place?" Ariq rubbed his eyes, dry from no sleep and desert air. He was talking to a wild cat.

As if to answer his question, Rosy ran off, escaping the first rays of sunlight. As she disappeared around the corner kicking up a cloud of dust, his phone beeped.

U up?

It was Jessenia. As soon as he replied **Y**, his phone rang.

"The bat genome data is all over **Bat Chat**…"

Now he regretted sitting in the dark and talking to Rosy. He should have been online. After all, most scientists lived in earlier time zones, and started their day long before Roswell did.

"…and scientists are coming to examine our bats. Our bats. They're flying in from Australia with lots of equipment and people."

"How did you find out?"

"We're going to meet them. Only Sofia must stay with her mother, so she can't drive us. Can you take us?"

"It's not even six o'clock yet. Did they invite you? Aren't you just going to be in the way?"

Jessenia's voice got louder and the words shot out faster. "They'll need us. We know the caves…and the bats. Those are *our* bats."

No one expected him at the clinic for hours. And most likely those scientists had Lily with them. Still this seemed ill-considered and impulsive. "You know I can't drive you without permission slips."

"We have them! We have Mrs. Santana as chaperone, but she doesn't drive. We're packed, ready to go. We're perfect for this! We know mist nets and how to take a punch biopsy. Real scientists are coming here, this is our chance."

He stood up and retraced his steps to the parking lot.

She continued, "Please. So much better than staying in Roswell and waiting for aliens."

That did it. He might be a fool online, but he'd help his students in Roswell. "I'm on my way, but I can't stay. I have to get back here."

BAT CHAT

———🦇———

PLUS FREQUENTLY ASKED QUESTIONS

? *When did bats evolve?*
Mammalian evolution took off after the K-T extinction 65 million years ago. This fifth major extinction was the end of the dinosaurs. An impact near Chicxulub, Mexico left a crater over 100 miles across and caused this.

By this time, primates (people) had split off. About 15 million years later, Bats went their own way, leaving cats, dogs, horses, and cows to evolve later. Like birds, bats evolved lightweight bones, which are rarely preserved in the fossil record making the exact story difficult to discover. Much of bat evolution is based on DNA analysis.

For more, check out www.batworlds.com

 Syms Covington: Did everyone see the announcement from Geneva?

 Canuck: You betcha. Took them long enough to say something

 Morcego: Forget that Did you see the dude from New Mexico?

 John Snow: He might have something

 Popo: He's not the first person to sequence a chiroptera genome

 Kitty: Give him some slack He's just an amateur Are his ideas any good?

 Syms Covington: I got him the sequencers

 Radar Rat: IDK but Im rooting for bats to be the heroes here

 Dreamtime: Good on the bats

 Capt Contagious: Lots of scientists are looking at bats I'm sure some will look at the data from Roswell There might be something there

3. LILY

CARLSBAD, NEW MEXICO

Private Glenn had begun to treat Lily as if she was some kind of healing angel. In his gratitude for her "cure," he was a bit annoying, helping her with her herb bundles as if she was suddenly broken, carrying her backpack for her. It would have been amusing if she didn't have to be careful about falling over him every time she turned around. Finally the Sergeant ordered him to assist with the mist nets, and Lily could walk without her grateful shadow.

The New Mexican desert was hot, like northern Australia. But unlike her home area, the air was parched, and there were very few trees.

The first evening, all of them sweating freely, they caught several thousand bats. The Mexican Free-tailed bats were so tiny compared with her Little Red Flying Foxes, she was amazed. Their name was "little" but the foxes had wingspans as much as a meter wide. The Carlsbad bats were very much smaller, lighter and had a wingspan of less than half the fox's. Two or three dozen equaled a single fox's weight. *This is how they can live on tiny bugs, while my foxes want tasty fruits,* Lily thought.

They were insect feeders, so were equipped with echolocation systems that were quite new to Lily. She had only worked up close with fruit bats before, so it was not only fun work, but educational, as they took the tiny punches from each wing and put the samples into Dr. Darnell's little test tubes and sealed them. One for each bat. No wonder he had so many sample cases.

"They'll be back to collect these samples and us, as soon as they deliver your Australian ones to the CDC in Atlanta," Dr. Darnell said. "So we need to move as quickly as we can here."

There were other researchers examining the bats—and their guano as well. Dr. Darnell spoke with biologists who were taking guano samples, looking at all the bacteria from the floor of the caves where the bats roosted.

These bats enjoyed caves, Lily's bats enjoyed trees. But of course, just because they were both bats, there was no reason to expect them to have the same kind of homes. Lily's bats ate fruit. They did not need echolocation to find their prey, like the New Mexico bats did. She grinned to herself, imagining little fruits flying around in the outback. That would make an amusing dreamtime story.

The Carlsbad bats worked hard—by comparison, her Foxes were a bit lazy. She imagined trying to depict that aspect in her paintings.

Lily used Dr. Darnell's working lights to examine the Mexican Free-Tail's faces, noting the wrinkles around their mouths, the difference in the shapes of the noses.

In her opinion, the Little Red Flying Foxes were much cuter, but the Mexican Free-Tails were probably a bigger boon to the environment. They ate millions of mosquitos and other pests every night.

———

Their second day at Carlsbad, a group of younger students appeared, sent by Ariq to help gather bats and mingle with real scientists.

One young woman ran over to Lily and hugged her. "You must be Lily!" she said, sounding much younger than Lily had first thought.

"Yes?"

Laughing, the girl said, "I'm Jessenia! One of Ariq Temuujin's students!"

"Oh, you are one of the ones studying bats," Lily said, trying to remember what Ariq had said about the girl. Hadn't she seen her in **Bat Chat**, too? "You are in high school?"

"Yes. We get extra credit for research projects. I love your accent."

"These bats are popular right now," Lily said, feeling a little overwhelmed.

"Yeah. And Ariq wants you to come to his hospital as soon as you can, so we're supposed to help collect and sample with you and whoever you are working with."

"Dr. Darnell, from the Center for Disease Control."

"Oh." Jessenia's face closed down. "They aren't very happy with us right now."

"Dr. Darnell seems nice enough. He gave me a ride to get here all the way from Australia," Lily said. "There are also some biologists looking at the bat guano."

"Well, I'm glad we can sample up here. The guano areas are pretty smelly, from the ammonia."

Lily nodded. "She was wearing a gas mask, the one we saw going down into the cave." She'd looked like an alien, like some of the oldest aboriginal rock art. Maybe those ancient artists had travelled through the dreamtime and seen such a thing from here and now.

Jessenia nodded. "It's just another amazing thing about these bats, that they can survive in such a toxic atmosphere. It's from the beetles, not the bats, though, so I'm surprised they're looking at the guano."

"Beetles?"

"*Dermestid* beetles—they feed on the fresh guano and on bats that die and fall. And there have been more dead bats than usual, so there're more beetles than usual, and more beetle poop, so more ammonia."

"Oh," Lily said, feeling even more overwhelmed.

Jessenia hardly seemed to stand still, hopping from one foot to another. "You're coming to Roswell soon, aren't you? Ariq really wants to have some of your medicine stew available."

"Yes. We should finish tomorrow, then I will need to find a ride there."

"Oh! You can ride with us, I'm sure. Or Ariq will come and get you."

"That would be good," Lily said. "Well, there seems to be plenty of people collecting, let's go work on the sampling." She smiled at the girl, who waved to the group of other students then turned and walked with Lily to Dr. Darnell's tent.

Lily was surprised the high school students were here on their own. Wouldn't Ariq come along to supervise? There was one adult with the students, or at least a woman who looked a bit older–maybe that was enough.

Hoping Ariq didn't have so many other problems he'd abandoned his bat project, Lily went to Dr. Darnell's work area, Jessenia tagging along.

The Sergeant was talking to Dr. Darnell when Lily rejoined them. "So we don't need to collect so many samples here, eh?" the Sergeant was saying.

"They want 5,000 here, only. Then on to Texas, to Bracken Cave, where we will take at least 5,000 more." Dr. Darnell shook his head. "They're on to something, but I'm not sure what. Most of these bats do not look sick—certainly not as if they have AIR." He included Lily in his glance, "Though you can never be really sure with bats. Anyhow, head office is more interested in quick, current samples than they are in volume."

"We certainly have caught at least that many already," the Sergeant said. "So it's up to you two, now."

"Three," Lily said. "This is Jessenia, an experienced bat handler from CRC. She can help." Dr. Darnell nodded, handed Jessenia a mask. They all masked up. To work.

———

By the end of the day, Lily's back and shoulders ached from the stretching of bat wings and releasing of bats. Small as they were, she nevertheless had a weird callous on her finger from holding them ready for release. Their tiny claws had brushed her finger many times as she tossed them back into the sky.

Finished at last, she washed her hands at the station the Sergeant had set up, and Jessenia followed her example.

She gathered her herb bags and her backpack. She double-checked her passport pocket, making sure her identification and passport were still there. Dr. Darnell had given her some kind of entry paper showing how she had arrived in the U.S., which she would need to go home.

She helped him pack up his gear. Then she sat at the soldiers' campfire one last time, Jessenia tagging along, quiet now, probably worn out, or perhaps in awe of the soldiers and the CDC man.

Dr. Darnell had arranged payment for Lily by collecting cash from the various soldiers and giving the Sergeant a check to cash to pay them back.

"Otherwise, Lily can't get her money until she goes home."

"Which I need to *go* home," Lily said with a smile.

"I really appreciate your help, young lady. And especially all the cultural things you shared. I've told the CDC offices about your stew ingredients, and they are quite interested in it."

Lily nodded. "I have learned a lot about bats," she said. "I love these little ones, they fly so fast and they have such funny faces. But my own flying foxes are still my favorite."

Dr. Darnell laughed and nodded.

The Sergeant stood up and reached a hand out to Lily to shake. "I appreciate you helping my man, here," he said. "It's been an education for us, too."

Lily shook hands and nodded at Private Glenn, who was still staring at her with worshipful eyes.

Abruptly, Jessenia jumped up and pointed to a cloud of dust approaching. "That's Ariq. He's arrived!" In the distance, they could see the headlights of Ariq's vehicle getting brighter, then the vehicle itself, shiny black showing through the tan dust.

Her ride to the next part of her adventure was here.

4. DR. BRIAN

MAPUTO, MOZAMBIQUE

R_X Dr. Brian heard the WHO news conference at the airport in Johannesburg. The general reaction there was calm. South Africans identified the problems of sub-Saharan Africa with the less developed countries to the north. The short airplane ride up to Maputo was noticeably empty. It seemed that South Africans were staying home.

His helpful self-powered carry-on seemed as lost as he was at the Maputo International Airport. He reclaimed his large luggage and stacked everything on a trolley. The customs agents were busy and his heart was racing. Rather than risk another syncope episode, he found a bench and waited for the crowd to clear and his pulse to return to normal.

He walked slowly through immigration and customs. His blue U.S. passport and a letter from Doctors with Helicopters seemed to smooth the process. The modern steel-beam and glass structure of the main terminal gave him confidence.

However, the large facility highlighted the unexpected low level of activity. Uniformed agents staffed the counters for over a dozen airlines, but most were idle waiting for non-existent passengers. He easily navigated the wide expanse, exited through electric doors, and looked for his driver.

Cars were driving in the same direction he walked. Oh, the wrong way, he thought. They drive on the other side of the road. He turned around and walked toward a line of waiting cars and drivers.

A few vehicles back, he saw a man with a hand-written sign saying **Medico Macalester**. Once settled in the car, he reflected on the lack of traffic. It felt like a quarantine zone. No one wanted to go to Maputo.

The AIR investigation had been going for years. Doctors with Helicopters must have known the risks in Mozambique. He felt tricked and trapped as his driver navigated the poor roads through this undeveloped country. He suddenly felt very old, and thought, I could die here.

———

Brian woke up at sunrise. One look at the crappy apartment Doctors with Helicopters had arranged reminded him of his sorry predicament. He was in a disease hot spot, isolated from western civilization, and most likely stuck in the last place that would receive any real help or make any contribution to the cure.

He looked at his phone. 5:00 AM. The internet had suggested September as the best month to visit Maputo, but he could already feel the temperature and humidity rising, both heading for the 80s. He raised his head and scanned his room: door, kitchenette, table, two chairs, window, another window, bathroom, closet. That was it, no air conditioner, no TV, no phone.

He got up, closed the windows, had a drink of water from one of the bottles the airport driver had left with him, used the bathroom, and fell back to bed. Thanks to his long flights and some arbitrary jet lag, with a pillow over his head and a light blanket he fell asleep.

He woke up eight hours later feeling refreshed and hungry. He looked out the window. From his tenth-floor room, he could survey the city along the broad *Avenida Eduardo Mondlane* to the Maputo Central Hospital with its green roofs.

From his vantage point, the area was beautiful with flower gardens and clean wide streets. Closer examination of the hospital showed few parking lots, and fewer cars. Instead of massive parking lots, there were grassy areas, concrete tree containers, and groups of people walking around.

After a shower and clean clothes, he ventured outside. He found a nice café. He pointed at a croissant and the espresso machine. He ate, drank, took his Malaria pill, and called that breakfast. A short walk brought him to the hospital.

With his passport and the letter from Doctors with Helicopters grasped tightly in his already sweaty hand, he entered the big double doors at the top of worn marble stairs. He showed the Portuguese copy to the guard. With a few more helpful assists, he arrived at a small office with a long list of non-governmental organizations on the door. This was his destination, the Visiting NGO Office.

He knocked.

An overweight man, dressed in white shirt and pants, looking like a colonial bureaucrat from central casting, grunted as he stood up and offered his hand, "Harold Charter. I presume you are Brian Macalester."

Brian shook he proffered sweaty hand, "Yes. Are you from Doctors with Helicopters?"

"No, I'm from Research Solution Suppliers. RSS to our friends. Something to do with rodent excrement to our detractors." Harold tipped his head back and laughed, again straight out of central casting. "We handle logistics for the good doctors and many others." He pushed his business card across the desk.

Brian recited his long experience and closed with, "I intend to find a cure for this disease, but I'm going to need some resources."

Harold sighed and looked at some spot on the wall above Brian's left ear. "That's very interesting. The good doctors have not authorized me to do anything about that. I was told you were going to run some clinical trials."

"What about the local development of investigational drugs?"

Harold sighed again, "I don't know what those are, but I do have several cartons being held for you. I shook them and they sounded like pills, lots and lots of pills." Harold looked around the small office as if someone might have snuck in while they were talking. He lowered his voice and smiled broadly. "If those are the *right kind* of pills, you might be able to make a killing on the black market."

Brian thought the man might have winked. What kind of con man was this? Research Solution Suppliers? Pills? He *shook* them? He thinks they're *street drugs*?

The man was an idiot and a crook.

Brian said, "Well you tell your people that this is a waste of my

302

time and expertise. If they can't do anything better, I may just have to go somewhere else to make my contributions. My time and experience are valuable, and appear to be wasted here."

Harold looked at his belly, "As I've said, I don't know anything about any of that, but I can tell you we have a lease on that room for six months. Here is the name of your liaison, Dr. Xavier. He's part of their research staff, expecting you tomorrow morning."

He mentioned nothing more about the pills, probably because Brian had ignored the illegal suggestion.

Brian reached over and took the business card and headed for the door without even saying, "*Tchau.*"

"One more thing," Charter called to his back. "I'm staying at the Radisson. I'll be in-country until tomorrow afternoon. Feel free to contact me there if you need anything."

Brian slammed the door. He found his reception disheartening, to say the least. But he'd spent so long getting there…he couldn't think about a strategic retreat…or getting on any more airplanes for a while. Maybe Dr. Xavier would redeem Maputo. Harold Charter certainly hadn't.

———

The following morning, he went to Dr. Xavier's office. Dr. Xavier seemed to be holding several meetings simultaneously in a mixture of Portuguese, English and something Brian couldn't identify.

"*Os pacientes estão morrendo.*"

"The internet says we have rabies in Maputo."

"*Temos viajar uma longa distância.*"

"I have 20 healthy people, we can help if you tell us what to do."

Dr. Xavier towered over everyone. Brian looked up at him and guessed maybe six-four or six-five. He seemed like the center of a circus carousel with a frenetic circle of minions bouncing up and down around him for attention. Like a calliope, his tune jumped around between melody and chaos.

After the insolent treatment from Charter yesterday, Brian was cautious and waited at the door to assess the situation. After a few minutes, he identified three groups.

First, there was a group in white coats with *Hospital Central de Maputo* badges. They seemed concerned about people dying. Brian figured this was due to Aerosol Infectious Rabies or they wouldn't be talking to an epidemiology research doctor.

Second, there was a young Scandinavian woman who seemed to be with an African man, or maybe a boy. He looked young, but what would a child be doing here? They spoke with a lot of urgency and authority, probably representatives of another NGO sent here to help with the global crisis.

Third, there was a small group, also in white jackets, but with UC San Diego badges. They must also be volunteers.

Seeing so many potential allies, he moved toward Dr. Xavier, and clapped his hands. Everyone got quiet and looked at him.

Encouraging. If he could get these people organized, maybe he could solve this and discover a cure. This just might be his chance to make a lasting mark in the pharmaceutical world.

"I am Dr. Brian and I've been sent to supervise some clinical trials for this new strain of rabies. Who's going to oversee the trial administration?"

The room again erupted in several discussions, until Dr. Xavier said something to the Scandinavian woman in Portuguese, who then had a discussion with the African in the language Dr. Brian couldn't identify.

The African man/boy moved closer to Brian, "I am Halid. I'm in charge."

Brian decided to ignore his youthful looks and just be happy to have someone experienced to do the study. "Great! Pleased to be working with you. What NGO do you represent?"

Halid did not respond. Neither did anyone else. He took this silence to indicate they were ready to follow his lead. After all, he was obviously the most senior person present.

Building on this apparent success, he continued, "One more thing. I need a chemistry lab and a staff of trained chemists. Since I'm here, I'm going to do real drug development and put

Mozambique on the pharmaceutical map."

Dr. Xavier seemed to know the Scandinavian lady, because he spoke to her again. After an extended discussion, they turned away from Brian as if more pressing matters required their attention.

Brian had expected his arrival to energize and focus the effort. However, no such urgency materialized, and Halid, ostensibly in charge of the effort to find a cure, put off their first meeting to the next day. Brian's initial elation faded when he discovered that Halid spoke little English.

———

Later that evening he called Penny in Matu Kiva, twelve hours away. "My welcome committee was a guy from RSS who just wanted to hand me an apartment key and a stack of shipping cartons, and went on his way."

She seemed interested in the details. "Was that Research Solution Suppliers? What was in the cartons?"

Brian checked the business card. "Yes, that's who he works for. Wasn't that Jake's company? Anyhow, this guy said the boxes contained pills. Pills for clinical trials. He shook the boxes. Can you believe that? He shook the boxes?"

Penny just laughed.

"And when he decided that they were pills, he told me I could sell them on the black market. Unbelievable."

Penny laughed again, but she sounded a bit nervous this time.

He moved on to his second concern, "I had no idea they already had an investigational drug for AIR. You have heard about AIR?"

"Oh yes. Not much of a problem in Polynesia, but everyone is talking about Aerosol Infectious Rabies. Each island has limited diversity, even though the inter-island diversity is high. New diseases from outside are always a concern here, individual islands are always at risk for a catastrophic outbreak."

Brian thought about this comment. "I understand. I don't think that is a problem here. I recall that the genetic diversity of southern Africa far exceeds the diversity of the rest of the world."

Penny laughed again. "I guess we here represent the few who traveled across the Pacific, the smallest subset of the limited genotypes who ventured out of Africa to settle the rest of the world. The genetic mother lode still lives in Africa. Maybe that is why they sent you there."

Brian proudly thought of how fast she picked up things and understood the implications. "Could be, could be."

He always felt better after he spoke to her. After all these years, it was nice to be in touch again.

————

The following day, he struggled to communicate with Halid the complexity of clinical trial administration. After several false starts, he finally boiled it down to a few instructions.

"I will prepare numbered envelopes with powdered medications. Each will be dissolved in bottled water for the patient with the same number, and only that patient. Each patient has a different number, which will match one envelope."

"Twice a day, someone will record each patient's temperature, heart rate, and general health."

"That report will be delivered to me each morning."

That was it. There was no discussion of controls, placebos, and blind trials. Brian would be responsible for all of that when he prepared the envelopes.

Throughout the training, Halid just listened passively, without any interaction, and not taking any notes. Even with such simple instructions, Brian was not confident that Halid understood.

Brian gritted his teeth and walked through the instructions again, trying to ignore the passive face. This was what it meant to be in charge—no one else was picking up responsibility, so Dr. Brian had to.

But they could run the trials, assuming everyone could match numbers and avoid cross contamination. Brian worried this could still be a complete waste of time.

Regardless, he had a small office and the boxes were delivered, so he spent the rest of the day preparing envelopes for the first trial. The pills came from four different lot numbers, so just to be conservative, he treated each lot as a different compound. He powdered the pills, and found some large bottles of vitamin C, which he also powdered for the placebos.

He left the envelopes for Halid to use in the morning.

5. HALID

MAPUTO, MOZAMBIQUE

Halid had seen Nga's relief when they met up with Ben. It had felt so good to get to the hospital and find people they knew. Ben had led them into the hospital building through a small side door to which he had the key. They followed him down hall after hall. Halid made sure to keep an eye on Mezi and the children who were walking at the back of the group. Mezi nodded at him. She'd made certain no one got left behind.

After walking for what seemed like ten minutes, Ben brought the group into a dormitory area—a single room with rows of small beds, each with its own tiny closet and cabinet between the beds. Nga smiled, "The TC dormitory. We will be safe, here."

Ben told them there were only four TCs in training. The Luambe group could use one end of the room, the TCs were at the other. They'd put their things in the small cabinets between the beds.

Nga abruptly sat down on one of the beds. "I'm not sure why I am so exhausted, but I think I need to rest."

Halid stepped forward. "Rest," he said, taking up the reins of responsibility. "I will get everyone settled, and we can assign chores." He turned to the big Malawian, "Ben, is there a place the people can cook?"

Ben made a face. "No, that's going to be a problem. The hospital kitchens are restricted areas, of course, so cooking and food preparation for the patients is clean and standardized. Perhaps we can find a place in one of the outside patios for you, but then firewood becomes a problem. You cannot build fires in here, of course."

"Of course," Halid said.

"I will make some arrangements for your wounded," Ben said, eyeing Wayya and others in the group. "I'm sure our physicians will be happy to see something besides AIR. I will be back later to let you know what we can do; for now, settle in and rest."

Nga's eyes closed almost before she was horizontal.

Halid walked with Ben back to the door they'd entered by. "Was the door we came in the closest to outside?"

Ben shook his head. He indicated a short hallway to their left that ended at double doors wrapped with a chain and lock. "Those doors actually lead out to a patio, but we were having problems with refugees sneaking into the hospital from there, so now it is chained." Ben rubbed his chin, a frown wrinkling his forehead. "I'll see what I can do to get it reopened."

Halid nodded. Ben pointed the opposite direction, to yet another hallway. "In that direction, turn left, then right, and there is a door to the front courtyard. But there are hundreds of refugees camping there, so if you would like to stay isolated, it is probably not a good place for you."

"All right, thank you Ben." Halid thought he'd seen some windows that might give them access to the back-patio area. He would explore.

———

Nga was still asleep when Ben returned the next morning, saying a meeting had been called. Halid shook her shoulder and she woke up, looking much more alert and like her normal self.

"Meeting," Halid told her, nodding toward Ben, who was speaking with Mezi and Wayya.

Nga got herself together and she and Halid followed Ben out. Mezi was organizing a game for the group's children as they left, marking out spaces on the tiled floor as a game board with some pieces of tape she'd found.

"Toothpaste, and brushes, and soap," Nga murmured, looking everywhere for supplies.

As they followed Ben through the maze of hallways, Halid counted turns and mentally marked landmarks. It was like following a trail through the forest they would want to retrace later. Ben walked into a room with a group of people crowded inside. A sign on the door where they entered read Dr. Pablo

Xavier, Epidemiology.

Dr. Xavier towered over everyone. He talked in a mix of Portuguese, English and native languages, none of which was Yao. There was a group in white coats with *Hospital Central de Maputo* badges. There was a small group, also in white jackets, but with UC San Diego badges. There was a bluff red-faced man shouting for attention.

"I am Dr. Brian and I've been sent to supervise clinical trials on an investigational drug for this new strain of rabies. Who's going to oversee the trial administration?"

The room again erupted in several discussions, until finally Dr. Xavier spoke to Nga. "Can your people take this on?" His eyes flicked toward the loud man, Dr. Brian, and back.

Nga looked at Halid. He wasn't sure what "this" was that they would be doing, but he wanted his villagers to feel like they were contributing, they were part of the hospital and its work.

"I think they can do it," Nga said. "Can you lead them?"

Halid stepped forward. "I'm Halid, I am in charge," he said, but his English stumbled and he finished in Portuguese, "The Yao will do this work."

"One more thing!" Dr. Brian said, loudly. "I must have a chemistry lab and a staff of trained chemists!" He went on, but Halid listed to Dr. Xavier as the tall man spoke to Nga again, in such rapid Portuguese that Halid lost the thread. After an extended discussion, Nga nodded.

"I will find a lab, I am less certain about chemists," she said, and they turned away from Dr. Brian as Dr. Xavier pointed to the small group of white-coats.

"These are my University of San Diego Residency staff. They are studying Internal Medicine, and will serve as adjuncts in the research and treatment plans." Nga and Ben nodded. Dr. Brian said nothing.

Halid stared at the man, who seemed simultaneously pompous and clueless. As if he felt Halid's eyes on him, the American turned and asked a question in English that Halid did not understand.

"I will see you tomorrow to do these tests," he said in his best Portuguese, hoping that answered the man's query.

––––––

It felt like a party on the patio, and Halid hosted it as his father would have if the guests were elders of a visiting village. The UC San Diego doctors practiced their Portuguese, interspersed with English, while the Yao taught them the names of foods in Chiyao. Dr. Xavier showed up with a dish he had filched from the hospital kitchens, called, "macaroni and cheese."

Halid had tasted cheese before, and decided he still didn't like it. Instead, he offered Dr. Xavier a skewer of grilled yam with a little spicy pepper. He saw Nga and Ben talking about the baked squash, which had been the hardest thing for the Luambe villagers to cook. They had removed a stepping stone and dug a hole in the dirt of the patio to make an oven. Mezi and Wayya had used Wayya's lap in the wheelchair to carry several bags of charcoal they'd found at the impromptu market that had sprung up across the street from the hospital. The charcoal was lighted and let go to coals before they put the squash in the hole with it. The skin was charred, but the meat of the vegetable was delicious and cooked just right.

Besides the squash, they'd also found some recognizable greens and a large fresh ocean fish they'd learned to clean and cook while aboard the *Sun Fish*. Freshly squeezed juice, milk for the children, and large bottles of water completed the meal. The San Diego people had brought their appetites and the water. Ben's tiny wife, Catia, had brought two chickens she had baked in her kitchen at home. Halid noticed the San Diego crew were mostly eating that. Recognizable food. Everyone seemed happy, and Halid finally felt his villagers were safe. Maybe they could help make a difference in finding a solution to AIR.

6. NGA

MAPUTO, MOZAMBIQUE

Nga helped herself to breakfast, nodding her thanks to Jojeza and Mezi who had cooked it. Ben finally managed to get ahold of the key for the patio doors. The chain removed, and the Yao became the gatekeepers. The dorm was fine for sleeping but everyone felt more comfortable gathered outdoors under the mimosa trees. She finished her breakfast of boiled grains with chilies and headed to the computer labs the TCs had access to. She pulled up her mask, making sure it fitted properly to her face.

She passed wards crammed with AIR victims, most of them in the very early stages of the disease. Hospital workers—all of them masked and gowned like surgeons—worked among them.

She had been right to fear their arrival in Maputo; they had gotten here at the same time as the disease they had been fleeing from. All that long way from Luambe, and here it was, even worse than it had been in the village.

She tried not to think about what the journey had cost them. She could do nothing about her bad advice, now, except make the best of being here. But it was hard to forget she was the cause of a lot of suffering for the Yao of Luambe.

She tried to focus on doing good. Or what she hoped would be good. How could she even tell anymore?

She had found an awesome laboratory for Dr. Brian's work. The United Nations Pan-African Forensics Laboratory, *Laboratoire de Médecine Légale Nations Unies Panafricain*, had been created to examine the bodies and data about the Rwandan massacres, where hundreds of villages, many thousands of people, had been murdered in a racial purge.

Since the end of the study the lab had stood vacant, its valuable but aging equipment left unused. It was even within walking distance of the hospital. She composed an email to the government agency now in charge of the lab, intending to get Dr. Xavier's approval before sending it. All they needed were permission and a key.

The chemists were a bigger problem. She had searched Maputo's job applicant sites on a tip from Ben, but found nothing. Plenty of massage therapists and herbalists, pharmacists and probable drug dealers, but no chemists.

One of the San Diego doctors stuck her head around the door. "Do you think you can assist with some exams this morning? We never got a nurse assigned to us... "

Nga blinked. "I only have to find these chemists for Dr. Brian, then of course I can help. You know I only have TC training, different from nursing."

The young woman nodded. "Halid is helping, too—so I'm sure you will be most welcome."

"Okay," Nga said, turning back to her computer screen.

"Try local schools," the doctor said. Nga thought her name was Greta, but she could not read the woman's name tag from that distance.

Nga nodded. "I'll find you as soon as I get something here. Where will you be?"

"Well, there's Dr. Brian's meeting, and otherwise I will be with Dr. Benson in the trauma ward."

Nga knew where that was. "Good, I will see you at the meeting if not before."

"Good, then." The doctor withdrew.

Out of desperation, she tried a Google search, typing "chemists, Maputo." Drugstores. Herbalists, again. And something called Khemistry Kids. She clicked on that. High school students. Prize-winning high school students, led by an obviously proud Dr. Armando Queiroz. She searched on his name. His training had been scientifically rigorous; she could hope he had passed that along to his students. Maybe they could do the job.

She wrote down the contact number and email address, then shut down the computer. They'd had computers and taught the TCs how to use them when she had trained years ago. This much newer computer was almost an entirely different gadget, but a few moments' lessons by a harassed tech lab student had set her on her way. The Mozambique government was doing its best to move the nation into the present, but its people still had to catch up. She imagined Anane trying to use a computer and grinned.

Her call to Dr. Queiroz produced a meeting for early afternoon.

She shook his hand. The plump gray-haired man had a wonderful smile. "We can do this; it is exactly what we have trained for. But we have no equipment, no laboratory." His Portuguese was good but tinted with a very strange accent.

"I have secured permission to use the old United Nations Pan-African Forensics Laboratory. Do you know it?"

He nodded. "I know of it; I have never been in there."

"I'm supposed to be getting the key later tonight. Dr. Xavier was able to acquire it." She bit her lip. "You will be working with an American researcher, Dr. Brian Macalester."

The doctor made a puzzled face. "Problem?"

How to say it? "Um, he is an *American* researcher."

"He speaks only English?"

"Yes." But that wasn't quite what she had meant.

"That is okay. I speak English, too."

She smiled at him. This is what made Mozambique great, people like him who were tolerant, hard-working and smart. And spoke six or seven languages.

"Well, I hope he is not too arrogant," she said. "He seemed to look down on everyone yesterday."

It was Dr. Queiroz's turn to smile. "It is good, we will do fine."

———

She'd assisted the San Diego resident physicians in the trauma ward for hours, especially helping with the pre-surgery explanations to Wayya. Wayya was irritated with all the discussions. She just wanted a foot that would work so she could walk. She would not have a wheelchair in the village— nor did she want one.

"Just an old wood foot will work," she said. "My papa's

brother had one, it worked fine."

"Well, we have better ones now," Greta said after Nga had translated. "But no matter what kind you have, we need to clean up your ankle before it can be fitted."

"Who is paying for this?" Wayya asked. The young woman was the exception who spoke only Chiyao, and a little Bemba.

"It is a charity organization," Greta said in her halting Portuguese. Then she looked askance at Nga. "They're not hateful about charity are they? I had some people who absolutely refused free treatments because they... "

"Were too proud?" Nga shook her head. When she translated for Wayya, the young woman burst into ironic laughter.

"The Yao are proud, not stupid," she said. Nga told Greta, who grinned.

"Good then," the young doctor said.

Nga was grateful for the resident's help. Greta was supposed to be working in internal medicine, but had volunteered to help in the trauma ward, the most desperate for physicians after AIR.

Wayya received the benefit of that. Other amputees were still waiting, with complicated and multiple amputations. Mostly from land mines, which were still a huge problem in some parts of Mozambique. The triage nurse had moved Wayya up the priority list to take advantage of Greta's help and to draw Nga into the ward. The land mine victims would be looked at, but once their initial surgeries were completed, there was no particular rush. AIR patients had pulled away most of the hospital staff, so this was a win-win situation for Nga and Wayya and the ward.

Later, Nga called Shelly, using the hospital's land line. It was TC business, so she didn't wince too much at the hospital footing the bill.

"The villagers have gone back to Lichinga," Shelly said. Just the sound of her voice was like a big hug.

"How did Salim do?"

"He improved quite a bit, and the other wounded also. They were fierce ready to re-take Luambe. No one had AIR, which I consider a miracle. The camp here has several hundred refugees now, so your villagers are safer back home."

"Yes. I hope they succeed without getting themselves killed. Salim and Anane are good people." "They are. I adore Anane. She is so patient and kind and good to Salim and all the villagers. How are things in Maputo?"

Nga could hear the worry in Shelly's voice. "Actually, things are going very well here. They are going to try some drugs to see what will affect AIR. We are housed in the TC dorm; oh—there are only four TC students just now. We definitely need to help with recruiting."

"Yes, I have been encouraging a couple of young men from the city here to go. It would be much better for them than their current jobs," she laughed.

"Pick-pockets?"

"And pimps. Ugh. What do you think about trying to rehabilitate some of the prostitutes here? A couple of them are extremely bright and ambitious. They could do very well in the TC program."

"That could work. We certainly need more trained people. I was helping as a surgical nurse today; it's crazy."

"You told them you were not trained for that, yes?"

"Of course, but the need is so great. And the surgeon is supposed to be doing Internal Medicine. What does she know about amputations? Enough I guess. She did a great job, and Wayya will be ready to be fitted for a prosthetic in a week or so."

"Oh, one of the San Diego students? They are still doing that Internal Medicine Residency program?"

"Yes, thank the stars. Most of them are working on AIR, but one is willing to work wherever she is needed. It will be an odd reference for her if she stays in Internal Medicine, though."

They both chuckled at that.

"So, what are they planning to fit your Wayya with? One of the land mine donations?"

"I'm not sure yet, but probably."

"We have a fabrication plant here in Nacala that is making a variation of the Jaipur foot. It's called a 'rolling joint' and it allows somewhat better movement. Wayya might be happier with that, out in the village."

"I'll ask about it."

"We'll be able to get her replacements here, if she gets that kind. She will need a new one about every five years."

"The rubber kind?"

"Yes. It's supported by donations. It's a small business, but the manufacturing plant seems to be in production continuously." There was a short pause, then, "How are your rape victims doing?"

"Tonan's wife and Jojeza are responding to the PTSD counseling. Miss Anderson is not; she is still a zombie."

"Oh, I was worried about her. Can she work as a nurse's aide or something? Some times that helps."

"She'll do anything someone tells her to do, but nothing more. It's like she's not even there any more, just her body standing there."

Shelly made a sad little noise in her throat. "So awful. We need teachers out in the countryside so badly, too."

"Yes." Nga saw Halid pass by outside the door, then return and gesture to her. "Shelly, I have to go. Keep safe. Wear your mask!"

"All the time," Shelly said. "And you, too. Hugs to you." Nga put down the phone.

"Oh, I didn't mean to interrupt," Halid said. "But I have news about Sami and Botte."

"Are they leaving the group?"

"Yes. Sami apparently has a friend out on the edge of town, who runs a towing company, for cars?" Nga nodded. "So they are going to help with that, and wash cars, and they can sleep in the back of the place as watchmen." Halid grinned sardonically.

"Good."

"And good riddance," Halid said, using the Chiyao terms for ridding the village of noxious pests.

She grinned back at him.

So...maybe coming to Maputo had been a good thing—at least

for *some* of the Luambe villagers. She kept thinking Jojeza would be a good candidate for the TC program, along with Halid.

BAT CHAT

PLUS FREQUENTLY ASKED QUESTIONS

? What are microbats?

Microbats are one of the two suborders of bats, formally called microchiroptera, yangochiroptera, or vespertilioniformes. DNA analysis is changing taxonomies previously based on anatomy. These bats are generally less that an ounce (15 gm) with a wingspan under a foot (30 cm).

Microbats live around the globe in the northern temperate regions. The largest populations in North America are Mexican Free-tail Bats, notably in Bracken Cave, and around Carlsbad Caverns, and Little Brown Bats. The largest populations in Europe are Pipistrelles.

These bats eat insects and migrate or hibernate in the winter. They use echolocation and have strange looking faces for this purpose.

http://www.batcon.org
http://www.bats.org.uk/

 Mongol Bataar: Anyone making progress on AIR?

 Fleming: I have a drug in trials. Can't say much more.

 John Snow: I have followed up on all treatments. Nothing promising yet.

 Capt Contagious: I saw some good results in from an herbal treatment in Australia.

 Mongol Bataar: I'm trying a treatment from Australia in the US with mixed results.

 Kitty: The Milwaukee Protocol helped my father.

 Syms Covington: So we need more research?

 Popo: Always more research.

 Radar Bat: Just so people aren't killing bats.

 Nina de la Ciencia: Yes, please don't kill the bats

 Morcego: I heard a rumor that the genetic work from New Mexico might be the key.

319

7. ARIQ

ROSWELL, NEW MEXICO

The sun dropped toward the peaks of the Sierra Blanca mountains as Ariq headed south to fetch the students from Carlsbad Caverns.

As Jessenia had predicted, much of the work had involved trapping bats in mist nets and punch biopsy collection. Even without an invitation, his students had infiltrated the teams by climbing the rocks like bears and expertly retrieving bats from the mist nets.

Ariq looked forward to seeing Lily, not that he'd have been able to pick her face out of a crowd. Aside from a short email, he'd had little news of the girl he was counting on to save his sick patients, especially Sofia's mom who was on the verge of coma or death. At this thought, he stepped on the gas and pushed his speed to over eighty. With the straight, flat highway still flooded with bright sunlight, he felt safe over the speed limit.

As soon as he arrived at the Caverns, he herded his allotment of students into his small SUV and secured their gear and Lily's luggage to the roof. He gave her the front seat, where she held the precious herbs for the stew close to her chest.

He was relieved to have finally met her in real life. IRL as the kids said. He wanted to hug her, but that didn't seem appropriate. Lily was subdued. He'd always imagined her as animated, full of energy. He found this strangely disconcerting.

Her coloring and features were different than he expected. He recalled she was only part aboriginal, so he'd thought she would blend in with the Hispanics and Native Americans. Instead, she was more African to his Asian eyes, except for the bleached white hair.

One thing reassured him. Her eyes. Her large, dark eyes seemed to glimmer with depths of energy and intelligence. As the sun sent beams through the car, those eyes reflected energy everywhere.

To his relief, she agreed to go straight to the clinic.

When the clinic came into sight, he became hypervigilant and anxious not to delay even an extra minute getting some stew into Louisa.

Instead of taking Lily through the impressive reception complex, he drove right past the main buildings to the old Area 51 Hideout dirt lot, potholes, and all.

He didn't even park. He drove right up to Louisa's room and stopped the car on the sidewalk, barely avoiding a crash into the stucco wall. At this point, he urged Lily out of the car, grabbed the bag of herbs and ran into Louisa's room. Lily followed, easily keeping pace.

Sofia stood as they entered. "I'm so glad to see you. Mama is shaking and panting." She turned to Lily. "Please help. The doctor wants to put her to sleep. They just can't. I'm sure she won't wake up."

Joni must have heard the commotion, because she suddenly appeared. "How can I help?"

Ariq replied, "This is Lily. Please help her make stew. She has the herbs." He put his arms straight out, passing the herbs to her. "I'll stay with Louisa and Sofia."

Sofia had not exaggerated. Louisa was having a seizure, already surrounded by a doctor and two nurses. One nurse had removed the IV to prevent injury from the tremors, while the other held an oxygen mask, connected to a small canister, in place. In the rush to open the annex, it had not been plumbed for oxygen.

When the doctor saw Ariq, he explained, "She's in critical condition. I've recommended we induce a coma. That's the only treatment that has worked in the past. She is too far gone to consent, and her daughter will not consent. I'm afraid we're going to lose her."

"Just wait. We'll have an alternative available in a few minutes. It can only be administered orally. We need her awake and alert for another twenty minutes."

The doctor looked unhappy. "I can relax her and maintain consciousness for a short period. But after that I insist on a protective, medically-induced coma."

Sofia yelled, "No, no coma! She'll die!"

He turned to the nurse, "Diazepam, five milligrams, IM, and two oral sprays of CBD aerosol."

He stepped back and looked to Ariq, "Good luck."

When Lily and Nizhoni returned, the doctor looked at the bowl of murky soup and frowned. Fortunately, Joni held the stew, because Sofia threw her arms around Lily.

At first Lily seemed shaken by all the excitement, but as soon as she sat next to Louisa and started feeding her with a small plastic spoon, she seemed completely calm.

Between spoons of warm stew, Lily leaned in close to Louisa and whispered. Sometimes it sounded like English and at other times like something else.

Before she consumed half the stew, Sofia's mother became quiet and the tremors stopped. Ariq feared she had died, but he saw her shallow breathing and she continued to accept more stew.

Everyone slept better that night.

———

Ariq felt good. Lily arrived and Louisa was receiving stew. This euphoria ended early the next morning when someone from the CDC called. Angry would have been an understatement.

"Didn't you read the nondisclosure agreement you signed? You are not permitted to speak publicly or publish anything without CDC review and approval."

Nondisclosure agreement? Ariq had no idea. What were they talking about? Why was the CDC calling? He had sent his MMWR disease data and made a few queries, but hadn't received any response. He wondered if this call had something to do with the sequencers. Jake and RSS had arranged the finances. Now he worried that he should have asked more questions.

"But people are sick and dying. I needed—"

"You? You are an administrator! We expected qualified

researchers to be using those machines."

So, it *was* about the sequencers.

"I can't begin to list all the regulations you've violated. You'll be lucky to stay out of jail!"

Jail? Ariq never expected glory, but incarceration wasn't on his list either. "What?"

"I can see you didn't read what you signed, but you'd better listen carefully to what I'm telling you now. First, someone is coming to reclaim the sequencers. Second, CDC is taking control of all the data generated by our machines. And third, and most important, you will not speak or write of this to anyone. Even this call is classified."

Classified?

Ariq didn't know how to respond, but hoped that some researchers had already downloaded his data to their own servers. Then the data would be out of his control.

This sounded serious. He wondered if they could revoke his Green Card. This was so outside his experience, he was mostly scared. Someone with the proud name from Ariq Böke should never be this scared.

He barely listened to the rest of the call liberally peppered with mentions of classified data, national security, and terrorism.

———

He held the morning staff meeting in a closed conference room. They were still standing, to keep the meetings brief, but there was a door between them and everyone else while he recounted his call from the CDC.

The staff had no interest or concern for this drama at the Chiropteran Research Center, but it was so heavy on his mind he had to say something before he could address the other issues.

Doctor Charles, being senior, began, "One of the reasons to be in Roswell is to avoid bureaucratic meddling from Washington." He paused, seeming to think, and then added, "And Atlanta," to make his intent clear.

Having made his point, he changed direction. "Everything

we're doing is proper…plus we don't have a big airport, any fancy hotels, or casinos, or even voters, so the CDC won't be visiting us anytime soon. Just ignore them."

Martina added, "I think we have the CDC, or maybe the NIH, to thank for the circus in the south, at the Caverns. I hear that in addition to the scientist flown back from Australia, and assisted by your science club, and the biologists, protesters have arrived from Texas. *Texas!*"

"I don't know if they are protesting the scientists or the bats. You'd imagine that if they thought one or the other carried a risk of AIR, they'd stay away!"

Ariq added, "Regardless we can be glad this circus, as you call it, is a hundred miles away."

He found the distance comforting. Protesters attracted to the clinic or, even worse, the CRC, would spook the Roswell planning commission. He'd never get approval to pave the Area 51 parking lot or plumb the annex for patient oxygen, much less consideration of the E-Ro development.

Martina seemed to bring every discussion back to the wedding.

"Lachy and I thought we'd have a small wedding ceremony at the Carlsbad Cavern amphitheater, but now the place is overrun with soldiers and protesters. Once again, we're open to suggestions. We'd like to do something soon."

Doctor Lachlan had surgery scheduled, so the wedding digression was short.

Ariq was ready to end the meeting and visit patients with nurse Nizhoni, when the conference room door flew open. In came a silly-looking man in tourist western wear. From a Stetson hat with a beaded band to snakeskin boots with silver tips, he looked like something from a dude ranch catalog. He even had a bolo tie with a large turquoise slider. Under each arm, he carried a pink box that everyone recognized as from 3D.

Ariq did a double take when he recognized him. It was Jake, the mystery man who often showed up without notice, but bearing gifts.

"Good Morning all! Jake the salesman here. The 3D special of the day is the New Mexico state cookie: *bizcochito*." He opened the boxes on the conference room table.

Ariq wondered if Jake was going to collect the sequencers. Then he realized that Jake wasn't dressed to crate the machines, drive a fork lift, or haul everything away in an eighteen-wheeler. In fact, the man wasn't dressed for much of anything, except maybe startling entrances.

While everyone ate cookies, Ariq pulled Jake over to a secluded corner. "What are you doing here? CDC called. They're going to take away our machines."

"I heard about that call."

Again, Jake seemed to know everything.

"The CDC is so funny. First, they want rush shipments everywhere. Next, they want everything shipped back to some warehouse. I'm just the sales guy. Most of this is between Research Solutions Suppliers and the CDC. I think the RSS lobbyists in Washington are also involved. Not sure. I just sell stuff."

Ariq picked up a *bizcochito*. The sweet cinnamon cookie crumbled when he took a bite. He brushed off his shirt and waited. Experience told him that Jake would go on without prompting.

"Anyway, my wife and I were taking a short break to visit Zuni, Hopi, and Anasazi ruins, so I thought we'd drop by to see how you were doing."

Ariq realized that standing behind Jake was a short woman with wavy blond hair, and an amused smile. "Are you going to introduce me to your friend?" she said.

"Oh, excuse me. Ariq, this is my lovely wife Dee. As you know, I travel a lot, so this is special to have her with me. As I told you, we're visiting the ruins. She collects pottery, both archeological and contemporary."

This guy could talk forever. Ariq finished his cookie and tried to lead him to the point, "So tell me, when are they coming to reclaim my equipment?"

"Oh, I could tell you stories about how long they take to do anything. RSS have nothing to do with that. The GAO will schedule packing and shipping and storage. If they put a rush on it, which they never do, the packing crew could be here in a month, and shipping a month later. Just forget about it. I remember once, not far from here—Los Alamos I believe, the entire process took four years. Longer than the Manhattan Project."

Once he understood that he could ignore the CDC call for the time being, Ariq was eager to get on with his patient rounds. Joni stood by waiting patiently. Ariq murmured his thanks and turned to leave when Jake started up again. Ariq listened politely.

"I can't believe they're recalling your machines. I listened to your online meeting. I've lost count of how many of those machines we delivered around the world in the panic leading up to the AIR announcement. You know I was there in Geneva when they broke the news.

"To make a long story short, you have done more with your equipment than anyone else has. Heck, there are machines in Mozambique that are still in their crates! RSS installers had been so busy. The wait time is unbelievable. I can't believe you got your system up and running with a group of high school kids. At least that's what I've heard."

Ariq smiled proudly. Joni moved closer to take in this indirect praise for her daughter and her friends.

"I've had calls from customers, you know scientists, around the world. You've impressed them all. They think your theories about extra B-cells and gene swapping are far out there, but they're impressed nonetheless. 'Quite something for someone without scientific training,' they say."

Ariq ignored the insult and jumped in with Jessenia's results, "You can tell anyone you speak to that we've seen viral immunity move rapidly through a colony. We have hard empirical data on this. Some mechanism must explain that."

Jake seemed to be thinking. Dee whispered something in his ear. Jake walked toward the door. "Well, nice to have visited you. I know you have a hospital to run. Keep up the good work."

So as quickly as they had burst in, Jake–and his wife–vanished. Ariq scratched his ear, wondering why Jake had even come in the first place. The man was an enigma.

———

When he visited Louisa Cortez with Joni, they found Sofia still sitting by her mother's side. Ariq feared for the worst. Louisa had died, hadn't she?

Sofia held her mother's hand gently.

Then he noticed she was smiling. In fact, they both were smiling.

Speaking softly, as if not wanting to break some magic spell, Sofia said, "*Ella está bien. Ella vivirá.*"

He looked more closely at Louisa. Her breathing was stronger. Her color was better. Her eyes were open and blinking.

Sofia continued in the same hushed tones, but with a solemn joy, like being in church, "That lady from Australia, she fed my mama the *sopa* and she talked to her and touched her. Mama is getting better."

Louisa said, "*Gracias a Díos.*" Mother and daughter hugged. Ariq turned to Nizhoni, "We need to find Lily and let her know."

For the first time, he felt at peace with his feeling about the strange girl from Australia, and what it seemed she could accomplish. The Roswell Orthopedic Clinic might not be staffed or prepared for sick people, Ariq might not be educated and trained, but good things were happening here.

ROSWELL, NEW MEXICO

Although they had "met" online and through Skype audio, Lily was still excited to meet Ariq in person. They chatted as the big vehicle drove the high school research team home from Carlsbad. Mostly they talked about bats, of course. Once Ariq had dropped off each student and the mom at his or her home, Lily settled back and prepared to get to know Ariq Temuujin.

They went straight to the hospital. Ariq was desperate for her to see one patient—the mother of one of his science students.

Lily's back ached and she was tired, but not sleepy—still a bit off because of what everyone called "jet lag" and what she called a disconnect from the dreamtime. She felt out of touch here, as if she had stepped outside the cloud that held the dreamtime. That was wrong. It should be with her, part of her, and her part of it. It shouldn't matter where she went, should it?

They'd made and administered the stew, then Ariq had taken her to his home, offering a 'guest room' for her to sleep in.

"If that doesn't work for you, we can get you a room at the motel. It's a little tacky, with lots of alien sci-fi stuff… "

"No, your house will be fine if we can manage that. I don't really have money for a motel. I can also camp out, if that's an option."

"Not necessary, unless you're uncomfortable with me. I have a kitchen, bathroom, the whole bit."

Lily was just glad to have a place to sleep.

The next few days were a blur of stew, sick patients, and bat work at the lab by the hospital. Lily thought the CRC would be a refuge, but it was not.

She was outraged by the number of bats in cages. "You cannot really get useful information from them when they are not in their native place, can you?"

Jessenia was obviously frustrated, trying to explain her project. "We are looking at details of genetics and trying to learn how the bats manage to maintain their health while carrying viruses," she said.

"I believe I understand that," Lily said, trying not to sound as angry as she felt. "What I don't understand is why the bats need to be kept here in cages. Don't you already have samples from them?"

"We do, but when something new—something like AIR shows up, we are interested in how the immunity is passed from bat to bat."

"So they should be with other bats," Lily said.

"They *are* with other bats," Jessenia said, sounding defensive.

"To be healthy, a colony needs to be all together. They groom each other, they breathe each other's air, they have their babies together. They take care of each other when they are sick. They even share food sometimes. None of that can happen when they are caged like this. Their cages aren't even next to each other!"

At that point, Ariq stepped in. "We are also trying out ideas for cures, Lily. We need a sampling of bats to see how the different species react, to understand how the viruses and the immunities are spread. Among species? Between species? These bats would not be found together in the wild."

Lily blinked, thinking through what he'd said. "If they aren't together in the wild, they *aren't* passing immunity between species," she said.

"Perhaps. But we don't *know* that. We're trying to understand a mechanism by looking at what happens when they're exposed to a virus. Do all species react the same? How do they compare?"

Lily stood in front of a big cage of flying foxes, looking at them in the dim light. At least the CRC tried to mimic natural conditions, the bats didn't endure bright lights, or unnatural lights like the fluorescents in the hospital. She nodded. "I guess I understand, but I don't like it. How long will they be here?"

"We have found that captive animals sometimes do very

poorly if they are released back into the wild."

"So, until they die, then?" Lily could feel a wall building between her and Ariq and his students. She didn't want to argue with them, but this wasn't right. The bats couldn't fly. They couldn't be together with their colony. This violated everything she knew from her observations and from what she had learned of the dreamtime and the bats' place in it.

"They are well-cared for, and they are helping to save human lives." Ariq spread his hands. "I'm sorry you didn't understand that's what we do here, Lily. I certainly didn't mean to cause you distress."

"It's not me," she said indignantly, "it's the bats I'm worrying about."

———

Her next day in Roswell, she met White Ears, Ariq's pony. He'd invited her to ride, but of course, she had no idea how, and had declined.

"I'll come watch," she said.

"I guess your people didn't have the option to learn about riding," he said.

"Kangaroos aren't really the right shape," Lily said, grinning. She pictured Obrey riding a kangaroo and had to laugh. "And dingos are too small."

"Same problem they had on the African continent—no appropriate animals. Zebras have weak backs and strong temperaments. We were lucky, in Mongolia."

Ariq backed White Ears up, just like he'd backed up his car to get out of the driveway.

"See, kangaroos can't do that."

"Do what?" Ariq rode the pony forward again, steering White Ears so Lily could reach the pony's head.

"Back up."

Ariq looked at her, a puzzled expression on his face. "Really? How do they get out of places?"

Lily shrugged. "They jump. Or don't get into places, or turn around and hop out. Their legs don't go backward."

"Hnh."

Lily touched the pony's soft nose and patted its head between the pricked ears. "Does he like being petted?"

"Not like a cat or a dog does, but she enjoys the attention. She thinks she is the most beautiful pony in the world."

Lily smiled. "She is. I hear you call her a pony. Is that different from a horse?"

"Ponies are smaller, and generally sturdier."

Of course, they used horses—and ponies, she supposed—at the *whitefella* ranches in the outback, but Lily had never been close to one. She watched the way the neat animal moved, and how Ariq sat upon her, fitting with her as though they were one. Then Ariq trotted off on his ride and she wandered around the open desert.

She pinched the leaves of plants, some pungent, some almost odorless. The ground was very sandy, instead of the red dust they mostly had at home. Lizards and birds and beetles were active, showing this was a desert, like hers, that supported many kinds of life. The early morning air was dry and cool, very much like at home.

After his ride, Ariq showered and dressed and they shared a simple breakfast of fruit and a bagel, which Lily had never tried before. It was chewy.

"I will cook dinner tonight," she offered. "I brought some dried foods I can cook."

"Do you eat meat?"

"Of course, but you have no kangaroo or snake or goanna— things I know how to cook. Fish, maybe."

Ariq nodded. "We can stop and pick up fish on the way home."

"You have fish in the desert? You have rivers?"

"We have rivers, and fish, and even ocean fish are flown in fresh each day."

"Mmm. I know how to cook river fish."

"Maybe some tilapia, then. Or trout."

Still feeling like there was a wall between them, a wall made of caged bats, Lily got into Ariq's van for the ride to the hospital, bags full of stew in containers by her feet.

She was startled when her telephone rang, drums thrumming "Hello?"

"Lily? Where are you? I've been trying to reach you for days!"

She realized she had never told her mother what she was doing, where she was going.

Was that a good thing or bad?

"Hello, mama. I'm sorry—I'm in the United States."

"What? What...where? I thought they had great cell phone coverage in America, but my calls did not go through. Were you in the bottom of a cave or something?"

Actually, she had been in a cave, but Mother probably didn't need to know that. "We were out in the desert, collecting bat samples."

"Oh. You and your stupid bats. That is so—ahh. Lily! Your Aunt Olivia is dead!" Her mother spoke the dead's name, just like *balanda* would do. That one fact made it clear, in a way Lily had never quite seen before, that Adjana had utterly abandoned the people's ways. "Pana needs you. I need you! We need to have a funeral service for her."

"I have done everything I can for your sister, Mama. Pana is with Pearl, which is the very best place she can be right now. She needs to be her own person for a while, to know what she wants. Pearl will help her with that. Her mother was angry at me; her anger has pushed me away."

"What are you talking about? She's your aunt! It's not like we have enough relatives to make a whole family, you can't just walk away."

"I have a whole family, Mama. It is just not exactly your family." Yes, that was so true that as Lily said it, she felt a warmth spread through her—the warmth of the dreamtime, of her people. Pearl, Obrey and Damon, June, Gima and his son and even his old battered truck. Kalinda from inside the dreamtime, and even Kutai and Minka, and all the people whose names she didn't know—those were her family. Maybe someday Minnakenna and

Jandry and the others at Ngukurr would be, also, but that did not matter so much to Lily, now.

"I have things to do here, Mama. I am not coming home for a *balanda* ceremony I wouldn't even be invited to if I weren't of your blood."

Her mother said nothing, but she could tell Adjana was crying. "Lily, please. I cannot lose you both."

"I'm sorry. I'm sorry you feel alone. I will come see you when I get back. But not now."

Her mother hung up. Lily turned her phone off and sighed. She felt cruel, as though she had a responsibility to go take care of her mother, go to the *balanda* funeral of the woman who had half-raised her, even though her aunt had begun to hate her. She felt bad for Pana, but not her aunt. And her mother clearly did not understand, and probably never would. But she remembered Pearl's words about choices.

It felt as though she had made hers.

———

Lily came through the open CRC door. She heard Ariq's students talking.

"Louisa is so much better today. I think Lily's stew must really work," Jessenia said. "Sofia just cried when she came in today and saw her mother so much better."

Lily stood quietly at the doorway into the room, unnoticed as yet. The other girl said, "She's so tiny!"

"Lily?" Jessenia laughed. "Yes she is. I love her little face, her hair."

"I didn't know aboriginals had white hair."

"Some do, but I think Lily said she bleached it, just for fun."

They became aware the subject of their conversation had come into the room at about the same time Lily was thinking maybe she should go out and come back in again, making more noise.

"So do you bleach it?" the girl asked. Lily couldn't remember her name.

"I did. It was an experiment. It's okay, but I think I will let it grow out."

"I want to dye mine red, but my mother would have a cow."

Cow? Lily shook her head. There were so many idioms in English, especially American English, that she did not know.

"My mother actually likes mine," Lily said.

"Oh, wow, that's fun, to have a mom that lets you do stuff."

Lily shrugged. "Sometimes doing stuff isn't so spiffy," she said, feeling very old.

The girls both gave her blank looks.

Spiffy? Where had she heard that word? Had she even used it right? The unnamed girl's phone rang, and Lily thought about her own phone, and maybe looking up words in the dictionary. Oh. Words!

"Please," she smiled at them. "There is something you can maybe help me with. I have these language tapes, but my tape player is dying. Do you think we can put the lessons onto CDs or maybe use my phone or something? I was going to ask Ariq, but you probably are better with technology."

"Um, well, we have to digitize them, then they could be put on your phone, then you can listen to them just like music," Jessenia said. "Can your tape machine play them one more time, do you think?"

"I hope so." She got the tapes and her player out and Jessenia looked it over. She carefully removed the cassette that was in the machine, then replaced it.

The other girl said, "You know, my papa could help with this. He still has working tape players and he's been converting all his old music to mp3's."

Lily felt hope, at last. "That would be so wonderful. These tapes were made by the last few Marra speakers in the world. I am trying to learn it to help keep the language alive."

"Oh, wow. That's so cool," Jessenia said.

"I can take them to my dad. He'll be even more excited to do it if he knows what it is for," the other girl said. She began putting everything into a plastic bag, which she put into her backpack.

"Thank you so much," Lily said. An awkward silence fell. "You said Mrs. Louisa is feeling better?"

"Yep. Sofia is so relieved," Jessenia said. "And most of the other patients are better, too. Your stew is helping."

"I need to get more supplies," Lily said. "I didn't bring enough." That was going to be a problem, because she was certain there wasn't anything here that she could substitute.

But she was beginning to think it wasn't just the stew.

Olivia had been given Pearl's stew. Pearl's had to be the best; she had been making it a long time, she knew the perfect proportions. But Olivia was now dead. Lily wasn't sure how much stew Pearl had been able to give the woman, though. Kalinda had been given stew, though not very much. She was dead.

June and Obrey and the soldier and Mrs. Louisa and Ariq's other patients were better. It wasn't making any sense. Was she making her stew wrong, but in a good way?

9. DR. BRIAN

MAPUTO, MOZAMBIQUE

℞ In just a couple of days, Brian fell into a pleasant routine. Up at dawn, he took a brisk walk to *Avenida da Marginal* where he could watch the sun rise over the Indian Ocean. Since today was Sunday, many people joined the parade to the beach. The crowd included extended families in bright clothes, women carrying baskets on their heads, girls in skirts walking dutifully behind, some carrying small children, and barefoot boys in t-shirts and shorts running everywhere like a swarm of puppies, occasionally kicking a soccer ball. *Bola de futebol.*

He wore slacks and a button-down shirt. Though some of the doctors at Maputo Central didn't wear ties, he still thought that one was appropriate for all occasions. As an important scientist from the United States, he had an image to uphold.

On the way back, he stopped at his café for breakfast. Even after only a few days, they recognized him and greeted him as "Doctor Brian," with their pleasant Mozambican accents.

He replied, *"Bom dia,"* or, *"Oi,"* when he arrived, and, *"Tchau,"* when he left.

With little else to do, he headed to the hospital, as he did every day. As he approached, he noticed a group of students, all in short-sleeved white shirts with navy-blue ties, maybe a dozen boys wore sneakers and slacks and a few girls wearing sandals and skirts. The ties, skirts, and slacks didn't exactly match, but still seemed to be part of a uniform.

An older man with wire rim glasses, prominent cheeks and a big smile walked toward him and took hold of his shoulders, "Dr. Brian, right? Nga told us we could meet you here."

Brian stood tall, but still found himself looking up at this man. Despite the gray hair cut close to his head, Brian guessed the man was ten years his junior. He had that bounce in his step and quickness of action that Brian associated with youth.

"Nga? Do I know Nga? Who are you?"

The man laughed. "Nga? Of course, you know Nga. Everyone knows her. Tallish? Blonde? You told her you needed chemists and a lab. Remember?"

Oh, that chaotic meeting with Dr. Xavier. He did remember the blonde. What did that meeting have to do with this man and all these kids? He cautiously replied, not wanting to commit to anything, "I guess I recall her. How does this involve you?" Brian waved his hand at the students, who now surrounded him and were all talking in languages he didn't recognize, "…and them?"

The gray-haired man, slightly overweight, especially compared to these skinny teenagers, did a Santa Claus belly laugh, "Me? I'm Armando Queiroz. You can call me Mando."

Dr. Brian backed up. The students had moved in too close for his American standards of personal space.

"I teach Chemistry. These are my students." He said something to the kids in a foreign language. They all got quiet and stood in two very straight lines. "You asked for chemists."

Everyone smiled. "We are chemists," they announced in unison in English.

Brian unconsciously shook his head. This was the way his days had been going, up and down, up, and down. After waking in a beautiful city on the Indian Ocean and having a delightful breakfast, teenage chemists. Chemists? Hah.

He already had Halid, a young man fresh from the countryside, who could barely speak English, administering a clinical trial with unknown drugs, delivered by the mysterious Research Solution Suppliers. His motto for Maputo had become: Nothing good happens after breakfast.

And now they expected him to do chemistry with Santa and his elves. He was going to call Penny and see if he could join her in Tahiti, anything to get away from here.

Mando went on, seemingly oblivious to the discouraged response. "Also, Nga found us a lab, a wonderful working laboratory."

Brian wondered again, who is this Nga anyway? How could

she find a chemistry lab? A lab wasn't something that would just be hiding behind a fresh vegetable stall or in some deserted alley. Besides, what might pass for a lab in this place, especially if high school students were chemists?

"If you could follow us, please. It is just a few blocks."

Brian had nothing else planned, and he was curious. And the day couldn't get worse, could it?

They headed away from the hospital. Brian followed. They were a strange sight, all in shirts and ties, heading inland on Sunday morning. He imagined they looked like a children's choir heading for some church.

No sooner had he had this thought than the students began to sing in the call-and-response style he recognized as blues or gospel from a Blues Brothers movie. No one gave them strange looks, but just to be safe and maintain his dignity, Brian stayed back.

After five or ten minutes of singing and walking, they arrived at a windowless, cinderblock warehouse. The sign on the door said, UNPAFL/LMLNUP. In much smaller letters, he read United Nations Pan-African Forensics Laboratory, *Laboratoire de Médecine Légale Nations Unies Panafricain*.

Brian re-read the word 'Laboratory.' He laughed to himself, and at himself. He thought, Look at that: a laboratory in some deserted alley.

Mando took out a ring of keys. He handed one to Brian. "You may do the honors; we already visited this morning, now it is your turn to be impressed."

This single-story cinderblock building was not promising, but the sign was encouraging. Someone had thought this was a lab. With hope, he unlocked the door and walked in. The children rushed pass him to switch on the lights. He saw a tiny reception area and a long hall.

Brian smiled, shook his head, and put his arms out at his side, palms up, in what he hoped meant, "What is this?"

Proudly, Mando explained, "Following the Rwandan Genocide in 1994, the international community could see that the investigations would last a long time. They build this forensics lab, close, but not too close, to those conflicts."

Mando did a slow turn, "Since 1992 Mozambique has been a peaceful garden in Africa. This lab operated for two decades. Now it is abandoned."

Brian found all this hard to believe, but couldn't help being impressed. It almost looked as if something good was happening after breakfast. Abruptly, two girls took his hands and half-led, half-dragged him down the hall.

Someone opened a door to the left. Suddenly all the kids spoke, in English again, "Conference Room."

On the other side of the hall, "Your office." A good-sized room, with a table, six chairs, a desk, and computer with a large flat-screen monitor. While he stared, another student added, "Best internet in Mozambique."

Further down the hall, a bigger room. The children's choir announced, "Analysis Laboratory." The students poured in. With very precise diction they ran around the room, "Look at this HPLC, high performance liquid chromatography." Another waved her hand, "See, GC-MS, gas chromatography mass spectrometer." Another student, standing by Brian's side said, "I hope you are not disappointed, but no nuclear magnetic resonance spectrometer, or X-ray crystallography."

By that point, the scope and quality of the lab overwhelmed him: far better than he could have hoped. Especially for an alley in Maputo, Mozambique.

When he got to the "Synthesis Lab," it was a blur of flasks and heating baths, and reflux condensers, lines for vacuum and dry Nitrogen supply, liquid nitrogen baths, rotary evaporators, and columns. The setup and the students running around naming everything in an eerie American marketing diction was dizzying.

He went over to a couple of gas cylinders, gave them a gentle tilt, and checked their tags. Unbelievably the weight indicated they were full, and the tags from Research Solution Suppliers showed they were regularly serviced and inspected. RSS seemed to be everywhere.

He couldn't believe his good fortune with the lab equipment, and the student's familiarity, in English no less. He wouldn't need to call Penny for a quick escape. For sure something good had happened after breakfast!

Feeling encouraged, Brian walk back to the hospital with Mando who had dismissed his students for the day. "Do your students have a lot of lab experience? They seemed quite at home in the lab and recognized all the equipment."

Mando pointed to a small shop. "Let's have some lunch and I'll tell you a story."

The food shop looked more like someone's kitchen. There was a single table with four chairs and a bench. Mando walked to a glass-front cooler and took out two 2M, pronounced dosh-em, beers. He nodded to the lady standing in front of the stove. She grabbed two ceramic bowls off a shelf and ladled a rice mixture into them. She added a few shrimps from a nearby frying pan.

Much of the local food was a variation on Portuguese. Brian decided the lunch was paella. A delicious roll which he already knew was called *paõ* accompanied the rice dish. So paella and *paõ* he muttered to himself. The spicy paella, with rolls from a wood-fired oven, and cold beer, balanced for a perfect lunch.

Mando began his story. "My students have never been in a laboratory before today. We cannot afford such luxuries for high school students here in Mozambique."

Brian thought, not in the United States either. He dipped his crispy roll in the paella and took a big bite of the soggy, spicy inside. "But they seemed to recognize everything?"

"We also cannot afford textbooks. At the beginning of each year, some friends in the United States send me a couple of old college textbooks together with two or three boxes of marketing and training materials from different equipment vendors, big boxes of manuals, brochures, and DVDs."

Mando looked at Brian's bowl; it was almost empty. He stopped talking to eat some of his own lunch.

Brian couldn't believe what he was hearing. "Do you mean that these high-school students learned chemistry with a mismatched set of college-level textbooks and a box of marketing literature?"

"Well, we do have internet. They watch a lot of YouTube videos and free lectures on edX. When a student finds something good, they present it to the class. These students want to go to university in the U.S. or Europe. I have worked as a chemist in pharmaceutical manufacturing in Europe, and my chemistry class can open doors for them, with the bonus of teaching them scientific English."

This detail of Mando's resume impressed and encouraged Brian, but he was cautious. As he had learned in his years working as an unappreciated chemist because he lacked a graduate degree, there were chemists and there were Chemists. This guy could have been a glorified janitor and dishwasher. With more than a little anger he recalled his own years working his way up because he didn't have the proper diplomas.

Brian cleaned his bowl with this last of his *paõ*. He leaned back and sipped on his 2M. He now realized that what he saw today was a game of matching pictures with captions from brochures.

"Okay, tomorrow we'll put your students to the test. We'll have some real work to do."

———

The next morning Brian met the students at the lab. They went directly to the analysis lab. The students, in their white and navy uniforms, gathered around Brian. "Here is the situation. They have sent us pills to test on the patients in *Hospital Central de Maputo*. Unfortunately, they have not told us what we are testing."

The students talked among themselves. They didn't seem happy, so they might have understood.

"Don't get mad yet. Being as they sent us so many bottles of pills, I'm pretty sure that they sent an approved drug, something surplus, just to see if it might work on this new Aerosol Infectious Rabies, which they are calling AIR."

The children repeated "air" with a Portuguese accent, not the

American accent they used for the lab equipment.

Brian paused. He wondered if their rapt attention was because they understood or were just polite.

"The bottles are all labeled with lot numbers which is good, but the bottles and caps are dusty which is not good. I'm afraid that the pills are not only surplus, but may also be out of date."

One of the students spoke up, "So once again, Africans are disposable test subjects. Why did we ever think that this might be something else?"

Brian admired these students working so hard to learn chemistry without equipment or even a consistent set of textbooks. He wanted to encourage them. "No worries. We'll figure this out. Today we're going to use this lab to determine what they sent us."

There were four different lot numbers. The pills looked the same, but he had no idea if they were. He divided the class into four groups and gave each group pills from their assigned lot.

With little expectation, he sat back and watched. One of the students found a supply of gloves and masks. Once they were all gloved and masked, he could imagine he was in a college class back in the United States.

The one thing he found different was the level of collaboration. When someone was stuck, or confused, the whole group discussed the problem, each bringing what they knew from their individual readings. This was the way they had to work all the time with their limited resources.

They were not ashamed to not know the answer, and many times they went to their teacher or to Brian for additional assistance. While all this group discussion might have slowed them down, in the end they made fewer mistakes.

They dissolved their pills in a few different solvents, prepared columns for the HPLC, transferred the results to the mass spectrometer.

By the end of the day, the teenagers, though he was finding it hard to still think of them as teenagers, had copied the mass spec peak graphs into lab notebooks and came back to Brian and their teacher.

"We recognize one set of peaks, it is an anti-viral drug called ribavirin. It is over 40 years old. We searched the internet and can't figure out what the others three are."

That they identified even one of the lots impressed Brian. He'd seen newly hired graduate chemists who couldn't do as well when they started. "Let me look."

Taking in their enthusiastic eyes and proud smiles, he repeated his invitation, "Let *us* look."

Looking at the different results, he was even more impressed. All four sets of peaks looked very similar. Less rigorous chemists might have declared all four compounds to be the same, but these students correctly recognized that the small differences were significant.

Feeling proud of them, he smiled, "Excellent. You are correct. I fear that they were all supposed to be ribavirin, but three lots have deteriorated—but differently, based on their various storage conditions. You know the structure of the ribavirin. Use that and the changes in the peaks on the other lots to find the other structures."

The students seemed excited with this assignment.

The students' stunning progress counteracted Brian's frustration with RSS for shipping old, out-of-date medications. Tomorrow he'd have some results from the trial.

Perhaps Halid might have some surprises.

———

That night he couldn't sleep, so he called Penny.

"You got me at my lunch break. What are you doing up so late?"

Brian had no time for small talk this late at night. "I'm afraid I'm going to kill someone. It looks like RSS meant to send us ribavirin to test, but they sent out-of-date, deteriorated pills. Instead of a human trial using an approved drug, I administered three different unknown molecules. None of these have been through phase I, safety testing. They should never have been administered to people."

The line went silent.

"Penny, Penny, are you there?"

Finally, "Yes. I don't know where to start. RSS messed up? How did you find out?"

Now he perked up, excited to tell her about the chemistry students, "Let me tell you how we discovered the bogus pills! They have put a great lab at my disposal, along with a group of high school students for assistants. These students are unbelievable. They did the analysis and identification. Believe it or not, high school students in Mozambique did the analysis! They are as good or better that most college grads I've seen."

Penny's voice rose in pitch and volume just like her mother's when she was excited, "That is good news and surprising." Then she stopped, seemed to be thinking, and continued in a serious voice, soft and deep, "Those tests are obviously illegal, unethical, and dangerous. I'd stop them as soon as possible, if I were you."

Brian agreed, and with his mind unburdened, he hung up and went swiftly to sleep.

10. HALID

MAPUTO, MOZAMBIQUE

On the "training" day, Halid had listened patiently as Dr. Brian yelled at him in English. He recognized perhaps one word in a dozen. He glanced repeatedly at Nga, hoping she was getting more than he was from what Dr. Brian was shouting. The UC San Diego doctor with long brown hair and merry eyes stepped forward and put a gentle hand on Dr. Brian's arm. She spoke to the red-faced man in gentle English and Dr. Brian subsided somewhat.

Nga turned to Halid and said in Chiyao, "He wants you to give each of the numbered villagers one of these packets and observe the results over several hours." She bit her lip. "Then I think he means for you to report to him if there is any effect." She held out a clipboard to Halid that had a list of numbers on it and columns of times.

"So, I need to make certain each packet goes to the person of that number, that they take the powder, then keep track of how it affects them on this chart?" he asked her, also in Chiyao.

She met his gaze and quirked her lips. "I think so, yes, that would make sense."

He reached out to Dr. Brian and accepted the large plastic bag full of small packets, each clearly numbered. "I only give them one time?" he said in his best Portuguese.

The San Diego doctor translated his question into careful English, and Dr. Brian nodded. His face was still flushed bright red, but his eyes did not look so angry now.

Halid nodded his understanding. "Then I check the people at these times," he pointed to the clipboard, "and write down my observation?"

Again, the translation, again the nods.

Halid smiled brightly and said, "This I will do." He made a little bow to Dr. Brian, trying to overcome his lack of respect for the man with a show of politesse—at least as well as a Yao could manage to an American, under the circumstances—and left the room at a brisk walk, hoping he looked a lot more competent than he felt to do the man's bidding.

Of course, he knew how to take a temperature and blood pressure. The tricky thing was the "general observation" column. Which was whether they seemed ill or not—to Halid. If that would be the same as what Dr. Brian thought, it would be difficult to guess.

Well, he had gotten the Luambe villagers numbered without fuss, but the other two native groups—in Wards 3 and 7—were going to be an ongoing problem. It was very difficult to ask those people to wear the number tags when they spoke no language in common. He had been surprised by how few other peoples had bothered to learn Portuguese. He had finally gotten help from Ben to explain that people must keep their numbers on.

When he had seen two young men laughing and exchanging their numbers, Halid had begun writing down descriptions or names or even their hospital admittance identification numbers from the wristbands of those who had them. Either the hospital had given up issuing wristbands, or they had run out of them entirely, for only two or three of the people in Ward 7 had one. He knew it was vital to identify who had taken what, or Dr. Brian's study would be confounded.

But it also needed to be a 'blind' study, so Halid did not know which compound was in which numbered packet. He just needed to keep the numbers straight with the symptoms or results.

He spent an hour writing up an auxiliary identification sheet for every number, which he could keep separate from the results he returned to Dr. Brian. Thus there would be no confusion about identifying any person's reactions to a powder that might be effective against AIR, if there were any.

He asked Jojeza to help him give the powders to the patients. They both put on the face masks that Ben and the hospital staff recommended. Jojeza made a face at the odd smell, but she tied it on covering her mouth and nose properly, and nodded at Halid.

They walked to Ward 3, to patient #1. Jojo stirred the powder from packet number one into a small glass of bottled water and they both watched as the subject drank down the entire glass. Halid consulted his identification sheets and made notes, and they ran baseline information on each person's temperature, blood pressure, and general appearance. Most of the people were well. A few had mild fevers. Only two had possible evidence of AIR, with high temperatures, sweating, and signs of deliria.

It took the two of them most of the day to hand out the treatment packets, so they were a little behind on the 6:00 p.m. observation. Halid realized they were going to need help or none of the observations would be done on time. He asked Nga to help, and noted on Dr. Brian's chart that the observation readings were done, in order, approximately eight hours after the first administration of the drug samples. After that, they were able to get them done more quickly and he was able to post results at four hours after the previous one, or twelve hours after first administration.

By then it was clear he and Jojeza and Nga were not going to be enough to do the job. They had to stop and eat and sleep some time. He enlisted the help of one partly-trained Yao-speaking TC and assigned Jojeza as the woman's assistant. He took on Miss Anderson. With dull eyes and an uncaring attitude, Miss Anderson nevertheless did a good job with the thermometer and blood pressure readings, while he wrote down simple observations, using the numbers and his identification notes as well.

In the morning, Halid did a final round of readings with Nga's help, then took his results sheet to Dr. Xavier's office to meet with Dr. Brian.

"Why are these crossed out?" Dr. Brian shouted. "Your notes are illegible!"

Halid grimaced. Yes, they would be illegible, since they were in Chiyao. He glanced at the clipboard to be sure he knew which patients Dr. Brian was asking about.

"Those were the two patients most ill, probably from AIR," he explained. "They died during the night."

"And what are all *these* chicken scratches?"

"They are my notes," Halid said calmly, reaching to take the page away from Dr. Brian. The man was not supposed to have seen that page.

"Notes!? Notes for what? This should be a double-blind experiment."

"Some of the people are not good about keeping their number identifications around their neck. And sometimes nurses remove them. So I am making sure I am observing and writing about the same person-number each time."

Nga translated again, remaining calm as Dr. Brian sputtered and fumed and then snatched the pages of observations from the clipboard so hard that some of the pages tore. He thrust the empty clipboard back at Halid, who took it, watching the torn corner pieces of paper as they fluttered to the floor.

He would not pick them up. He *would* not. The man was arrogant and rude. He turned and began to make his way through the group of other people who were crammed in Dr. Xavier's office, but Nga's voice stopped him.

"Thank you, Halid."

He glanced at her, nodded, rolled his eyes, and stalked from the room.

"He's not a real doctor, you know. Not an M.D., not even a Ph.D.," the black-haired UC San Diego resident said. "He's not affiliated with any University as an honorary doctor of any kind, either." The young man shook his shaggy head, reminding Halid of one of Imrane's spirit ancestor dolls. He smiled at Nga and Halid. He held the double doors open as they passed into the next hallway.

"He's embarrassing," the merry-eyed woman said. She'd asked them to call her Dr. Greta, to distinguish her from another Dr. Simmons currently at Maputo Central. Halid still had no idea if he should be calling them all "Doctor," but none of them seemed offended by what he said. In fact, all the doctors from UCSD had been friendly and pleasant. Dr. Greta went on, "I've reminded him twice that *he's* the limiting factor, since he only speaks English, and that you cannot be expected to understand every little thing he says."

"Especially if he shouts it," Nga murmured, rubbing her forehead.

"Indeed." Dr. Greta smiled. "I think you are doing splendidly in difficult circumstances."

The black-haired doctor laughed out loud, then put his arm around Dr. Greta and gave her a little hug. "Do you think we can have another one of those wonderful potlucks with your villagers again?" he asked, looking at Halid.

"We can bring more than water this time!" Dr. Greta said with a grin.

"I will certainly talk to Mezi and see what plans we can make," Halid answered. "I haven't seen her much the last couple days."

Nicolas nodded. "Yes. There's far more to do than we can manage, here, but everyone would enjoy a little time off from tending the ill and dying. It is necessary."

Halid said, "I'm glad you enjoyed the first time, and I will let you know what Mezi thinks. I've stolen her kitchen help to do these observations," he smiled at Jojeza, "and so I don't know what we still have on hand, for goods or people."

"Let me know what to bring," Dr. Greta said, and they parted.

Halid heaved a big sigh. "At least they are friendly Americans," he said. Jojeza smiled.

"He's a little like my papa," she said. "Always shouting, always angry like life cheats him somehow, nothing ever quite good enough."

"Your papa is a holy man by comparison," Halid mumbled. They made their way out to the patio where Mezi was supervising the children and the next meal.

11. ARIQ

ROSWELL, NEW MEXICO

Lily came to breakfast with her plastic bags of herbs.

"Is that all you have left?"

"Yes, just enough for one last batch of stew for Louisa and a few others. She is getting better. This should do."

"Can you use any of the plants that grow here?"

She walked over to his little-used and dusty front closet. He called it his coat closet; at the moment, it contained a couple of pairs of old shoes and a rain poncho to run to the mailbox during sudden downpours. When she opened it, he saw different sages and flowers hung to dry.

"I've tried some of your plants. They look similar, but they are different. Different to the tongue, to the nose, and to the hand. They even sound different when crushed."

After their arguments about releasing the bats, he took a conciliatory note. "Just like immune systems. After fifty million years, we've lost some immune system capabilities. I believe bats have a larger variety of T-cells and B-cells to fight off diseases. Evolution loves differences."

She closed the door to her impromptu drying room. "I will cook up some stew with the local plants." Short as he was, she still looked up to him, her small face framed by the startling white hair. "Similarities often outweigh differences. You should be looking for common threads. Weaving is about the strength of the yarn, not its color variations."

He wanted to agree, be agreeable. But natural selection, and thus evolution, depended on differences. "Even before sexual reproduction, simpler species used horizontal gene transfer to exchange DNA, mix things up, multiply differences. Bacteria and viruses still benefit from this cross-species sex. I think bats can do this."

Lily ate her breakfast of coffee and granola. She gave him a look he imagined was for ignorant children. He decided she lacked the education in Biology and Genetics to follow his argument. Unfortunately, his understanding wasn't that good either.

She finished her coffee, and gave him a half smile, "It is just not that complicated."

Unsure what to say next, he murmured, "I'm listening."

"Bats, people, all the animals, all the plants, live together in one big colony. We all take care of each other. It is like a circle–or, more like a cloud that we exist in together, one touching the next and next. How can we not affect one another?"

While he sipped his breakfast tea, he thought about what she said.

———

A big city news van greeted their arrival at the clinic, most likely from Albuquerque—but Las Cruces and El Paso were similar distances away. The truck with its satellite dish seemed like an excessive amount of technology to report from the low-profile Roswell Orthopedic Clinic. What rumors could have inspired them to drive such long distances?

He picked up his pace to a casual jog and headed for the news crew. They were interviewing some staff members. When they saw Ariq trotting up, the staff dispersed. Lily joined the group heading for the hospital, away from the news van. In the shadow of the satellite dish, Ariq stood alone. This sudden retreat of the others didn't faze the news team.

The cameraman pivoted toward Ariq. A fit young woman in a red suit, white blouse, and shoulder-length blonde hair positioned herself half facing the camera and half facing him. She wore high heels, so he looked up to her as she spoke, "Hello Mr. Temuujin. We're from KJNM in Albuquerque. You're the head administrator here. Right?"

Still puzzled about why they drove 200 miles, Ariq nodded. "Yes. You can call me Ariq. What brings you all the way to Roswell?"

He wanted to discuss the AIR patients, now that he had some good news thanks to Lily's stew. He'd skip the details, as Lily's methods were a conundrum.

He also hoped to showcase *los cientificos*, especially Jessenia's latest project, suddenly relevant because of AIR. The science club made good television, too, featuring telegenic youngsters—who had now gathered around him, just out of sight from the camera.

"We heard you were doing some important genetic research."

Oh. The CDC had clearly told him not to talk about this. On the other hand, they'd already recalled his equipment. What else could they do? There had been threats of deportation or jail, but both Jake and Chucky had assured him that Roswell couldn't be important enough to wake up the sleeping bureaucracy, even if he had done anything prosecutable–which was arguable.

He pressed his lips tight. He needed time to think. Had things gotten so crazy that that he based his decisions on a wild salesman like Jake or a middle-age surgeon like Chucky…and looked for science from an Australian aborigine?

"Genetic Research?" he asked just to stall.

"We watched your online announcement and a confidential source informed us you are being gagged. What are they hiding? Is New Mexico going to be bombed like that outbreak movie?"

Outbreak again? Where did they get these ideas? Making an on-the-spot decision, Ariq decided to give them an interview. After all, the internet never forgets, so they already had access to everything. Hopefully, he could clear some of their misconceptions.

"Our little Chiropteran Research Center has decoded the full genome for the Mexican free-tailed bat. This is the first time for any bat."

At this point one of the *los cientificos* proudly interjected, "And our data has been downloaded over 300 times. People are interested."

That was news to Ariq and emboldened him. He smiled at his students, listening to the reporters talk among themselves about b-roll footage of bats. The news folk seemed to prefer bats to the strange science of genetics.

The reporter returned to Ariq and his students. "That sounds important. We've heard that New Mexico is a *hot spot* and those bats were the *reservoir*. Are they going to bomb Carlsbad Caverns?"

He ignored the bomb question, but with the mention of reservoirs, he came to life, "Bats are carriers for hundreds of viruses. That's what our research is about."

"Do you have a cure for the AIR germs?"

He took a deep breath, trying to be patient, "No. Bats have a more complex immune system than other mammals, including humans."

The lady in the red suit looked at the cameraman, "Are we mammals?"

He replied, "I don't know, let's just find a story."

She returned to Ariq, "Did you find the cure to Aerosol Infectious Rabies?"

"No, but Roswell High School science students have shown bat colonies acquire immunity very efficiently. A bat colony is like a single organism. When one part of your body acquires immunity, very soon all of you is immune. If you get a measles shot in your right arm, your entire body becomes immune. You cannot later get measles in your left arm."

This analogy came in the pressure of the moment. He liked it.

"A bat colony works like this. First, a few bats fight off the disease, but shortly afterward, they all learn how to do it."

"Wow," the fit young reporter turned away from him, "That sounds good to me."

She looked right into the camera with a big smile, "So there you have it. Thanks to research right here in Roswell, New Mexico, all we need is one person to beat AIR, and they can pass it on to everyone else. Stay tuned to KJNM for the latest breaking news that matters to you and your family."

Ariq yelled, "NO! You've got it all mixed up!" But they ignored him, packing up and walking away. He heard the reporter tell her cameraman they should film Carlsbad Caverns before the bombs dropped, and then get safely home to their own beds. He called out to her, but she didn't seem to hear him, nor want to, climbing gracelessly into the news van and rolling up the window. She never stopped talking long enough to listen.

———

As the reporters retreated, Ariq realized that Lily had disappeared. He was glad that the reporters hadn't interviewed *her*. The heavens only knew what kind of story the reporter would have made up. He ran to the CRC, expecting she would be with the bats.

Sure enough, he found her in the dark room that simulated a cave. She didn't seem bothered by the humidity and smells of so many animals.

"Lily, are you okay?"

She wiped her eyes, took a deep breath, and stood up. He thought she was crying, but instead she seemed to get taller and calmer. "You have to let them go. They are very unhappy."

Did she have some weird way to communicate with them?

He explained all the precautions they took to keep the bats healthy. He proudly explained the Animal Welfare Act and Standards for Laboratory Animals and how the animal care at the CRC exceeded all the relevant regulations.

"Not impressed," she spoke to him like he was a naive child. "Bats need to live in their colony to be healthy."

He showed her the checklist and record of veterinarian visits and special food, and temperature control. He sensed her disappointment that he was so misinformed, like she'd never imagined such ignorance.

He reflected that her arguments were like what he'd said to the news reporters about bat colonies and immunity.

Now he wondered where that idea came from. He had thought the pressure of the news interview had forced a burst of creativity, but maybe not….

"Those bats can no more live in cages than your hand or foot can."

He looked at her with new respect. She had convinced him. He had just told the news lady what he'd learned, what she had taught him, essentially. "Lily, I will let these blasted bats go if it will make you happy." He feared she'd immediately start opening cages. "But this isn't the right time. Later, and besides, after so much time in cages, I doubt they are strong enough to return to their colonies…if they can even find them."

She smiled like someone who knew an important secret. "Prepare to be surprised."

Then she added, "You're so focused on your fancy machines, you're missing the most important part of the story."

———

Over the next days, Ariq pondered the implication of "one big colony." The morning staff meetings became more routine as the number of critical AIR cases decreased. A few died, but even more recovered, including Louisa and someone who received stew made with local plants. The discussions moved from life and death to scientific curiosity. Everyone was interested in Lily, who was like a reverse Typhoid Mary, spreading health.

"Is Lily curing these patients?"

"How is she doing it?"

"Why aren't the people back in Australia also getting better?"

Ariq didn't let this take up too much time.

He stopped expecting the FBI or immigration to show up, and relaxed a bit.

Eventually Martina announced, "We're not waiting any longer. The wedding will be at the court house. So, it will be on a week day."

Lachy added, "All we need to do is find a place for a party afterward."

Martina frowned and said, "*Reception.*"

Ariq had little interest in the wedding. He left them to it.

Instead, he pondered the science. Why had some recovered, while others died? Were the bats the cause or the cure? What about Lily's stew? He felt as puzzled by the cures as the deaths.

Just because Lily's arrival foreshadowed the recoveries didn't mean she caused them. More credible, the AIR cases caused her to arrive—that being clearly true.

Could it be that bats weren't just reservoirs of disease, but they were also reservoirs of immunities, reservoirs of *cures?* How did the bats propagate immunity throughout the colony?

Was the colony really a single organism? Was the story he made up for the news reporters truer than he imagined?

He returned to the staff discussion.

Martina said, "The reception could be *here.*"

Deciding he hadn't missed anything, he imagined the clinic as "One big colony."

12. DR. BRIAN

MAPUTO, MOZAMBIQUE

R_X The curtains of Maputo Central Hospital waved out the open windows and a long line of sick patients floated away, their IV, breathing and feeding tubes fluttering behind them like so many streamers. A cappella gospel music filled the air and the men and women danced to the melody, stomping their feet according to the bass line. Down *Avenida Eduardo Mondlane* this ethereal parade floated toward the ocean. All landed among the fishing boats and walked into the ocean. As the waves broke, their life support tubes dissolved and they cheered, dancing and singing out to sea until they too were gone.

The tropical sun flooding into the windows woke Brian from his dream, and he felt lighter and more optimistic. Today good things would happen after breakfast, lots of them. He barely spoke at his café as he rushed through breakfast. With the sun at his back, he almost ran to the hospital, breaking into a sweat and panting long before he arrived.

As he reached the flower gardens across from the main entrance, the sky darkened and thunder echoed between the buildings. A flash of lightening reminded him of his midnight call to Penny.

Today he would take charge, forget Doctors with Helicopters and the mysterious, ubiquitous RSS. He would stop the drug trials with rogue, untested compounds. There might be no glory for preventing another ill-advised test on innocent Africans, but he and Penny would know that he took the high road and avoided another Tuskegee syphilis experiment.

He walked past the hospital to the lab, rehearsing his speech to the students. You are the best! Not your fault– Try not to be too disappointed—

He imagined hugs and tears, followed by a quick escape back into retirement. He might move to French Polynesia to be with

Penny.

———

When he arrived at the lab, the students were waiting for him. Hyacinta and Sebastian, the leaders, he the tallest and she the shortest, stood at the door. They both spoke at once. "Radicals! Hydroxyls! Nitrogen! Look: phosphorous substitutions! And peroxides!"

Other students added to the cacophony until Gabrielle, almost as tall as Sebastian, but so shy and quiet that she often seemed to disappear, pushed through the crowd, and took Brian's hand. She led him into the building. Either from surprise or respect for the tall girl, everyone fell in behind, even Thomas, who always had some funny diversion.

The parade ended at the conference room. Even with everyone quietly in line behind her, she still hadn't found her voice. Brian looked around the room. They had taped pieces of paper covered with lines and numbers to the cinderblock walls. He recognized bonding energy calculations and chemical structure diagrams. These were their synthesis pathways. Looking at the results, he knew that they'd stayed late into the night.

On the big conference room table were molecular models. Ball-and-stick models. They must have found the modeling kits somewhere in the lab. Balls lacquered to a high sheen for atoms and springs for bonds. He immediately recognized the black carbons and white hydrogens.

They'd done it! They'd decoded the unknown compound structures. As expected, each of the alternate compounds was just a single substitution from ribavirin, a phosphorous for a nitrogen or a hydrogen for a hydroxyl.

The room became silent. Gabrielle faded to the back. The usual leaders returned to the front. Every one of those deep, dark eyes, stared at Brian. Each face had the half smile which said, "I did good, didn't I?"

Brian decided he could wait to cancel everything until after lunch. "Good job. You are the best. I am taking you all to lunch to celebrate!"

Everyone cheered. He noticed again that they always seemed to be hungry. The closest place he knew was the food shop around the corner, so he took them for paella and *paõ*. The lady had enough bowls, but most of the students had to eat sitting along the side of the road. No one seemed to mind. The leaders took the bench by the table. He sat in one of the chairs, and shy Gabrielle took another. The remaining chairs were left for other customers.

Halfway through lunch, there was a commotion outside. Sebastian jumped up to see what going on. After a few minutes, he returned with an envelope which he handed to Brian. "These are the first test results, just sent over from the hospital."

Brian tore the envelope open. His eyes rapidly scanned the page.

One of the compounds had an effect! He looked up, "People got better. We found a cure. We're going to save the world!"

Hyacinta translated. Everyone cheered. The students were on a roll. Outwardly he celebrated with the students, but inside the unethical drug test weighed on his conscience.

He had the key to decoding the results in his pocket. The double-blind design assigned each patient a unique treatment code, so only mapping the effective treatments back to the actual compound would uncover the answer, but he didn't dare look at it in such a public setting.

Additionally, he worried about which compound had had the effect. He hoped that it was the old but normal ribavirin, and not one of the mutants, and please, please, not the placebo. He still regretted his decision to experiment with unknown compounds— but something had helped!

———

Back at the lab the students dispersed, some to take naps in quiet corners, and others to clean up the lab after the long night. He retreated to his office to decode the test results.

The good news was that the effective compound was not the placebo. A few placebo patients improved, but that happened regularly, so he ignored those results. Unfortunately, it was not the ribavirin either. As with the placebo, a few of the ribavirin patients also showed improvement, but not at a rate higher than the placebo, so he felt safe also ignoring those results.

It was the compound with the phosphorous for nitrogen substitution that accounted for most of the good outcomes. He wondered what crazy storage conditions had led to that substitution, for that was not the easiest synthesis pathway even when you wanted it.

He puzzled what to do. It was too late to call Penny. He replayed everything she had said about how unethical and dangerous it was to go straight to human trials with an unknown compound.

His years of experience had shown him that the FDA established their approved screening regime, first testing for safety using chemical and cellular screens, and then animal models, and then small scale human Phase I trials, for a reason.

He'd seen, first hand, dire results, including birth defects and deaths, even when developers rigorously followed the procedure. Skipping safety testing was crazy and criminal. He was old enough to remember the Thalidomide babies born with flippers instead of hands and feet. He didn't want to be responsible for a similar tragedy.

On the other hand, he'd already cracked the egg. *All the king's horses and all the king's men.* He'd accidentally authorized one round of human testing and the result was positive. With all the people dying around the world from AIR, how could he ignore this possible cure?

He wanted to go forward with the new compound which he was already calling ribavirin-P for the substituted phosphorous. He examined himself for conflict. Was he afraid to lose the credit if he sent his results back to Doctors with Helicopters? Or would they just ignore him with such flimsy results?

Did he want to save the glory for the students in Mozambique? Was this a selfish and dangerous decision? Pride before the fall?

For several hours, he went back and forth, and in the end,

urgency convinced him to go forward. Not only would he go forward, but he'd have the students synthesize some more variants for testing.

He brought the students together and explained the plan. They would identify the lots of ribavirin-P. They would use that stock to synthesize two alternatives: ribavirin-P1 and ribavirin-P2. As soon as they could complete this, the second round of trials would begin.

———

He woke up again in the middle of the night. This time with nightmares of babies born with flippers swimming into the ocean and sharks devouring them. He thought to call Penny. The time was right, but he didn't want to argue with her about human trials of unknown compounds vs. potential cures. Especially given the apparent fatality rates of AIR.

He spent a few hours on **Bat Chat** lurking in different discussions of Aerosol Infectious Rabies, and finally fell back to sleep, only to wake up before dawn, too early for breakfast at the café. After some instant coffee and local granola of cassava chips and cashews, he headed for the lab, hoping that the short walk would clear his head, so he might catch a few hours' rest before the students arrived.

When he turned up the narrow road toward the lab, the hospital blocked the rising sun and the way darkened. As he approached the lab door, he could make out shapes at the sides of the road. They were the chemists, his high school students, fast asleep.

He stepped lightly to avoid waking them. He didn't like them sleeping in the street, but his own grogginess let him empathize with them. In the lab, Gabrielle greeted him. Given the early hour and her general demeanor, he whispered, "*Bom dia*. Did you know students are sleeping outside, in the street?"

She gave him a small smile, "Of course. They can't sleep inside. Too many lights. Too much activity. And machine noise."

She thought for a moment, and if looking for the word in

English, "…and the laboratory must be kept sanitary, sterile."

"Can't they go home to sleep?"

Now she gave him a patronizing adults-have-such-strange-ideas smile that seemed to be universal world round. He remembered getting that same smile when he'd asked Penny why she wore torn jeans.

However, Gabrielle was more respectful and polite than an American teenager. "They live too far away. Bus fare is too expensive. The weather is fine. Many people sleep outside."

She turned around and led him to the conference room. Thomas was sleeping under the conference table. She nudged him with her bare foot. He jumped up, banged his head, said something to her that Brian didn't understand, and started to roll around the floor as if he was in dire pain. This performance only lasted until he saw Brian, at which time he stood up, made a little bow, and left the room.

Left alone with the taciturn Gabrielle, he surveyed the conference table. In addition to the ball-and-stick models of the ribavirin, ribavirin-P, and the other compounds bequeathed to them by RSS, there were two more models for the new compounds. In front of the ribavirin-P there was a beaker of perhaps 100 CCs of white powder, almost a half-cup. Good work he thought.

Then he noticed smaller beakers in front of the new compounds. Each contained perhaps 20 or 25 CCs of white powder, enough for ten or twenty patients, depending on the concentration. While he was doing the math in his head, he realized they'd synthesized *both* compounds *overnight*. He had some miracle chemists, here.

Thomas returned. It looked like he'd washed up, somehow found a clean shirt, and straightened his tie. Brian grinned at the two students. "You did it! You synthesized both compounds overnight!" It never occurred to him that they might have made a mistake or synthesized the wrong compound. He'd seen their collaborative style. With so many students checking every step, he couldn't imagine a problem.

Thomas took an elaborate bow, swung his arm out, and spun in a circle. *"Nós fizemos isso. Nós todos fizemos isso. Nós todos fizemos isso juntos."* When his grand gesture was complete, he said, "We did that. We've all done it. We all did it together."

Brian got the point. *"Obrigado!* Thank you." With the compounds in hand, all doubt evaporated. He picked up the valuable beakers and retreated to his office to prepare the envelopes for the second trial.

———

When the envelopes were complete, he put them in a plastic bag and collected the students. They all walked toward the hospital.

Street vendors were serving breakfast, so he looked at the students and asked, *"Pequeno almoço?* Breakfast?" He knew the answer, and since he'd missed his regular morning meal at the café, he was also ready for something.

The students favored one vendor, speaking to her in a language he didn't recognize. He figured the women belonged to a tribal group in common with many of the students. Tribal connections seemed to be very important in Maputo.

He gave the women a couple of American twenties, and all the students got a cup of tea and a sandwich, either egg or fish.

While they all stood around eating and laughing, he asked the leaders if they could deliver the envelopes to Halid. Sebastian and Hyacinta went off with the valuable package that they'd spent the night preparing. By the time they returned, the others had finished their morning snack and Brian collected them in a small circle.

"I didn't know you were sleeping in the street."

Several students spoke up, echoing Gabrielle's earlier response that many people slept outside, especially during the good weather.

"Well, I have an idea. Can you come with me?"

He led the students into the morning sun, toward the ocean and his apartment.

He took out his apartment key and said, "Locksmith? Key

cutter?" This seemed to be beyond their vocabulary. He tried Google Translate on his phone and came up with, "*Chaveiro, cortador de chave, serralheiro.*" Finally the light went on for Thomas. He did a back flip and led them down a narrow alley to a small alcove.

Brian knew they were in the right place when he heard the painful screech of grinding metal. He didn't know his teen numbers, so he handed his key to the key cutter and said, "*Vinte.*" Twenty would be too many, but that was the best approximation given his limited language skills.

In a half-hour, they were on their way again.

His plan was to have them sleep at his apartment. It wasn't great, but it had a thin carpet on the floor, a bathroom, and a kitchenette. As they walked toward the building, he distributed keys and answered questions as best as he could.

"Sleep with you?"

"You are not of my tribe!"

"Joke? American joke?"

"We can cook."

"*Obrigado.*"

"*Obrigado.*"

Eventually they understood and each one held a key as they walked up the nine flights. Once inside they swarmed the small apartment, looking everywhere, checking the stove, and the sink, and the bathroom, pointing to the hospital out the window.

Hyacinta announced in her best formal English, "Dinner is served at seven o'clock."

13. LILY

ROSWELL, NEW MEXICO

 Lily spoke to Obrey late that night, asking about his health and their friends.

"I'm doing great," Obrey said. "Damon hasn't gotten sick, but a lot of other people are. Pearl could use your help."

"I actually need her help," Lily said. "I'm almost out of herbs. I brought so much, but it didn't last very long."

"She's got Pana and June out gathering, but they really need everything we can collect to use *here*."

"Well. I'll keep harvesting locally, though so far nothing here has the same effect."

"Um. Your mother called."

"Yes, I talked to her. She also wants me to come home, but you know, I'm helping my bat friends here." Although they weren't exactly friends of the bats, were they? Lily scowled.

"Well, there's been a lot of interest in your paintings. We've had reporters and government people here, and they flew in some nurses and doctors."

"From Darwin?"

"From Sydney. Darwin has some sickness, but nothing much in Sydney. Yet. Anyhow, some of them have been in here for coffee and such, and have asked about your work. I sold the black and white one for more than you were asking, 'cause two different people wanted it."

"Oh, that's one of the ones Ariq liked." She realized she had missed being able to paint, to sing her songline in colors. "That's good. I think I still don't have enough to pay for airfare home."

"How much is it?"

"Something like $2000 U.S. More in Australian dollars."

"Maybe we should raise the prices on these."

"Okay. I was thinking about doing that at the Coop, too, since so many are selling."

"Good thought. Any idea when you'll be back?"

"I don't think I'm going to do much good here without herbs, so probably not too long."

"Good. I miss you."

Lily felt a definite pang. "I miss you, too, Obrey. I'll let you know when I'm coming back."

Using the last of her native herbs, along with some of the local sages she had picked behind Ariq's house, Lily made up what felt like a final batch of stew.

Only three of Ariq's patients were ill now. She had enough for them.

"But I'm now out of everything," she told Ariq, who stood beside her at the stove in his sunny kitchen.

"Maybe it's enough," he said. "Louisa is going home this morning. You've really helped."

"I've helped the people. But your bats are still in cages."

"I can't do this research in the wild, Lily."

"That's the only place your research makes sense! The bats are a colony, they need to be together. That's the way they should be studied—how they live."

Ariq shook his head. "Then I'd need to bring the entire colony into the CRC for study, and that's just not practical."

"And I would like that even less," she said, handing him the plastic container, "but at least they would all be together." He held it while she spooned stew in, set it aside when it was full and got another one. "That's why I didn't mind Dr. Darnell's sampling method—the bats weren't taken away, just separated from their colony for a short time. Yours are imprisoned for life. You are just killing them."

"They're not dying!" Indignance plain in his voice, Ariq slapped the filled container down and stomped from the room.

Why couldn't she convince him? Lily rubbed her temples, then picked up the ladle again and finished emptying the stew pot. Maybe it was time to go home.

———

Lily walked into the CRC office and set down her herb bags presently filled with empty stew containers. She saw Ariq looking at a computer and some printed papers.

"Ariq, it sounds like you are still thinking you need to keep these bats here."

"My study is far from finished; these results are helpful, but they are still not answering my question."

"Your question?"

"Okay, the bats clearly transfer immunity to diseases from one to another, that is now an established fact." He waved a hand indicating the computer screen.

"And also why they should be together."

"That's what is required for the immunities to transfer, yes. But *how?* That's the question. What is it about their genetics that makes bats' immune systems so different? What is the mechanism they use for transferring immunity? And by the way, this is a whole entire colony of pipistrelles, my friend assured me," he waved at one bank of cages with the little British bats in them.

"Well, that part is good. But, if you are studying genetics, you don't need these bats anymore."

"If the different colonies and different species transfer immunity in different ways, I need a sampling of bats. We still don't know if they are all doing the same thing."

"I understand that, Ariq. But why do you need these bats in these cages now? You have already taken samples, multiple samples," Lily said, waving at the boxes of specimen test tubes with wing punches in them that partially covered one wall of the CRC main room. The other wall was covered with caged bats. "Why would you need more samples from these bats?"

"For one thing, to see if they've spread immunity to the viruses I've exposed them to."

"Haven't they already been tested for that? Didn't you find they are all immune to those new viruses now? I thought that's what you said."

"Yes. I said that, and they are immune."

She spoke slowly to control her anger with his thick-headed

stubbornness.

"Then why are they still here?"

————

Lily hitched a ride with one of the high school student's parents to an art supply store. She used some of the cash Dr. Darnell had given her to buy canvases, her favorite colors of acrylics and a couple decent brushes. She was not traditional enough to try and paint with a chewed stick, though it did add interesting character to the details of paintings she had seen done that way.

Her customers seemed to like the more modern, cleaner look— they were less interested in authentic aboriginal art than getting a painting in the colors they wanted. With lots of dots. She assumed Americans would prefer the same.

Ariq had shown her the wall in the hospital that, in his opinion, cried out for three or four pieces of black and white and red art.

Art she could make. Would make. It was her ticket home.

She walked past Ariq's house, past the last back road of Roswell town, past the arroyo, out into the desert. She used her bare foot to brush a sandy spot clear of thorns and sticks and stones, then sat down.

She plugged the earphones into her phone and turned on the Marra lesson that the science club student had fixed up for her. The sound was actually better from her phone than it had been from the tapes, through some wizardry of electronics.

She pronounced words and set out her canvases.

Six hours later she had the outlines of four different paintings done. Of course, filling in the dots and lines of dreamtime movement was going to take at least that long again, but she was satisfied with her progress. She gathered her gear and walked back to Ariq's house in the dusky light, carefully balancing the almost-dry canvases in each hand, her paints and phone stuffed into her backpack slung over her shoulder.

She cleaned her brushes and left them sitting in a container from Ariq's recycling bin to dry. She set her paintings carefully on his porch to finish drying before she began the next stage of painting.

She walked around Ariq's house, thinking of shiny black eyes, folded wings, wire cages.

She cooked dinner, baking a big squash she and Ariq had gotten at the grocery store, in the traditional way—on a bed of coals outside in Ariq's sandy backyard, with hot rocks piled around it. She made also a traditional bush food of soaked and stewed seeds and dried mango, cooked over the stove.

Ariq was quiet during dinner, so she kept silent also.

Afterward, they had tea and talked.

"I am thinking the bats share breath, and that is how they spread immunity," she said.

Ariq looked at her as if she had sprouted horns, then the worry frown lines on his forehead deepened and he stared fiercely at his feet resting on the table in front of his sofa.

She licked her lips and went on, "That would explain why it takes a bit of time, but they all become immune eventually."

Ariq nodded, still frowning.

"I am also thinking that is maybe why some of the people who receive stew get better and some do not. Certainly the ones they put plastic tents over, like my teacher's friend, died, while those we were able to touch and talk to while we gave stew got better."

Ariq nodded again. "That could be it."

After a long silence, she said, "I've made reservations to return home, tomorrow night."

That jerked him out of his thoughts. "Oh. So soon?"

"I have no more stew, and, well, there isn't much here for me to do now. I'm needed at home."

He nodded. "Your flight leaves from Albuquerque?"

"Mm."

"I'll drive you."

"I need to spend tonight at the CRC or the hospital, to finish the paintings, and say goodbye to the bats."

"Okay."

"Can you drive me back there? I need to bring all my canvases and paints and my backpack."

"Of course."

14. DR. BRIAN

MAPUTO, MOZAMBIQUE

R_X At bedtime, the reality of more than a dozen students sharing his studio apartment hit Brian. His narrow bed suddenly seemed extravagant when compared with students sharing his floor. He alternated between wanting to send them back to the street and feeling guilty for his privileged position. He considered his age compared to their youth, his education and importance compared to their—. He got nowhere with these lines of reasoning. He couldn't rationalize his comfy bed. Finally he put his mattress on the floor, which several students eventually shared. He curled up on the vacated wooden platform.

Surprisingly, he had his best night of sleep. No nightmares. When he awoke in the middle of the night, he navigated around the sleeping bodies to visit the bathroom. The gentle breathing of sleeping children reminded him of visiting Penny's childhood bedroom. He felt like a parent to these children.

When the sun awakened him, he looked around. The students had gone. The only record of his overnight guests were neat piles of personal belongings. Some toilet articles like soap, shampoo, toothpaste, or small towels peeked out from the stacks.

He noticed buried within some piles were tampons or pads, and in others condoms, and some even had both. He felt just a bit creepy spying on them like this, but they had clearly made no efforts to hide anything. He recalled that education in Mozambique combined with other responsibilities, and some of these students were in their late teens, some maybe older. So, not children, young adults.

Looking at his large suitcase and his robotic carry-on bag, the comparison again made him feel privileged, and possibly a little bit stupid. He promised himself never to forget these students and to make sure they received credit for their contributions finding ribavirin-P that was going to stop the AIR pandemic.

When he got to the hospital, he saw his assistants—he could no longer think of them as children, or students—in the park across from Maputo Central Hospital. They were eating a breakfast of fruit. He recognized papaya, bananas, and mangos, all of which were plentiful, cheap, and grown locally. Other hospital staff joined them.

He recognized Halid in the center of an excited group that seemed to include not just hospital staff in their MCH uniforms, but also the visitors from UCSD. He didn't understand the discussion which seemed to be a mixture of something and Portuguese, but as soon as Halid spotted him, he ran over waving a thick envelope.

"We've done it! Everyone is getting better! Here's your report."

Brian accepted the envelope, upset that they hadn't followed the protocol, afraid that their incompetence was going to ruin his results. "It's too soon for results from the second trial. It just started yesterday afternoon. The drug can't work that quickly." He thought to say something about pharmacokinetics and metabolism, but restrained himself. Such details would be wasted in this crowd.

One more time he regretted that Doctors with Helicopters had sent him to Africa. The smiles of the Khemistry Kids somewhat mitigated his disappointment.

Halid and his cheerful band ignored Brian's concerns. "The cure is tribal. The Yao are healers. Together they can take care of the rest."

Barely hiding his disgust, Brian told Halid, "I'll look at your report. Don't get too optimistic. Science doesn't work like that." Now he knew why he had to be in Maputo. He needed to maintain scientific discipline and counter their primitive tendencies to magical explanations.

Halid held his ground. Incredibly, this uneducated child, who could barely speak English, and a few days ago had not even heard of a clinical trial, now stood up to Doctor Brian's experience and expertise. "We understand science. We sent Yao DNA to America for analysis." At this point the UC students smiled.

Brian looked at the San Diego students. "Did you really send DNA samples to the United States?"

The American interns answered in unison. "Yes, of course. We have DNA sequencers here, but they haven't been unpacked, so we sent out samples to the Chiropteran Research Center in New Mexico."

He scowled and shook his head, "Bat research center? New Mexico?"

———

Back in his office, Brian opened the envelope and spread the pages on the conference table. He assigned his chemists to help with the data analysis. He relaxed once the work started. At least he could count on his chemists. While Halid's group preferred magical thinking, his group began serious data analysis without any preconceived bias.

By lunchtime, they had graphs for each patient and composites for each treatment option. It didn't take long for him to see that the results were chaos, clearly indicating faulty trial administration.

Not wanting to waste their effort, he used this as a teaching moment. "What do you see in this data?"

Hyacinta spoke first. "The results for the different treatment options are all the same."

Sebastian added, "Some subjects seemed to be improving before they were even given any medicine. Should we just forget them?"

Everyone started talking at once. Brian noticed Gabrielle holding a small stack of graphs. "Gabrielle, what do you have there?"

"I did what Sebastian suggested. Here are the results just for the sick people." She held up the four graphs, for each of the experimental compounds, and the placebo.

Brian summarized, "Good idea, but the results are the same. Clearly the trial has been a mess. What do you think went wrong?"

They discussed among themselves for a while, until Thomas picked up a stack of papers and dramatically walked across the room bumping into people, knocking things over, and spilling the rest of the pages off the conference table. Once he had everyone's attention, he did an exaggerated trip and fall that was actually a skillfully executed backflip. All the papers he had been carrying flew into the air.

He got up, dusted himself off, took a bow, and said, "Just like that. Like that they did it."

Everyone laughed.

When the laughter died out, Brian went back to his lesson. Modeling the many failure analysis meetings he'd attended at Miller & Miller, he taped a piece of paper to the wall and picked up a marker. "Exactly what went wrong?"

Hyacinta started, "They could have mixed up the patients and the drugs, or even just written the results wrong."

He wrote Bad Data on the paper and explained, "This category includes the multitude of errors that could contaminate the data. This category includes: sloppy writing, transcription errors, unit confusion."

He took a few minutes to recount how mixing up meters and feet caused the Mars Climate Orbiter to crash back in 1999.

"Anything else?"

Sebastian suggested, "Maybe they mixed up the drugs. We didn't give them pills. We gave them powders that could have been mixed up."

He wrote Contamination on the paper. "Very good. We are working with small amounts here, milligrams. There are lots of ways to mix things up. They were dissolving the doses in water. Residuals can cause contamination."

Gabriella seemed a bit embarrassed to add, "They could have touched each other."

He wrote Not Following Protocols. He summarized the procedures to protect staff from patients and patients from each other.

In the end the group convinced themselves that Halid and the staff didn't have the discipline and they shouldn't have been surprised that the results were mixed up.

Brian chastised himself for letting them run the test unsupervised. It had been a mistake to be so careful about the double blind part of the test at the expense of all other considerations. He rationalized this mistake because he'd never seen such incompetence by test administrators.

He went to sleep that night hoping they had enough compounds for a third trial.

The next morning, the students served breakfast in Brian's apartment and they all walked together to the hospital. He was happy to discover they had enough compounds for another trial, and they decided to run that trial themselves.

With a plan in place and confident they had discovered a cure, if only they could run a clean trial to prove it, everyone was cheerful. They sang as they ambled down the road to the hospital.

They called a meeting with Halid, the American interns, and the others. Brian brought a big basket of fruit as a peace offering.

"We looked at the data. We think that the envelopes were mixed up, or maybe the patient numbers were exchanged. It is also possible that there was some cross exposure."

Brian's students stood in three straight rows and listened respectfully. Everyone else responded differently, from angry and insulted (primarily the Americans) to confused or bored. Halid had a smug smile.

Brian tried to continue, bringing up hand washing, face masks, and careful record keeping. When he realized that he'd lost control of the meeting, he closed with, "We'll be back tomorrow to run another trial. Please prepare a list of patients that are still sick that we can use."

15. HALID

MAPUTO, MOZAMBIQUE

"Yes, I plan to stay here and enter the *técnico de cirurgia* program, if it is still in effect." Halid glanced at Dr. Greta, who was still smiling at him.

"Oh, I am pretty sure your government will never stop that program; the TC's have been life-savers throughout all this, even though there were only four of them here, and now you and Nga."

"Good, because I believe Jojeza wants to stay also."

Hearing her name, Jojo looked over at them, still wielding her ladle, serving up soup to villagers and a few hospital staffers. He waved at her and Dr. Greta laughed, then went to chat with the other two residents who had come to the potluck lunch. They'd brought chicken this time, that Nicolas and the merry-eyed doctor had baked. Seven whole chickens, with a crispy, spicy coating. It had been swiftly eaten up by Luambe villagers and hospital personnel alike, and had tasted wonderful alongside Mezi and Jojo's savory multi-vegetable soup.

Halid finished wiping his hands clean and picked up his clipboard. He couldn't stall any longer. They were due at a meeting.

It was going to be very difficult with "doctor" Brian today. The results weren't just mixed-up looking. It was more confusing than that. Every Luambe villager, and *all of Wards 3 and 7* were *well. Cured.* No signs of AIR remained among those people. Maputo Central was kicking them out, to make room for new, sick patients.

Even though Halid was certain this was a huge success medically, he had a feeling that to Brian it was going to be another *experimental failure.* Again, Halid had carefully followed the numbering procedure and administered the test drugs to the matching numbered patient. Again, he and the others had observed and recorded health data for each of their patients, number by number.

And this morning, every one of them was *well*, even those who had previously shown definite symptoms of AIR. There weren't any sick people left for another test.

Halid knew he had given the test patients different treatments—that was how Brian had organized the test. He knew the patients came from five different ethnic groups, from six different origins, including locations in Mozambique, Malawi and South Africa. They were all different ages, in all different stages of human development and health.

The only thing this batch of "cured" people had in common with each other was—Halid and Jojeza, Nga and Miss Anderson.

He knew what he had to tell "doctor" Brian. But the man was not going to like it.

———

"None of the Luambe villagers was ever even really sick," he said, and Dr. Xavier translated. "All the patients are now well. The Yao are not only naturally immune to this, we appear to be the reason the others are better."

There was silence in Dr. Xavier's crowded office.

Brian's face got redder and redder. Halid wondered if the man's head would explode, like the squash his aunt had once overbaked.

Dr. Xavier looked from Halid to Brian and back. "That is an extremely interesting result," he said to them.

Brian shook his head. "No." He continued shaking his head. "You've screwed up the trials again!" He waved his arms. "Don't you see? Something, one of the tested substances has cured these people, and you have made such a mess of the data, I cannot even tell which one!" He practically growled, smacking the clipboard with the results pages against the back of one of Dr. Xavier's office chairs as the doctor quietly translated. "You have completely destroyed this experiment. It will have to be run again, on an entirely new batch of patients." He gritted his teeth. "Without your 'help'!"

Halid shrugged. "I did exactly as you asked. I recorded everything. The drugs were given properly. The results do not have anything to do with the drugs, I am thinking. They have to do with who gave the drugs."

Dr. Xavier raised an eyebrow. "They weren't even all Yao, Halid." He cleared his throat, still speaking in his smooth soft voice. "You said Miss Lind and Miss Anderson assisted. They are not Yao."

"They are not Yao," confirmed Halid, "though Nga has lived all her life in my village, Miss Anderson has not. But they merely were present, each along *with* a native Yao. Miss Anderson helped me. Jojeza helped Nga. Though we did wear masks, we saw the patients over and over again."

About a half-dozen people all tried to speak at once.

"You are saying you think you and Jojeza spread the cure?"

"It wasn't the drugs?"

"What was being tested in the trial?"

"Did they all eat the same foods, come from the same villages? Maybe it's more than the Yao… "

"Just STOP!!!" Brian yelled. "This is stupid, unscientific speculation!" He waved his arms broadly, including the entire room. "You should know better! You are all physicians! You don't speculate, you prescribe and test and observe. One of these drugs has helped, people are better. But you have suddenly devolved into mysticism! Natural immunity spread through social contact? Please!"

Halid saw the black-haired San Diego resident bite his lip, and Dr. Greta's mouth made a firm straight line. It was impossible for him to tell if they agreed with Brian or not. Dr. Xavier stood quietly, eyes blinking rapidly while he apparently thought things through. He was the epidemiologist, after all. He should have the best clue what was going on, shouldn't he?

Halid was certain he was right, but with no training and no formal titles to his name, he was also pretty sure he wasn't going to be heard. He quietly turned and left the room.

It was time for the Luambe villagers to return home. Maybe Nga could help him figure out how to get them there. He and Jojeza would remain, to learn the formal TC program, which he was looking forward to.

So long as he needn't work with the red-faced man.

16. ARIQ

ROSWELL, NEW MEXICO

They arrived at the hospital after dinner had been served and the evening rounds completed. The grounds were quiet. Bats flitted after bugs attracted to the meditation garden, and a distant coyote protested the silence.

Lily listened to the yips, then turned to him. "Dingos?"

"Coyote," he said.

"Sounds a bit like a didgeridoo, but higher. Yelpy."

"When there is a group of them calling, it's called a sing," Ariq said. "But they're usually solitary."

"Mm," Lily said.

Together they moved her backpack and art supplies into the lobby. He had wanted to give her an appropriate goodbye, but her plan to leave tomorrow overwhelmed his procrastination and indecision. She'd even cooked the final dinner.

One at a time, he carried each canvas with all the care and gratitude he felt, but couldn't put into words. He barely dared speak, for it seemed like every time they talked, they'd argued, about bats, about disease, about colonies. More than anything else he wished for some mutual closure.

Realizing nothing more would happen tonight, he left her to complete her paintings.

The next morning, something interrupted his sleep.

Phone? Yes.

What time is it? Early.

"Hello?"

Lily. "Two packages for you. From Africa and Mongolia."

"Africa?"

"Yes, Mozambique."

He didn't expect anything from Africa. "I'm on my way."

The Mongolian package had to be from his father, mostly likely ɘMɘɘ's long-awaited hospital records.

He jumped out of bed, and threw on some jeans and a blue oxford shirt. Even though it was Saturday he still had to maintain appearances. He grabbed some left-over dinner for a quick breakfast. He'd get coffee at the hospital.

When he arrived, the Roswell Orthopedic Clinic hummed with activity setting up for the wedding reception. Marti sent the last-minute invitations by email on Friday,

Join us on Monday to celebrate our wedding. 11:00 AM in the ROC reception space. Light snacks will be served.

He sighted Lily across the room and raised his hands palms up while looking around the room. She understood his question and pointed toward the CRC. He ran out the back door past the waterfalls, almost knocking over one of the patients attracted to the unusual wedding commotion.

The package reminded him of the one from Lily with a hand-written address and lots of string. It seemed heavier, so probably not dried herbs. He examined the stamps, Mozambique, and the postmark, Maputo. Wasn't that the capital?

Jessenia and Sofia walked in while he was opening the package. It contained about a dozen glass vials, a melted blue ice pack, and a note in neat block letters with words crossed out and corrected. The note read:

I am Halid from Mozambique. These samples are from Yao people. Yao people do not get sick. People living in Yao villages do not get sick. Please look at this Yao DNA.

Ariq had seen hints of this in **Bat Chat**, but having the DNA samples in his hands made it real. Now he had three data points that he desperately wanted to put together in a straight line.

He handed the note to *los científicos*. "What do you think?"

He kept talking while they read, "First, Lily's stew. Second, there were the Mexican free-tailed bats in Slaughter Canyon. A few developed immunity and then they all did. Now the Yao in Mozambique might be something like those bats in Slaughter Canyon."

"Lily's stew. Our bats. These Yao people in Mozambique. These three cures must be related."

Sofia thought for a moment, "Do scientists always try to connect everything like that?"

Ariq smiled, "Yes, it's called Occam's Razor. The simplest explanation is the right one."

Jessenia jumped in, "I can see how the bats and the Yao are similar, but the stew?"

Sofia suggested, "Well they all conferred immunity. Lily's stew seemed like a miracle, saving my mother."

Ariq defended his scientific method. "Probably not a miracle. I've kept careful notes and squirreled away samples. We don't have a mass spectrometer or even the most basic chemistry equipment, but if we did, I think we could find the answer."

"Lily herself is not certain it's the stew," he continued. "She suggested maybe it's breath."

"Something in the air," Sofia said. "Hmm."

Jessenia, not one to get distracted, brought the discussion back on topic. "Forget chemistry. This Halid suggested a DNA analysis. We can do DNA analysis. We're good at that."

They couldn't do much else than sequence DNA. They didn't have equipment for any other avenues of investigation. No scanning electron microscope, no x-ray diffraction, no mass spectrometer—so DNA sequencing it would be.

General Indecision and Colonel Delay never won any battles.

Since he was ignoring the CDC, they might as well run the sequencers one more time. He didn't have a sample of Lily's DNA, but he had lots of samples from the Yao. So, they would set the sequencers to work on those. It would take time, but they had plenty of that.

He laughed, "If your only tool is a hammer, everything looks like a nail. Let's do it!"

More *los cientificos* had arrived, and everyone began prepping samples.

While the students worked, he opened the packet from Mongolia. His thoughts to get advice from the clinic doctors evaporated when he saw the few pages of disorganized notes. Test results and patient observations shared the pages with TV schedules and gossip—no order, no timestamps, no signatures. He couldn't even tell if ɘмɘɘ's health was improving or otherwise.

———

Ariq returned to wedding central. The bride-to-be rushed around giving everyone orders.

He found Lily. "We are all so glad for your visit. Especially Sofia. You saved her mother." He opened his arms wide. "Your paintings are perfect. This enormous area of open beams and glass needed some color. We can't drill holes in the sandstone walls to hang them, but we'll think of something." Then he gave her the check he'd had Martina cut the day before, for the art. He felt awkward. Lily seemed so also.

She seemed a bit shy about her art. "My color palette works well here. Your environment reminds me of back home. I'm glad you like the paintings."

Ariq felt like a teenager making small talk at the prom, afraid of a lull in the conversation. He'd been debating whether to mention the bats. He had released the Mexican free-tailed bats. He needed to arrange for the pipistrelles and flying foxes to be shipped over an ocean, so they would take longer. He wanted to tell her, but he didn't know how to bring the subject up without starting another argument.

Maybe during the long trip to Albuquerque…. Then he realized that he'd have to stay with the DNA analysis. He'd have to make other arrangements for her travel to the airport.

He didn't want to bring that up either.

He shut up. Martina had everyone's attention anyway.

"Joni, you have the scissor lift, can you hang Lily's paintings?" Martina called. "I'm thinking of long wires hung down from the ceiling beams."

"I've seen that in the Santa Fe galleries. We'll take care of it. Don't you have to head out to Albuquerque soon to pick up your dress?"

Marti held up an old-school clipboard. She went silent a moment, perusing her list. "We're on schedule. If you can take care of deliveries, Lachy and I will head out."

Joni nodded. Marti put down her clipboard. "We're off to pick up my dress and a few last-minute items. I'll see some of you tomorrow and all of you on Monday."

She realized Lily stood next to her. "Except Lily."

At that point everyone said goodbyes to Lily.

Ariq stepped up and spoke to Martina. "I was supposed to take Lily to the airport, but I have to stay here. Can you take her?"

Martina blinked, putting a hand on Lachlan's shoulder as she turned to Ariq. "Of course! We're already going to the airport to pick up my mom. We need to leave very soon, though."

"I'll get my things," Lily said.

Ariq stammered, "The paintings are great, Lily. Thank you so much for your help with the stew and everything." He gave her awkward hug while she slid the straps of her backpack onto her thin shoulders. She gave him a small wave. He waved back and still feeling awkward, he headed back to the CRC and the DNA sequencing. It was a lot easier to talk to her on **Bat Chat**.

Ariq sat with the science club in the CRC listening to the sequencers, the buzz and the click of the servomotors, now in unison and then in counterpoint, playing a meditative symphony as the machines fell in and out of synchrony. He impatiently counted the minutes before he'd have something to feed into BLAST. He knew he wasn't needed to watch the automation, but it took his mind off the abrupt goodbye, and the fact that Lily was returning to Australia. Nothing he had hoped for had worked out between them. Except for the stew.

A call from Julia Whitey in Washington DC interrupted his reverie.

"I'm calling again to thank you for saving my father. Now that the course of AIR is known, I realize how lucky he is to be alive."

He said, "Thank you," but his head was spinning. What did she mean by the *disease course is known*?

She continued, "Between the residual immunity from his rabies shots, and your brilliant use of the Milwaukee Protocol, you saved him."

He thought it was more lucky than brilliant, but didn't say anything.

"I don't know how much you hear out there in New Mexico…"

Evidently not much, he thought.

"…but almost all of the early infections were fatal."

"We're a little out of touch out here. Have you heard anything else?" he hoped his probing seemed innocuous.

She switched over to a conspiratorial whisper. "There are discussions about how your genetic analysis was faulty. People are saying things like, 'What can you expect from an administrator and a bunch of high school kids?' They aren't completely laughing because your bat DNA sequence provided the missing puzzle piece. I don't think they want to admit it, they'd still be lost if it wasn't for you and those kids."

She laughed.

At this point he put the call on the speaker phone.

Ariq smiled, "So we did something useful?"

"Useful? Not just useful, important!"

The science club quietly cheered and there were high-fives all around.

"What was wrong with what we did? Why were they laughing at us?"

Julia got serious, "That story about bats splitting off from the other mammals fifty million years ago…"

Ariq protested. "That's true! I read it on Wikipedia!"

"Yes, but the idea that they had a unique immune system… Empirical data didn't support that conclusion. The implication that bats were somehow special and unique— That kind of mystical exceptionalism doesn't sit well with the scientific community."

Ariq was silent. He regretted he'd made such a mistake.

"Regardless, scientists around the world downloaded your bat sequences and compared them. They compared them to everything."

"They found that the immune system genes from your bat sequence might be rare, but they are expressed in other mammals, some mice, a few primates, and most importantly in Australian aborigines and some tribes of sub-Saharan Africa, a nexus of high genetic diversity."

His heart pounded when she said, "Australian aborigines." He thought about the Yao DNA sitting in his sequencers. He concluded someone had already sequenced the Yao and the aborigines. What *los científicos* and he were doing now was unnecessary.

"Many scientists were working over the weekend to find the connection between these rare immune systems and a treatment for AIR."

Ariq thanked her for the update and tried to end the call.

"Wait, one more thing! That data about immunity in that bat colony…Slaughter House Canyon, right?"

No one corrected her. Ariq just thought Vonnegut would be laughing.

"Anyway, everyone is saying that showing how immunity spread through the colony—almost like the immunity propagation in a single organism—was just brilliant. You should congratulate the students who figured that out."

With that, the call ended, and the high school students cheered loudly and jumped around. He turned to them. "Put everyone's name on the research from Slaughter Canyon. This is going to be the science fair project for the ages."

That night he took them all out. They ate pizza and drove into the desert to watch the tiny bats on their journey. Everyone talked about science and college and, of course, bats.

17. DR. BRIAN

MAPUTO, MOZAMBIQUE

R_X Brian opened one eye and looked out the window. The green hospital block gleamed in the bright morning sun. Too bright. He had overslept. The stress of the clinical trials had left him exhausted. He had slept soundly, even though he woke drenched in sweat. The night had been exceptionally warm.

He rolled over and noticed that the Khemisty Kids had also overslept. He smiled. Sleeping in on a Saturday morning was universal. They had been working hard, pulling all-nighters to analyze the compounds and again to prepare for the trials.

When this was all over, he should host a celebration.

Regardless, he really wanted to run one more trial. Patients were improving; they were close.

When he stood up, he got dizzy, and sat down. "Hey sleepyheads, it's time to get up."

They stirred. Some grumbled. Others buried their heads under their makeshift pillows.

"We need everyone. Remember, *we're* running the trial this time. No more mistakes."

The leaders, Hyacinta and Sebastian, got up and walked over to where quiet Gabrielle curled up in the corner. The three of them whispered.

The grumbling stopped. Everyone got very quiet. Thomas jumped up and everyone frowned at him. There were no flips or falls. He sat down.

All eyes turned toward at Gabrielle.

She started, "Doctor Brian…"

Everyone looked serious. He wondered what was going on, why would Gabrielle be the first to speak.

"Last night we went to the hospital. We talked to everyone."

Now Sebastian spoke up, "We spoke to the patients, and the nurses, and the doctors."

Hyacinta added, "Even the people who clean and those also who cook. Everyone."

Brian looked at Gabrielle, trying to imagine where this introduction was leading. He didn't want to repeat the discussions from yesterday. Case closed. His chest tightened at the thought of another round of recriminations and debate.

He took a friendly tack. "I'm sorry you wasted your time. I had hoped you were out partying. It was Friday night after all."

Gabrielle ignored this comment, "We reviewed all of Halid's documents and procedures." She spoke so softly, everyone had to be still to hear her. Brian leaned forward. She continued. "There were no errors."

She folded her arms across her chest. "No errors," she repeated.

Brian took a deep breath and quickly recapped everything he'd said yesterday, finishing up with, "Nothing else can explain the results."

Now it was his turn to cross his arms. "Nothing."

He looked around the room. The Khemistry Kids were unmoved by his logic and experience.

They looked to Gabrielle, their spokesperson.

She walked over to him. He had to turn to stay facing her. "We're sorry, Doctor Brian. We have enjoyed working with you. We learned so much."

Here it comes. His heart was beating out of his chest. He moved away from her and grabbed his chest.

She continued, "We'd love to support you and administer another round of testing, but we can't. There are no more sick patients at the hospital. No more people to test. *Everyone is cured*."

He couldn't think. His attention flashed back to North Carolina, and the warnings he'd received. He gasped, "Heart attack. Heart attack."

He felt he was going to pass out. With his last bit of strength, he pointed to his phone, "Call Penny, Penny, my daughter."

18. LILY

———◆🦇◆———

ROSWELL, ALBUQUERQUE, NEW MEXICO

———

🦇 Lily had set the black and white and red paintings against the wall they were to be hung on and tried to "feel" the space, looking at the balance of color, space, and style. A few creamy tans and pinkish beiges picked up bits of color from the wood, walls, and floors. But something wasn't quite right. They were out of balance with the room, or each other, or something.

The clock said four in the morning. She left the paintings and went back into the CRC. She folded her legs and sat on the floor of the dark room, listening to the bats. This was the time of day they would normally be returning home from a night of feasting. She could hear them hopping and fluttering in the cages.

"You will go home soon," she promised them. The Mexican Free-Tails had already been released.

She wouldn't be able to take the black flying foxes with her as she had hoped, for they'd be classified as pets and need to go through quarantine. But if they were scientific study animals, the shipping process was different. Dr. Darnell had been surprised by her call asking for help, but said he would make sure the CDC sent the proper papers for Ariq to use. Jessenia had promised to make sure Ariq got them prepped and shipped properly. Lily would pick them up in Katherine and take them home to Roper's Bar.

She'd also more or less bullied Jessenia into making sure Ariq followed through with the pipistrelles, and she'd also applied pressure in **Bat Chat** to be sure there was follow through.

At peace with herself and the displaced bats, she relaxed into what felt like the most genuine dreamtime sequence she'd felt since she had landed in the U.S. She *could* touch the dreamtime from here.

She was swept up into memories—or a dream—or the song of

389

life—and into the bats' dreaming, where they flew full of life, to feed on blossoms and fruits, others on mosquitoes and flies. They were connected in a path that could be felt and almost seen, connected to the earth and the elders of the dreamtime and the peoples of the present.

She walked the path, the songline, the earth dusty and red beneath her feet.

———

When she woke, it was to the memory of a buzzer sound. Then she heard it again, and a banging on the outside door of the CRC.

She got up and opened the door. A man stood there with two packages.

"These are for Ariq Temuujin…?"

Lily nodded.

"Please sign."

Lily signed her name on the form and the man handed her the boxes.

One was from Mongolia, but the other had an odd return address: Mozambique. Wasn't that in Africa? She called Ariq and told him what had arrived.

"Okay, I'll be there in a bit."

Lily washed her face in the CRC lab sink, brushed her teeth with her finger, and went outside and over to the hospital lobby.

She found Martina standing there staring at her paintings, which still rested on the floor, unhung.

"Oh, Lily, these are wonderful!" Martina exclaimed.

"They aren't quite finished yet," Lily said, smiling at the older woman's enthusiasm. "I realized what they needed last night."

She sat on the floor and mixed a pinkish gray paint. To each painting, she added two of the semi-circles that represented women. Lily and Pearl.

People and bats.

Then she signed them, with a stylized version of her name. When she looked at them against the wall, they were just right.

She was a bit disappointed that Ariq barely looked at them

when he ran in, looking for her.

"Oh, nice," he said. Then, "Where's the boxes?" he asked.

"In the CRC, by the sink," Lily said.

Martina had returned, and was admiring the paintings again. "That gives me an idea," she said. "We can use a little red in our decorations for the wedding." She grinned at Lily. "I'm so glad you got them finished. Can you tell me anything about what they mean?"

Lily explained, about the Mataranka pools, and the palm trees, and the bats. Then about the bush tucker, and what each food was and how it was used. She pointed to the women markers and said, "This is my teacher and me." Finally, in the one painting she had included one in, she pointed to a space-alien-looking figure. "This is an ancestral spirit, or elder."

"Oh, I'm glad you told me. A lot of people around here are going to think that's an alien from outer-space."

Lily grinned. "Maybe it is!"

They were still laughing when Ariq ran in and gave Lily a quick hug. "I'm so sorry I won't be able to drive you to Albuquerque today; I need to run these samples through the sequencer while we still have it."

"I suspect the CDC isn't going to get around to picking it up any time soon," Martina said.

"I'd rather not risk it," Ariq said. "The answers to AIR are in there, I just know it." He turned to Lily. "Thank you so much for bringing your stew to my patients. I have been re-thinking my whole life, thanks to you."

Lily blinked, not knowing what to say. "I'm glad the patients got better," she finally managed.

———

As much as she felt things were not good between her and Ariq, Lily still felt odd to spend her last day with the two people she knew least well at Roswell.

Martina chattered pretty much nonstop on the drive to Albuquerque, mostly about her and Dr. Lachlan's plans for the wedding and afterward. She made some effort to include Lily, but that felt awkward to them both.

Lily spent most of the time looking out her window, watching the New Mexico desert sweep by. It was like, yet unlike her own desert. There were fewer trees, more scrubby shrubs, and open spaces. Ariq had warned her to watch out for rattlesnakes and scorpions when she had walked around, but she had not seen any. Nor coyotes, though she had heard them "singing" one of her first nights here, at Carlsbad.

She realized she'd never gone inside the Caverns to see any of the formations. She did have a brochure from the park that showed photos. It seemed majestic, but strange.

Albuquerque was a lot bigger than Roswell, bigger even than Darwin, so Lily was treated to the sights of the largest city she'd ever seen. A lot of the buildings were of the style she pictured when she thought of the American west: adobe walls smoothed by hand and painted desert colors. Almost her colors, but not quite. To her eyes, they needed more ochre, less dark reds and browns.

Lunch was Mexican style food; Martina let Dr. Lachlan pay for all of them. Lily had something called a chimichanga, which was crunchy on the outside and full of interesting veg and meat on the inside.

Then they awkwardly stood around awhile and asked if Lily minded being at the airport hours early. They really couldn't in good conscience drag her around Albuquerque while they finished their wedding shopping. She thanked them, and sat happily in the airport, reading email on her phone over the free airport WiFi.

She thought about her paintings, about walking in the desert, and realized her metaphor about the bats and people being in a circle, or a cloud, was wrong. The interaction, the life between them was not a separate thing, floating in the sky. It was part of the world, must be grounded in the world, just as her feet were, walking in the red dust of home.

She tried to figure out how to word that explanation to include in her thank-you text to Ariq. Then she remembered Pearl laughing at her when she'd tried to explain things about aboriginal life to Dr. Darnell. It wasn't so much that there was a taboo, it was that it was simply very hard to explain. The dreamtime was an aboriginal concept that they had grown up with, just as Ariq had grown up with his sense of western science.

She wasn't going to be able to explain her "colony" idea to him, not in a way that he could believe it. It was possible they would *never* quite understand one another. The realization fascinated her.

Then her phone ding'd. Jessenia had shown her how to do all kinds of things on her phone, and Lily laughed when she received a "selfie" from Obrey showing the blank, empty walls in his coffee shop and himself with a pleading expression on his face. It would be so good to see him.

She slept on the plane, transferred in Los Angeles, slept, transferred again in Sydney after a longer sleep, and finally saw the Darwin airport. The plane that took her to Katherine was small and friendly, and full of natives and *balanda* alike. As they touched down at the tiny Katherine district airport, all she could do was grin.

19. ARIQ

ROSWELL, NEW MEXICO

Sunday morning Ariq arose early, eager for news to corroborate the call from Julia Whitey. For what seemed like the thousandth time, he checked for news online. Nothing. The only interesting search hits were copies of the report posted by *los cientificos*. For lack of something else, he reread their report about the bats in Slaughter Canyon Cave.

He proudly read the names aloud, Sofia Cortez, Jessenia Sanchez.... After the names, they listed their affiliation as Roswell High School and Chiropteran Research Center. For a contact, they included their CRC Gmail account and the phone number at the CRC lab.

Since the big news channels had nothing to say, he went to **Bat Chat**.

Citizen science saves the day.
Great science doesn't require big budgets.
Curiosity killed the epidemic.
Gratz to *los cientificos* and khemistry kids.

Los cientificos certainly referred to the Roswell High science club, but he didn't know anything about the Khemistry Kids. A quick search didn't help. He gave up on returning to sleep and walked through the house turning on lights, starting the shower, and making coffee.

Drinking hot coffee in the shower clarified his thoughts. Since his houseguest had left, his modest home felt larger and colder, less like home. Lily had to be in Australia by now.

He found some granola that Lily had left. Along with a second cup of coffee, that comprised an early breakfast.

He walked out to the paddock thinking of an early morning ride, but the sun hadn't peeked over the horizon yet. White Ears slept on the ground, snoring, for one of her brief deep-sleep naps. No ride this morning.

Ariq put out some hay and oats, and drove to the CRC. Since

the report had listed that phone number, someone should be there to answer calls…if anyone called.

He stopped at Desert Dessert Delights. They didn't open this early on Sunday, but his experience and nose knew Dee and her crew were already baking. Sunday meant family dinners and church social hours, so a lot of baking, early. He knocked on the back door.

"*Beunos dias*, Dee."

"*A usted también*. Big wedding tomorrow."

Wedding? Ariq had forgotten about the wedding.

"Yes, we're all looking forward to your cake. Sorry to bother you so early."

"*De nada*."

"Can I get a dozen of whatever cookies you're baking, and an order of fry bread."

"Just wait here. Shall I put it on the clinic's tab?"

"Not this morning."

He handed her a couple of bills and walked back to his car with a warm pink box of mesquite shortbread and a paper plate overflowing with fry bread.

He'd finished half the bread by the time he arrived at the clinic.

The hospital lobby looked festive. Red and White ribbons festooned the wooden beams spanning the high ceiling. Lily's paintings seemed to be floating midair next to the wall, suspended by nearly invisible wires.

Outside, tables and chairs surrounded the fountain. Wet pawprints announced Rosy's earlier presence. Ariq walked toward the meditation garden and tore off a particularly greasy piece of fry bread to leave for her in case she was still around. If she'd left, the chipmunks would happily clean up.

As he approached the CRC, he heard talking. He recognized Jessenia and Sofia's voices among others. He had not been the only one wondering if people might call. The phone speaker cut through the silence.

"University of Cape Town here."

Sofia said, "South Africa. Wow. What time is it?"

"Late afternoon. We wanted to congratulate on your insight. With all the concern about mutated virulent viruses becoming airborne disease vectors, we never considered that the same might happen to attenuated viruses."

Ariq looked around the room. The students smiled and laughed—they were not hearing new information, but it was nice to hear confirmation.

"Your data made us think of an airborne vaccine."

Jessenia jumped in, "Do you think that is really what is happening?"

"Oh yes. A few years ago, UCT sequenced the full Natal long-fingered bat genome. We can see an MHC genotype that might facilitate this mechanism. The European Molecular Biology Laboratory database has our sequences."

Ariq opened the box of shortbread and the students helped themselves. No one looked directly at Ariq or mentioned that UCT had obviously completed a full chiropteran genome years before the CRC had. Ariq was torn between joy for the Slaughter Canyon success and the embarrassment that UCT had preceded his Mexican Free-tailed bat genome.

UCT continued. "We wanted to let you know that we found similar MHC genotypes within the Yao people of Mozambique and Malawi, but not Tanzania. You can easily check our data which is also at EMBL, and the National Center for Biotechnology Information GenBank."

"Oh, thank you for letting us know," Jessenia said.

Ariq slowly walked over to the sequencers. He typed a few commands into the console to terminate the work on the samples from Halid in Mozambique. Ariq ate the last bite of fry bread, greasy and cold. Too little, too late.

That set the tone for the next couple of hours. The University College of Dublin together with the Greifswald University of Germany sequenced the Greater Mouse-Eared bat. Kunming University in China had sequenced the Little Brown bat of North America. The CRC could not even claim the first bat in the Americas.

As Ariq had suspected from Julia's call, the Australian National University answered any questions about Australian Aborigine DNA. They confirmed the now familiar MHC variant.

He took solace that Lily already had departed when he learned all the experiments with the caged bats were useless. Only the Slaughter Canyon data collection paid off. Ariq put on a happy face, as the students accepted congratulations and gave interviews.

KJNM called. The students told about being chased by the bear and how they had thought something had contaminated their data, and how their two youngest students had suggested the previously unthinkable: contagious immunity.

In the morning, they heard mostly from Europe and Africa. Eventually the United States woke up. Universities and corporate research labs offered *los científicos* summer internships. Several colleges recruited the new seniors, especially Jessenia.

———

Roswell Orthopedic Clinic was the place to be. Everyone gathered waiting for the happy couple to arrive from the small ceremony at the Roswell Court House. Ariq observed that the midday-Monday reception challenged the fashion sense of this diverse community.

Nizhoni wore a dress with a bold weave in bright reds, purples, and blues, with turquoise-and-silver jewelry. She waited outside by the fountains surrounded by Jessenia and her friends. Girls and boys alike wore blue jeans and tee shirts with bold southwestern designs. Joni just smiled as the kids all told her about their scientific successes.

Mayor Smyth and the city council chose to arrive in their Sunday wear, dresses for the women and jackets for the men. They seemed uncomfortable and congregated away from the crowd, around the stone benches in the meditation garden.

The hospital staff had arranged split shifts for the day, so everyone could spend some time at the reception. Fancy scrubs were the uniform of the day. ROC provided everyone with corporate scrubs in the hospital colors of desert brown and sandstone red. Today bright colors and patterns set the tone, along with shiny material. He had never realized scrubs were available in satin and silk.

When the limo arrived, the couple waited while everyone crowded under the red and white ribbons for their grand entrance. First to enter were Dr. Thompson in a white tux, and Martina's mother wearing a long lace dress in beige.

The five children followed, all in purple—the three girls in short party dresses, and the two boys in jackets and ties.

Finally, the bride and groom in classic white and black.

Everyone cheered.

During his toast, Chucky heaped compliments on the couple both personally and professionally. He ended with, "Fine professionals like this give me confidence in the future of this hospital, even after I retire. After years in the desert, I am looking forward to relocating to Hawaii."

The City Council admired the fountains while Dee helped to serve the cake. Immediately following, they said their goodbyes, but not before cornering Ariq.

Jorge spoke, "We've been talking to PopulistHealth in Minnesota. They now understand we like our town the way it is and are not interested in becoming a destination for hip replacements."

Ariq scanned at the group. No one returned his glances, not even Dee, whom he had thought of as a friend.

Mayor Smyth said, "We've worked out a deal. The President will declare the land east of town a Federal Preserve. PopulistHealth will withdraw."

Now he understood the unfriendly calls from corporate. They had nothing to do with sick patients or any clinic activities. It was all about profits and politics instigated by lawyers and lobbyists. On days like this, he wished for the return of the Mongolian Horde.

He walked with the planning commission toward the parking lot in silence, unable to find anything to say. His phone rang. He expected it to be another useless call from Minneapolis and intended to ignore it.

It wasn't. International.

"Please excuse me. I have to take this."

He let the phone ring a couple of more times as he retreated to a far corner of the now deserted meditation garden.

"*Сайн байна уу.*"

His father.

"Эмээ is on her deathbed. You need to return home."

He didn't see any purpose of mentioning the useless Mongolian hospital reports he'd received. The time had obviously come. He could not delay any longer.

"I will be there."

Rosy looked down from the top of the wall.

He smiled at the cat. "They're going to build a park for you."

Rosy stretched and yawned. With a flick of her stubby tail, she headed east into the new Federal Preserve.

BAT CHAT

PLUS FREQUENTLY ASKED QUESTIONS

? *Are bats friends or foes?*
Vampire bat species only live in Central and South America and rarely attack humans. They live in small colonies; a few hundred. Mexican Free-tail bats colonies numbers in the millions.

Bats harbor harmful diseases, including rabies and lyssaviruses. However, interactions between humans and bats are rare.

Microbats eat insects that they find through echolocation. How many? A colony might consume 250 tons in an evening. They control pests without dangerous chemicals.

Megabats are important pollinators and seed propagators.

Bats are our friends.

http://www.batconservation.org

 Dreamtime: **Long trip Lots of airports Happy to be back home**

 Mongol Bataar: **My grandmother is very sick I'm also going to take a long trip home**

 Fleming: **Me too. If I could figure out where home is, I'm ready to go**

 Syms Covington: **Tell me about it I feel like a nomad, home is where I lay my head.**

 Mongol Bataar: **Dreamtime-the last of the bats are on their way home to England and to you.**

 Morcego: **We saved the world, I get to travel to University of Cape Town. They invited me and they are paying!!!**

 Nina de la Ciencia: **Me too, travel and I'm going to be on television.**

 Kitty: **No travel here, but my dad has recovered from AIR and is coming to visit**

 Canuck: **It's been an exciting time in bat chat Nice to have met you all**

 Popo: **Sim adeus amigos**

 Nina de la Ciencia: **Si adios amigos**

 Radar Rat: **Our friends live to fly another day.**

20. BRIAN MACALESTER

MAPUTO, MOZAMBIQUE

R𝒳 His nose itched. He moved his hand to scratch it, but he couldn't reach. It felt like a dream, a frustrating dream. His chest hurt. He held his chest. His heart beat against his hand. He was alive. He wasn't dreaming.

He reached for his itchy nose again. This time he felt the restraints. He wrinkled his nose and realized he was wearing an oxygen mask. He wanted to tear the mask off and shout for a nurse. Then he remembered removing his IV and his mask, lowering the bed rails, and collapsing on the floor before several nurses appeared.

He had trouble recalling what happened next.

Did he tell them that he was a doctor? Did they call Penny? Did he tell them he had discovered a cure for AIR? Or that he needed to run another trial?

Then he remembered what Gabrielle said, he'd run out of subjects. Somehow, in a declared global-epidemic hot spot, Maputo Central Hospital had run out of sick people.

His arms fell to his sides and the restraints relaxed.

———

Later, feeling better and thinking clearly, realizing he'd escaped death again, he reviewed his situation. First, he really should have delayed going to Mozambique for further medical evaluation and possible surgery for an implantable cardiac defibrillator. As the doctor in North Carolina had suggested.

He'd foolishly flown over ten thousand miles away from the best medical facilities. His heart rate increased.

With his increasing pulse came an insistent beeping from his monitor, and two nurses. One nurse removed his oxygen mask. *"Você está bem?"*

He took several deep breaths to calm himself and nodded. One nurse checked his urinary catheter and the other offered him a straw to sip some fruit juice. He couldn't identify the juice, but it calmed him.

He pressed his tongue against the top of his mouth. Mango, maybe, he thought. Yes, mango.

He liked Maputo with its seemingly endless variety of fruit juices, sunny flower gardens, and fresh fish. And the pleasant morning walks to *Avenida da Marginal*. He replayed the successes of the Khemistry Kids. Then he thought about Halid and Nga and how they messed up his research.

But no, he realized. That's not what happened. As the Kids had explained, Halid had done everything by the book. Any problems with the trials belonged to Brian, or their test materials.

Right from the start, he shouldn't have administered those untested drugs. When the results didn't support his hypothesis, he surely should have abandoned the experiment, but instead he had pushed ahead.

Why had he risked his own life by coming to Mozambique, and once there why had he placed the lives of so many others in jeopardy? He looked around the ward where he lay: sick, innocent people, sick just like him. He regretted the way he'd treated them, and their friends and families.

But I am Doctor Brian, and I have the experience and the expertise, who are they to question me?

He heard himself, maybe for the first time. His arrogance embarrassed him. His heart raced.

My heart is trying to kill me.

Faster beeping this time, and then the nurses were back. This time they added something to his saline IV drip.

He fell back asleep repeating, *I am not the doctor. I am not a doctor*.

He slept fitfully, dreaming in flashbacks of prideful behaviors throughout his long career.

———

"Sit up. You've been sleeping for over thirty-six hours. Have some lunch."

Brian smelled charbroiled steak, something he hadn't had since that breakfast in Papeete with Penny. That seemed so long ago.

"Do I have to feed you?"

He opened his eyes. It was Penny.

"What are you doing here?"

Then he looked around. He was in a small airplane. He realized he could hear the dull roar of the jet engines, smell the recycled air.

"We're taking you home."

Brian. Plain Brian. Not Doctor Brian. Happy-to-be-alive Brian relaxed, ready for someone else to be in charge.

"Mom and dad–I mean, step-dad—are here, too. Dad hired this jet. You know it's pretty hard to get to Mozambique from anywhere, especially Tahiti."

Brian just nodded. He looked past Penny and sure enough there was Darlene, looking better than ever.

"Hi Darlene. Nice to see you again."

"Hi to you. I believe you know my husband, Jake."

Brian blinked. He rubbed his eyes and blinked again. Sure enough, there was Jake-the-salesman standing with his arm around Darlene's waist.

Even the new Brian, the one who could already feel his heart rate rising, couldn't be quiet when faced with Jake, especially with his arm around Darlene's waist, standing close to Penny.

"What are you doing here? Did you know RSS sold out-of-date medicines? Did you know RSS never installed the equipment you sold?"

Jake tried to interrupt, but Brian was shaking and shouting. Penny leaned over and hugged her father like a mother calming an upset child.

Brian continued, "People were dying around the world, and you were just profiting as much and as quickly as possible."

In a brief pause, Jake responded, "You are right. When I discovered what they were doing I quit. I quit. I quit so fast, I forfeited my final commission check. A substantial check."

Jake waved his arm around the cabin. "The check would have

been more than enough to pay for this jet we hired to come rescue you."

Brian listened. He tried to be calm. To not be a privileged, arrogant ass. He was practicing his new self. He tried to consider things from Jake's point of view.

Jake continued, "I was working day and night, thinking I was helping to solve the rabies epidemic."

Darlene added, "And he did help. The sequencers he got for that little hospital in New Mexico decoded the bat DNA and helped lead the way to the solution."

Jake also explained how he'd been testifying in Washington and Brussels against Research Sciences Solutions.

The discussion took a hiatus when the pilot announced for everyone to buckle their seat belts for takeoff.

———

Jake and Darlene sat together and Penny sat with Brian.

"Where are we going?"

"We're on a short hop to Jo'burg and then we'll fly commercial to Papeete."

Brian wondered about that hospital in New Mexico. "What did they discover in New Mexico?"

Surprisingly, Penny had the answer, "Well I don't understand the details, but evidently bat colonies are able to propagate immunities from bat to bat."

"So the colony responds to an infection as a single organism?"

Penny smiled, "Yeah, something like that."

About then the pilot announced they were preparing to descend into O R Tambo airport in Johannesburg. As they approached, the pilot mentioned that a high school science and math teacher became such an important person that they named the airport after him.

Brian thought about retiring again, maybe teaching high school.

Since they were on a private jet, their schedule let them board their flight to Narita without delay.

———

Once on-board, Brian had access to several English-language news broadcasts. He started with the American networks. They covered the RSS scandal, the CDC and NIH talking about their contribution to the AIR breakthrough, and a human-interest story about a group of high school students in New Mexico who were the first to observe contagious immunity in a local bat colony.

This confirmed what Jake and Penny had told him. He looked across the aisle at Jake and Darlene holding hands, and smiled.

When he switched over to the BBC, they were carrying a story about an aboriginal girl from Darwin Australia who somehow ended up in New Mexico and contributed to ending the AIR pandemic with her aboriginal treatment methods.

At this point, Brian turned to Penny, "Have you been watching the news? Everyone is stealing the credit for stopping the epidemic."

She gave him an angry look, "I thought you'd finally learned your lesson. Are you still looking for praise and glory?"

"No, not me. I was thinking about the people in Maputo. I'm certain everyone would still be scratching their heads without the detailed reports from the Maputo trials."

"Have you watched anything but American reports?"

"The BBC? Not much."

Since they were flying to Narita, the entertainment system featured news from Tokyo. This didn't help. Tokyo emphasized the Asian angle. In between rebroadcasting American and British stories, they told the story of some guy from Mongolia who was in New Mexico. At this point, Brian just laughed.

"Penny, you know New Mexico hasn't been so much in the news since the Manhattan project."

Penny just laughed.

He scrolled through the in-flight entertainment system's news choices. At the end, Brian found South Africa. It was number twenty-three, after Singapore, Malaysia, and Vietnam. They had the stories Brian was hoping for.

———

"I am Yaseen Botha, and today I have Armando Queiroz, a chemistry teacher from Maputo. Can you tell me a little about yourself?"

"Yes, during the time of wars, my family sent me to Tallin, Estonia, to study. After I graduated, I stayed to work for a pharmaceutical company."

Yaseen wasn't interested in history, so he moved the story forward with, "I understand that when Mozambique settled down, you returned, but the only job you could get was a high school teacher. How did your students get involved in an international research project?"

"Mozambique was a hot spot for AIR, so it was natural that Maputo had a part in the research. They needed Chemists, and my students were available. They are keen on chemistry and all belong to the high school science club. They call themselves: Khemistry Kids."

Yaseen laughed and turned to the camera, "For those of you out there who aren't up on the latest Maputo teen culture, that is Khemistry Kids, with two K's." The camera showed a picture of the students in their school uniforms.

Moving on, he asked. "I understand Research Solution Services victimized your group along with so many others?"

"Yes, we had cartons of medication which were unlabeled and unknown. My students had to analyze the compounds to determine what we had, and when we found some promising leads, they had to synthesize enough for a test."

"I see."

Armando had lost the interviewer, but he continued anyway. "The American in charge, Brian Macalester, said my students were better than graduate chemists in the United States."

Brian looked at Penny, who was watching over his shoulder, "Those kids were good."

Yaseen wrapped up with, "So that is how chemists in Maputo helped save the world. They have all received scholarship offers from universities around the world. In fact, two of Mr. Queiroz' students start here at University of Johannesburg after the winter break."

———

The next story featured a popular South African news personality, Sameera Chetty. Brian remembered seeing her on Maputo TV where she presented stories in Portuguese. In fact, this interview was in Portuguese with English subtitles.

"Halid, doctors and researchers around the world are singing your praises."

Halid sat quietly, so Nga responded. "Halid is our village headman, and he did what was required. Someone needed to lead the trials at Maputo Central Hospital, so he did it."

"Well he did a great job. There were rumors of natural immunity from New Mexico, and Australia, and a few other places, but no one took it seriously until they saw Halid's data."

Halid's chest puffed out while he stared at his feet, with a mixture of pride and embarrassment. "Doctor Brian told me what to do. I just followed his instructions."

Brian cringed at the "Doctor." Penny laughed at her father's new found self-awareness and embarrassment.

Sameera needed to carry the story for these modest and bashful people from the countryside, "You should realize that your careful records made the difference between scientists laughing off stories of tribal medicine and taking it seriously. On behalf of many around the world, I want to thank you."

Halid finally spoke up. "Don't forget Nga. If she had not led the Yao on the long trip to Maputo, we would have been a pocket of immunity unknown to the outside world."

She had finally found a topic that animated these two. The interview went on with the many trials on the way to Maputo—counting fish, paddling canoes, riding the train.

Sameera closed with, "There you have it, how a Yao headman, a Swedish missionary, and a Maputo science teacher worked together to save the world."

Brian looked to Penny, "So I did okay?"

She took his hand and smiled.

ARIQ EPILOGUE

ORKHON VALLEY, MONGOLIA

Albuquerque, Phoenix, Los Angeles, Tokyo, Beijing, Ulaanbaatar. He had plenty of time to think. Too much time. Эмээ's spirit had left her earthly body by the time he arrived.

He sat next to his father in a Soviet-era farm truck for the drive to their village. They spoke in Mongolian.

"I'm getting old too." His father's face and hands echoed this truth. Эмээ had been close to one hundred. His father was not that old, but neither was he young.

As they headed west, Ariq found the green hills comforting.

"How long will you stay?"

The conversation got ahead of him. The language came back familiar and pleasant, but the words to reply would not form. He silently repeated his father's question. *How long will I stay?*

He thought in English. He thought in Mongolian.

His mute musings abruptly ended when the pickup truck arrived in Orkhon Valley. Only a few thousand people inhabited his village, but it seemed like everyone knew his story and wanted to talk to him.

He visited the local hospital. He observed the haphazard scheduling and record keeping reflected in the chaotic reports he'd received. Several people explained. The Ministry of Health promoted the director to a larger hospital, and they hadn't located a replacement for their small facility.

A few tasks took precedence over this pleasant visiting.

At the top of the list was his grandmother's funeral.

In order for эмээ to become again, her most prized possession, the one holding her to this world, had to be given away. The lama and his father decided this worldly attraction was her book of healing from before the revolution and the Russians.

It had to go to someone who would treasure it. If the recipient did not strongly grasp the book, эмээ's spirit would not let go. They assigned Ariq this task. He received the book with a sense of gravity matched with gratitude.

Each night he read the ancient healing traditions. One ritual involved touching and breathing on the sick person. This reminded him of Lily's stew ritual. Each day his admiration for the old ways expanded.

As he discovered more hidden wisdom, he could feel his grandmother letting go and becoming again.

Another task at the top of the list was the local science fair. The teachers pressed for the visiting Mongolian scientist to judge the competition. Unfortunately, Ariq had planned a short stay, and the fair date was much later. Everyone compromised. The students would complete their projects under a tighter deadline, and Ariq would delay his return.

Ariq erected a small *ger* in an open field adjacent to the school grounds. The door, lattice frame, roof poles, felt insulation, canvas cover, and ropes, so many ropes to hold everything together. Memories of annual migrations to the high pastures returned as his temporary house rose, and an empty field became home. Like so many generations of nomads before him, Ariq was home.

Day by day, hour by hour, students found him to ask questions about their experiments. In between the student visits, nurses and doctors recruited him to apply for the director job. He explained that he now lived in New Mexico. He told them about *los cientificos*, the 3D bakery, Nizhoni, the aliens, the clinic, Rosy the bobcat, and White Ears; he couldn't leave White Ears.

All this faded away on the day of the science fair. As a judge, Ariq did not have favorites, but a few students left strong impressions.

One was Naiman. When her family moved to the high pastures for the summer, she wandered the hills following the sheep. Over the years, she collected "fossils" and as she got older, she learned to recognize over 200 sheep bones from skulls to small vertebrae to tiny phalanges. Every so often, she found something different.

Her science project proudly presented some true fossils,

including a dinosaur phalange related those found at the Flaming Cliffs. Ariq couldn't help feeling her enthusiasm as she explained each sample, mounted in a cardboard box, and labeled with careful printing.

Switching from the past to the future, Gurban compared the felt traditionally used to insulate *gers* with modern foam alternatives. Ariq marveled at the small model *gers* he used to test winter and summer insulating properties. Gurban could barely stand still as he explained the benefit of one type of foam sheeting. Not only had he done the experiments, but he also had acquired the franchise to sell this foam in the Orkhon Valley.

There was such a fire and joy in these students, that Ariq marveled he could have ever thought of the Orkhon Valley to be a dull backwater.

That night a committee representing the Ministry of Health visited his *ger*. They made him an offer. They couldn't pay much, but they did offer to transport White Ears to Mongolia.

That night he weighed their offer. He considered returning to medical school, in honor of ɘʍɘɘ's wishes. The success of the CRC gave him a once-in-a-lifetime chance to become a real scientist.

Los científicos and the clinic drew him back to Roswell. But did they still need him? Jessenia's science fair project exceeded all expectations. Sofia had left for college. Another teacher could keep the science club going.

Roswell Orthopedic Clinic would not be expanding. Martina could run the place. He fell asleep in doubt and confusion.

He woke to the sound of sheep and goats grazing outside his *ger*. In the insight of morning half-sleep, he realized he was an okay teacher or scientist, and if he went back to med school, he could be a mediocre doctor. However, he was a *great* administrator, he knew how to organize and the people loved him.

The Mongolian students' enthusiasm and curiosity tipped the balance for Orkhon Valley. When the Ministry of Health agreed to free up a day each week from the hospital directorship to work with the Orkhon Valley students, he agreed to stay. With the decision made, he felt a great tension slip away. He was home, and soon White Ears would be too.

NGA EPILOGUE

LUAMBE, NIASSA, MOZAMBIQUE

Nga smiled to see Salim standing erect, his staff of office planted firmly into the ground. Of Imrane there was no sign. She did not ask about the man, or his supporters, or what had happened. She just hugged Anane and gave a little bow to Salim in acknowledgment of his authority.

"The Yao are the heroes of this story," she said. "And the Luambe villagers especially." She met Salim's steady gaze. "Without your people, an answer to the plague would have been difficult to find." She reached out and took Anane's hand. "*You* are the answer, your blood, your Yao heritage, your village and others where Yao blood runs strong."

A tiny smile formed on Salim's face as the previously silent villagers stirred at this news. Of course those who had returned from Maputo had already begun to tell what happened, but this meeting was the confirmation, the official announcement to Salim.

After a brief silence, "Must we meet all the people of the world, then?" Anane asked quietly.

"From your blood, they have derived a medicine. It cures those infected, and will protect everyone who hasn't gotten AIR yet."

"It is like magic," Anane murmured. Then even more softly, she said, "Imrane was almost right. *Our people* are the answer— not *him*—but we have cured ourselves."

Nga nodded. "This is true. And the Luambe villagers who went to Maputo have begun to cure the world."

Salim and Anane both looked at Wayya and Tonan and Kimi and the others who had gone to Maputo and returned. The headman smiled largely, opened his arms, officially welcoming them back into the village. Many hugs were exchanged.

Behind Nga, Mezi stood with a hand on each of her children's shoulders. After a few moments with his villagers, Salim turned to her; she stood apart, holding her children back.

412

Mezi took a breath. "My husband was a traitor to you, and my parents are dead. I will understand if you wish myself and my children gone." Mezi's face was very pale, her knuckles white as she gripped the children tightly.

Nga said, "Mezi helped keep the wounded villagers alive. She cooked and took care of all the village children at the hospital while Halid and Jojeza and I worked."

Anane stepped forward, making the decision before Salim could speak or move. The village headman's wife wrapped Mezi, Teleza and Mu into her hug.

Salim spoke then. "Of course you are welcome. We have lost too many. You have a place here, it is your home."

Little Teleza burst into tears and ran forward to hug her friends who had stayed behind in the village. Mezi's tears ran silently down her cheeks as she watched her children. Muluzi bounced the black and white football Ben had bought him, catching the eyes of the village boys. He was so small and pale among them, Nga's heart quailed a moment, as they surrounded the little boy, and took him in. Squeals and shouts soon punctuated the parents' conversations as the lively game of football spread over the slope below the ruined TC building.

Smiling, Anane took Nga's hands. "And you, will you stay?"

Nga bit her lip, shaking her head. "Halid and Jojeza are taking the TC training. Halid is partly trained already, he may be able to get though in much less than three years, and of course he will return to you, until he marries. Jojeza said she wanted to come home to Luambe, to stay, after she finishes her training."

"And you?"

Nga sighed deeply and turned a full circle, looking at the village, the burnt, tangled wreckage of her parents' house. She shook her head. "I will always see that, even when it is gone," she said.

Anane nodded. "All of us will, child."

Nga tried to smile when Anane said that. She wasn't that much younger than Anane in years, that she should be called a child. She wasn't that much younger in hurt and life and love either.

"I have my friend Shelly in Nacala I am going to help. She and I have a plan to get more *técnico de cirurgia* into Maputo for training. It is a project I have been wanting to do for a while, once Halid was trained." She rubbed her forehead with her thumb. "Ben Kalagho will come here once a week until Halid is finished training. They are moving from Malawi to his wife's village near Lichinga."

Anane nodded, then moved to stand next to her husband.

"Good," Salim said. He moved his staff to his other side, so he could rest his arm on Anane's shoulder. "Your Shelly saved my life, so we could return and save our village," he said. "Ben will be welcome here, but we have also a *mundunugu* from Tekane village who will come. It is good to have both."

Nga nodded. She wanted to walk down the hill to the terrible dirt road where the rattletrap truck was parked, now. She was ready to go. Dr. Xavier had given the truck to get the villagers home and to use as a TC-candidate "bus" to be stationed in Nacala.

She was eager to drive it to the clinic, to Shelly and home.

"It is good," she said.

BRIAN EPILOGUE

OMO'A, FATU HIVA, MARQUESAS ISLANDS

R_X Brian sat outside the clinic this morning in the shade of the broad leaves of a banana tree. He waited to help the older patients with mobility problems, usually pushing a wheelchair. The sandy paths on the island discouraged anything with smaller wheels. Even so, navigating a wheelchair through Omo'a was not for the fainthearted or frail.

He had volunteered to help in the office, but, except for tourists, few people spoke English. Those who did only spoke commercial English. They could sell the wide range of handicrafts produced locally, but not discuss where it hurt or why.

He was studying French, but he really needed to learn North Marquesan.

That morning, Manihi showed up with her baby girl for six-month shots. While mother and daughter went inside, her five-year-old son, Rainui stayed outside with Brian.

Brian and Rainui kicked a soccer ball while teaching each other vocabulary. *Vai* is water and *tahi* is one. Rainui seemed to be learning faster than Brian, but ultimately the task was to keep the boy occupied, especially when his little sister screamed from getting her shots.

In the afternoon, Brian sold wood carvings to tourists at the dance exhibition. Some of the tourists were polite, others rude. The other vendors knew to send the rude ones to Brian. He had a special understanding of arrogant tourists and could not only calm them down, but usually sold them more of the villager's works, and at better prices.

Best of all, in the evening he had dinner with Penny at her home. Often, she worked late clinic and Brian had dinner with one of the families. He had settled into the role of surrogate grandfather.

Tonight, Penny was cooking and had invited a nice man from

the French consulate. Nice enough that Brian could imagine his own grandchildren, but he knew enough to keep his mouth shut.

LILY EPILOGUE

KATHERINE, AUSTRALIA

Obrey's big smile was the same, but the rest of him looked different to Lily. At first she thought it was because she simply hadn't seen him for days, but then she realized he was wearing new clothes. He still wore jeans, but they were new. And his bright red shirt was new, as were his flip-flops.

They arrived at the Casuarina Café, and Lily was startled to see four or five people inside.

"Business is good!" Obrey said. "I am sorry for the sickness, but it has brought many people here."

"That's good," Lily said. But she worried about what happened when all those people went home.

As if he had heard her, Obrey said, "A lot of locals have been coming in, too—I think maybe people didn't know the café was here, and now they think it's a great place, so we are popular now." He made his crooked grin and said, "I think my papa helped. He started coming here with some of his friends. They sit and talk. It makes the place look busy, even if they don't buy anything. I set up tables outside so they could smoke out there, the old guys."

"I see. I'm glad, Obrey, it's a nice cafe."

"Your paintings helped, too. The newspaper did an article on your work; I saved it so you could see what they said. Then people came to see the paintings and stayed for coffee." He smiled. "But we're out of paintings, as you can see." He walked to his cash register and took out an envelope, handed it to Lily.

It was full of cash and checks.

"Thank you. I've sold all my new work; all I have is a couple awful old ones I think I will throw out. But I will have at least one for you tomorrow. Now– "

"Now you need some sleep," Obrey said.

She had been going to say she wanted to see Pearl, and Pana, of course, but she realized he was right. Even though she had slept most of the time on the planes, she was exhausted.

"Pana can wait one more day, Lily," Obrey said. "She's fine with Pearl, although your mother– "

"What?"

"She's been here since the *balanda* funeral for your aunt. She's going through your aunt's house, going through her things."

"Those are Pana's things, now."

"Yes. It is good you are home."

———

It was cool that night, so Lily decided to sleep inside her shed. She woke to the sound of a cloudburst, thunder and lightning and heavy rain crashing down. Glad for her roof and floor and walls, she snuggled back under her blanket and fell asleep to the rhythm of falling rain.

In the morning the storm was gone. She walked to the showers enjoying the fresh, sweet air. Walking back, she was as fresh and clean as the air, her hair still dripping like the trees.

The sun shone down, rays of bright light striking crystal rainbows from the drops on leaves and branches.

She made a painting of it, outlining the storyline, including the bats in the tree above her shed house. She didn't usually do casuarina trees, since it was mostly palms at Mataranka, but today she painted what was in front of her. She even made a small blank rectangle to represent her shed.

She had cleaned and packed up her brushes and paints and was waiting when Obrey pulled up. He handed her a latté, helped put her portfolio with the new painting she'd begun and a couple blank canvases in it into the back seat. She set her paint box on the floor by her feet and savored the coffee.

"Pana?" he asked.

"Yes, that would be good."

"I know you have things to take care of, but I wanted to let you know I have a new plan for part of the Café," Obrey said.

"Oh? What is that?"

"A game center," he said.

"What's that?"

"A place where people can come and play video games. Damon suggested it. They have them in Darwin, and lots of them in big cities, but there's nothing like that here."

"People will come to play games?"

"Yes. And compete on teams, and buy coffees and computer time! But I must build a wall, and block off the windows in that section. Damon says it needs to be dark. He has a dozen friends who already want to start coming for it."

"Mmm. Well there certainly isn't anything like that in Katherine already," she said and Obrey laughed.

"Maybe you can help me with it," he said. "Once you've filled up the other wall with paintings, that is."

"Yes," Lily said. "I've one started, it will be done tonight."

"With the new wall, there will be more room for paintings, too," Obrey said. "But I've got to block the windows on that end, and figure out how to add the wall without aggroing the owners."

———

Pearl and Pana were working outside under Pearl's lean-to where gourds and herbs hung to dry. A couple gourds clacked together in the light breeze. Pana's little face was scrunched up in concentration, and Lily was grateful Pearl had found a way to distract her from constant mourning.

What was it like to lose a mother? A chill descended on Lily, and she vowed to give her own mother a big hug when she saw her later that day, no matter what else was going on.

"Lily!" Pana sprang to her feet and ran to hug her cousin. Lily hugged her back, patting the girl's narrow shoulder. Pana's tears wet her shirt in silence. Lily let the hug go on, since that was what Pana seemed to need.

"So, what is the desert of New Mexico like?" Pearl asked.

"Some same, some different," Lily said. "I brought you herbs. They have many different kinds of salvia. Sage."

Pearl nodded. She studied Lily while Pana finished her long

hug. Then Pearl smiled, a gentle knowing smile.

Pana stepped back. "Lily, I don't know how to ask this, but your mother... "

"Is in your house," Lily said. "I know, Pana. We will go there in a little while and I will talk to her."

"Is she taking things?" Pearl wondered.

"Some of the things actually belong to her," Lily said, but I know she is worried about Pana. She will not take things that are Pana's."

"June Araminty says the house belongs to Pana now."

Pana looked at Pearl, tears building in the corners of her eyes. "What will I do with a whole house?" she asked.

"Live in it," Lily and Pearl said at the same time. Pearl's eyes smiled at Lily, and Lily nodded back at her teacher.

"Auntie Pearl and I will help you, Pana. You need to go to school, and also learn how to take care of your home."

"Aunt Adjana wants me to go to Darwin with her."

Lily shook her head. "That will not happen, unless you want to. I think you belong here." Lily thought of the self-assured high school girls in New Mexico. They were real scientists. She wanted Pana to have that chance, those choices.

"I talked to little Pana," Pearl said. "I explained that she must decide someday, Darwin or Katherine or someplace in country. But not yet." Pana glanced from Pearl to Lily and back.

Lily nodded. She helped Pearl finish tying off a couple bundles of herbs and hung them. Then they got ready to go to Pana's house. This was going to be hard, Lily thought, telling mama she must go back to Darwin alone.

―――――――

"My friends are here, mama, and Pana's are here too. Bad enough her mother is gone, but she should not be forced to leave behind everything and everyone else she knows. She wants to stay here."

Adjana looked at Lily, then at Pana, then at her hands, red and rough from cleaning. She sighed. "I know that. I am glad for that, Lily, Pana." She looked at them in turn. "If Lily is here with you, then I agree. But not if you are gone for weeks, Lily. That is not right."

"I do not plan to be gone again, but even if I am, Pearl is here. Auntie Pearl has much she can teach about the people, about life, so if she chooses to not live the *balanda* life, she will know something else."

"As you have chosen."

"I have."

Lily's mother's expression drooped into sadness, but she nodded, accepting that. "I am glad you know what you want."

"Darwin is not so far," Lily said. "And I have my wonderful phone," she smiled at her mother.

Adjana smiled back, eyes tight. She turned to her niece. "Pana, there is one dress and one piece of furniture I gave to your mother that I would like to take back home with me," she said. "I've tried to clean and organize everything so it's easier for you for a while."

"And Lily and Aunt Pearl will help," Pana said, much more assertively than Lily would have expected.

"Yes," Adjana said. She bit her lip and walked to the table where a bottle of lotion sat. She squirted some into her palm and rubbed it into her fingers, the backs of her hands. The scent of jasmine filled the air. "Fei will be here later this afternoon to drive me back to Darwin. Maybe we can go to lunch until then?"

Lily smiled. "That sounds nice. My treat, since I'm such a famous and rich painter, now."

Adjana laughed. She seemed sad and proud, at the same time.

Pana reached for Lily's hand and Lily then reached for her mother's, now soft and scented with lotion.

———

"You're expanding the menu, too?" Lily shook her head. "Maybe it's too much all at once. You're going to have to get a cook. And a server, maybe."

Obrey shook his head. "Nope. It's just some more snacky foods, cut lunch, pizza. I can get them fresh from Damon's friend, she runs that organic foods place on Diamond Road."

"Organic pizza?" Lily wondered.

"It's good, I've had some. We can warm it up in the oven. Also I'm getting a microwave for those little sausages in buns that Damon likes."

"So fancy," Lily teased. "Just don't get any bagels—they're too chewy." She made a face.

"Okay! No bagels. I don't think Damon thinks those are gamer food anyhow. Crackers and cheese, the cut lunch sandwiches, things they can eat with one hand."

Lily rolled her eyes, pretending to be upset about their manners.

With no warning, Obrey's arms enfolded her in a gentle hug. "I missed you so much. I wanted you to be here to help me plan, Lily."

Her arms went around his sturdy shoulders and she stood on her toes and leaned upward to plant a tiny kiss on his cheek.

"Oi! Don't let me interrupt anything," Damon said, coming through the door, arms full of bags and a box. "We just have a ton of lumber outside that needs to be brought in—but we can work around you!"

Laughing, Lily and Obrey went to the door and helped carry the supplies in. Damon stopped on his second trip in and stared at the two large paintings Lily had hung that morning. "Wow, Lily. Those are amazing."

"Thank you," Lily said. "They are truly my own dreaming."

"Yes, they are," Obrey said, smiling his crooked smile.

In the paintings, bats fluttered among the palms, bright eyes shining. A casuarina tree shaded a mysterious rectangle, two women seated below. Beside them, yams baked on coals.

"What do you think about trying to coax some of the gamers into learning Marra?" she asked. "It would be fun to tell them we have a whole new group of speakers, when we drive the bats to Roper Bar."

"Uhhh…" Damon said.

"Tell them it's a secret language. Not even the old men know it," Obrey suggested.

"That might work, actually," Damon said, and Lily laughed.

TO THE READER

Please accept the authors' gratitude for finding and reading our book.

We are independent authors and appreciate how difficult it is to select our book from the flood of offerings. As independent authors, we are significantly dependent on reader-to-reader recommendations.

If you enjoyed our novel and wish to support independent writers, we would appreciate any posts on social media, and especially an all-important Amazon review.

http://amzn.to/2k8qJgi

You might also be interested in **Plague of Equals: A science thriller of international disease, politics, and drug discovery (Pandemic Mysteries #2)** by J. Oestreicher and D.R. Oestreicher

Available in all Amazon stores: ISBN: 978-0-9631755-4-0

http://amzn.to/2jEwdyp

Thank you.
    J. and D.R.

APPENDIX: BAT CHAT IDENTITIES

RESULT OF DIGITAL FORENSICS

The investigation of the good (Acquired Immunity Syndrome) and the evil (Research Solution Suppliers) eventually pointed investigators to Bat Chat. The following is the consolidated results of several digital forensics efforts. The UK Data Protection Act prevented individual identification of a couple people.

Australian IP Addresses

Captain Contagious is Dr. Darnell, a biologist and epidemiologist with the CDC. Digital forensics note: He posted from Darwin, Australia; Roswell, New Mexico; and Atlanta, Georgia.

Dreamtime traced to Liliadja Dhuwa Waters (Lily). Lily is a healer, dreamer, and artist from Mataranka in the Australian Northern Territory. She is patient zero for the Australian family of Acquired Immunity Syndrome. Digital forensics note: She also logged on briefly from Roswell, New Mexico.

Mozambique IP Addresses

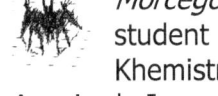*Popo* is registered to Armando Queiroz, a secondary education science teacher in Maputo, Mozambique. He worked in pharmaceuticals in Estonia during the Mozambican Civil War. He is the advisor and mentor to the Khemistry Kids. Digital forensics note: Popo is the Swahili word for bat.

Morcego is registered to Maputo Secondary School student Gabriella. She is one of the leaders of the Khemistry Kids who helped discover the African family of Acquired Immunity Syndrome among the Yao tribe. Digital forensics note: Morcego is the Portuguese word for bat.

Canadian IP Addresses

Canuck is a deleted account created by Natalie Jenkins of Alberta, Canada. She is the mother of an early victim of Aerosol Infectious Rabies, her five-year-old son Ian. She was one of the first people to suggest non-animal transmission of rabies.

Roswell, New Mexico IP Addresses

Mongol Baatar links to Ariq Temuujin. Ariq grew up in Mongolia under Soviet rule. He went to college in Colorado and was the Administrator at the Roswell Orthopedic Clinic in Roswell. Digital forensics note: Baatar is Mongolian for hero.

Niña de la Ciencia belongs to Jessenia Sanchez. She is a senior in high school and her science fair project helped show that Mexican Free-tail bats transfer immunity throughout the colony. Digital forensics note: Niña de la Ciencia is Spanish for science girl.

East Coast United States IP Addresses

Fleming is used by Brian Macalaster. He is the pharmaceutical chemist instrumental in the development and testing of Ribavirin-P in Maputo. Digital forensics note: Ian Fleming wrote the James Bond novels, and Alexander Fleming discovered penicillin. While this account's registration lists New Jersey, investigators observed activity around the world, especially Maputo.

Syms Covington is one of several accounts associated with Jake Abbott. Jake was the top salesperson for Research Solutions Suppliers until he quit. With his global contacts, Jake sold DNA sequencers around the world, including Maputo and Roswell. Few of these machines were unpacked, but the units in Roswell proved to be important. Digital forensics note: Syms Covington was Charles Darwin's cabin boy on the voyage of the Beagle.

John Snow is a CDC account used by Mark Gereben. Mark is the director at the Center for Disease Control and

Prevention in Atlanta who coordinated research related to Aerosol Infectious Rabies. His research started while the disease was still a mystery and continued in the aftermath of the WHO announcement. Digital forensics note: John Snow was the first epidemiologist.

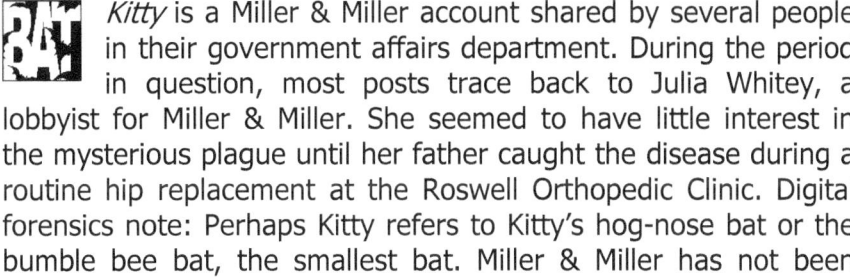 *Kitty* is a Miller & Miller account shared by several people in their government affairs department. During the period in question, most posts trace back to Julia Whitey, a lobbyist for Miller & Miller. She seemed to have little interest in the mysterious plague until her father caught the disease during a routine hip replacement at the Roswell Orthopedic Clinic. Digital forensics note: Perhaps Kitty refers to Kitty's hog-nose bat or the bumble bee bat, the smallest bat. Miller & Miller has not been connected to the RSS scandal.

United Kingdom IP addresses

 Batty. Zoo docent?

 Radar Rat. Bat conservation advocate?

ACKNOWLEDGMENTS AND CREDITS

———

Many people and organizations (knowingly and not) contributed to this work of fiction. Acknowledgment here does not imply an endorsement, review, or even knowledge, of this book. If this book has piqued your interest in bats, here are some good sources.

Bat Conservation International (www.batcon.org).

Bat Conservation Trust (www.bats.org.uk).

Bat Conservation and Rescue QLD Inc. (www.bats.org.au).

Several people across the Internet provided information on medicinal chemistry. We would like to thank each individually, but unfortunately, our lengthy writing process has lost all record of these generous people. You know who you are and you have our gratitude.

We also want to thank our family: for information, support, and understanding: Jason, Jennie, Lenny, Matt, Roseli, and Samantha.

We must mention these two who still believe this book is about cats, not bats.

Chapter graphics

Ariq's horse by Mercedes Yrayzoz vectorized by T. Michael Keesey (Creative Commons Attribution 3.0 Unported) from PhyloPic.org.

Chapter title bat by Rigby471 (Public Domain) from Wikimedia.org.

Bat Chat avatars copyright by Jason P. Schumacher.

Brian's Rx by Nevit Dilmen (Creative Commons Attribution-Share Alike 3.0 Unported) from Wikimedia.org.

Halid's Mozambique flag by authors.

Lily's bat by Yan Wong (Public Domain Dedication 1) from PhyloPic.org.

Nga's Caduceus by Nyo (Public Domain) from Wikimedia.org.

Maple Leaf by Canadian Flag (Public Domain).

The question mark is from font Arial Rounded MT Bold.

United Nations logo by Shizhao (Public Domain) from Wikimedia.org.

Cheerwine is a trademark of Carolina Beverage Corporation.

ABOUT THE AUTHORS

The authors grew up in Oakland, CA and Long Island, NY before meeting in Salt Lake City. J. raised three wonderful children while making time to publish poems and short stories. D.R. researched Silicon Valley startups. Today they live in Southern California with their two cats. They enjoy international travel, reading, and writing, and gathering a different perspective from the magical minds of their grandchildren.